YELLOW ROSE

LONE STAR LEGACY

BOOK 2

THE YELLOW ROSE

A Novel

GILBERT MORRIS

INTEGRITY®
PUBLISHERS
Nashville

THE YELLOW ROSE

Published by Integrity Publishers, a division of Integrity Media, Inc., 5250 Virginia Way, Suite 110, Brentwood, TN 37027.

HELPING PEOPLE WORLDWIDE EXPERIENCE *the* MANIFEST PRESENCE *of* GOD.

Scripture references are from the King James Version of the Bible (KJV).

Published in association with the literary agency of Alive Communications, Inc., 7680 Goddard Street, Suite 200, Colorado Springs, Colorado 80920.

Cover Design: The Office of Bill Chiaravalle, www.officeofbc.com
Interior Design/Page Composition: PerfecType, Nashville, TN

Library of Congress Cataloging-in-Publication Data
Morris, Gilbert.
   The yellow rose / by Gilbert Morris.
      p. cm.
   ISBN 1-59145-112-4 (trade paper)
   1. Texas—History—Revolution, 1835-1836—Fiction. 2. Triangles (Interpersonal relations)—Fiction. 3. San Jacinto, Battle of, Tex., 1836—Fiction. 4. Mothers and daughters—Fiction. 5. Indian captivities—Fiction. 6. Women pioneers—Fiction. 7. Widows--Fiction. I. Title.

PS3563.O8742Y45 2003
813'.54—dc22

                                                    2004005455

Printed in Canada
04 05 06 07 08 TCP 9 8 7 6 5 4 3 2 1

DEDICATION

To Betty Jo Grant—A *real* southern lady with grace and charm to spare!

(And to all the members of her Wednesday group
of crafters—bless them all!)

PART ONE:

DIABLOS TEJANOS

CHAPTER
ONE

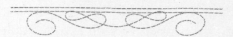

Spring had come to Texas in April of 1836, painting the plains with riotous colors. As Clinton Hardin walked steadily toward the house, he took no notice of the iridescent colors that spread out and dotted the landscape. The pale sunflowers raised their heads, making yellow dots across the land, and snakemouth, with their pale pink blossoms, added a delicate splash of color as Clinton strode by. He moved through the bright orange red of what he called "pleurisy root." Farther off, the tall purple spikes of the heelaw, used by most people to cure wounds, added their sharp splash of color to the scene.

At the age of fifteen, however, Clinton was not particularly given to studying the natural beauty of wildflowers. His mind was much more taken up with important theological matters. Ever since he had been soundly converted during a revival meeting in Arkansas, he spent little time considering the minor things like the beauty of earth and food. Most of his thinking and his conversations with other people were focused on the more significant truths of religion.

The evangelist, a tall gangling man with a sunburned face and a voice like creaky thunder, had been named Edward Jardice. His theology had been simple—"Turn or Burn." Jardice had scared the wits out of half the population of Clark County, and the baptismal service that had taken place in the Caddo River after his meetings had been one of the largest ever recorded for miles around. The river had been at almost flood tide, so it was a dangerous affair to be immersed. Reverend Jardice had sent out "feelers"—young, strong swimmers who entered the waters and probed the river for sinkholes. It wouldn't do to lose a fresh new Christian to a mere river!

A pleasant memory came to Clinton as he shifted the sack with four rabbits on his shoulder and found a more comfortable position for the double-barreled shotgun he bore in the crook of his right arm. He knew he would never forget the moment when Reverend Jardice had slapped him under the chocolate brown waters of the Caddo River, and he had come up feeling like a new human being.

The memory warmed Clinton even more than the heat of the April sun overhead, but the pleasant memories were suddenly interrupted by the sharp sound of a dry buzzing. Stopping at once, Clinton snapped out of his reveries to see a large rattlesnake coiled ten feet in front of him right in the middle of his path. The rattlers made a blur as the sound spread itself over the soft spring air, and the head was pulled back in the striking position.

Though Clinton had many fears, he was absolutely fearless where snakes were concerned. He could not understand why people acted as they did at the mere sight of a reptile. He took them merely as a minor irritation and disposed of them with whatever was at hand—a hoe, shovel, or a stick, and more than once simply by a kick of his heavy half boots. Once he had even startled his older brother Brodie by letting a five-foot rattler strike at his foot. He had reached down quickly and picked him up by the tail and beat the snake's brains out against a tree. Brodie Hardin had a healthy fear of snakes himself and had turned pale and could hardly speak. Clinton had stared at him, then shrugged. "It weren't nothin' but a snake, Brodie."

Now, almost casually, Clinton lifted the shotgun and dropped the sack of dead rabbits. The shotgun had a healthy kick, so he held it firmly and pulled the trigger. The explosive roar filled his ears and riddled the snake, driving him backward. With the ease of experience, Clinton cocked open the gun, removed the hull, and shoved in a new shell. Then he picked up the sack and continued walking, kicking the mangled carcass to one side. He stopped for a moment and stared at it, saying with immense satisfaction, "Well, devil, how you like that? I reckon that'll take care of you."

The devil occupied a great deal of Clinton's thinking, and he saw every snake as simply an emissary of the evil one. He was totally convinced that the devil was as real and as corporeal as his brother Brodie, or his uncle Zane, or any other human being. As he stood staring down at the fragments of reptile that were left, he was filled with a desire to come face-to-face with the devil. "Well, Satan, you red-legged rascal," he said with a touch of arrogance, "you think you got my family hog-tied, but I'm tellin' you right now that you ain't gettin' nary one of 'em! If you'd just show yourself, I'd give you what I just gave that no-good creepy varmint."

Clinton was totally convinced that one day the devil *would* appear, and the two of them would have it out, and he had not a shred of doubt about the outcome.

Moving on down the path, Clinton thought of his family with apprehension. Ever since he had been baptized, he had considered himself as the spiritual head of the Hardin household. A touch of sadness brushed his mind as he thought of them. He thought first of his father, Jacob. He had not known his father well, for Jake Hardin had been a wandering man and had spent little time with his family. He had, in fact, abandoned them, gone to the mountains, and married an Indian woman with whom he had two children. They were all dead now. His father's Indian family had died of smallpox in the mountains, and Jake had been killed a month ago by the guns of the Mexicans at the Alamo. Clinton grieved considerably, for his pa had shown little sign of being anything but a sinner. His mother was different, though. He had some hope for her. True, she steadfastly refused to be baptized, but she, at least, said that she knew the Lord.

Brodie, who was four years older than Clinton, showed little interest in spiritual things, which bothered Clinton considerably. Brodie was so enamored with a young half-Mexican woman named Serena Lebonne that he had no time for thoughts of the devil or of God or of heaven or hell. As for Moriah, Clinton's seventeen-year-old sister, the thought of her made Clinton shake his head. "She's plumb given over to vanity," he muttered and thought of the time when he had caught her putting powder on her face. He had rebuked her sternly about pride, and they had gotten into quite an argument. But he was at least satisfied with his baby sister Mary Aidan, who, at the age of four, had not yet come to the age of accountability, though Clinton was already sharing his faith with her whenever he could.

Walking over the crest of the hill, at the foot of which lay the Hardin house, Clinton picked up his stride. He had been thinking all morning of things he could say to his uncle and aunt, his mother's brother and sister. Zane Satterfield and Julie Belle Satterfield were the targets of much of Clinton's hardest preaching lately. Julie Belle had been a saloon woman and had announced without shame that she intended to be one again as soon as the war with the Mexicans was over. Zane Satterfield was a criminal. He had escaped from a prison and fled to Texas to avoid the law. "You're not gonna get 'em, devil!" Clinton announced loudly and looked around as if he expected Beelzebub to be standing to one side grinning at him.

He hurried on toward the house, stopping long enough to hang the sack of rabbits on a tree far enough away so that the flies would not be drawn inside the house. He kept a loose grip on the shotgun, and when he stepped up on the porch, he found a huge dog lying squarely in his path on the threshold.

"Bob, git outta the way," Clinton said impatiently. He had little hope that Bob would move. The dog was mammoth, weighing eighty pounds, and was an unusual brownish-red color with long, floppy ears and a tail strong enough to almost knock a person down when he wagged it. Bob had been rescued by Moriah, who took in any sort of injured animal, and so the hound had become part of the Hardin household. Bob spent a great deal of his time sleeping. When he went to sleep, he looked dead, for his mouth would hang open and he hardly appeared to be breathing. His other peculiar habit drove everyone crazy. He loved to sit on the feet of anyone he found standing still. Bob was awake primarily when it was time to eat or when one of the family was threatened. At a moment like that, he could be a frightening sight with a mouth somewhat like a shark.

"Git out of the way, I said!" Clinton lifted his voice, but Bob merely grunted and did not even open his eyes. Clinton considered dragging him out of the way but then shrugged his shoulders and stepped over him. Bob did not move as Clinton stepped into the house. For one moment, Clinton stood there glancing at his family, who were all seated at the large table eating. His mother, Jerusalem Ann, was standing by the big fireplace, taking a pot off one of the hooks that held it over a bed of glowing coals. The house was adobe and had been there when the Hardins had bought the land. It had one huge room, which served for cooking, eating, and general living, plus three small bedrooms. The walls were penetrated by pegs, from which hung *ollas,* pots, pans, rifles, and whatever else anyone in the family felt like decorating them with. A large fireplace dominated one end of the room, and three windows on the other two walls let in pale rays of sunlight.

"You'd better set down here, Clinton, before these hogs eat all the grub," said Clay Taliferro. Everyone had to learn how to pronounce Clay's unusual last name as *Tolliver.* He was a man of average height, with his tawny hair worn long and tied with a piece of leather. He had sleepy, light blue eyes, and they crinkled when he smiled, as he was doing now, until they almost disappeared. He had a wide mouth and high cheekbones, and a deep cleft marked his prominent chin. Right now his face was somewhat pale, as he had been wounded at the massacre of Goliad and had escaped alive only by a miracle.

"Come set down, boy, and tell me how many deer you brung in."

Placing the shotgun on pegs over the doorway, Clinton turned and said, "I killed four—" He broke off, for his sister Moriah had risen from the table where she was eating and moved toward the fireplace. Clinton stared at her with horror and burst out, "Moriah, you go put on some fittin' clothes!"

Moriah Hardin, at the age of seventeen, had been emerging out of adolescence for the past two years. She had dark red hair, brown eyes, and the strong build of her mother. The dress she wore was indeed a little tight, but new dresses in Texas were hard to come by, as they had been in Arkansas. Moriah's budding figure was made prominent by the tightness of the dress, but she was aggravated by Clinton's constant preaching.

"What's wrong with this dress?"

Clinton shook his head fiercely. "Why . . . why, it's down right in-decent! That's what's wrong with it. Why, you don't look no better than Jezebel!"

"You mind your own business, Clinton!" she snapped.

"Well, I reckon it *is* my business. You're my own sister. I'm a Baptist, and we don't stand for women runnin' around practically naked."

Moriah shook her head with disgust and then turned to her mother. "Ma, you tell him to hush."

Jerusalem Ann Hardin, at the age of thirty-four, did not look like a woman who had borne six children. She was a strong-bodied woman and looked at least five years younger. The hard life had not marked her as it had many pioneer women, and she retained the same clear complexion that she had enjoyed as a young girl. Her eyes were green, and she still had a trim waist and a fully developed figure. "Leave her alone, Clinton. Sit down and eat."

"Why, Ma, I'm ashamed of you puttin' up with Moriah like that! You got to make her act decent."

"She is decent. Now, sit down, Clinton."

But Clinton was beyond persuasion and continued to preach at Moriah until finally Brodie became disgusted. Brodie was almost a foot taller. Indeed, he was one of the tallest young men in the community. He was not filled out yet, as he would be later on, and he had the auburn hair and green eyes of his mother. "Clinton, you are the most cantankerous human being I ever seen. If we throwed you in the river, you'd float upstream! Ever since you been baptized, you ain't been fit to live with. Now, sit down and eat or leave."

Clinton stared at Brodie defiantly. "I expect God will strike some folks dead for the way they're acting." He turned and left the room, stumbling over Bob, who did not even rise up and bark.

"Ma, is he *always* going to be like that?" Moriah sighed. "He used to be so nice. But ever since he got religion, he's been impossible!"

Jerusalem set down a plate before Mary Aidan, who had been taking the argument in with large eyes. She stared up at her mother and began to shovel the grits into her mouth, her throat working as she swallowed.

"Mary Aidan, don't eat so fast. You've eaten so much your belly's tight enough to crack a tick on."

"More!" Mary Aidan smiled. She was a cheerful, happy child and the pride of all the Hardins.

"Well, what's wrong with him, Ma?" Brodie grumbled. He forked a piece of beef, stuck it in his mouth, and chewed on it. "Sometimes I think he's dumb as last year's bird's nest! It's gettin' so I can't even live with him."

Zane Satterfield, Jerusalem Ann's older brother, laughed. "He's just like his pa, Brodie. Whatever Jake did, he did it full steam." Zane suddenly was aware that a silence had fallen over the room and knew that the family was not yet used to the idea of Jake being dead. Jake had been gone for long periods, for years, more or less, but this time he wasn't coming back, and that made a difference. "He's a good boy, Clinton is. He's just all taken up with religion. He sees it as his duty to save the rest of us and keep us all on the straight and narrow line."

"He's driving me crazy with his constant preaching," said Julie Belle Satterfield, who was twenty-nine and had the same reddish hair and sparkling green eyes as her sister. She had full lips, a provocative body, and a rebellious spirit. She had never been known to back down to anyone, and now she shook her head, her lips drawn in a straight line. "He's a pest."

Jerusalem shook her head as she sat down and began to eat. "We have to love him," she said firmly. "He's my son and your nephew, Julie. That's what counts. No matter what any of us do, me or anyone else, all the rest of the family has got to show love."

Julie stared at her sister, then got up and walked outside without another word.

Zane watched her go, then shrugged. "I guess Julie and me needed that, sis. We're the outlaws of the family, me the jailbird and Julie the bad woman."

"And there's me," Clay said, grinning. "I reckon I ain't got much credit up at the pearly gates either, but Clinton never gives up on me."

Jerusalem smiled at Clay. "And you never get angry with him, Clay. I appreciate that. I know he's a trying boy, but I'm hoping one day he'll get past that fire-and-brimstone stage. You know, I've often thought," Jerusalem Ann said quietly, "if he had heard a sermon about the love of God, he would have been a gentler convert. All he knew was that one evangelist, and he just got the wrong one to mold himself after." She suddenly got up and left the room, and everyone knew that she was going outside to talk to Julie.

Brodie shook his head mournfully. "Well, Ma's right, but Clinton is peskier than chiggers. As a matter of fact, I'd take the chiggers any time over his blasted preachin'!"

Clay walked down toward the river and found Clinton there, as he had suspected. Clinton was fishing, which he did with every free moment he had. Clay came up and sat down beside him.

"Caught anything?"

"No."

Clinton's answer was terse, but Clay ignored it. "You know, I've been thinkin', when this shootin' war with the Mexicans is over, you and me might make a trip to the mountains where your pa and me used to trap. You've never seen the high country, have you, Clint?"

"No, I never have." Clinton relaxed slightly. All the rest of the family was irritated with him, but Clinton could not seem to help being what he was. Clay Taliferro, however, was different. It had been Clay who had come back from the mountains and stayed until, at Jerusalem Ann's request, he had led them to Texas in search of Jake Hardin. Clay had become such a part of the life of the Hardins that when strangers came by, they almost automatically assumed that Clay was Jerusalem Ann's husband. Clinton sat there listening as Clay spoke softly for a long time about the things that they might do in the mountains. He finally said, "I know I'm a pain in the neck, Clay—but I can't help it!"

Clay smiled and, doubling up his fist, struck Clinton fondly on the shoulder. "Don't fret yourself, Clint—they's a whole tomorrow out there that ain't even been touched yet!"

CHAPTER
TWO

Looking up from the dress that she was mending, Jerusalem fixed her eyes on the approaching rider and then smiled. "Look, Mary Aidan, there comes your gentleman friend."

Mary Aidan was sitting flat on the porch with her legs stretched out in front of her. She was wearing an old shirt of Brodie's that came down halfway to her knees and had been cut off at the elbows. Her red hair, fine as gossamer, caught the afternoon sunlight, and she jumped up at once and ran down the steps. "Rice," she cried. "Rice!"

Rice Morgan stepped out of the saddle, patted the gray on the shoulder, and then draped the lines over a sapling that had been tied across two posts to make a hitching post. He turned quickly, and a smile lit up his face as Mary Aidan ran straight toward him. He caught her under the arms and tossed her high in the air and laughed as she squealed. Rice squeezed the child and gave her a kiss on the cheek, saying, "How's my best girlfriend?"

"Rice—play with me!"

"All right. I don't have a thing in the world to do but to play with pretty girls." He carried her up the steps and took his hat off and tossed it on the floor, then sat down flat as he said, "Hello, Jerusalem."

"Hello, Rice." Jerusalem took in the figure of the man who sat there. Rice Morgan's actual name was spelled R-h-y-s when he had lived in Wales, but everybody thought it was *Rice,* so that was what he had become. He was a trim man of five feet ten, well-built, with a deep chest and strong muscled arms. Years of hard work in the coal mines in Wales had formed his upper body, and he was stronger than most. He had jet black hair, direct gray eyes, and when he smiled, two creases appeared on each side of his mouth. He was a neatly handsome man but seemed to have no knowledge of the fact. He also had the fastest reflexes of any man that Jerusalem had ever seen. She had seen him sparring with the young men, and he had merely laughed as he pulled his head out of the way of their blows and softened his own. She knew that he had done some prize fighting in Wales, although he rarely spoke of that.

"This is my baby. Her name is Abigail," Mary Aidan said, holding up the rag doll that Jerusalem had made for her. "You be the pa, and I'll be the ma, and she'll be our baby."

"I think that's a good arrangement." Rice nodded. "We'll pretend that I've just come home from work and am playing with Abigail."

Jerusalem put her sewing down in her lap and sat there quietly watching the gray-eyed man play with the red-haired girl. There was something pleasing to her about the way Rice could adapt himself to the world of a four-year-old. She did not know many men who could do it, and of her own children, only Brodie could unbend at times to play with his younger sister.

Julie stepped out of the house and came over to sit down in a cane-bottom chair. "Hello, Rice," she said. "We haven't seen you in a while."

"I'm not Rice. I'm Pa. This is Ma, and this is Abigail."

Julie smiled. "Oh, I see. Sorry. I made a mistake."

The two women sat quietly and saw that Rice Morgan had no embarrassment at all about sitting down on the porch and playing with the child. Jerusalem never remembered a time when Jake sat down and played with the children like this. He had taken the boys hunting on occasion, but never had he known how to reach out to Moriah.

The game went on for quite a while, and finally Mary Aidan crawled up into Rice's lap and asked him to sing for her. He had a fine tenor voice and sang one of the well-known ballads from the old country. Mary Aidan was tired, and soon she put her head against his chest and went sound to sleep.

"I declare, that child is worn out," Jerusalem said. "Put her up here. I'll hold her, Rice."

"She's all right where she is."

"You're good with children," Julie observed. "That's a rare thing in most men."

"Well, devil throw smoke! Why wouldn't I be good? Didn't I raise my own four brothers and sisters?"

"You raised them? What about your parents?" Jerusalem inquired.

"My pa, he got killed in the coal mine when I was only thirteen, so it was up to me to step in and help."

"What about your mother?"

"Sickly she was most of the time, and so I had to learn to do women's work as well."

"Most men wouldn't have done that," Julie said.

"Well, there is dull you are, Julie Satterfield! A man does what's to be done when it comes to family," Rice said as he stroked Mary Aidan's hair gently.

Both women noticed how his hands were almost square and looked very strong. There was an old scar on one of them, and Julie said, "How'd you get that scar?"

"Foolishness."

"I'm surprised you were ever foolish, Rice. You're so proper now."

Rice grinned at her. "Go and scratch. I've had my share of foolishness like all men. Where is everyone?" he said, looking around.

"Clay's fishing with Clinton down at the river, and Brodie's gone to make a fool of himself over a girl."

"Well, I will go to my death," he said. "Brodie is a fine boy. He'll not make a fool of himself over a skirt."

"That's what you think." Julie grinned. "You don't know near as much about women as you think you do, Rice Morgan."

"Saying nothing against him, I was. But he's a fine broth of a boy. He's got more sense than to go wild over a female."

Both Jerusalem and Julie broke forth into laughter.

His feelings slightly hurt, Rice stared at them. "Well, why are you laughing? Am I a rat with green teeth, then?"

"Rice, the only person who knows less about women than you do is Clay Taliferro," Jerusalem said. She shook her head in dismay and said, "You'd better stick to your preaching and leave women alone." Getting to her feet, Jerusalem reached over and picked up Mary Aidan. "I'm going to put her down for a nap. She sleeps like Bob. I'm afraid she's died sometimes." She left and went into the house.

For a moment there was silence between Rice and Julie. Finally, Julie said, "Rice, I think you'd better warn Brodie about Serena."

"Why would you say that?"

Julie was examining a slight cut on her thumb. She did not answer for a moment, but when she looked up, there was a strange expression in her eyes. "Because she's like me."

"Like you in what way?"

"She's got it in her to be a bad woman."

"Oh, there is dull you are! All of us have meanness in us."

"No, it's different," Julie said. "Look at Jerusalem and me. Did you ever see any two women more different? She's good and I'm bad."

Rice ran his hand through his black hair. A lock of it fell down over his forehead, but he paid no attention. "I don't agree with you about yourself. We can be what we please, Julie. You've got something in you that's good."

"Jerusalem was right. You're a fool about women." Julie might have said more, but then Zane Satterfield stepped out of the house, accompanied by Jerusalem.

"Hello, Rice. You have any news?"

Rice got to his feet and picked up his hat. He held it, tapping it against his leg, and shook his head. "Santa Anna is on the march toward here. Everybody's running like rabbits."

"You can't blame them after what happened at Goliad," Zane said. "Santa Anna turns those soldiers loose, nobody will be safe. What about Sam Houston?"

"The word is," Rice said, "that he's gathering men to make a fight of it. As a matter of fact, I'm on my way to join him."

"You're going to join the army!" Julie exclaimed, staring hard at him. "How can a preacher be a soldier?"

Rice looked embarrassed. "I guess I'll have to put my preaching aside. I wouldn't be able to live with myself unless I did what I could to help make this land fit to live in."

"I'll go with you," Zane said. "Both of us might as well be fools." He turned and looked toward the river and said, "I don't know about Clay, if he's able to go."

Clinton and Clay had appeared down the path that led to the house. Clinton was carrying a string with some large catfish on it, and when he came closer, he held them up and said, "Look here. We caught some big ones. Ma, let's have fish for supper."

Jerusalem smiled. "All right, but you'll have to clean 'em. I purely hate to clean catfish."

The meal had been so good that Clay had pronounced it a sockdolager and had gotten no argument from anyone. Julie and Jerusalem and Moriah had ganged up on the cooking and fried up not only a mountain of fresh catfish but also prepared the rabbits along with fried potatoes, hush puppies, and a huge platter full of wild green onions that flavored the meal.

Clinton had not said anything to Moriah about preaching to her, but once during the meal he said, "I know how much you like fish, Moriah. I caught these just for you."

Moriah smiled. She loved her brother when he was not throwing one of his religious tantrums and reached over and squeezed his arm. "I sure appreciate it, Clinton. You're the best fisherman in Texas."

The talk soon turned to the upcoming battle with Santa Anna and his well-trained troops, and how Rice and Zane were going to join the fighting. The conversation had not gone far before Brodie, who'd said almost nothing since returning to the house from his visit, declared loudly, "I'm going with you two."

"Son, you don't need to be running off to fight," Jerusalem said, but she saw that Brodie's face was set in a determined expression. *That girl is giving him a hard time, and he's going to show her what a fine man he is.*

But there's no point to tell him that. "Just stay around a while longer. You'll have plenty of chance to fight."

"No, Ma, I don't mean to disrespect you, but I need to go with Zane and Rice."

Everyone at the table, with the exception of Mary Aidan, knew exactly what was happening. Brodie, at the age of nineteen, was physically tough, but emotionally he was overly sensitive—especially where Serena was concerned.

Clay had said little during the meal, but he saw the stubborn streak that held Brodie and decided to wait until after dinner to say anything. Jerusalem had gone out on the porch, where a breeze was blowing, to churn butter. Clinton had stayed inside to help clean up. As Clay sat down and watched Jerusalem churn, he was aware that she was the one woman in his life that he felt most comfortable around—at times. At other times she had a way of making him feel totally out of step and embarrassed, and he could not say why. He had said once to Rice, "That woman can pin me to the wall with just a look!"

"I'm worried about Clinton," Jerusalem said. "His religion is too harsh."

"He's got a good heart. He's just caught up in something that's real to him. Give him some time. He'll change."

"I hope you're right, Clay. I know there's such a thing as judgment, but I've known some Christians who were so hard that you could strike a match on them."

Clay did not respond. He sat there quietly, trying to think of some way to speak of what was in his heart. The trouble was he didn't *know* what was in his heart. He only knew that this woman stirred him in a way that no woman ever had.

"Have you seen the way Rice looks at Julie?" Jerusalem asked abruptly.

"Why, I don't reckon I have."

Jerusalem shook her head in disgust. "You can see further than any man that I've ever known with your eyes, but you can't see what's right in front of you. He's fallen in love with her. That's what he's done."

"But he's a preacher, and she's—" Suddenly, Clay found himself in over his head. He had started to say, "She's a scarlet woman," or something of that nature, but he found he couldn't say that to Jerusalem. He added lamely, "Well, she's pretty wild, Jerusalem. It would never work."

Jerusalem was not satisfied with Clay's response. "I don't think you know any more about women than he does."

"Than who does?"

"Who were we talkin' about? Rice Morgan. He wouldn't be the first preacher to get his head turned by a pretty face."

Clay chewed thoughtfully on his lower lip. He put his finger on the scar beside his mouth, something he often did when he was nervous, and said, "Well, to tell the truth, I have noticed that Rice looks at Julie from time to time."

"Oh, you have!"

"Yes, and he has no business doin' it."

Suddenly, Jerusalem stopped churning. She half turned and faced Clay. He was caught by her motion and found something in her eyes that disturbed him.

"How have you been looking at me, Clay Taliferro?"

Clay flushed, knowing that he was doing exactly what angered and embarrassed him. He could not think of a single reply.

Jerusalem laughed a good hearty laugh and said, "Did you think I didn't know you're looking at me the same way?"

Clay dropped his head for a time, unable to meet her gaze. After a moment, he looked up and shrugged, trying to speak as nonchalantly as possible. "Well, I guess I knew it, but I thought no matter as long as nobody said anything."

"Clay, go away! You are the champion dummy where women are concerned!"

Inside, while Jerusalem and Clay were talking, Julie said, "I'm going out to the garden, Rice."

"I'll go with you," Rice said. He followed her out the back door, and she picked up a hoe. "I'll do that," he said, taking it from her. He went down to the garden and began to hoe for a time. He started to speak of what was going to happen when the war was over, and Julie suddenly interrupted him.

"Don't get serious about me, Rice."

Surprised, Rice turned to face her. He held the hoe in both hands, resting it on the ground, and studied her. She was not just beautiful on the outside, which everyone saw. He saw something that others did not, something deep inside her, which drew him. He could not define it even to himself, and finally he said, "Why not? You must know I'm beginning to care for you."

"I'm a bad woman, and you're a good man. People are what they are, and nothing can change it."

"No, you're wrong about that, Julie. We can choose. We can be different if we want to."

"I wish I could care for you, Rice, but when two people come together, a man and a woman, one of them may drag the other one down. I don't want to be the one who drags you down. You're one of the best men I've ever known, but you don't know me."

Rice stood there for a moment, and then he shook his head. "You're wrong, Julie. Each one can help the other choose to be better. I'm going to fight with Houston, but I'll be back." He looked over toward the house and said, "I hope Jerusalem will leave the ranch. It won't be safe here."

Julie felt weary. These talks with Rice always seemed to drag her energy down and cause her to think on things she'd rather not have to confront about herself. "She won't do that. She loves this place, and she's stubborn."

Lucita Lebonne looked up and saw Brodie Hardin approaching. She stood beside the house, holding the clothes that she had hung out to dry, and waited until he dismounted. She was thirty-four now, pure Spanish, and still beautiful, with glossy black hair and warm brown eyes. She had lost her husband to sickness, and it had been the Hardin family who had kept her and her two children, Mateo and Serena, from abject poverty. Jerusalem and Clay Taliferro had brought her from the shack, where her husband had spent his last days, and seen to it that she got a land grant from Stephen Austin. Clay Taliferro had been her husband's friend in the old days, and he had been kind to her, helping her after her husband had died.

"Buenos días," Lucita said. "How are you, Brodie?"

"I am fine," Brodie said. He stepped off his horse and removed his hat, the breeze ruffling his hair. He looked very young, but he was tall and lean and strong.

"How is all your family?"

"Well, I guess they're kind of scared like everybody else. I reckon Santa Anna will be here pretty soon with his army."

"Will your people leave, do you think?"

"I don't reckon anybody could make Ma leave." Brodie smiled. "She's as stubborn as a blue-nosed mule."

"And Señor Clay, is he recovered from his wound?"

"He's lots better. Zane and me and Rice Morgan are going to join General Houston."

"It is sad that all this has come. I had hoped for peace," Lucita said.

"I guess we all did." Brodie shifted uneasily and then said, "I'm never gonna forget what your son did for me at Goliad. If it hadn't been for Mateo, me and Clay would have both been butchered."

"I'm glad he was there to help."

The two stood there awkwardly, then Lucita said, "Serena is out at the barn milking. I know you didn't come to see an old woman."

Brodie grinned crookedly. "You ain't an old woman, Señora. Not you! I don't know why you don't get you another husband. I know you've had chances."

"It is too soon," Lucita said.

"Well, I'll go mosey down to the barn."

"You can stay for supper."

"Thank you, ma'am."

Serena was milking the goat, but she heard footsteps coming. Looking up quickly, she saw Brodie and smiled. "Brodie, I'm glad to see you."

"I'm glad to see you, too." He came over to stand beside her and watched as she continued to milk. "I never could milk," he said. "Clinton can beat me a mile."

"I expect you're too rough," she said as she aimed the stream of milk into the pail.

Brodie stood there, making conversation, as she asked him about his family. He told her about the herd of cattle they were building up to sell at market in New Orleans, and then asked, "Have you heard from Mateo?"

"No, not a word."

"I ain't forgot how he saved me and Clay there at Goliad. That was a bad time. I thought we were goners for sure."

Serena set the bucket down and then turned to face him. There was an air of glowing health about her. Her hair was pure black, and she had strange-colored violet eyes. It was these eyes that drew men as well as the curves of her developing body. She was eighteen now and a full-grown woman. As she watched Brodie, she knew exactly what was going on. *He wants to kiss me, and he's afraid to.* She said, "Mateo is a good man, but he is a firm believer in Santa Anna and the cause to rid Texas of the Americans."

"I'd sure hate to be in a battle and look up and see Mateo on the other side. I don't know what I'd do."

"It mustn't come to that," Serena said. She reached out and put her hand on his chest, and she saw his eyes flare suddenly. He stepped forward, put his arms around her as she had known that he would, and kissed her. It was an awkward thing, and she stepped back, laughing, and said, "You're a naughty boy, Brodie Hardin."

"I'm not a boy. I'm a man."

"A man! Well, I'm glad to hear it." Brodie reached out for her, but she evaded him. "You mustn't do that anymore, Brodie."

"Why not? Serena, you know how I feel about you. I want to marry you."

Serena knew of his intentions, for he had spoken of them before, but for all of his height and strength, he still seemed like a little boy in her sight. "No, you don't want to marry me. You're too young."

Brodie stopped and stared at her. "You're making fun of me, and you're getting to be a flirt, Serena."

"I am not!"

"No? What about Jeff Bettis?"

"What about him?"

"You think I don't know that he comes calling on you?"

"He comes calling. What of that?"

"I don't like it."

Serena felt sorry for Brodie. She liked him a great deal, as she liked all of the Hardins. But she was not ready to marry yet. Brodie was so infatuated with her that she felt smothered at times by his constant attention. "I don't want any more talk about marriage. You're too young."

Anger flared up in Brodie, which was an unusual thing. He was usually gentle natured and sweet tempered, but he had thought about nothing but Serena for weeks now. While he had been gone with the other young men to fight with the Texans against Santa Anna, he had done little but dream about her. And when it looked as though he would be shot, she was the one who had been on his mind. "You ought not to torment a man," he said roughly and turned and stalked blindly away. The bucket was in his way, and his boot bumped against it, spilling the milk. He gave it a kick and left.

Serena followed him and watched as he mounted his horse and rode away at a furious gait. She shook her head and turned to find her mother watching her.

"What happened, Serena?"

"Nothing. He wants to marry me."

"And how do you feel?"

"Oh, I like Brodie, but that's not enough. He's going to fight. He may never come back. You know that."

"If you love him, you should give him something to hope for."

"That would be cruel, Mamá. I don't feel that way about him. He'll find somebody else to love." She stood there watching Brodie disappear and then said quietly, "What's going to happen to us when Santa Anna comes?"

"Mateo will see that we're not harmed."

"But what about the Hardins? He can't help them."

"I hope they will leave," Lucita said quietly. She looked in the direction of the Hardin ranch and shook her head. "Santa Anna will not spare them—he will not spare anyone!"

CHAPTER
THREE

Clay gave a sudden jerk that brought a pain to the wound high on the left side of his back. He had been dreaming of Goliad. It had been a massacre, for the Americans had been marched out from where they had been held captive, and then the Mexicans had opened fire on them. The Mexican rifles had laid a staccato crackling sound in the air. He had seen the blossoming crimson wounds in his fellow Texans as they had fallen under the murderous fire. The worst part of the dream was that he and Brodie had both been hit. Brodie had taken a bullet in the head, and just when he had, the boy had let out a pitiful cry that had gone right to Clay's heart.

Clay sat straight up, favoring his left shoulder, and put his hand over the wound. The bullet had gone almost all the way through, making a neat hole in the back and a bulge in the front. Fortunately, it had missed his lung. Brodie had used Clay's bowie knife to slit the skin and pop the bullet out. The wound had been painful, but Clay had kept the ball for a souvenir. Now, as he sat there with cold sweat on his brow, he shook his head and muttered, "I could do without them blasted dreams. They ain't good for a feller."

Sleep was gone, so he lifted his legs and put his feet on the floor. He sat there for a moment, waiting for the pain to subside, then with a grunt he stood upright. He slipped into his pants and had trouble buckling the belt because he still had considerable pain when he tried to use his left arm. Finally, he put on his shirt, but let it hang out. He managed to put on his socks, using mostly his right hand, then slipped his feet into the boots. He glanced over and saw Zane, with whom he shared the room, lying flat on his back, straightened out as if he were a soldier standing at attention. It puzzled Clay how a man could sleep like that. He himself usually curled up into a ball, but every man has his own ideas about such things.

Moving quietly, he left the room, walked down the hall, then stepped outside on the front porch. The air was cool, and over in the east, he could see the faint red rays beginning to tint the morning sky. Looking up, he stared at the stars for a moment. Somehow the stars seemed to be closer in Texas than they had been in Arkansas. It had been that way in the mountains, too, where the air was thinner. For a moment he stood there picking out the brightest stars, wishing, not for the first time, that he knew their names. *I should have been a sailor. They have to know the stars to get where they're goin', but I'd hate to be cramped up in a little ship for months at a time. I don't see how those fellows stand it.*

He stepped off the porch, enjoying the freshness of the breeze. Texas was a dry country, but the rainy season had now come upon this part of the land. The rivers were up, and even now the ground was soft and mushy under his boots. As he walked out away from the house, a sudden movement caught his eye. He was an alert man, for the constant threat of danger in the mountains had sharpened his senses. Even though he was no longer so much in danger of the mountain Indians, he was cautious about sleeping close to a fire when camping out. He always moved back into the safety of the dark shadows.

The movement came again and a slight sound. Clay recognized that it was coming from the two graves of Jerusalem's sons that had died in Arkansas. He saw that she was sitting there on a bench that she had asked him to make, and he moved toward her slowly. Brodie had told him once that, when back in Arkansas, she had spent a lot of time sitting beside the graves of her boys and the rest of her people who had passed away. He halted and thought about how Jerusalem had never complained about anything on the trip from Arkansas, but three times she had mentioned that the hardest thing about the move was to leave her boys so far behind.

Her words had bothered Clay for a long time, and when he had made a trip to New Orleans, taking a herd of cattle for cash money, he had headed for Arkansas, bought a wagon, and exhumed the two boys. The caskets were crumbling, so he had bought new ones and then put the remains in them. For a while he had considered bringing her parents back. But she had never spoken of them, so he contented himself with bringing the boys. He had been apprehensive on the way back, not knowing if he was doing the right thing. But he knew by her tears, when he told her what he'd done, that for once he'd done something right.

From far away the sound of a coyote howling plaintively at the coming dawn broke the silence. Clay moved forward and deliberately shuffled his boots as he walked and cleared his throat as he approached the bench Jerusalem was sitting on. She turned to look at him, but she did not speak. Clay came to stand off to one side, then she made a gesture toward the bench, and he moved over and sat down beside her. He noticed that Bob was sitting on her feet. It had always amused Clay that the rangy dog loved feet and would sit on anybody's except those who posed a threat to the Hardin family.

Jerusalem remained as still as a statue. Her eyes were fixed on the two graves and the two stones that she had had made by one of the neighbors. She turned to him and said, "Clay, it was a noble thing you did bringing my boys here. I will always be grateful to you for that."

Clay saw that even in the breaking light her face was drawn. He was embarrassed and didn't know what to say. Finally, he murmured, "I was glad to do it, Jerusalem Ann." The two sat there, neither of them speaking. Clay knew that she was thinking of her boys and wondered what sort of long thoughts she had, if she were still remembering them as infants, or as they were beginning to crawl and creep around. But the memories were there, strong and sharp, and Clay suspected they would never go away from her.

Suddenly, Clay thought of Jake with a touch of anger. Jake had died with William Travis and Jim Bowie and Davy Crockett defending the Alamo. *He died an honorable death,* Clay thought, *but he shore did make a sorry life! I don't know how a fellow could go off and leave a woman like*

Jerusalem Ann and the kids like he had. Clay had gone over and over in his mind about why Jake would do a thing like that, but there was never any answer. He had known men like that before, men who just couldn't keep still, and Jake had, evidently, been one of those wandering types. He pushed those thoughts from his mind and sat there quietly until he heard Jerusalem Ann start to weep.

She was not a woman who cried a great deal, and Clay could not think of anything to say. He longed to comfort her, but he just sat there. After what seemed like a long time, she stopped, took a deep breath, and pulled a handkerchief from the front pocket of her apron. She wiped her eyes, blew her nose, and then turned toward him. The morning light was clearer now. He could make out the green eyes, well shaped and deep-set, that so fascinated him. The crying had not ruined her face as it does for some women.

Finally she said, "Men hate a weepy woman, and so do I."

"Grief takes you like that," Clay said softly.

"Yes, it does. It all caught up with me, my two dead boys, my parents dead—and Jake dead now."

Clay almost asked her, "How did you feel about Jake and his runnin' around and his Indian family?" But he knew better than that. He knew that Jerusalem had forgiven Jake for all the pain he had caused her and the kids. He waited until she gathered her thoughts and began to speak again.

"You know, Clay, I really loved Jake at first. He was one of the finest-looking men I'd ever seen, but it wasn't just that. He loved me, Clay, and I thought that he always would, so I married him." A silence interrupted her then. It was as if she were remembering those days, and then she continued, her voice soft, but filled with pain. "He was a wandering man, Jake was. At first he just made short trips, was gone only a week or two, but then he stayed longer and longer until finally he'd be gone for a whole year."

Suddenly, Bob lurched off, barked sharply once, and dashed off toward the copse of cottonwood trees down by the river. Clay had not seen anything, but he knew dogs could smell and see and hear better than any man. They both heard the dog barking at something, probably an armadillo.

"I've been tryin' to think," Jerusalem Ann said, "how I felt about him, and I found out that I had two husbands." She shook her head as if in wonder at the thought. "The first husband was the Jake that I first loved and who loved me. But the second was the stranger who would come in now and then, and who would always be leaving on some trip to the mountains. I guess I knew he would wander off after a while, and I can't love a man I can't hold, Clay."

Clay listened as she continued to speak to him for the first time of her marriage to Jake. She told him how when the children were born Jake seemed to be proud of them and promised to be there for them. But then whatever it was that drew him away from her would come upon him, and he would leave. She had learned to recognize the signs and tried her best to do whatever to keep him home. She did not think it was another woman. She thought it was just simply that he was one of those men born with a wanderlust like Daniel Boone and that breed of adventurous pioneers.

She gave a strained half laugh and turned and put her hand on his arm. "Poor Clay. Here I am weeping and spilling over with my troubles."

Her hand tightened on his arm, and he turned around. He saw a strange look in her eyes, one that he could not identify, and she was watching him intently. He could not imagine what was on her mind.

"Most men would take advantage of a woman who's having a weak moment like this."

Clay saw that she was waiting for him to speak. He cleared his throat, for in all truth she had touched on a sore spot. He had wanted nothing more than to put his arms around her and pull her close. The thought shocked him, and he put it away, saying, "Why, Jerusalem, I'd never do a thing like that."

Jerusalem stared at him, not saying a word for a long moment. He grew uncomfortable under her gaze.

"No, I guess you wouldn't."

Clay could not read what was in her expression. She seemed almost disappointed. He changed the subject quickly and said, "I've been thinkin' about what to do about Santa Anna. What I think is that we all better git out of here as soon as possible."

"I'm not leaving here, Clay," Jerusalem said.

The sound of Jerusalem's voice was like a door closing firmly and the lock clicking.

Clay tried to argue. "You know soldiers are bad when they are loot-
ing and raiding. You've got young'uns here to think about."

"I'm not leaving, Clay. I didn't come all the way to Texas to run
away." She got up and stared at him for a moment, as if something had
been left unsaid. He stood up with her, but she did not speak at once. She
stood there looking out over the land that had become home to her, then
she said, "I've got to go get breakfast." She turned and walked away without another word, leaving Clay standing there.

He did not move, and Bob returned and sat down on his feet. He
looked down and shook his head. "Have a seat, Bob. Make yourself at
home. While you're there, why don't you tell me what that woman's got
in her mind."

Bob looked up and leaned heavily against Clay's knees. His tongue
lolled out, and he barked, "Woof—woof!" softly and then pulled his
tongue in and looked away back into the woods.

Knowing that the men would have a long trip on their journey to join
Houston, Jerusalem fixed a large breakfast that could not only be eaten
early, but the remains could be taken in a poke. She fixed cat head biscuits,
so called because they were about as big as a cat's head. Clinton had
brought back a passel of squirrels, which he had cleaned, and she fried
them up along with a big potful of grits. She also fried large slices of ham,
and draining off the excess fat, she added a little water to the drippings to
make red-eye gravy, which the men all loved. As she cooked, she listened
to the men, who were talking about Houston. Brodie was excited, and she
heard him say, "Just wait until Sam Houston gets them Mexicans where
he wants them. Why, there won't be a live Mexican left in Texas!"

Clay was drinking coffee out of a big mug, and he shook his head
slightly. "Don't reckon he'll be doin' much of that for a while."

Brodie said in a shocked tone, "Why, of course he will, Clay. Ain't
nobody can get the best of Sam Houston."

"I reckon Clay is right," Zane said. He was standing up, leaning
against the wall, holding Mary Aidan, who was pulling at his long hair and
chattering constantly.

"Why do you say that, Zane?" Clinton asked. He was still disappointed because he was not accompanying the men, but he knew that when his mother spoke in a certain way, the subject was closed. "I thought you admired Houston."

"I do," Zane said. "I think he's the toughest man in Texas, but he won't be able to do a lot except retreat."

"Retreat!" Brodie exclaimed. "Sam Houston wouldn't run away! He's no coward!"

"He ain't got much choice, Brodie," Clay shrugged. He sipped the coffee and said, "Right now all he's got is a few men, and Santa Anna's coming with thousands of trained soldiers. It would be a slaughter if Houston threw what few men he's got against Santa Anna's army."

"I never thought about going to find Houston and then just retreatin'."

"Houston's smart. He's fought Indians, and he knows men. He knows Mexicans, too," Zane said. He grimaced as Mary Aidan gave his hair a yank to get his attention and smiled down at her. "You are aggravatin', Mary Aidan. Now, be still."

Rice had not said much during the discussion about Santa Anna's approaching army. He had been watching Julie while the others had been talking, but now he said, "I think Zane's right, Brodie. It's not always muscle that wins, but brains. I found that out fighting men bigger than myself back in Wales."

"Did you get whipped?"

"Did I get whipped? Certainly, I got whipped. Nothing to buy a stamp for, I was, but I did learn how, when you got an opponent that's bigger and faster and stronger than you are, you have to be smart."

Julie said suddenly, "I'm surprised that a preacher would fight."

Rice Morgan gave her a look that was almost belligerent. "A man must fight or let him put skirts around his knees!"

Jerusalem interrupted then by saying, "Come to the table. Breakfast is ready."

Brodie went to the table and sat down, but he was thoughtful, disappointed even. As the women set the plates of food on the table, he waited until Morgan asked the blessing, but his mind was still on the battle that was to come. He had pictured himself along with Rice and Zane and others charging the Mexicans and driving them away. The thought of running in retreat was shameful to him, and he could not believe what he was hearing.

Everyone ate heartily except Jerusalem, who seemed to have no appetite and contented herself with seeing that the food and the plates were replenished and the coffee mugs full. When they were almost finished, she suddenly straightened up. "Someone's coming."

At once Zane was up, and he made for the door. He grabbed the rifle as the others stood up from the table. When he looked out, he said, "It's okay. It's the professor."

"Fergus?" Clay said, his eyes suddenly alert. "That's good news." He moved outside along with the rest and laughed. "It looks like he's picked up some other Indians along the way."

"Yes, and Comanches at that," Zane murmured. He kept the rifle in his hand, but then laughed. "Depend upon Fergus to pick up Comanches. Everybody else is tryin' to kill 'em, and he's tryin' to make pets out of 'em."

They waited until the two wagons pulled up in front of the house. The first wagon was like none that could be bought anywhere, for Professor Fergus St. John Nightingale III had converted it to a rolling home. It bowed out over the sides in a strange fashion, and the canvas was tight as a drum over it. Inside was a bed, a small cabinet for whiskey, a stove on which small meals could be cooked, and a bookcase, filled with all kinds of books. The other wagon was driven by a short, chubby man who took off his hat, showing his bald head. This was James Langley, Fergus's servant, as his father had been.

The three Indians were mounted on fine horses that any man would desire. They did not smile but stared silently at the gathering in front of the cabin. The Comanches were the most fierce of all the Plains tribes, and these were armed with muskets and looked thoroughly dangerous.

"My stars and garters, if it's not the Hardin clan," said Fergus. He was a man of forty-nine years, tall and skinny, but hearty. As he got down off the wagon, his long arms and legs made him look like a spider. He had a homely, long, horse face and the brightest blue eyes that any of them had ever seen. His nose was large like the prow of a ship, and his normally pale complexion was cooked red by the Texas sun. He came forward, a smile of delight on his face, greeted the women with a bow, shook hands with all the men, kissed Mary Aidan, and then said, "By jove, it's jolly good to see you all again."

"I didn't think you'd show up here, Fergus." Jerusalem smiled. "Don't you know we're in the middle of a war?"

"Oh, I heard about it. Nothing to be troubled about, my dear lady."

"Who are your friends?" Clay asked, motioning toward the Comanches. "These are different ones than you had before."

"This chap here is Fox." He indicated a tall and lean young man. "This one is called Young Man Afraid of Thunder. I just simply call him Young Man." Young Man was short and muscular, with a pair of eyes as black as obsidian. "And this is Paco. It means eagle. He's small, but a rather violent fellow. They're teaching me the complexities of the Comanche language. You know I wanted to study Comanches all along."

"Have them get down. We've got plenty of breakfast left," Jerusalem said.

"Jolly decent of you. They're always hungry." He turned and spoke to the Indians in rather awkward words, but they slid off their horses at once. They kept their rifles in their hands even when they went inside. The cabin seemed very crowded, but it didn't seem to matter. The Indians ate everything that was put before them, belched loudly, and kept their guns clutched in their hands.

It was Clay who discovered they could speak some English. "Why do you put up with a white man, Fox?"

Fox said with a gleam of humor, "He not afraid of us. We don't understand him."

Young Man Afraid of Thunder belched loudly. "When we understand him, maybe we kill him."

"No, we will never understand him," Paco said.

"We don't know what Santa Anna's doing, Fergus," Zane said. "We're going to join up with Houston."

"Well, Paco there has seen Santa Anna's army. He wasn't very much impressed."

"Where did he see them?" Clay asked quickly.

Paco began to describe the location where he had seen the army. He stopped once to drink some more of the coffee, which he appeared to like a great deal, and then continued.

When Paco had finished, Clay said, "They're gonna pass pretty close to here, I think."

"I hope not," Zane said. He turned and said, "Fergus, would you stay here and help take care of Jerusalem and the family?"

"Nothing would give me greater pleasure."

Clay looked at the Comanches and at the tall, lanky Englishman and at James Langley, who he knew was a fine shot. "Well, I reckon one butler, one Englishman, and three Comanche braves is just about right to take care of any Mexican army that would make the mistake of coming this way."

Jerusalem stood beside Zane and reached up and pulled his head down and kissed him, saying, "You take care of my boy, you hear me, Zane?"

"I'll do my best, sister."

Brodie was embarrassed, and when his mother came over and hugged him and kissed him, he said, "Don't worry about me, Ma."

"You mind Zane and don't be foolish, you hear me?"

"Yes, Ma."

Jerusalem moved over to Rice and put both hands on his shoulders. "You come back safe, Rice Morgan."

Julie had said good-bye to Zane and Brodie, but now she came over to Rice and smiled. "That's no way to send a man off to fight." She reached up, pulled Rice's head down, and kissed him soundly. "There! There's something for you to fight for."

Clay laughed out loud, for Rice's face turned red. "I'm glad she's tormentin' *you* for a while, Rice. It gives me a break." He suddenly turned serious. "Save a few of them Mexicans for me. I'll be along in a few days."

But Jerusalem said, "No, you can't go, Clay."

Everyone was shocked. Zane grinned and punched Clay with his elbow. "Mind what that woman says, Clay. She's as stubborn as a blue-nosed mule."

"You go to grass, Zane Satterfield!" Jerusalem said.

"Guess we'd better get going," Zane said. The three men mounted their horses and rode out. Brodie looked back and waved just before they disappeared around a turn in the road shielded by the trees.

Jerusalem watched them go and saw that Clay was staring at her. She folded her arms in front of her and said, "No, you can't go. I need you here." She waited for Clay to speak, and when he was utterly silent, she turned and walked into the house.

Julie was amused by the scene. "Well, Clay, are you going to mind her?"

Clay huffed and looked angry. "I reckon I'll go when I get good and ready."

"I don't think you will, not if Jerusalem says no."

Clay stared at Julie, offended, and looked down at Bob, who had come to sit on his feet. He shoved Bob away and walked off stiffly. Bob immediately went and sat down on Julie's feet. She leaned over and stroked the rough fur and said with a smile, "I reckon Clay Taliferro knows about as much about women as you know about draw poker, Bob."

CHAPTER
FOUR

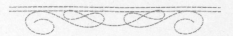

F inding General Sam Houston proved to be more difficult than any of the three men had imagined. They wandered for several days through the hill country across the Colorado River and the Guadalupe River. The rainy season had brought both rivers up, and the ground was spongy. They passed by the rolling hills and steep cliffs, and as they rode along a natural fault, they could see miles of the country spread out to the horizon. Brodie was shocked at the enormous expanse that made up Texas. The rocky ground was dotted with live oaks, blackjack, and mesquite trees, and the chains of lakes that sloped away cut their way through canyon walls so steep that a squirrel would have trouble climbing.

All the time they were searching for Houston, Santa Anna found himself unable to take advantage of the defeat of the Alamo. Although William Travis had died in the battle, he had given Sam Houston valuable time, and the army of Santa Anna had been cut to pieces. An arrogant man, Santa Anna was ready to start out in pursuit of Houston with whatever men he could gather, but his officers persuaded him against it. Forced to wait for reinforcements, his delay allowed Houston to gain still more time.

Darkness had fallen when the three found themselves at the break of one of the many streams. The water was high, so Zane said, "We better stay here tonight."

Brodie was relieved. He was younger than the other two and had thought himself as tough as any man. But Zane seemed to be made of iron, and Brodie was ashamed that a preacher, such as Rice Morgan, could endure hardness better than he could.

The three made camp back from the stream and built a fire, although they had nothing to cook. Zane doled out the last of the squirrel and ham and biscuits Jerusalem had sent with them and said, "We'd better shoot somethin' tomorrow or we'll go hungry."

Brodie slowly ate the sparse rations, making them last as long as possible, and washed them down with the coffee they had made. "Shore wish I had some of Ma's grungers."

Rice looked at him strangely. "Grungers? What's that?"

"Why, that's molasses cookies, Rice."

"I wish I had some myself. There is hungry I am!"

"I'm worried about Ma," Brodie said. "I hated to go off and leave her and the others."

"Well, it's a dangerous time, but I feel better with Fergus and those three Comanches there," Zane said.

Suddenly, Zane got to his feet, staring out into the darkness. "Somebody movin'," he said. He reached down, picked up his rifle, and checked his powder. The others did likewise. They all moved away from the fire, and Zane whispered, "Sounds like a single horse, so I don't reckon it's no army."

A voice called out, but none of them could make out what was said.

"Who's out there?" Zane called loudly.

The horse moved in closer, and a figure was outlined against the sky. "Who are you?" the visitor called out.

"There's three of us. What do you want?"

The voice was strange, high-pitched and scratchy. "Somethin' to eat wouldn't be bad, if you wouldn't mind sharin'."

"Come in slow," Zane said. He stood there like a cocked pistol, and the others were on their guard. The horse came forward slowly, obviously worn out. The rider was a tall man with a slouched hat down over his face, and his clothes were soaked and worn. "You fellows lost?"

"We ain't lost. What about you?" Zane asked. "Where you headed?"

The stranger stepped off his horse. He had a rifle in a buckskin sheath, but he made no attempt to remove it. He had a pistol on his right hip, but he was staring at the two men carefully. "I'm Deaf Smith," he said.

Zane suddenly exclaimed, "Deaf Smith! Come on in to the fire, man. We got no grub, but we got plenty of hot coffee."

"That'd go down good."

All three of the men had heard of Deaf Smith. He was the one man in the world that Sam Houston trusted completely. Smith had lost some of his hearing as a result of fever as a child. As far as Sam Houston was concerned, Smith was the best scout in all of Texas, or anywhere else. Now, as he came forward, Brodie kept his eyes fixed on the legendary Smith. He could not wait and said loudly, "We're huntin' for Sam Houston. We aim to join up with him."

Smith seemed to relax. "Well, he needs all the men he can get. Where you fellas from?"

Brodie said, "I was at Goliad, but me and another fellow, we got away. My pa was killed at the Alamo."

Smith did not answer until Zane poured him a cup of coffee. He drank it down as if it were lukewarm, although it was scalding hot. Wiping the back of his hand across his mouth, he said, "Well, he died in good company. I lost good friends there. Jim Bowie was a good friend of mine. We're gonna miss him in this here war that's comin'." He looked at Brodie and said, "So, you was at Goliad. Well, Santa Anna made four hundred martyrs there, and he stirred everybody up all over the country. There's men comin' in from Louisiana and Arkansas, but I don't know if they'll be in time."

"How far away is Houston's camp?"

"Too far to make it tonight. We'd better bed down here. We'll ride in first thing in the morning. I got some news for Sam."

"What do you think he'll do, Mr. Smith?" Brodie asked eagerly.

Smith looked up into Brodie's face. "You're a tall one, ain't you, boy? Well, we ain't got enough to do much with, so I reckon we'll back off until we can get Santa Anna in some place where we can fight him like we want to."

"I've been tryin' to tell the boys," Zane said, "you can't fight trained soldiers unless you've got some troops that know how to handle it."

"You're right about that, but Sam, he'll find a way. He always does."

★   ★   ★

Santa Anna had a young woman in his tent, as he almost always did. Mateo Lebonne was outside speaking with one of the adjutants. Mateo tried not to think about Santa Anna's constant pursuit of señoritas. Mateo was worried about what was going to happen next. He had almost idolized the general and was waiting anxiously for his leader's next orders. He leaned forward and lit a cigar from a burning stick that he picked up from the fire in front of the tent.

"What do you think the general will do, sir?" Mateo asked.

Colonel José Martina was a short, rotund man with a fierce mustache that turned up slightly on each side. He caressed them now as if they had some sort of special meaning. Then he grunted and said, "He told all the officers this morning that he's going back to Mexico City."

"Mexico City! He can't do that. Everything will fall apart without him."

"Of course it will. It took the whole staff to convince him to stay here. He only stayed because we found the pretty young woman there to keep him occupied. That's his weakness, one of them anyway."

Mateo stared at the officer. "What does that mean?"

"I'm talking too much, but he doesn't have enough respect from these *diablos Tejanos*—the devil Texans, and that's exactly what they are."

"We whipped them at the Alamo."

"Yes, and we lost seven or eight hundred men doing it." The colonel shook his head. "The report the general sent in was a little misleading. He said we lost seventy men and the Texans lost six hundred."

Mateo stared at the colonel. He could not answer, but he knew that it was probably true. The general had a creative way with words. He was an immensely popular man in Mexico, and he had gotten that way partly because he was able to inflate his own deeds at the expense of the truth.

At that instant General Santa Anna came out and walked over to the two men. "Give me a cigar, José."

Martina fished a cigar out, and Mateo reached down and grabbed another small twig. He lit the general's cigar, and Santa Anna winked at him. "A little recreation does a man good."

The lieutenant smiled. "Nothing wrong with recreation."

"You have a sweetheart, Mateo?" Santa Anna asked idly. He had become fond of Mateo Lebonne. The young man had come to him and offered to serve as a scout. At first Santa Anna had not been impressed, for Mateo was half-Mexican. His father was a gringo. Still, the young man had a fierce loyalty to Mexico and to Santa Anna himself. He had tried the boy out and found him to be faithful, loyal, and a fierce fighter. Now he turned and said, "Are you anxious for the next fight, Mateo?"

"Yes, my general. We should go after them at once."

"Exactly what I tried to tell my staff. They say we've got to wait for reinforcements. Bah, we have enough force here to wipe up the Texans."

Mateo was thinking of the Alamo and the fierce fight that less than two hundred men had put up against such odds. "I don't know, my general. You remember the bodies of our men around the Texans. The *diablos Tejanos* fought indeed like devils."

Santa Anna blew smoke into the air and said disdainfully, "They are running like scared chickens. We will destroy them all, although General Urrea has been trying to change my mind."

"About what, my general?"

"About our military tactics. I have decided to divide the army into five divisions. That way we can cover more territory as we make our advance. We're going to sweep down and head for the border. I'm giving orders to burn the towns, to kill anyone who stands in our way. When we reach the Sabine River, we will have driven every Texan back to the United States, and we will never permit them back again."

Mateo Lebonne knew there was no limit to the self-confidence of General Santa Anna. He also had serious doubts about the project that the general had laid out to those under him. Mateo had learned, however, that Santa Anna did not suffer criticism gladly, so he simply nodded.

Brodie did not know what to make of Sam Houston and his army. They had found him outside of Gonzales on the Guadalupe River. It was mid-morning, and the rain was pouring down. When Brodie saw the tents and lean-to shelters spread in the piney woods, he was disappointed. "Is that the army?" he shouted.

"That's it," Deaf Smith said. He grinned at the boy and said, "What'd you expect, a bunch of men in fine uniforms marchin' in order?"

"No, sir, I didn't expect that."

"I think you did," Zane laughed. "Well, we found Houston if he'll have us."

"Oh, I'll expect he'll have you. You fellows wait here," Smith said. "After I make my report, I'll see that you get somethin' to eat and get you signed up. But the general usually likes to see his volunteers. He may want to talk to ya."

"I'd like to meet him," Zane said. "I've heard a lot about him."

Sam Houston sat at the camp desk feeling uncomfortable on the small stool. Houston was six feet three and two hundred and forty pounds of hard muscle. His face was stern, for he had done the hardest thing for a soldier to do—which was to order a general retreat. He knew that the small army he had gathered would never win over Santa Anna in a war of maneuver in the field. He also preferred to pull the enemy away from Mexico as far as possible, crossing the defensive rivers as they fled. He also was planning how to accumulate more soldiers to strengthen his forces.

The loss of all of Colonel Fannin's men at Goliad had been a hard blow. He had needed those five hundred men, but now they were gone, lost by the actions of a foolish, ill-trained man. Lifting his head, Houston listened to the rain falling on the tent. The rivers were up, and the population of Texas, for the most part, was on the run. Santa Anna had started a panic to drive the colonists across the frontier. The entire population, frightened and horrified by the tales of the army's atrocities, were now fleeing. Many able-bodied men had joined Sam Houston's army, but the women and the children and the old men were left to fend for themselves. Wagons and horses and those pitifully on foot, carrying what they could, headed east, leaving a pathetic litter as they fled from the Mexican army.

Houston looked down at the letter he was writing. He had been under personal attack by many because of his retreat. The president of the republic wrote, "The enemy are laughing you to scorn. You must fight them. You must retreat no farther. The country expects you to fight. The salvation of the country depends on your doing so."

Houston was writing back to Rust, the Secretary of War. He had said plainly that he was holding no council and that he was consulting with no committees. The last line of the letter said, "If there is a failure, the fault will be entirely mine."

Houston leaned back and thought of the hostile army that faced him, demanding to fight. He had retreated down the Brazos River past San Felipe and ordered the town burned. He had left part of his small army to guard the crossings over the Brazos, but he had no real battle plan. His only hope was to bring Santa Anna to battle in a way to his own advantage. He had fallen back, and now he was waiting for the enemy to make a mistake. He heard the sounds of voices outside the tent, and one of them was familiar, the screechy voice of Deaf Smith. Houston felt relieved, for Smith was the one man that he trusted more than any other. When Smith stepped into the tent, Houston said, "It's good to see you, Deaf. Sit down and have a drink."

"Don't keer if I do, General. It's been a wet, muddy, cold rain out there."

Houston poured whiskey from a bottle. The two men drank, and then Deaf said, "I brung three able-bodied volunteers back with me."

"Only three? I wish there were three thousand," Houston said.

"Well, they ain't, but I have some news for you." Deaf Smith reached into his inner pocket and brought out a leather pouch. He handed the pouch over to Houston and watched as the big man read the contents. Smith would follow Sam Houston anywhere, even into perdition, and it pleased him to see the light on the craggy face of his leader.

"Where'd you get this, Deaf?"

"I took it from a Mexican courier. I thought you'd be interested."

Houston got up and began to pace the ground. The tent was leaking, and the water dripped down on his head, but he paid no attention. "We can do something with this information."

"I got even more news than that. You'll like it, Sam."

Houston reached over and pounded Deaf on the back, nearly upsetting him. "You're better than Santa Claus. What is it?"

"We won't have to fight the whole Mexican Army," Smith said.

"Santa Anna's dividing his army up. As far as I can tell, he's split them into four, maybe five, divisions. They are scattered all over creation."

"Why would he do that?"

"They're all spread out hittin' the ranches and the farms, drivin' the people before them. It ain't a pretty sight, General. I feel right sorry for our people."

Houston's face grew stern. "So do I, Deaf, but this will help."

"What do you got on your mind?"

"How big is Santa Anna's division, the one he's leading himself?"

"Maybe seven, eight hundred men. Of course, he could be joined by reinforcements."

"We've got to get him before they all join up. If we can nail Santa Anna, the rest will collapse."

"I reckon you got you a plan in your mind," Smith grinned.

Sam Houston rubbed his head and then stared at Smith. "I do, and it's gonna take a miracle to make it work, but it's the only hope we got. Come here, Smith. Let me show you on this map what I think we've got to do."

The two men moved to the table containing the small map. Houston began to speak, pointing with his finger, and showed Deaf the strategy he had in mind. When he finished, he turned and said, "What do you think, Deaf?"

"I think we'll eat 'em alive. And the army's ready, too. They're tired of retreating. They want to fight, General."

"That's good, because that's exactly what they're going to do!"

Finally Smith came out of the tent and said, "You fellows come in and meet the general."

Brodie walked in, following the other two. When he got inside the tent, he stood silently eyeing the big man who was seated before a rough desk. He wore deer skin clothes, Indian moccasins, and stared at them with eyes hard as any Brodie had ever seen.

"Where you men from?" Houston asked.

"I'm from Arkansas. This is my nephew. He's from Arkansas, too," Zane said.

"I come from Wales, General," Rice said.

"From Wales? Well, there's some good fightin' men come from that part of the world. You come to fight, did you?"

"Yes, sir," Rice said. "My name's Rice Morgan, sir."

"Well, Morgan, I'm glad you're here, and your names, fellas?"

"Zane Satterfield, and this here is Brodie Hardin."

Houston stood up and walked over, his eyes level with those of the young man. "Well, if you ever fill out, you'll be quite a man. How old are you?"

"Nineteen, General."

"You'll be a little bit older before this is over with. Smith, sign these men up."

"We heard you were givin' land to any soldier that'd stick it out," Zane said.

"That's right. Six hundred and forty acres each."

"That sounds good to me, General."

The three men turned and walked out, and Smith introduced them to a tall, lanky man named Hank Henley, who had a full beard. "Sergeant Henley, these men will be servin' with you. See if you can find some grub and teach 'em what you can before the trouble starts."

Henley stared at Smith. "You think we're gonna fight soon?"

"I wouldn't be a bit surprised."

"Good," Henley said with satisfaction. "I'm tired of retreating. I come to kill Mexicans, not camp out in the woods."

"Reckon you're gonna get your wish," Smith said. He gave the three a wink, then turned and walked away into the darkness.

CHAPTER
FIVE

Acloud of dust rose as the cavalry and the infantry began to form into position. Santa Anna stood straight as an arrow watching his troops prepare to move out. Behind him Mateo Lebonne was also watching, but with much different feelings. Mateo knew that Santa Anna was thinking of gaining another victory. He had won the Battle of the Alamo at a high cost, but the general was never one to worry about losing men. Now he had divided his army up into five divisions. After waiting for some time, he was ready to implement the rest of his plan, which was to drive the Texans all the way across the Sabine River. Then Mexico would own Texas, and the *diablos Tejanos* would be gone from Mexican soil forever!

Mateo had given himself to the liberation of Texas. He had left his home, his family, and joined General Santa Anna as a scout. He had pledged his strength and his mind and his soul to the same cause. But he could not help but be troubled about what happened to those he loved who were in the path of the juggernaut. He had saved Clay and Brodie from certain death during the massacre of Goliad, but it could just have easily gone the other way. His two good friends could have suffered the same fate along with the other Texans who died there. Now he listened carefully, for Santa Anna had gathered his generals together, and his eyes flashed with excitement as he began to speak.

"You are the arm of God to destroy our enemies," he cried out. The troops around could hear as well as the generals who surrounded their leader. "Burn their towns. Kill their stock. Kill anyone who opposes you. Mexico for Mexicans! Death to the devil Texans!"

Cheers went up, and many of the officers of the cavalry lifted their sabers, which flashed in the sunlight.

Mateo could not enter into the celebration. He was certain that the Texans were doomed, and he worried about his mother and his sister. He was troubled also about the Hardins. It had been the Hardin family who had saved his mother, his sister, and himself from poverty when his father had died.

Santa Anna turned, and his face was flushed. He saw Mateo and came over and said, "It's a glorious day, Mateo. We will see the dead piled high."

"Yes, my general," Mateo said. He thought quickly and said, "Perhaps I could go with General Almonte. I know that territory well that he will be following."

"No, I need you with me. We will leave at once, and I intend to scout out Houston. Then I will kill him and all those who stand with him." Santa Anna's eyes flashed, and he smiled cruelly. "We will see the blood of these Texans. Come, I want you to go in front of my column. Ride quickly and find Houston for me." His hand came down on Mateo Lebonne's shoulders. "You have a fine future, Mateo. Now, go!"

General Juan Almonte had led his division on the north side of the sweep toward the Sabine River. He had been obedient to Santa Anna's orders to burn everything in sight, and his men had killed those they found. There were few of them, and Almonte was disappointed, as were the men, who had looked forward to massacring the fleeing Texans.

"Lieutenant Alanso!" Almonte called out. He waited until the young lieutenant rode up to him and saluted. "Yes, my general."

"Take a detail farther north. I have received word from our scouts that there are several ranches there. You know what to do when you find them."

Lieutenant Alanso laughed. He was a handsome young man with many sweethearts and had a brilliant future in Mexico. Not only General Almonte but also President Santa Anna had his eye on this young man who came from a noble family. His eyes gleamed, and he laughed. "They run like rabbits, General."

"You know what to do with rabbits, Lieutenant."

"Yes, my general. I will rendezvous with you just this side of the river. There will be nothing left alive where I travel."

Lieutenant Alanso drove his men hard. They rode all morning and by midafternoon had found two ranches, both of them deserted. His men burned them and took what loot was left. At two o'clock a scout came riding in, his face covered with dust. It was hot, but he ignored it, and a smile came to his lips as he said, "I have found a ranch over there, Lieutenant Alanso. It is deserted, I think."

Alanso stretched in his saddle and laughed. "I wish all soldiering were this easy, Sergeant. Come, lead us to it."

He spurred his fine horse and led his troopers, twenty-two of them, at a fast gallop. His mind was not really occupied with the ranch they intended to destroy. He was thinking ahead to the time when the entire army would come against the ragtag troops that Sam Houston was supposedly gathering. Alanso knew that his men had found whiskey at the last ranch they had burnt to the ground, and many were half drunk, but this did not trouble him. *I will sober them up after we burn this ranch. Perhaps there will be a fresh beef or two there. Then we will ride ahead and rendezvous with the general.*

Professor Fergus St. John Nightingale III closed his eyes with ecstasy. He was seated in a copper tub, his spidery arms and legs hanging over the edge, and his man James Langley, from time to time, dipped down into the soapy water with a ladle and poured it over his master's head.

Clay was watching this phenomenon with disbelief. He shook his head and said, "I don't see how you can worry about takin' a bath when there's about five thousand Mexicans about to drop in on us. We need a bath about like a cat needs a wedding license."

"Oh, I say, old chap, don't worry. Our Comanche friends are keeping track of them. I don't know how it is, but those fellows seem to make themselves invisible. They could hide behind a pocket watch, I do believe."

Clay got up and stared off toward the south. He shaded his eyes but still could see nothing. "It bothers me, them Indians. I ain't used to trustin' them."

"Oh, you can trust these fellows. They'd like nothing better than to collect a few scalps. Better they get the Mexican scalps than ours!"

Suddenly, Fergus rose up out of the tub and stood there gazing off into the distance. James Langley stood to one side with a large, fluffy towel, which the professor wrapped around himself.

Julie had been watching the scene. She had been on the front porch sitting there with Jerusalem, when she suddenly laughed. "Look at that crazy Englishman. I never saw such a long, skinny man in all my life. He's skinny as a rail, but he's tougher than he looks."

"I'm glad he's here, Julie, but those Comanches scare me." Jerusalem was thinking, at that moment, about the time she had been kidnapped by the Comanches. If Clay had not come and taken her out of the camp of one of the most fierce war chiefs of the Comanche, she knew she would be dead by this time.

Julie got up and watched as Langley began handing Fergus his clothes. He wore the fanciest clothes that had ever been seen in Texas. They perhaps were fitting for Windsor Castle, but not in this place. "I'm worried about the men," Julie said.

"So am I. Zane and Brodie are country bred, but Rice is no soldier. I don't even know if he can shoot. Well, God will have to take care of them," Jerusalem said. She suddenly straightened up. "Look."

"What is it?"

"See that dust over there? I think it's the Indians. Come on. Let's go see what they found out."

Julie followed Jerusalem to where Fergus was putting on a top hat. He turned to beam at them, saying, "Nothing like a bath to invigorate a fellow, I always say."

"Well, I say I hope them Indians found out something about the army," Clay said. He stood there looking, and the three Comanches pulled up. Young Man Afraid of Thunder slipped off his horse, keeping a firm hold on his rifle. Clay had never seen him without it.

"Soldier come from there," Young Man said, pointing back over his shoulder.

The other two Indians dismounted, and Paco said, "Smoke behind them. Burning houses, I think."

"How many?" Clay asked quickly.

Paco held up his fingers spread wide, closed his fists, then opened them again.

"About twenty," Clay murmured. "Could be worse. How long before they get here?"

"Not long." Young Man grinned suddenly. "Many scalps."

Fergus smiled brightly. "I say, this is exciting! A bit of sport."

Clay said sharply, "This is no game, Fergus." It seemed natural that he would take charge, and he began to speak rapidly. He noticed that Moriah had come out of the house along with Clinton, and he waited until they were close enough to hear his words. "We've got to make them think this place is deserted. We'll all get under cover where we can't be seen. They've got to think nobody's here."

"And what then, Clay?" Clinton said.

His eyes were big, and his face was pale.

"We'll let them ride in. They may send a couple of advance scouts, but if they don't see anybody, they'll wave the rest of the troop in."

"What's the plan, Clay?" Julie asked.

"I'll knock the officer out of the saddle. Nobody shoots until then."

"Without warning? That's not sporting!" Fergus protested.

"It'll give them time to understand we're serious. I'm telling you, Fergus, this is no game. We'd better get them all. As soon as you hear my shot, everybody take a man out. Be sure you don't shoot the same man twice because it's got to be quick. If they get away, they'll bring the rest of the army boiling back here." He paused, then ran his eyes over the group. "Well, there's me and Clinton. You Fergus and your man, that's four. Three Comanches—that makes seven of us. I wish we had more."

Jerusalem said at once, "I can shoot as good as most men, and so can Julie. That makes nine."

"I can shoot, too," Moriah spoke up. "Zane's been teaching me, so we have ten."

"I don't think you women ought to get involved with this."

Jerusalem caught his eye and said, "What do you think will happen to us if we don't stop them?"

Clay knew exactly what was on her mind, and he held her gaze for a moment.

Finally, she said impatiently, "Don't argue with me, Clay."

Clay laughed. "All right. I'm the general here. I'm going to place you all where you can't be seen, but where you can get a clear shot. I'm not sure we've got enough muskets."

"No problem there, old boy," Fergus said. "I've got five sporting rifles besides my own. Should be able to blast the blighters with no trouble, eh?"

The afternoon shadows were beginning to fall as Clay placed his people in position, but the azure sky was marked by diaphanous clouds. He had thought it all out carefully, and though Clay sometimes seemed lackadaisical, now he moved with decision. In the back of his mind was the knowledge that if his decisions were bad, they would all die. But he let none of this show in his expression. "Moriah, I want you and Clinton upstairs. Each of you take one of the windows up there, but don't let yourself be seen. Don't poke your muskets out until the right time."

"All right, Clay," Moriah said and turned to go.

"I want to stay down on the ground, Clay," Clinton said. "I ain't sure I can shoot so good shootin' down."

"You can't afford to miss, Clinton. Now, don't argue with me. Get on up there and be sure you don't let yourself be seen." He did not wait but turned to say, "Julie, you and Jerusalem take the two windows on the first floor. You heard what I said to Moriah and Clinton. If they see a sign of a weapon, they can pull back, surround us, and we won't have a chance."

"All right, Clay," Jerusalem said. "Come along, Julie."

"Fergus, why don't you and James take the barn."

"Where are you going?" Fergus asked.

"Right over there at that smokehouse. Remember now. You wait until I fire the first shot before you cut down on them."

"What about my Indian friends?"

Clay had been thinking about the Comanches. He looked at the three who were standing there regarding him, all holding their rifles. "I never saw a Comanche that could be seen if he doesn't want to." He smiled.

Fox, the tallest and leanest of the men, returned his grin. "That is true," he said. "What do you want us to do?"

"Find you a place where you can't be seen. When I knock the officer out of the saddle, get you a man apiece. I'm hoping the rest of them will turn and run. Don't let any of them get away, or they'll bring other soldiers back."

Paco nodded firmly. He seemed to be the leader of the three. "Good. We will take all their scalps."

"You are welcome to anything they've got, including their guns," Clay said. "Now scatter."

Clay waited until the Indians seemed to vanish from sight. He looked up at the upper windows of the house and saw nothing, and then at the bottom two windows. Everyone was hidden from sight. From the barn he could not see a sign of the two men hidden there. He walked to the middle of the yard and said, "Can you all see me clear?"

"I could blast you right where you stand," Julie called out.

"Well, don't do it."

Suddenly, Jerusalem said, "I see some dust clouds, Clay. I think they're coming."

"All right. Remember everybody," he shouted, "don't let yourself be seen until you see me knock my man out of the saddle. If you do, we're in trouble." He moved back quickly to the smokehouse, stepped inside, and closed the door. It was dark in there, and he heard the hum of insects but ignored them. He had already found a gap between the boards, and he held his own musket up but did not insert it through the opening.

He stood there looking and found himself wishing that he could pray. It was not the first time that he had envied those who seemed to have this privilege. He discovered that his hands were trembling, and he was shocked. He looked down at them and murmured, "I didn't think anything in the world could make me do that." He knew, however, that it was not fear for his own life or even for the men. It was for Jerusalem and the women. He knew what would happen if his plan didn't work, so he bowed his head for a moment, pulled his hat off, and stood there in the murky light that filtered through the cracks. "Lord," he said, "I got no business calling on You—and I don't for myself—but I'd appreciate it if You would take care of the womenfolk." He finally shrugged his shoulders, put his hat back on, and then moved to watch as the Mexican soldiers drew closer to the ranch.

Lieutenant Alanso pulled the troop up, and as his horse moved restlessly, he stared at the house.

"It's deserted, sir," his sergeant said.

"I think so. Go take a look, Sergeant."

The sergeant eagerly spurred his horse forward. He rode at a full gallop, raising a cloud of fine dust, until he came to the yard in front of the house. He stepped off his horse, tied him at the hitching post, and then went straight into the house. He had his rifle in his hand, and he looked around and saw no one. Quickly, he whirled and went back on the porch. "There's nobody here, sir," he yelled toward the others, who had remained a distance from the house.

Alanso nodded. "All right, men. Let's burn the place." He brought the troop to a gallop until they were all gathered in front of the yard. Alanso laughed and said, "No women for you this time, men, but we'll catch some for you soon enough. Take what you want from this place and then burn—"

He did not finish his sentence, for a bullet struck him directly in the mouth. As he fell from his horse, he faintly heard the fusillade of shots, and he died before he touched the earth.

Julie whispered, "That soldier's coming in the house."

Jerusalem said, "Quick. Hide, Julie." She watched as Julie ran down the hall, and then quickly she ducked into the storeroom. She was breathing hard, and fear crept up on her of what would happen if Clay's plan did not work. She stood perfectly still, the musket in her hands. As she heard the soldier's foot strike the porch, she pulled the hammer back, which made a slight click in the stillness. She knew she could not shoot until Clay gave the signal, but she stood there thinking of Moriah and Mary Aidan and even Julie. She found herself holding her breath, and then she heard the heavy steps come inside the house and walk around. For a moment, her breathing stopped. She was afraid he would come and jerk the door open. She reversed her grip and held the butt forward, planning to strike the man in the face if necessary.

And then she heard the soldier go outside and call something to his officer. Quickly, Jerusalem lowered the rifle, and she heard the troops yelling at one another. She heard the soldier move inside again, and suddenly a shot rang out from the outside.

That's Clay's shot, she thought. She stepped outside, and the soldier whirled to see her. He grinned and moved toward her, but Jerusalem lifted the rifle and pulled the trigger. The shot caught him in the chest and drove him over backward. He dropped his musket, but even as he lay there with blood pouring from his chest, he was struggling to remove his pistol from the holster. At once Jerusalem came forward and put her hand on his arm. He looked up at her and said something about his mother, then his eyes glazed and he went limp. "Julie, get in here!" she shouted.

She turned and began to load her rifle. She saw that several of the soldiers were on the ground and were returning the fire, although they could see nobody. They were shouting and screaming. Jerusalem finished loading, and lifting her rifle, she took dead aim and knocked one of the soldiers off. She turned to reload, but then something slapped her on the back. She thought, *Who could have hit me?* But then the slap drove her to the floor, and the searing pain came.

Clay had shot two of the soldiers, but he saw one of the Mexicans whose horse had been shot get up and run for the house. He burst out of the smokehouse at a dead run, ignoring the pain in his side. The soldier saw him, turned, and drew his saber. He started for Clay, but Clay pulled the heavy bowie knife from his belt and threw it with all of his strength. It caught the soldier in the stomach, and he stared at it. He lifted his eyes, and Clay saw that he was very young, not over sixteen, it seemed. He did not wait to see the man fall but glanced around and saw that seven of the soldiers were riding away furiously. Two of them fell as they reached the outer perimeters of the yard, and Clay was shocked to see arrows coming from their bodies. As the other five fled, the three Comanches appeared out of nowhere and rode after the soldiers at full speed, uttering wild screams.

Suddenly Clay turned, for Julie had come out of the house. "Jerusalem's been shot!" she cried.

Instantly, Clay felt a chill. He ran inside past Julie and found Jerusalem lying facedown, and her back was bloody.

The wound was evidently high on her back. Without hesitation Clay reached up, grabbed the neckline of her dress at the back, and ripped it open. As he tore away the undergarment, he was aware that Julie was standing over him.

"Is she dead, Clay?"

"No. It ain't bad, Julie. Thank God! It hit her a glancing blow, but she's losing blood fast. Go keep the men out of here, and you and Moriah get some water and some strips of cloth to bandage this wound."

Clay hardly heard the voices as Julie kept the men locked out. He was aware that Mary Aidan had come and was watching him, her face white. "She'll be all right, honey. I just have to do a little bandaging." When Moriah came back with water, he said, "You take Mary Aidan out. She don't need to see this."

Julie was there then with cloth that she was tearing up.

"Make a pad that I can put over this track."

Julie instantly folded the cloth until it was long enough to cover the wound that had plowed a furrow into Jerusalem's upper back. "It didn't hit her straight on. It would have killed her if it had. Are you all right, Jerusalem?" Clay said.

"I'm . . . all right."

"I know it hurts, but we've got to get it bandaged to stop the bleeding."

Clay washed away the blood with the water Moriah had brought, took the bandage, and carefully put it over her back. He hesitated then and looked up. "Julie, maybe a woman ought to do this. It's got to be tied around in front. You'd better do it."

"Nope," Julie said. "I'm no good at things like that. You go right ahead."

Clay hesitated, but Jerusalem said, "Go on, Clay. Do it." She sat up, gasping from pain, and pulled her dress down until it hung around her waist. Clay was behind her, and instantly he took some of the long strips and began to pass them around her body. He put one over her shoulder and several high over her chest. Even as he did, he could not help notice that her back was as smooth as a young girl's. It was strong and well-formed, but he put that out of his mind.

When he tied the last bandage behind, he said, "You can pull your dress up now."

Jerusalem pulled her dress up. It was torn in the back, but she held it up in front, then turned to face him. She saw that Clay's face was flushed. "Well, I guess you've seen a woman's back a time or two."

"Well, I reckon not under these circumstances. We got off lucky, but I wish it was me that got nicked instead of you."

"I'm glad it wasn't."

Clay licked his lips and said nervously, "When I saw you lyin' on the floor with blood all over your back, I like to have died, Jerusalem."

Jerusalem stared at him curiously. "Did you, Clay? Why did you feel like that?" She saw him struggle for an answer, but he was unable to find one.

"I reckon they'll be worried about you. I'll go fetch 'em. That bandage will have to be changed pretty often."

Jerusalem smiled then. "Well, I've got a good doctor. You can take care of that, I expect." She saw Clay stare at her blankly, then he shook his head and turned and hurried from the room. She smiled as she watched him go. "It's good to see you shook up even if it takes a bare back to do it, Clay Taliferro!"

CHAPTER
SIX

Sam Houston stood looking at the dispatches that Deaf Smith had just arrived with. He had taken them from a Mexican courier. When Houston looked up from them, there was a gleam in his eyes. "Well, Deaf, I reckon it's time to find out who's the big dog."

"Reckon so, General." Deaf gestured toward the messages. "According to these, you ain't likely to catch Santa Anna with fewer men. I doubt he's got more than seven, eight hundred in his column."

"But he'll have more if we don't take him now."

"What's your plan, General?" Deaf asked.

"I'll tell you, Deaf, but then you keep it to yourself. I don't want the men to know what's going on until it happens." He pulled a rough map out of the desk drawer and laid it flat on the table. "Okay, here we are. Up here is the San Jacinto River, and over here is Buffalo Bayou. That's where we are now."

"You're right about that. It looks to me like we've got ourselves caught in a trap."

"If Santa Anna moves in, he'll come in from here, you see, and he thinks he'll have us trapped. And in a way he will."

Suddenly, Deaf Smith laughed his high-pitched eerie laugh. "I think I got your meanin', Sam. Our boys can't run away this way because the river's there. They can't run this way because of Buffalo Bayou. They could take off toward Harrisburg, I reckon."

"Not if you take some men and burn the bridge." Houston smiled grimly.

Deaf Smith stared at the general. "We'd be trapped for sure, wouldn't we?"

"That's right, but that's my plan. Keep it to yourself. We let Santa Anna's column come in right here alongside Lake Peggy. I don't think he'll come chargin' in. I think he'll set up camp and wait for reinforcements. If he does that, then we've got him."

"What if the reinforcements get here before we can attack?"

"They better not," Houston said and smiled frostily. "That would ruin my plan, and I do hate to have my plans ruined. Go burn that bridge, Deaf, but don't spill my plan to anybody."

Santa Anna's scouts had finally discovered the location of Sam Houston and his small force. They had brought the word back, and Santa Anna had made them repeat their report several times. "You say he is trapped in between this river and this swamp?"

"Yes, General. There is a bridge, but it's very small. If you attack head on, they would have no place to run. They would be trapped."

Santa Anna was an impetuous man, but something about this situation set off an alarm. He believed the scouts and moved his men into place and studied the map carefully. The area was barely three square miles and was roughly triangular, bounded on the northeast and the northwest by the San Jacinto River and the Buffalo Bayou. It was open on the southwest, but the ground was marshy along the margins of the waterways, where the land was cut with shallow ravines. On the night of the twentieth of April, Santa Anna encamped on the southeastern corner of the plain up against an arm of the San Jacinto River. He walked about and studied the terrain, wishing that the reinforcements would arrive soon. He walked along the line and inspected the placement of his soldiers. The Matamoros Battalion covered the front, which extended from the edge of Lake Peggy on the east for about twelve hundred yards, running into a little copse of woods and then curling toward the southwest. He had only one cannon, a six-pounder, but word had come that more were on the way. On his right flank, he placed five companies, and on the left five more. Somewhat back of these he made his personal camp with the lancers of his escort. His entire force amounted to no more than six hundred and fifty, perhaps, seven hundred men. He had no reserve, just himself and his staff, but he was expecting six hundred reinforcements under General Cos to arrive within a few hours and did not anticipate any serious enemy action before then. He studied the terrain and then went back to his tent, where a young señorita had been brought in to keep him company until the battle started.

On April the twenty-first, Houston held his war council. He had planned to attack on the morning of the twenty-second, but the army was rebellious. They voted company by company to fight immediately, and Houston was secretly pleased. He whispered, "Better they think the attack is their idea, Deaf."

"I reckon you're right, General. I don't know how many men we're facin', but we got nearly a thousand here. They couldn't have many more than that. The thing that bothers me is how we gonna march a thousand men on a bright, sunny day across a mile of open ground. Them Mexicans ain't militia over there. They've been in battles before and know how to fight."

Houston did not even answer. He had made up his mind, and his bridges were burned. "We'll form 'em up right now," he said decisively and began to place his men. He had sixty horsemen mounted under Mirabeau Buonaparte Lamar, a fierce fighter. Lamar's orders were to keep the Mexicans from breaking across the prairie. Next, he installed two small companies of Texas regular army with one gun to support each wing. Then Burleson's first regiment, the Texas backbone of the army, took its place in line. Then Moseley Baker's riflemen and finally Sidney Sherman's second with a corps of Kentucky men.

Houston had thought his plan out carefully and stationed the men in a line only one man deep. In the center floated the republic flag: a five-point blue star with the motto *Ubi Libertas Habitat Ibi Nostra Patria Est*—"Where Liberty Lives There Is Our Homeland." Houston then mounted his huge, white stallion Saracen and looked down the line. They had readied their equipment and formed their companies. Now astride Saracen, Houston took up his position in the center of the line. At three-thirty he drew his sword and waved the army forward. There was no band, but two men, a black drummer and a German fifer, began to play, and the men began to sing along with it. The only tune they knew was a bawdy tune played and sung in brothels:

Will you come to the bow'r I have shaded for you?
Our bed shall be roses all spangled with dew.
There under the bow'r on roses you'll lie
With a blush on your cheek but a smile in your eye.

To the tune of a song usually sung in the houses of ill-repute, the Texans, tired, dirty, bearded, and terribly angry, leveled their long rifles and marched forward across the open plain. Brodie looked to his left and saw Sam Houston astride his white horse. His knees felt weak, and he gripped his musket so hard that his knuckles were white. He moved forward with the battle line and said to Zane, who was on his left, "Zane, I guess you'd better know now I'm scared plumb to death."

"So are the rest of us." Zane turned and grinned. "The older you get, the better you get at coverin' that up."

"You'll be all right," Rice said, who was on Brodie's right. "Listen to that song. Not a very good fighting song."

Neither of them said anything else, and there was a strange silence as the line advanced across the plain. Brodie could not believe that the Mexican army was not there to meet them. A slight hill stood between the two armies with some scattered oak trees, but even so, it was amazing that there was not line after line of armed, uniformed soldiers waiting there to attack them.

It soon became apparent that Santa Anna's overconfidence had led him to post no scouts and no sentries. Most of his troops were fast asleep. None of the senior officers were aware of the advance of the Texans.

Brodie found himself in a strange mood. He knew he could not run. He could not bear the thought of his friends seeing him fleeing like a coward. He seemed to be caught and marched on with the rest of the advancing men in his company. They emerged from a ravine in the center of the plain, and there, not five hundred yards away, lay the Mexican lines. He saw the tents and men moving about and the horses picketed far to his right. His mouth was dry, and his throat seemed to close up, but Zane laughed.

"Will you look at 'em? They act like they're out on a blasted picnic! They don't even know we're coming."

"Well, devil throw smoke!" Rice said and actually laughed. "Look at them! They act like men in a play."

Suddenly, a bugler somewhere to the right sounded the alarm, and men began scurrying around. A cannon cut loose with grape shot, but the fire was too high and went over the heads of the advancing troops. The Texas artillery opened up then. The two guns called the Twin Sisters unlimbered and let fly at two hundred yards in the Mexican lines. Lamar's cavalry began swinging around to the right as a feint, and the infantry rushed forward. As the Texas line moved forward, the gunners manhandled the Twin Sisters to within seventy yards and then brought them into action. As they opened fire, Brodie heard a cry go up and down the line, and he heard himself shouting. He moved forward at a trot and heard Zane say, "Look, Houston's gone down." He turned to see Sam Houston's horse down, but Houston mounted another horse and pressed on, shouting and waving his sword as his men advanced.

All up and down the line, the Texans were shouting, "Remember the Alamo! Remember Goliad! Remember the Alamo!" Suddenly, the line dissolved, and every man ran screaming toward the enemy. When they were no more than twenty yards away, the Texas rifles began to explode in a tremendous roar. Brodie drew his rifle, pulled the trigger, and saw one of the fleeing Mexicans fall down. The eight hundred rifles had left gray uniforms of the dead and dying scrambled all across the trampled ground.

Time seemed to cease for Brodie, and he screamed and charged forward in a battle madness. He stumbled over a body once, and his face was no more than a foot away from the dead man's. He saw an ant on the face of the dead man, crawling along the lower lip, and the sight sickened Brodie. He got to his feet dazed, reloaded his musket, and pushed forward. Somehow, he had gotten separated from Zane and Rice. He moved forward, and what he saw was not like the battle he had envisioned.

Brodie had always pictured a battle with two sides facing each other, shooting and reloading, but there was none of this at San Jacinto. It had become a massacre! He saw the Mexicans screaming and fleeing, but laughing Texans shoved bayonets through them as they tried to flee. Other Texans were using knives, and some were even taking scalps.

The Mexican army had simply dissolved, and there was now nothing but murderous death.

Brodie had no heart for murder and was sickened by the brutal butchery. He moved forward, watching in horror and disgust at what he saw. A battle was one thing, but Goliad had been no worse than this. He remembered the fear that had filled him when he thought he was going to die, but now he felt a strange sympathy for the Mexican soldiers who were dying by the hundreds.

"Rice, have you seen Brodie?"

Rice looked up, his face black with powder. "No, I thought he was with you."

"This battle is over," Zane said grimly. "You go that way, and I'll go this way. We've got to find Brodie. I'd never be able to face Jerusalem if anything happened to that boy."

Mateo had not been aware of the charge of the Texans until he heard the cannon go off. He grabbed his rifle and waited for the officers to put the soldiers into order, but there seemed to be no order. Santa Anna and his colonels under him ran about shouting conflicting orders. Some of the soldiers, Mateo saw, simply threw down their arms and begged for mercy, and the rest fled.

Though the Mexicans dropped their weapons and tried to surrender, they were clubbed and stabbed, some of them on their knees. Everywhere were the high-pitched shouts and screams of the Texans, "Remember the Alamo!" The cries of vengeance frightened the Mexicans even more, and they fled, but there was nowhere to flee. They were trapped between the bayou and the river. Mateo ran, but men were dropping all around him. He turned and saw a huge soldier coming at him with a saber no doubt taken from a Mexican officer. He had a full beard, and his teeth were white as he grinned and shouted, "Here's for the Alamo, you dirty Mex!"

Mateo knew there was no escape. He stood straight and dropped his hands at his side. He had no weapon, and he waited for the blow to strike him dead.

Suddenly, the man grunted and fell headlong down on his face. Mateo was shocked, and he looked and saw a man holding a rifle with the butt reversed. He had struck the soldier with the saber in the head—and then Mateo whispered, "Brodie!"

Brodie lowered the rifle and looked down and saw that the soldier he had struck was stirring. "Thank God I didn't kill him," he said. "Come on, Mateo, let's get out of here." Mateo seemed unable to move, so Brodie grabbed his arm and started leading him away. The screams of the dying filled the air. As they moved forward, a Texan started toward them, his eyes on Mateo. Brodie lowered his rifle and said, "This is my prisoner." He saw the soldier waver, then turn and run toward a group that was butchering Mexicans in the bayou. Turning to Mateo, he said, "It's a good thing he didn't know this musket's empty. Come on."

They reached a group of men led by General Juan Almonte. He had managed to hold them together and surrender to one of Houston's officers, who stood there keeping them from the massacre going on all over the battlefield.

"You'll be safe now," Brodie said.

Mateo swallowed hard and felt a weakness in his legs. "You saved my life, Brodie."

Brodie looked into Mateo's face. "Well, you done the same for me and Clay over at Goliad. I figured I owed you."

"We're even, then." Mateo looked around and saw the proud army of Santa Anna being butchered. "It's all over," he said. "General Santa Anna's either dead or captured."

"Well, I'm proud of it," Brodie said. "Now you and me won't ever have to shoot it out."

The two young men stood there until finally Zane and Rice came running up. "You okay?" Zane demanded.

"I'm all right. I'm glad to see you fellas made it. You remember Mateo."

"Sure do," Zane said. He wanted to ask questions, but he saw the pain in the young Mexican's face. "Well," he said, "I guess—" He looked over the field and said, "I guess this pretty well ends the war."

Brodie felt a gust of relief. *I'm glad of it,* he thought. Aloud he said to Mateo, "Now we can go back to livin' again."

PART TWO :

STAR RANCH

CHAPTER
SEVEN

A sickening smell hung in the air, for after the battle of San Jacinto, the Texans had refused to bury the dead of their enemies. The bodies of the dead swelled, turned black, and their distended stomachs burst the buttons of their uniforms.

Brodie could not eat, and in all truth, neither Zane nor Rice had much appetite either. Everyone was shocked at the overwhelming success of their attack on Santa Anna's army. The Texans had lost two men in the battle, and of the thirty wounded, several more were fairly sure to die. Over six hundred dead Mexicans lay scattered across the field, and General Almonte surrendered the rest. The captured Mexicans were sitting on the ground, dazed by the horror that had overtaken them by surprise. Brodie had withdrawn from the battlefield to get away from the stench of the dead, but late in the afternoon he heard cries that he could not identify. He straightened up and ran back and saw Rice and Zane standing there, watching something and grinning.

"What is it?" Brodie demanded.

"It's Santa Anna! There he is right there!" Zane exclaimed.

Brodie stared at the captive, who was heavily guarded now by a half-dozen armed Texans, and gasped, "Is that really him? Why, he don't look like nothin'!"

"They found him hidin' in a canebreak over by the bayou," Rice said.

Zane nodded and grinned even broader. "I don't reckon he'd have been found out, but when they started bringing him back, all the Mexis started calling out, *'El Presidente.'* "

The man who was the center of attention, the president of Mexico, was not very impressive. He was unshaven and dirty and wearing the tunic of a Mexican private to try to hide his identity. Many of the Texans were crying out, "Hang him! Hang the butcher!"

Sam Houston was sitting underneath a tree with his wounded leg stretched out, his eyes fixed on Santa Anna. He ignored the cries from the angry soldiers, looked around, and saw some carrying coiled rope ready to carry out the execution. Deaf Smith stood off to one side, watching the dictator with a grin fixed on his lips.

Houston lifted his voice. "Quiet down, men. Try to act like soldiers."

"Let's hang him, General. Remember the Alamo! Remember Goliad!"

Houston did not even answer. The crowd grew quiet, and Brodie leaned forward so as not to miss a word of it. Sam Houston would not have minded in the least hanging Santa Anna except for one fact—there were still four thousand Mexican troops in Texas, over half of them within fifty miles. Houston's mind was working rapidly, and he understood clearly that hanging Santa Anna might satisfy the blood lust in his men, but it would do nothing toward helping free Texas. He was wise enough to realize that hanging Santa Anna would only make him a martyr, and his troops would go on a murderous rampage all across Texas.

"General," Houston called out, "I'm glad you've survived."

Santa Anna, whose face was pale, as if all the blood had drained, took courage at these words. He stood straighter and bowed from the hip. "General Houston," he said. "I surrender myself and my men to you without reservation."

"Mighty nice of him," Zane whispered, "seein' he ain't got no other choice."

"Why is Houston being so nice to him?" Brodie whispered back.

"Sam Houston's a fox. The corpse of Santa Anna ain't no good,"
Zane said. "He'll trade with him."

Indeed, that was exactly what happened. Houston treated Santa Anna
with all courtesy, and the two even shared a pipe of opium. Santa Anna and
Houston got along surprisingly well, and in the end the terms Sam
Houston demanded were simple. In return for his life, Santa Anna signed
a public and secret treaty with the Republic of Texas. He swore personally
never to take arms against Texas and that all hostilities between the two
nations would cease immediately. He also agreed that the Mexican Army
in Texas would withdraw below the Rio Grande and that all American prisoners would be released.

Zane turned away, and the other two followed him. "Looks like we're
about done here, with the treaty now signed and everything," he said.

"Are we going home now?" Brodie asked.

"I expect we will. We'll hang around for a little while, but if you ask
me, there won't be any more fightin'."

"I think you're right," Rice said. "Besides that, I doubt that General
Houston can afford to keep an army. Texas is a republic now, but there's
no money."

"The army will scatter if they don't get paid," Zane observed. "I
expect that's what we'll do, but we'll wait to see what happens."

The three waited a week, but it soon became apparent that there would be
no more military action. On Monday morning Zane had made the decision. "We'll pull out today, but first we'll see if we can get a word with the
general."

They found Deaf Smith and persuaded him without difficulty to let
them have a word with Houston. The three were admitted to Houston's tent. He was sitting with his leg propped up. His wound was
severe and had taken its toll on him, but he was genial enough. He listened as Zane explained that they needed to get home to take care of
their womenfolk, and he nodded, saying, "I understand, men. I appreciate your loyal service."

"What do you think will happen next, General?" Brodie piped up.

Sam Houston smiled at the young man. "I want Texas in the Union, but it's going to be hard to get in. Not everybody's going to greet us with open arms. We'll make it in the end, though, or my name ain't Sam Houston."

Zane saw that the general was tired and weak and said, "General, if it ain't too forward of me, I'd like to know about the land you promised to those who joined up."

"You're going to get it." Sam Houston nodded. "Six hundred and forty acres each. It'll take a while to get the paperwork done, but you leave your addresses with my adjutant, and as soon as I can do it, every soldier who served at San Jacinto will own a piece of Texas. Good luck to you, men, and stay available. I may need you in the days to come."

Zane laughed. "You just send for us, General. We'll be back."

"I wish I didn't have to leave you here, Mateo." Brodie had stopped by where the prisoners were being held, and they admitted him without difficulty.

The guards were lax, and the one that Brodie had spoken to said, "Wait a few days and they'll all be loose. We ain't got nothin' to feed 'em anyway."

Mateo had greeted Brodie without enthusiasm. He was leaner than ever, and his face was drawn. He wasn't the same young man Brodie had known. With Santa Anna's defeat, something in Mateo seemed to have died.

"You're going home, Brodie?"

"Yeah, we're pullin' out today. I'll be going to see your family. You want to write 'em a letter?"

"No, but give them a message for me."

"Sure. Be proud to."

"Tell them as soon as I'm released, I'll come. But I'm going back to Mexico."

"You're leaving Texas?"

"There's nothing here for a true Mexican," Mateo said bitterly.

Brodie studied the face of his friend. Mateo had always been a handsome, cheerful young man, full of life, but the loss of the battle had changed him. He was filled with a bitterness that was almost palpable. Brodie hated to see it and tried to find some way to encourage him.

"I expect this'll all blow over now that everything's settled."

Mateo stared at Brodie. "Things are not settled," he said. "We lost the battle, but there will be others."

Brodie was rather shocked. "Why, the war's over, Mateo. Santa Anna signed a treaty."

Mateo Lebonne stared at Brodie, and his eyes were hard as agates. "Not for me," he said softly. "For me the war will never be over." He shook himself and tried to smile. "Thank you for saving my life, Brodie. Tell my family that I'm well. I will see them soon. Good-bye."

"Good-bye," Brodie said and could not think of anything to add. He turned, and as he walked back to where Zane and Rice were getting ready to leave, he thought, *Mateo's had a hard bump. I hope he can get over it.* When he reached the horses, he swung up into the saddle.

"You ready to go home, Brodie?" Zane asked.

"I am, and I hope I never have to fight in no other army." The three turned their horses west and rode out of the camp at a fast gallop.

CHAPTER EIGHT

Twilight had come now, and the low hills to the west were turning dark and edged against the sky. The flatland to the east slowly foreshortened as the night's shadows crept over it. Jerusalem sat quietly beside the graves of her boys, watching as the sun slipped below the horizon. As she sat there in the dusk, a sadness came over her. The silence seemed to nurture it, for only the cry of a night bird, always a sad sound to her, broke the stillness of the land.

She stared at the graves, and her sadness turned bitter. It overwhelmed her as she remembered when each of her sons had died. Those days of mourning and grief had drained her of all strength to perform even the simplest of tasks. And for days she had fought to control the desperate screams she wanted to utter. She had wanted to shake her fist at God and demand why He took her boys, but the bitterness and anger had remained trapped inside. She thought she had gotten beyond the worst of what she felt. The wild anger that would come upon her at first had passed away, washed into the river of time that she had navigated. Now, however, she felt a loneliness and emptiness gnawing at her heart. She could not help but think what Bobby and Hartsell Lee would have been like if they had lived. Much like Brodie or Clinton, perhaps. She always had them pictured in her mind as they were when they had passed beyond her hand. Bobby died at six of cholera, Hartsell Lee two years earlier of that same horrible disease, which seemed to reach out and strike almost at random.

The fear of losing her own again had gripped her when Brodie had ridden out with Rice and Zane to join up with Sam Houston's army. She loved Zane, as she loved Julie, but he was a grown man, toughened by time, while Brodie seemed to her little older than when he had run about the house barefooted in a single shirt, his eyes bright, his voice crying out. Looking up at the sky, she searched the infinity beyond the few stars that were already beginning to twinkle.

"Oh, God," she whispered, "why did You take my boys?" She spoke aloud involuntarily, and then brushed a hand across her face, trying to dispel the shadows in her mind. She expected no answer from God, for she had prayed this prayer a thousand times.

Suddenly, she was startled as the big hammerheaded tom cat that had been adopted by Moriah leaped into her lap. She stroked the battle-scarred face, and the cat began to purr loudly. He shoved his face against her hand, and she doubled up her fist so that he could push against it.

"Well, Smokey, you look pretty bad," she said quietly. Her fingers traced the scars on Smokey's head, and the purr seemed to intensify. "All those fights for a little romance. Was it worth it, do you think? Or have you forgotten now all that tomcatting around you've done?" She sat there speaking quietly to the cat, when suddenly Bob appeared. The huge dog cast a resentful glance at Smokey, whom he hated, and sat down on her feet.

Smoky turned, and his paw shot out and raked across Bob's jowl. He did not draw blood, but Bob's eyes glowed, and a deep, vicious growl began rumbling in his throat.

"You two stop that or get off of me!" Jerusalem scolded, slapping both of them on the head. They both settled down to a temporary truce, but Jerusalem knew that it would last only as long as she was there.

A coyote began to howl far off, and Jerusalem felt an answer in her heart—which was filled with loneliness. She stroked Smoky's head, and he settled down, but her thoughts suddenly turned inward. She had been thinking, ever since Brodie left, how she would handle it if he were killed in battle. And now she shoved the thought away and fiercely tried to think of the things she had to do, the meal that she would fix for dinner tomorrow, the need to build a fence to protect the chickens from the coyotes and other varmints that roamed the plain. Anything to think of but losing Brodie! She could not bear the thought of that!

She was not a woman given to a great deal of introspection, but at times, she did have those moments of contemplation, wondering what it was that made her the woman that she was. As she sat there, she realized that the feelings for Brodie were mixed with something else. Her thoughts turned to her marriage with Jake, which had been bittersweet all those years he was gone. He had not been a good husband—in fact, he had been a very bad one. But still, when she thought of those times when he came home from his long wanderings, she remembered how she had responded to him fiercely. She knew she was a woman of great passion, and when Jake had left for those long periods, she had missed his touch. And even now she longed for a man to love her completely.

"I miss having a man."

Jerusalem whispered these words aloud and then suddenly felt ashamed. "Why, I must be a hussy to say such a brazen thing!" She tried to push the thought away, and yet it would not leave, and she began to wonder if other women craved physical love the way she did. She well understood that it was only part of a marriage, but it had been a part she had mostly been denied. Not long after marrying Jake, she had understood that she loved him more than he loved her. All the years that they had been together, she had tried to win his love. When he was home, she had pleased him with her affection and warmth. But he had neglected to tell her so, for he had not been a man who said such things.

Suddenly, a fragment of sound came to Jerusalem, and she grew still, shoving her thoughts aside. The sound grew louder, and hope grew in her. It was still light enough to see the two horsemen that approached, and her heart gave a lurch. *Only two,* she thought. *Was one of them killed?*

She got up immediately, shoving Smoky up from her lap and pushing Bob away. The horsemen grew larger, and soon they were close enough so she could see that it was Zane and Brodie. She thought for a moment with fear of what had happened to Rice, but the joy of seeing Zane and Brodie pushed that away. She saw Brodie step out of the saddle, and she rushed toward him. He was smiling, and when she got to him, she was overwhelmed with emotion but did not want to cry in front of them.

Brodie laughed, saying, "Well, Ma, I reckon you're glad to see us."

Zane stood by smiling at the scene and said, "I bet you hope Serena gives you that kind of welcome."

Jerusalem turned and went to Zane, and kissed him soundly on the cheek. "I've been worried about you both."

She had no time to say more, for the others came running out of the house. Mary Aidan ran straight to Brodie, who snatched her off her feet and tossed her high in the air. She began peppering him with questions, and Julie asked, "Where's Rice?"

"He went on into town," Zane said. "He had some kind of business to see to."

Moriah went to hug Brodie and said, "What was it like? Did you fight? Was there a battle?"

"Don't pester them with questions. I know they're starved," Jerusalem broke in.

"That's right," Zane said. "We ain't had a good meal since we left here."

Jerusalem took a deep breath, then released it. "Come on inside, and I'll fill you up." She had a thousand questions swelling inside her that she wanted to ask. She looked at her brother, who smiled and nodded his head in a knowing fashion. They would talk later. She wrapped her arms around both of them and walked into the house.

CHAPTER
NINE

A pale blistering sun beat down from overhead, heating all the earth, an implacable melting ball in a cloudless cerulean sky. The air was thin and still, and far off Clay could see a cloud of fine dust raised by wild horses. As he lay tilted back in his chair, he watched the heat waves dancing in layers along the soil. At his feet Bob lay as if dead, which was customary with him. The big hound had basically two motions, either lying like a dead dog or growling and charging inexorably at something or someone.

A restlessness had taken hold of Clay in a way that he had experienced several times in his life. The wound he had taken at Goliad had slowed him down so that he had been unable to work. Simply sitting around the house watching the women wash clothes and cook was not his idea of an exciting life. For some reason he felt that something had come to an end for him. He had thought about how his life had had purpose when he had come back from the mountains to bring money from Jake to Jerusalem and the family. He'd had no intention of staying more than a few days, but somehow he had wound up agreeing to help them leave Arkansas and head for Texas in search of Jake. That had been a challenge that he'd accepted, and he managed to keep them from getting scalped and help them get established.

After arriving in Texas, he had thrown himself into the effort of keeping the family together—and had even taken on looking after Gordon Lebonne's family after he had died. It had been a chore seeing to all these responsibilities. When he had ridden off to join Sam Houston's army to take part in the battles against Santa Anna, that had been exciting.

But there was nothing interesting sitting on a chair on a front porch and watching Bob as if he were dead. He felt like giving Bob a poke with his heel, but he knew Bob would not move unless he kicked him hard. "You are a worthless, triflin' dog and ought to be chopped up and fed to the fish, Bob. What do you think of that?"

Bob didn't even move a muscle, and Clay shook his head in disgust. "You and me are about the same. More dead than alive."

For a time he sat there thinking about the mountains, and, as always, he remembered the good times he had spent there. Sure, there had been danger, but part of the excitement was the adventure he had experienced living there. The weather was hot enough in the summer, but it was a dry heat that didn't bother a man. And in the winter when the cold crackled, a man could spit, and sometimes it would freeze in the air with a snapping sound—now, *that* was weather! He thought with longing of the cold mountain streams, cold enough to make a man's teeth hurt. He also remembered times when he thought he would get scalped, but even those he remembered fondly. He had never felt more alive than when he was matching his wits and his eyes and his legs against the Cheyenne.

Maybe I ought to go back to the mountains. I hear they found gold out in California. Maybe I ought to go try to fill my pockets up with nuggets. He toyed with the idea, and as he did, he saw Julie come out from around the house. She had been boiling clothes, washing them, and now she had come to hang them on a wire that was strung between two big walnut trees that stood to the east of the house. His eyes narrowed, for he saw that she was wearing a pair of pants and a man's shirt. He recognized the pants as belonging to Clinton, who had outgrown them—and noted with appreciation that Julie filled them out thoroughly. A smile touched his lips as he watched her fasten a dress to the line and then a petticoat and then a pair of men's drawers. He thought, *There's somethin' downright unseemly about hangin' men's underwear alongside of women's, but that wouldn't bother Julie none.*

He tilted back, enjoying watching her. Though she could be difficult at times, he was fond of Julie. He never knew what she would do next, although whatever it was would be fairly audacious. He liked that about her, but he was careful around her. He knew he would have to answer to Jerusalem if he ever took up with Julie.

He heard a shout and brought his chair down and twisted to the right. Clinton had come sailing out of the barn, shouting as he approached. Clay grinned, for it amused him to watch Clinton's religious fits. He was convinced that one day Clinton would calm down, but right now the young man had all the fiery heat of an evangelist.

"What do you think you're doin'?" Clinton shouted, coming up to Julie. She turned to face him and did not answer for a moment. "Don't you know you'll go to hell for wearin' forked pants?"

Julie laughed. "I never read that anywhere in the Bible."

"Well, it's there somewhere," Clinton said loudly. "It ain't decent. You get in the house right now and put on a dress like the Bible says."

"Go on about your business, Clinton. I'm going riding when I finish this, and I can't ride in a skirt."

"You ain't goin' nowhere in them pants! It's downright scandalous!"

Clay leaned back, his eyes slitted, and his lips turned upward in a grin. "Give it to her, Clinton," he murmured. "Let's hear you rip and roar and see how far you get."

At that very moment Jerusalem came out, no doubt drawn by the sounds of the two shouting at each other. She stopped on the porch alongside of Clay, took in the scene, then turned and looked at him. "Why don't you stop that, Clay?"

Clay looked up slowly and said innocently, "Why, if they was my young'uns, I would, but they ain't."

His answer angered Jerusalem. She was irritated with Clay anyhow, for ever since he'd come back from the war with Santa Anna, he had been impossible to live with. Even after his wound had healed, he'd done very little work, and now the irritation that had been growing in her boiled over. "Clay, you've been moping around for days now doing nothing but complain. It's about time you acted like a man."

Her words gave Clay a guilty feeling, which he hated. He jumped to his feet and shoved his hat back on his head. "I reckon I'm the judge of what I'll do around this place."

"Well, go do something worthwhile. You're acting like a spoiled brat."

Clay glared at her. "I reckon I will do something worthwhile. I guess I'll just go into town, have a few drinks, and play some cards." He whirled and leaped off the porch, and her words followed him.

"Good, you won't be underfoot."

Jerusalem watched him as he headed for the barn and knew that she shouldn't have said what she did. She owed Clay Taliferro more than she could ever repay for all he had done to help her, but he was hard to live with at times. Putting him out of her mind, she moved across the yard until she stood in front of Clinton and Julie.

"Clinton, what's wrong with you?"

"I wish you'd look at them pants she's got on, Ma. She ain't no better than a hussy! Why—"

"You leave her alone, Clinton."

Clinton stared at his mother, affronted. "I'd think since you're her sister, you would be more interested in her." He turned around and stalked toward the house, slamming the door as he went in.

Jerusalem turned and eyed Julie, who was watching her warily. "Don't start on me, Jerusalem. You know how he is."

"I know, but be patient with him."

"It's easier to be patient with a chigger than it is him," Julie laughed. "Did you hear what he said? He said I'd go to hell for wearing forked pants. Now, where did he get a hare-brained idea like that? If that's the worst thing I ever did, I'd feel pretty good."

"Well, they do make you look pretty—obvious."

"Let him look the other way."

Jerusalem shook her head, knowing that it was useless to talk to Julie when she was in a mood like this. Going back into the house, she found Clinton in the kitchen drinking a glass of water thirstily. He gave her a hurt look, and she went over to stand beside him. She noticed how tall he was getting. In a few more years, he would be a big man like his father. She knew he really was sensitive to anything she said. Julie had said many times, "He's nothin' but a mama's boy." His soft side did not bother Jerusalem, for she liked the obvious affection Clinton was capable of showing. She waited until he was through drinking, then reached out and took his arms. His eyes were even with hers now, and she said, "You're growing up, Clinton. Before you know it, you're going to be big like your pa and strong like he was." She smiled and reached up and ruffled his hair. "And good looking like he was, too."

As she had known it would, this sudden gentleness on her part melted Clinton. "Aw, Ma," he said. "That ain't so."

"Yes, it is." She ran her hands down his cheeks and studied his face. "You look so much like him it frightens me sometimes." She continued to talk gently to him, then gave him a hug. "Try to understand Julie. I know she's a pain at times, but it doesn't do any good to fuss at people, son." She stepped back and shook her head. "It's what's on the inside that has to change."

At that moment they heard the sound of a horse running hard, and Clinton turned and looked out the window. "There's Clay," he said. "Where is he goin' ridin' so hard?"

"Probably to get drunk," Jerusalem said.

Clinton swirled around. "To get drunk! Why?"

"Because I nagged him. I should have learned by this time, Clinton, that Clay's a man, and he's got to make a fool of himself from time to time." A reluctant smile turned the corners of her lips up. "It's in all men. Once in a while it just has to break out."

Clinton was staring at her incredulously, and then his eyes danced. "What about women?"

Jerusalem laughed and said, "No, we're all sweet and soft-spoken and nice all the time. Haven't you noticed?"

Clinton laughed aloud. He had a crooked grin, the exact replica of Jake's, which brought memories back to Jerusalem. "Well," he said, smiling broadly, "women are taken pretty easily by serpents."

"Now, was that a nice thing to say to your poor, old mother?"

"You ain't poor, and you ain't old either."

"Why, that's the nicest thing you've said to me all day! I'm gonna make you a pie of your very own. You don't even have to let Brodie have any of it. What kind will it be?"

"Apple!"

The Dry Gulch Saloon was not particularly attractive, but it was the biggest one in town, and Clay had made himself at home for the past two hours. He had been drinking steadily and playing cards, and a woman, whose name he now forgot, was sitting beside him, egging him on. He had been winning steadily, and one of the losers, a tough-looking man named Hack Dempsey, stared down at the winning hand Clay had tossed down in the middle of the table. He stared at his own hand, threw them down with a curse, and watched as Clay, moving leisurely, reached out and dragged the pot in.

"You're too lucky, Taliferro."

"Why, Hack," Clay said, pronouncing his words very distinctly, as drunks will usually do, "you hurt my feelings. Poker ain't luck. It's all skill."

Dempsey cursed again and poured himself a drink from the bottle on the table. He was a large man, a little overweight, but obviously tough. The scars on his face were proof that he had been in some fights in the past. "I'm sayin' that it ain't luck, and it ain't skill either."

Clay reached over and put his arm around the woman and pulled her close. He put his head next to her ear and said, "Lena, I think Hack is hinting around that my card playin' ain't exactly on the up and up. Is that what he's sayin'?"

"Why, honey, he wouldn't say a thing like that."

Hack cursed again. "You win one more pot, and I'll do more than say it."

"You don't understand," Clay said. He almost said *unnerstand* but pronounced the word very carefully to show them that he was not affected by all the of liquor he had downed. "I win at cards because I have a pure heart, don't you see?" He laughed at Hack's expression and said, "I don't think you have a pure heart, Hack. I think you are a mean man."

"You're gonna find out!"

At that instant Clay looked up at a man who had just entered the saloon. He blinked his eyes and had some effort focusing, then he carefully stood up, saying, "Don't nobody leave. I'll be back in a minute to show you how a pure-hearted man can win at cards."

"You'd *better* come back. I'm gettin' even," Dempsey snarled.

Clay walked carefully, holding himself erect, over to where Brodie stood. "What are you doing here, Brodie? This is no place for a young man to be. It's only for us people who have pure hearts." He laughed at his own joke and said, "Come on to the bar. I think they got some sarsaparilla."

Brodie grinned and followed Clay to the bar. He leaned up against it, and Clay said, "Clyde, give me a drink of whiskey, and give my boy here a sarsaparilla."

"I don't want no sarsaparilla, Clay, and you ain't my pa."

"Why, son, I'm the same as your pa. Ever since your poor dad died, I just felt like you was my own son, and I'm gonna look out for you. I surely am. I want you to have a pure heart like me."

Brodie laughed aloud and said, "I'll have a whiskey."

Clay studied Brodie owlishly and finally nodded, saying, "All right. You can have *one* drink, but that's all." He took his own drink, tossed his head back, downed the whiskey, and then pulled at Brodie. "Come on. I'll teach you how to play cards." He walked back to the table, slumped down into his chair, and said, "Pull up a chair there. This here is my friend Brodie. I'm gonna teach him how to play cards, but he can't have but one drink. Don't be givin' him none, you hear me?"

"I hear you," Dempsey grunted. "Now, play cards."

The game began, and Brodie drank the whiskey. It was not his first drink, despite what Clay was thinking. He watched as Clay played, and when Clyde came around with a bottle of whiskey, he let him fill his glass.

"Remember now. You can only have one drink," Clay said, his speech a bit slurred.

Brodie took the drink and grinned at the woman sitting with Clay. "I bet when you were my age, you had more than one drink."

"When I was your age," Clay said, swinging his arm around in a grandiose gesture, "I went to church every Sunday. And I helped old ladies across the street."

Brodie drank his drink, and Clay said, "Well, that's one, and that's all you get, Brodie."

"Sure, Clay," Brodie said as he sat back and watched the game go on.

The bartender brought drinks several times, and each time Clay would say, "That's right, Brodie, you can have one drink."

By the time Brodie had enough drinks to make him feel numb, a hard-faced young woman had come to sit on his lap. Clay could barely sit in his chair, but he was still winning hand after hand. He looked up and screwed his face up, trying to focus on Brodie. "You can have one drink, Brodie—unnerstand?" He looked around at the rest of the players and said, "I'll allow him just one drink a day."

The young woman named Lena, who was sitting on his lap, giggled. "Is he always this way?"

"Sure," Brodie said. "We get drunk every day like this."

Clay handled his cards awkwardly but managed to win a large pot. Hack Dempsey threw the cards down and shouted, "You cheated!"

Clay could barely sit up. He swayed as he stood up and started walking around the table. "I . . . I can't allow you to talk to me in that manner, Hack. We can't be friends with talk like that." He took a wild swing and missed Hack by a foot. Hack Dempsey drew his arm back and struck Clay a tremendous blow that caught him right in the mouth and drove him backward. Everyone in the saloon turned to watch, and Brodie pushed the girl off his lap and tried to stand up. He found he could barely do so.

Clay struggled to a sitting position. His mouth was bleeding, and he looked up owlishly at the big man who stood over him. "Have you had enough, Hack," he demanded, "or do you want some more of the same?"

Dempsey laughed and launched a kick that caught Clay in the ribs.

Seeing Clay groaning on the floor, Brodie got angry. He picked up the half-full whiskey bottle by the neck, lifted it, and brought it down on Hack's head. The bottle broke, and Hack collapsed to a sitting position. Instantly, one of Hack's friends came over and hit Brodie and knocked him down. Brodie remembered getting up, and he remembered shouting and screaming as a fight broke out. He staggered as he tried to throw punches, but he received more than he threw, and then one of Hack's friends landed a blow in Brodie's jaws. All he saw was a blackness engulfing him as he fell to the floor.

* * *

Jerusalem looked up to see Serena, whose face was tense. She had ridden in, jumped off her horse, and come running to the house. She seemed so terribly upset that Jerusalem said, "What's wrong, Serena? Somebody sick?"

"No, it's Clay and Brodie."

Instantly, Jerusalem straightened up. "What's wrong with them? Are they hurt?"

"I don't think so. Just beat up pretty bad. They got drunk in the Dry Gulch and started a fight, so the sheriff threw both of them in jail."

Jerusalem stood absolutely still. "Thank you, Serena," she said.

"I don't think it's anything very serious," Serena said. "Just fighting and disturbing the peace."

"I'm glad you came and told me."

"Do you want me to go with you and get them out?"

"No, I'll take care of it."

Clay lay flat on his back on the cot, and Brodie sat on the floor, his back against the adobe wall of the jail. Both of them had been sick several times during the night, and there was no one to clean up the mess. Brodie held his head very still, for every time he moved, it was as if someone had drilled a hole right through the center of it.

The jailer, a tall, lean man named Andy, appeared at the door to their cell. "Well," he said in a loud voice, "you boys are gettin' out."

"Could you speak a little quieter?" Clay whispered.

Andy laughed. "Come on, Taliferro. You've been sprung."

Clay rose up to a sitting position, swung his feet over the edge of the cot, and sat there staring at Andy. His eye was a colorful shade of purple and rose, and the dried blood on his face gave evidence of the fight the night before. He stood up slowly, for his head hurt something fierce. He looked over at Brodie. "Are you all right, Brodie?"

"No."

"Well, me neither. Let this be a lesson to you. I told you only one drink!"

Brodie shook his head and got to his feet and leaned against the wall. "Why, you've had enough lessons. You should have had better sense."

"You fellows can argue when you get out of here. Come on, if you can walk."

The two moved carefully out of the cell and walked down the short hall. As soon as they stepped in the office, both of them saw Jerusalem standing waiting for them. The sheriff was there, too. He had some money in his hand and glared at the two.

"If I was you, ma'am, I'd let them two stay in jail for a week or two. Why, they made a wreck out of that saloon, and there's some fellers who're gonna be out to get even."

"I'll be responsible for them, Sheriff. You don't have to worry."

She turned without another word or another look at either of the men and walked outside. Brodie muttered, "I'd druther be shot as face up to her."

"So would I," Clay said, "but it's got to be done." The two walked outside and saw that she had brought the buggy into town. Their horses were tied to the back of it. Clay walked over and said, "Jerusalem, it was Brodie's fault."

"My fault! What do you mean?" Brodie yelled and then grabbed his head. "It was *your* fault! You're the one who started the fight."

"I didn't neither, and if you'd just had one drink like I told you, none of this would have happened."

Jerusalem said, "There are your horses. Get on them if you can. Come home and get cleaned up."

After Clay untied the horses, she stepped into the buggy, spoke to the team, and then pulled off at a rapid clip. Clay stared after her and was shaken. He had never seen her like this. "I ain't goin' back, Brodie. I'm goin' prospectin'."

"I'm goin' with you."

"No, you're not. That's your home and she's your ma."

They got into an argument, and finally the sheriff came out and said, "Do you two want to go back to jail?"

"No, I don't reckon I do," Clay said. He stared at Brodie and seemed to slump. "Come on. Let's go take our medicine."

The two managed to get on their horses and turned and rode out of town at a slow walk.

* * *

Zane and Julie both enjoyed the sight of Brodie and Clay dragging in. They seemed to have been waiting for them, and when the two almost fell off their horses, Zane looked at their battered faces and said, "Well, I see you two have been enjoyin' yourselves. You should have invited me along for the fun."

"Shut up, Zane!" Clay snapped.

"Why, Clay, what a mean way to act." Zane pretended to be hurt.

Julie came over and lifted Brodie's face. He had kept his hat on and his head down, and when she examined the cuts and bruises, she said, "Listen, the next time you two want to go in and have fun, don't leave me at home."

"Leave me alone, Aunt Julie."

Mary Aidan came sailing out and threw herself at Brodie. He did not bend over to pick her up but tried to turn away. She looked up at Clay then and saw his battered face. "What's wrong with your face?"

"I fell down," Clay said loudly, then turned and walked away toward the barn. Brodie followed him, and Clinton was right with them, preaching at them at full steam.

"You'd better leave 'em alone, Clinton," Julie said. "They're liable to whip you like they did all those other people in the saloon."

Julie went inside and found that Moriah and Jerusalem had been watching. "They look terrible and they smell worse," Julie said. "You gonna whip 'em, sister?"

"I feel like it," Jerusalem said. "But it was partly my fault. I nagged Clay."

"Men don't need much naggin' to raise the devil," Julie said.

Moriah was worried. She had caught a glimpse of Brodie's face and said, "It's not like Brodie to do something like this, Ma."

"He's sullied up over Serena," Jerusalem said. "I guess I can't blame him too much. When I was about his age, I lost a beau of mine to another girl. I wanted to scratch her eyes out. I probably would have with just a little encouragement, but I just cussed her out."

"You did that, Ma?" Moriah was shocked.

"I did worse than that, but I'm not telling. Come on. There's work to be done."

The evening meal was rather strained. Clay and Brodie had cleaned themselves up as best they could, but their faces were puffy and scarred. Clay could barely turn from a blow he had taken in the ribs. Zane thought it was hilarious and made mild remarks about fighting in saloons. "The wages of sin is getting your face busted. At least that's been my experience."

Jerusalem gave him a stern look, and Zane shrugged and ceased teasing. Moriah, who was serving, stopped more than once to put her hand on Brodie's neck, and she gave him a smile. He tried to smile back, but it hurt his face.

As for Clay, he did not say a single word. Indeed, he did not even look up. He was deeply ashamed at what had happened, not so much for himself, but for dragging Brodie into his drunken foolishness. He could not look Jerusalem in the face nor anyone else, and despite Julie's effort to cheer him up, he refused to speak. Finally, Jerusalem, who had been helping Moriah serve, sat down and finished her meal. She looked around, and as she did, a silence fell on the room. Only the sound of flies buzzing was audible, and Jerusalem took a deep breath, then said, "We're leaving this place. I've decided we're going to raise cattle."

"We don't have enough land for that," Zane protested.

"I know that. We can't do it here."

"Ma, we don't know how to raise cattle," Moriah said.

Jerusalem said, "There are a million cows wandering around Texas and probably that many wild horses. We can sell out here and buy a lot of ground up north. We catch some cattle and horses and brand them."

Clay had raised his head, and his eyes were fixed on Jerusalem. One was almost swollen shut, but he said quietly, "You think the Comanches will agree to let you do it?"

"It can be done," Jerusalem said.

"This is a family matter, Jerusalem," Clay said. He half rose to leave, but Jerusalem's voice caught him.

"No, you can't leave," she said.

Clay stared at her, and for a moment the two seemed locked in some sort of struggle. Clay sat down slowly, and Jerusalem repeated, "No, you can't leave. You've got to go find us a place."

"Why me? Why not send Zane?"

"I want you to go and find some land where we can raise cattle, Clay."

Clay stared at her and then finally made some sort of helpless gesture with his hands. "All right, I'll go find you a blamed ranch—but after that I'm goin' lookin' for gold."

His words did not seem to bother Jerusalem, for she smiled and said, "You're too hung over to leave tonight, but you can leave early tomorrow morning."

Clay was up before dawn, dressed, and when he went into the kitchen, Jerusalem was already there. She had cooked flapjacks, which he liked best of any breakfasts. She smiled as he poked holes in them with his finger, then filled them with the dark molasses. He always did that with pancakes and biscuits. She sat down with him while he ate.

"Does your mouth hurt?" she said.

Clay reached up and touched his mouth. "I don't know as I hurt any place particular. Just kind of all over."

"I hate to send you out like this, Clay, but you're the only one that I can trust."

"You can trust Zane."

"He's never done anything right yet, but I've got hopes for him."

"Well, my record ain't none too good, Jerusalem."

"You'll do it," she said. "I know you will."

Clay finished his breakfast, got up, and said, "Guess I'll go saddle my horse."

"I'll put some grub up for you to take. You may be gone a long time."

She turned to gather the food, and Clay went out to the barn. He saddled his horse, and when he went back, he found her on the porch. She had gathered some of his clothes and tied them up in a tarp. He fastened it on behind his saddle and put the bag of food over the saddle horn. His rifle was shoved into the boot.

The two had not spoken much, and finally he turned to her, but before he could speak, Jerusalem came forward. She put both her hands on his shoulders and said, "Be careful, Clay. I can't spare you." She put her arms around his neck and kissed him hard on the lips, lingering for a time, and then turned and walked back into the house without another word.

Clay stared after her and then felt a weight on his feet. He looked down and saw Bob sitting on the toes of his boots, as he always did. He looked up and barked, "Whoof!"

Clay laughed. "That's my sentiments, you mangy critter! Now, git off my feet." He shoved Bob away, stepped into the saddle, and took one final look at the house. He reached up and touched his lips and thought for a long time, then turned the horse around and said, "Come on, Caesar, let's go find us a ranch."

CHAPTER
TEN

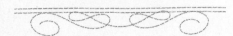

The sea of grass stretched for miles before Clay and faded into an undulating brown wave toward the horizon. The scorching heat pressed down upon him and made a thin, unseen turbulence as he rode his weary horse toward the town he had spotted earlier in the day. The cry of a flight of blackbirds made a harsh incantation as they flew overhead. For weeks he had traveled across Texas, passing rivers turned to dust, and had slept in buffalo-rutted depressions. He licked his lips and smelled the odors that drifted to him, a combination of baked grass and sage and bitter, strong dust. Two hours earlier he had lain down and drunk from a tiny stream fed by a trickle from a spring. He was exhausted and felt the burning sun on his skin. His errand had taken him long distances, and he let Caesar take his own gait as he rode toward the town. Clay sat easy in the saddle, even-balanced to save his horse, while his eyes searched the endless land. Once he caught sight of a fleeting herd of wild mustangs racing somewhere across the land.

Caesar suddenly lifted his head, snorted, and quickened his pace. Clay smiled, leaned over, and patted the sweaty shoulder of the animal. "I think you smell somethin' good in that town. Maybe like water." He straight-ened up and glanced around. "Must be a hundred and fifteen degrees out here." His saddle was too hot for comfort, and the sun hitting the metal on his bridle sent painful flashes across his eyes.

Thirty minutes later he rode into the town that was perched on the side of the Brazos River. He had been riding all day, and now his shadow ran before him as he entered Jordan City. A slight smile twisted the cor-ners of his lips up, and he murmured, "Not much of a city here. Just barely a town." It huddled beside the river, facing the desert, a double row of buildings, with other buildings scattered around. Clay's eyes moved from side to side as he rode between the lines of buildings. Most of them were painted, but the paint was faded out by the blistering sun and scoured by the sands when the winds came. One of the signs said simply "Hotel," as if there were no other hotels in the world. Across the street was another building that proclaimed itself only as "Stable." Turning Caesar toward this building, Clay murmured, "They ain't very proud of their town. Don't even think about puttin' their names on their businesses."

He stepped out of the saddle and stretched himself wearily. When a short, chunky man with a black patch over one eye came out, Clay said, "Grain him and give him a rubdown."

"Cost you extra." The reply was brief and laconic, and his eyes looked over horse and man carefully. "Looks like you had a hard ride."

"Pretty hard. Where's the best place to eat?"

"Hotel. My name's Jeffries. You be here long?"

"No, not long."

Jeffries seemed to be concerned for some reason. Perhaps he was just prying. His single eye was bright as a crow's, and he asked, "You goin' far?"

"Not too far, I guess. Take care of this horse. He's a good one."

"I always do," Jeffries said in an offended voice. He asked quickly, "You got business here, I take it."

Clay grinned. "Not quite sure. I'll let you know as soon as I make up my mind." He saw the light insult brush across the man and laughed. He pulled his saddlebags and blanket off the horse and started toward the hotel. The town was asleep, it seemed, although he could hear the tinkling of a piano from the saloon. He stepped inside the hotel and found what he had expected, a worn, tired lobby with stairs with rickety steps leading to the second floor. To the right was a bar, and to the left was some sort of a drawing room for ladies. A tall, thin man with a hook where his right hand should have been greeted him amiably.

"Howdy, just get into town?"

"Just got in. You got a room?"

"Got all the rooms you want. Put your name down right there, friend."

The hotel clerk watched as Clay signed, then looked at the name. "Reckon you say your name Tol-e-ver instead of Tal-i-ferro?"

"That's right."

"You must be from the South."

Clay nodded and said, "I need a bath and a shave and something to eat and a little recreation."

"Take number eighteen upstairs. You can get a bath and a shave down at Charlie's Barbershop down the street on the right. The best place to eat is here in the hotel, if I do say so. Golden Lady Saloon is where you might find a game."

"Thanks."

Clay climbed the stairs, aware that the man was staring at him. Strangers were always interesting in these out-of-the-way towns. Clay opened the door to room eighteen and found it no better nor worse than he had expected. A worn carpet, a bed with a sagging mattress, a washstand, and a chair. He tossed his bedroll down on the bed along with his saddlebag, looked at the bed, and was tempted to simply lie down, but he needed to sluice the weariness out of his tired body. Turning, he went down the stairs, nodded to the hotel clerk, and walked down the street to Charlie's Barbershop.

He had a long bath in a copper tub, luxuriating in the warm water. After thirty minutes, he got out and dried off with a fresh towel. He put on fresh underwear but merely shook the dust out of his shirt and pants. After paying his fifty cents for the bath, he went back to the hotel to get something to eat. Being in the saddle all day had given him a hearty appetite. He entered the restaurant and sat down at a table, and a middle-aged Mexican woman came and took his order. When the food came, he was surprised to find that it was very good. The steak was fairly tender, and the beans that went with it were well done and spiced. When he had finished, he left the payment for the meal on the table and walked out of the restaurant and headed for the saloon.

The afternoon had gone now, and dusk was coming. The sun seemed to melt into a shapeless bed of gold that painted the tops of the mountains off in the distance. The air was becoming cooler, and he stood for a moment outside the Golden Lady Saloon, watching the colors of the land run and change along the horizon. He watched the shadows creep up to the eaves of the building and the houses farther out on the prairie. The dusty road took on soft, silver shadings. The day's heat was running out of the earth, and it felt good to Clay. He took one more look at the dust that whirled in the flat of the street, then turned and pushed through the double-hinged doors of the saloon.

Raucous sound and smoke filled the place, and Clay had no doubt that this was the most active place in Jordan City in the evenings. It was still early in the evening, but the place was half full. His eyes ran over the blackjack game to his right, a poker game closer to the wall, and a roulette wheel that no one was using, watched over by a sharp-eyed man in a fancy vest. He moved over to the bar, and the burly barkeep came over. He had heavy shoulders, a thick neck, and a pair of steady gray eyes.

"What'll it be?" he asked pleasantly.

"Some beer would help wash the dust out of my throat pretty well."

"You got it."

Clay took the beer and drank it slowly. He was not much of a drink-ing man, and his last escapade with alcohol had embarrassed him. He looked the crowd over, wondering if he would have to wait till the next day to find someone who could tell him about the possible land for sale. Several men were at the bar, but none of them seemed particularly inter-ested in conversation.

Clay moved his head to look around at one of the poker players, and his eyes narrowed. A slight smile containing a little bitterness, perhaps, touched his lips. He drained the beer and put the glass down, then walked over and moved slightly to the right of a medium-sized man wearing a red calico shirt and a gray hat pushed back on his head.

"Hello, Lou."

The man with the gray hat turned around quickly and was surprised when his eyes saw Clay. He didn't speak at first, and the other three men playing at the table became interested. One of them, a well-put-together man with black, curly hair and smoothly shaved cheeks, said, "Introduce us to your friend, Burdette."

Lou Burdette did not move. He held his cards in his hand, but he seemed to have forgotten them. Finally, he nodded and said, "I didn't expect to see you, Taliferro."

"It's been a long time. When did you leave the mountains?"

"Two years ago."

"Well, if Lou won't introduce us, I'll introduce myself," the black-haired gambler said. "I'm John Barr. Everybody calls me Frisco."

"Clay Taliferro."

"Glad to know you, Taliferro. This is Charlie Hake, and this here is Prince Daniels. Sit down and take a hand."

"Thanks," Clay said. He pulled a chair over from one of the tables while Hake moved over to make room for him. "You two were in the mountains together," Frisco said.

"Been a while," Clay nodded. "Those were good times, but I guess I was glad to get out of it with my hair." He turned to face Burdette and said, "You still running with George Macon?"

"No. George took an arrow in his liver and died on the Little Missouri." The words were grudging, and the three men at the table could sense Burdette's animosity. "Are we gonna play cards, or are we gonna talk?" Burdette grunted. He was a tall man, lean almost to a fault. His skin was burned dark by the sun, and he had black eyes and hair to match. There was a wildness in him that lay underneath a thin veneer of civilization.

Clay joined in the game then and, as usual, found himself winning. He was a fine poker player, drunk or sober. He had proved that only recently. As the game continued, he studied the other men, as he always did. He had learned to read the eyes of those who played cards with him, noticing that a man could not really control the little movements of his eyes and his eyelids. A good hand would always bring some sort of reaction, the lids slightly pulling down and the pupils growing larger.

As they played, Frisco Barr, without being at all pushy, carried on a conversation with the other men. He was a better card player than the other three and often drew out when Clay had a good hand. He also gave a good bit of information about the town and the surroundings. "Not much of a town now," he said cheerfully, "but it's a good spot on the river here. One of these days it'll boom."

"Not if the Comanches don't agree to it," Charlie Hake grunted.

"They pretty troublesome?" Clay asked, studying his cards.

"They can be pesky." Hake shook his head. "They rode into town a year ago and just about held us hostage. Rode off with three women and one young boy. Never did catch 'em."

"Hard to catch a Comanche," Clay remarked.

At some point Clay mentioned that he had come from close to San Antonio, and at once Frisco asked, "That Alamo was quite a business. Don't suppose you were there?"

"No, I was at Goliad, though."

"Goliad! That was a rough thing, from what I hear."

"It was pretty bad. General Portilla's men massacred most of us. I was lucky to get away. Not many of us did."

Burdette took no part in the conversation, and his eyes often glanced at Clay as he studied his cards. He had thin lips that he kept pulled into a fine line except when he was speaking, and he threw his cards down violently whenever he lost a hand. His eyes seemed to glow with an inner fury.

Clay remembered this man well. They had not been partners, and at one of the meetings of the trappers, the two of them had gotten crossways. They got into a fistfight, and when Clay had whipped him soundly, Burdette had pulled out a knife. Clay had pulled his own knife, and when Burdette had gotten a slash across his neck—the scar was still there—he had backed off. Clay was careful after that not to turn his back on Lou Burdette. He knew the man was like a wounded animal seeking an opportunity to strike back.

Burdette was drinking steadily, and after two hours, he was starting to get more aggressive. Clay remembered he was always belligerent when he was drunk.

Finally, Clay pulled in the biggest hand of the evening, and Burdette cursed and threw his hand down in anger. "You were always too lucky at cards to suit me, Taliferro."

"Take it easy, Lou," Barr said quickly. "Let's keep it friendly."

Burdette smiled and cursed again. "I've always said you cheated at cards."

A silence began at the table and spread all around the room, for Burdette's words had been loud enough for everyone in the saloon to hear. Clay was watching Burdette's eyes. He saw them suddenly change and knew that Burdette was going to pull his gun. The men at the table did not even see Clay move. They saw Burdette hitch his arm up and pull his pistol half out of the holster. Suddenly, the gun was in Clay's hand, aiming right at Burdette's heart. Burdette paused and his face froze.

"I ain't pullin'," Burdette said.

Clay studied him for a moment and then reholstered his gun. "Second thoughts are usually best," he said mildly.

Burdette glared at him, shoved his chair away, and walked stiffly out of the bar.

"Well, I take it you two don't enjoy the warmest friendship in the world." Frisco grinned.

"I never saw anybody do that to Burdette," Prince Daniels said, staring at Clay. "It ain't over, though."

"It is as far as I'm concerned," Clay said. He gathered his winnings, and Daniels and Hake stood up from the table and left.

Frisco said, "How about a drink?"

"Just one. I'm tryin' to quit." Clay grinned.

"Wise idea." Frisco signaled the bartender, who brought over a bottle and two glasses and poured them full.

Clay took the glass and stared at it. Then he grinned and held it up. "Here's to clean living," he said.

Frisco laughed. "I can see you're a man of peace and would like things to be like that." The two men drank, and then Frisco studied the other man who sat loosely in his chair. "Lou Burdette's a pretty tough fellow, but I guess you already know that."

Clay had decided that Frisco Barr was a man that could be trustworthy, at least as trustworthy as any gambler could be. "Maybe you can help me out, Barr," he said. "I'm lookin' to buy a place."

"What kind of a place?"

"Looking for a place to raise cattle. It's not for me. It's for a family down closer to the Gulf, an Austin settlement. They want a big place, but they don't have much money."

"Nobody in Texas has much money now. I'm about to starve to death at my trade."

"You don't know of anything?"

Barr poured himself another drink but did not touch it. He twirled the glass around in his fingers, studying it as if some sort of answer lay in the amber liquid. After a moment he said, "I may not be doin' you a favor to tell you about a place I know."

"Try me."

"Well, Burdette works for a man named Kern Herendeen. He's got the biggest ranch in this part of the country. He's pretty big potatoes around these here parts."

"He wants to sell his place?"

"No." Frisco smiled. "He wants to make it bigger. He's been trying to buy another ranch to add to his. It belongs to a fellow named Tucker Howard."

"Howard's place for sale?"

"Not to Herendeen. He'll never sell to him."

"Why not? Sounds like he's got the money."

"Bad blood between the two." Frisco sipped his drink and then shrugged. "They had trouble over a woman a long time ago. Howard was going to marry a woman named Margaret Hendricks, but Herendeen came along and took her away from him. Married her. She died a year ago. But Tucker hadn't spoken to Herendeen since he stole his woman away from him."

"How big a place he got?"

"Pretty big. I'm not sure. I think somewhere around ten thousand acres. Maybe more."

"You know what he wants for it?"

"No, I don't. He's let it go down. He stopped runnin' cattle. Most of 'em were run off by rustlers, or the Comanches took them." He finished the drink and shrugged and said in a quieter voice, "There are some rumors that say Herendeen took some of them himself."

Clay sat there for a moment in his chair. "Maybe I'll talk to Howard."

"Might work out for you. I hope so. Tucker told me he'd sell to the devil before he'd let Kern Herendeen have an inch of it. If you ride out to see Tucker, tell him I sent you. We've known each other a long time."

"All right. Thanks. I reckon I'll hit the sack."

"Good luck. I hope it works out for you."

Frisco watched as Clay left the room, and the bartender came over and picked up the glasses. "The fastest thing I've seen with a gun. He could have blown Burdette away."

"Yes, he could," Frisco murmured. "He's thinkin' about settling around here. Be interesting to see how him and Burdette get along, won't it?"

CHAPTER
ELEVEN

A small tribe of Cherokee had lived close to the Hardin family in Arkansas. They had been peaceful, not like the Plains Indians, and were ready to learn how to farm and to become civilized. One of the recipes Jerusalem had picked up from them was Cherokee Indian bean bread. It was late afternoon, and she had thought about making a batch of bean bread, so she had boiled dried beans in water until they were tender. Now she poured boiling beans and some of the soup into a large pot. She had decided to make bean dumplings instead of baking it, so she lifted the pot and put it over the open fire in the fireplace. She covered the pot and went about preparing the rest of the meal. As she did, she could not keep from thinking about Clay and wondering if she had done the right thing. The choice had been hers, but now everything was in Clay's hands.

For the next hour she worked in the kitchen, cooking up a huge bowl of grits and a batch of squirrels that Clinton had shot.

Bob had been lying in the doorway, as if dead, which both aggravated and amused Jerusalem. She walked over and picked up one of his heavy legs and then let it drop back. Bob did not stir. "You are the craziest dog

I ever saw!" she exclaimed. She picked up his head. He opened one eye slowly and stared at her, but when she dropped his head, the eye closed, and he immediately went back to sleep. "I believe you've got the sleeping sickness."

It was quiet in the kitchen, which was unusual. Clinton had insisted on taking Moriah, Mary Aidan, and Zane fishing while Brodie and Julie rode over to see the Lebonnes. The quiet seemed to seep into Jerusalem, for it was a rare thing in her world.

Suddenly, Bob rose up and faced the door, a low growl in his throat. "What is it, Bob?" Jerusalem asked. She walked over and put her hand over her chest when she saw Clay riding in at a slow trot. She stood there watching him, thinking about how this man had become such a part of her family. Jerusalem's feelings for him were mixed. She was a lonely woman needing a man's touch and a man's presence, and this troubled her, but she could not seem to put the idea away.

Stepping out on the porch, she said, "Welcome home, Clay." She waited until he stepped up on the porch and put out her hand. He took it and held it for a moment. She squeezed it and said, "Come on in. I know you must be worn out and hungry."

"Well, I am, for a fact. It just come to me a minute ago, Jerusalem. I ain't twenty years old anymore."

Jerusalem smiled as he took a seat at the table in the kitchen, and she began to fill a plate for him. "What made you think of that?"

"Well, when I was twenty, I could have made a little ride like this and then gone and danced all night. That's all passed me. I'm an old man, worn out and not much use for anything."

Jerusalem laughed and set a platter full of fried squirrel in front of him and a huge bowl of grits. She put some fresh butter and salt out to mix with the grits and then dipped out some Cherokee bean dumplings. "Get on the outside of this. It'll make you feel twenty again."

"Cherokee bean dumplings, my word! I swan, that's just what I need! Set down and eat with me."

"No, I'll wait for the others." She filled a glass up with buttermilk, and he drank it down without stopping. She refilled it, then sat down and said, "Don't eat so fast. You'll kill yourself."

"Sure is good, Jerusalem." He began to eat more slowly, and finally when he shoved his chair back, he nodded with admiration. "Plumb good, Jerusalem." He smiled at her. "I got somethin' to tell you, but I reckon I'll wait for a spell."

He often did this to tease Jerusalem, saying he had something on his mind, but he wasn't going to tell her until the next day. She reached out, picked up his little finger, and bent it back. "You tell me right now, Clay Taliferro, or I'll break this finger."

"Stop that, woman. I need that finger!" Clay did not pull his hand away but held her, suddenly reversing the grip so that he was holding hers. "You'll have to ask me nice before I tell you."

"Please tell me, Clay."

Clay could not help but think of how much this woman had stirred him. He studied her for a moment, noting her long, composed mouth. He knew she had a temper that could charm a man or chill him to the bone. The fragrance of her hair came to him then, and he noticed the swing of her body and even the warm tones of her personality. She made a provocative challenge. He had never met a more complex or unfathomable woman, and as he held her hand, he noticed her quick breathing and the color that ran across her cheeks. He also knew she was the kind of woman who could draw a pistol and shoot a man down if necessary and not go to pieces afterward, for she had a courage and simplicity that he had found only in Indian women.

"Tell me, Clay."

"All right. I found a place . . ."

Jerusalem listened as Clay gave her the details but was aware that he was still holding her hand. He had strong hands, and she could feel the vitality that ran through the man.

"Well, it's got a house and some outbuildings. It's got good grass. But the best thing, Jerusalem. It's right on the Brazos River. Won't never have to worry about a drought."

"It sounds wonderful, Clay. How big is it?"

"Well, ten thousand cleared and an option to buy another ten thousand."

"Twenty thousand acres!" Jerusalem was stunned. "How much does he want for it?"

"Like I say, he won't sell to Herendeen, who's the only man that's got the money to pay what it's worth. I reckon it's worth forty thousand, but Howard says he'll sell for ten thousand. He just wants out, but he's got to know in a month. He's leavin' and movin' on."

Jerusalem pulled her hand away. "Why, Clay, we couldn't get more than two thousand dollars for our land here."

"I know it," Clay said. He chewed his lower lip thoughtfully. "I found another place that we could get for about that, but it ain't much, Jerusalem."

Jerusalem sighed, knowing there was no way she could come up with that kind of money. "Thanks for going, Clay," she said, standing up then and facing him. "I guess you'll be going looking for gold pretty soon."

"Oh, I guess I can hang around a little while. I ain't in that big a hurry to get rich."

None of the Hardins had any hope whatsoever of getting the Howard place in the north on the Brazos. Clay had explained it to the whole family, and Zane had stared at him. "Why'd you even fool with talking with the man? We'd have to hold up a payroll to get that much money."

The others had been no more positive, and Clay grew glum. "I reckon I shouldn't even have mentioned it, Jerusalem, but it's about the nicest place I ever saw. I wish I had the money. I'd buy it for you."

"That's like you, Clay," Jerusalem said.

"I can go look again if you want."

"No, I don't think you should. We'll just wait a spell."

As the days passed, Jerusalem thought of little else but the place Clay had found. She made him describe it in detail several times, and since he had a gift for putting things into words, she began to long for it. Dreaming of a place large enough to start a ranch where her family would have land for years to come made itself at home in her heart. She could almost see it the way Clay had described it. The sweep of the river moving in long, slow curves, and the tall grass spreading out as far as the eye could see. Even the house that Clay said needed a lot of work seemed to be just exactly what she wanted.

There had not been many things that Jerusalem Hardin wanted in life. She had wanted a husband, of course, but had been disappointed in her marriage to Jake. She had never complained about the lean times on the hardscrabble farm in Arkansas. Work and hard times didn't bother her. But deep inside she wanted a place where she could put roots down, and she knew that this place she lived on would not do. There was no room to expand to leave parcels of land to children and grandchildren, and she longed for land to call her own and to hold her family together.

Six days after Clay returned, she was sitting in the small graveyard, thinking of the place on the Brazos. No one disturbed her there, as usual, and it was too early in the morning for most of them to be up. The sun was rising in the east, making a faint line of pale crimson, and the air was still. Jerusalem tried to think about what she should do. Finally, she took a deep breath and began to pray. It was a halting prayer, for she did not know God that well. After a while she spoke out loud, "God, if You'll give me this place that Clay has found, I'll serve You all the days of my life."

As soon as she prayed, something stirred within Jerusalem. She knew that something was wrong with that prayer. For a long time she sat there, wondering what it was, and it finally came to her. All around her was silence, but inside her heart a realization dawned on her.

She whispered, "No, Lord, I didn't mean that. I can't bargain with You. I'm going to serve You all my life—even if I don't get that place that Clay found."

She sat very still then, and tears came to her eyes. She repeated her words aloud, "I mean it, Lord. I'll serve You no matter if I have to live in a hut. It won't matter. If You want to give us this place, I'd appreciate it. But I want to serve You and love You no matter where I live."

Jerusalem knew that she had come to one of those places in life that mark the end of something—and the beginning of something else. She had believed in God most of her life, but now she knew that her belief had not been strong enough. She let herself be as still as she could, waiting in the silence for God to speak again. But all she felt was a peace and a new certainty, and then a new joy began to fill her heart. She straightened up and smiled as she looked up into the sky. "I'm ready, Lord, for anything You want me to do."

As Fergus Nightingale III pulled up in his wagon, followed by James Langley in the companion wagon, he did not get the horses stopped before Clinton was scrambling up into the seat with him. "Go on down to the river, Fergus."

"To the river? Whatever for?" Fergus demanded. "What's going on?"

Clinton's eyes were sparkling, and he was quivering with excitement. "It's Ma," he cried out. "She done gone and got converted. She's bein' baptized in the river this mornin'. I just came back to get her some dry clothes. We all forgot about 'em we're so excited."

Fergus laughed. "You have made a convert, have you, Clinton?"

"It wasn't me. Ma came to it all herself. She didn't even have to go to no revival or hear no preachin'. She got converted sittin' out in her little cemetery. Come on, Fergus, whip them horses up."

"Right you are. I wouldn't want to miss this."

"Maybe you need to get baptized yourself, Fergus," Clinton said.

"I was sprinkled, lad, when I was a mere baby."

"Why, that ain't no good!" Clinton shook his head vigorously. "You need to get plunged right down under the water. Every bit of you! Why, when I was baptized in the Caddo River, the preacher didn't get one of my feet under. It kind of popped up, and I made him do it all over again. I didn't want my foot to go to hell."

Fergus laughed. He had learned to appreciate this young man with his excessive religious vitality and strange ideas.

"We shall see, my boy, but I'm happy for you and for your mother."

Rice Morgan stood at the bank, dressed in a pair of jeans and a white shirt. He had taken his boots off and was smiling at those who stood gathered around. He had a Bible in his hand, and he was reading from the book of John. Now he looked around and said in his quiet, warm baritone, "This is a happy day. Not only for those who are to begin their walk with the Lord Jesus, but for their friends and family. They say a journey of a thousand miles begins with a single step, and the four here this morning who have come to manifest their determination to follow Jesus are taking their first step."

He turned and walked out into the water until he was waist deep and held his hand out. There were four of them, including Jerusalem, and Rice baptized each one of them heartily and with enthusiasm. As each one went down under the water, Clinton's voice could be heard roaring, "Stick 'em under deep, preacher! Make it wet!" At other times he would holler "Amen" or "Hallelujah." His excitement added some spice to the meeting. Clay stood beside Brodie and was holding Mary Aidan so she could see.

"Is he going to dip Mama next?" Mary Aidan whispered to Clay.

"I think he is, darlin'."

Jerusalem was wearing an older dress. She had wisely sewed some stones into the hem of it so it would not float up. When she went out to stand in front of Rice, he reached out and turned her so she was standing sideways. He put her hands together, held them, put his right hand on her back, and said, "In obedience to the command of our Lord and Savior Jesus Christ, I baptize you, my sister, Jerusalem, in the name of the Father and of the Son and of the Holy Ghost."

Jerusalem felt herself going back, and then the warm water closed about her. She went down deep, but Rice Morgan's hands were firm, and he brought her up in one swift motion. She heard Clinton hollering, and when she passed her hand over her face, she looked to see her family standing there. They all seemed very serious, and she lifted her hand then and said, "Praise the Lord. I'm a happy woman this day!"

Jerusalem waded ashore, and within the shelter of blankets that the women held up, she put on her dry clothes. As soon as she stepped out, Clinton was waiting for her. He put his arms around her and lifted her off the ground, squeezing her hard. "Good for you, Ma."

Others came forward to speak to her, and Clay came last. He was still holding Mary Aidan, who held out her arms, and Jerusalem took her. "I'm right happy for you," Clay said quietly.

"Thank you, Clay. Now," Jerusalem said, "let's all go to the house. We've made a feast."

* * *

Fergus had enjoyed watching the baptism. He had never seen anyone immersed completely, and the sight down at the river had fascinated him. He joined them all at the house and ate heartily. While they enjoyed the meal, Clay told him all about the situation with the Howard land and ended by saying, "It doesn't look like she's going to get it, Fergus."

Fergus was eating apple pie, and he finished a morsel and then wiped his lips delicately with a snow-white handkerchief. "Doesn't seem right. I think she deserves that land." He stood up and walked over to Jerusalem. She looked up, and the others around her fell silent, looking at the tall Englishman who towered over them all. "I've heard that angels sometimes show up when they're needed."

Jerusalem was puzzled by the statement, for the Englishman often made strange statements at times. She smiled and said, "I think that's true, Fergus."

"Shore, it's true. Read your Bible," Clinton insisted loudly. "I've been waitin' for one to show up."

"I'd like to see one myself." Jerusalem smiled.

Fergus did not smile, but humor glinted in his eyes. "I have the feeling that, perhaps, *I'm* an angel."

"No, you ain't no angel." Mary Aidan popped up and stared at him. "You ain't got no wings."

"Well," Fergus shrugged, "perhaps I'm just a beginning angel just learning how. But, I have just heard, Mrs. Hardin, that you have a desire for a home on the Brazos River, but you have no way to get it. Perhaps I've never mentioned it to anyone, but I have scads of money. And I feel that it is imperative that you have that place."

"Why, Fergus—"

"No, let me finish. You're going to get your new home. I'm going to lend you the money." Fergus then laughed. "If I were a *real* angel, I'd just give you the money. But since I'm not, just an Englishman, I'll lend it to you at a low interest rate. If you don't pay, I'll foreclose on you," he said fiercely. "Not much of an angel, am I?"

Silence filled the room, and Jerusalem suddenly stood up. Tears were running down her face, and Fergus was embarrassed. "Oh, I say, don't do that."

It took Jerusalem some time to get control of herself, and finally she said, "Thank you, Fergus. You're the kindest man I know."

"Not at all! Not at all! When will you be leaving?"

"As soon as we can," Jerusalem said. "And you'll have to take us there, Clay, just like you brought us here from Arkansas."

Clay was smiling. "Well, I reckon as how I can do that." He winked at Mary Aidan and said, "Maybe I'm an angel, too."

"No," Mary Aidan said and turned her head to one side. "You ain't an angel."

"How do you know?" Clay teased.

"Because angels don't get drunk and get throwed in jail."

CHAPTER
TWELVE

W hoa up there, boys! I reckon we've done arrived in the
promised land."

After pulling the mules forward, Clay turned in the seat
and studied Jerusalem's face. He had drawn the small caravan up so that
the lead wagon, which he drove with Jerusalem and Mary Aidan by his
side, stopped directly in front of the house. He had pointed the house out
to her twenty minutes earlier, and she had not said a word but had
watched with a rapt expression on her face. Mary Aidan was asleep in
Jerusalem's lap, her face pressed against her bosom, but Clay saw that
Jerusalem was not even conscious of the child. *She looks like she's puttin'
her eyes on heaven for the first time,* he thought. Aloud he said, "It ain't no
palace, Jerusalem."

Jerusalem took her eyes from the house for a moment, and when she
turned to face him, he saw that the hint of tears was in her eyes.

"It's fine, Clay—just fine! You done real good."

Clay got out of the wagon and saw that behind him Brodie had pulled
up the wagon and, he and Julie were climbing out. Moriah and Clinton

had stopped their wagon, and he could hear Clinton talking even from this distance as he and Moriah piled out. Farther behind, Zane was leading the horse herd, and even farther back were the cattle they had picked up, herded by four Mexicans that had been hired to make the trip.

The mules were so tired that they simply stood there, not needing to be hitched. Clay walked around and reached up and said, "Let me have Mary Aidan." He took the child, threw her over his shoulder, and suddenly looked down, for Bob had sat on his feet. "Get off of my feet, you lazy critter!" he grumbled and kicked at Bob. The large dog stared at him woefully and then lay down and went promptly to sleep.

Jerusalem was aware of the sounds of voices as her family came forward, but she was staring at the house. Clay had described it to her as well as he could, but men can't see things as women can. She stood there for a moment and took in the structure, a two-story house divided on the first floor by a door with two windows opening on each side of it and two corresponding ones on the second floor. The roof was made of tin, which was rusty, and tin also covered the long porch that ran the length of the house. It was a frame house painted white once but was peeling now in spots and showing the silver gray of the wood beneath.

"There's the barn over there," Clay said, pointing to the left. "And over on the other side is a smokehouse and a spring house already dug."

"I love it, Clay! I'm glad they left the trees standing." She looked at the huge walnut tree in the front yard and the two pecan trees that shaded the west and the north of the house.

Clinton's voice overrode everyone else. "Well, what are we waitin' for? Let's go inside and have a look around."

Jerusalem laughed. "All right. Let's see our new home."

The tour did not take long, for the house was not that large. The bottom floor consisted of three areas, a large room with a stone fireplace dominating one side, a sink on the back, and the other half was composed of one bedroom and a cupboard and workroom, which also included an ancient wood-burning stove.

A stairway was on the east side, which led up to the second floor. The second floor had a narrow hallway with four bedrooms. There was a great deal of laughter as everyone chose their bedroom. Zane and Clay shared one bedroom, Julie and Moriah another, Brodie and Clinton a third. The other would remain empty for guests, Jerusalem insisted. Her own bedroom was down on the first floor.

"Well, it's going to take some paint and some work to put this house together," Zane said as he looked around. "It looks like nothin' much has been done to it in a spell."

"Who lived here before, Clay? Why is it so run down?" Moriah asked.

"Tucker Howard. He was gonna marry a woman, but she ran off and left him. He built the house for her, as the story goes, and I don't reckon he did anything to it later. A bachelor is a sorry excuse for keepin' house."

"It'll look wonderful in no time," Jerusalem said. "Now, let's get moved in."

For two days everyone worked like whirlwinds, and Zane took the Mexicans to ride out and round up more cattle. "If we're gonna get rich, we'd better start grabbin' all these free cows we can," he said, grinning. "When we get back, Brodie, you and Clinton can brand them."

He left on Thursday morning, and on the next day, August the nineteenth, Jerusalem and Clay rode into Jordan City to record the deed that had been left at the lawyer's office. The payment had already been made, so all that was necessary was for Jerusalem to sign it.

Jordan City was only six miles south of the house, and the road followed along close to the river whose banks were covered liberally with pecan and hickory and cottonwood trees.

"It's nice to be near a river, Clay."

"Clinton will like it. He'll get all the fishin' he wants." He turned and smiled. "I don't think you hit the ground since we got here. You really like this place so much, Jerusalem?"

Jerusalem did not answer for a moment, and then she said, "It's the oddest thing, Clay. You know, I tried to make a bargain with God at first. I told him if He'd let me have this place, I'd serve Him. Then I realized that was wrong . . . it was selfish. I told Him I'd serve Him whether I got it or not. But somehow this place is different from any land I've ever known. Texas is my home now."

"Well, it's big enough," Clay said, sweeping his eyes over the plain. "Full of longhorn cows, coyotes, Comanches, scorpions, and snakes."

"Oh, it's better than that, and you know it!"

"Well, if you like it, then it suits me fine." He motioned and said, "There it is. The metropolis of Texas. Jordan City." He grinned wryly and said, "Took lots of nerve to call it a city. They might have called it Jordan Junction or somethin' like that."

Clay drove straight into town and noted the considerable activity about the town. "Must be havin' a hangin'," he said, "or a party of some kind. Not much, is it?"

"I'm glad it's here, though. Only six miles from the ranch. That's no distance at all."

"You're talkin' like a real Texas woman." Clay grinned. He drove down the broad street, stopping at a two-story building. "Our lawyer, Gentry, has an office upstairs," Clay said as he helped Jerusalem out of the wagon. As soon as he had tied the reins to the hitching post, they turned and climbed the stairs and entered the lawyer's office.

Micah Gentry was a fat man bursting out of his clothes. He had a wild mop of brown hair and a beard to match and bowed swiftly two or three times as Clay introduced Jerusalem.

"Well, now, Mrs. Hardin, we're mighty proud to have you in the country. Here, you sit down right here while I get these papers out." He saw to it that Jerusalem had a seat, scurried around through a mass of papers that littered his desk, and finally nodded. "Here it is. Let me tell you. You got a real buy on this ranch, ma'am. I don't know as I ever knew anyone gettin' a better bargain."

"That's good to hear, Mr. Gentry. Where do I sign?"

Jerusalem signed the four papers and was about to stand up when the door opened and a big man walked in.

"Oh, Kern. Glad you came by," Gentry said rather nervously. "Like for you to meet some newcomers. This is Mrs. Hardin, and this is her foreman, Mr. Taliferro. You know, the ones that bought the Howard place. This here is Kern Herendeen."

Jerusalem had risen and was studying the man who had entered the room. He was an inch over six feet and in his late thirties, she judged. There was a hardness and a strength in the man, and she noticed he was roughly handsome. He had yellow hair with a slight curl and unusual hazel eyes. His mouth was broad and firm, and he had a determination in him that he made no attempt to hide.

"I'm very happy to meet you, Mrs. Hardin. I heard you were coming."

"Thank you, sir. It's good to be here."

Suddenly, Herendeen smiled. "I suppose you heard I tried to buy your ranch from Tucker."

"I did hear something about that."

Herendeen shrugged. "Well, my loss is your gain. But we'll be neighbors, you know. My own place is just across the river from yours. When the river is not up, you can ford it, and we'll be visiting, I hope."

"I hope so."

Kern Herendeen turned to face Clay and nodded. "I understand you scouted the place out, Taliferro."

"I'm just Mrs. Hardin's errand boy," Clay said idly.

"Well, you found her a good one."

Jerusalem smiled and said, "It's good to meet you, Mr. Herendeen. I'll look forward to seeing you again. Thank you very much, Mr. Gentry."

Clay nodded at the two men and left with her. "What'd you make of him?" he asked.

"Mr. Herendeen?"

"Yes."

"He's a very forceful man."

"I think you're right about that," Clay said dryly. "From what I hear, he's used to having his own way. I'm surprised he took it so nice; you're getting the place he wanted so bad."

"Well, he didn't have much choice. Tucker would never have sold to him, so you said."

Clay said no more, but Jerusalem wanted to do some shopping. The choice of shops were not very extensive in Jordan City, but she did manage to buy several items that she needed. When they went back toward the wagon, before she could get in, a voice called out.

"Mrs. Hardin . . ."

Jerusalem turned and saw Kern Herendeen approaching. He stopped in front of her, removed his hat, and said, "I have to go right past your ranch on the way to the ford. Why don't you ride along with me, and I can show you some of the interesting sights."

Jerusalem hesitated but wanted to be a good neighbor. "Why, that would be very nice. Clay, you go on ahead."

Clay nodded and without a word got into the wagon and drove off.

"Taliferro's not much of a talker, is he?"

"Oh, sometimes he is."

"Well, he's going to have his hands full. Ranching's not easy. Come along. Get in the buggy."

He helped her into the buggy and climbed up and sat down beside her. Taking up the lines, he said, "You're close to town. We're trying to get a church started here. I'm not much of a churchgoer myself, but I donated the materials."

"Why, that's very generous of you, Mr. Herendeen."

Herendeen turned and smiled at her. "We're not much on last names. I know it's a little soon, but I'd like it if you would call me Kern."

Jerusalem did think it was rather soon, for she had just met the man, but she nodded. "All right, and I'm Jerusalem."

"You have a family?" he asked as he slapped the reins on the horses. "Tell me about them."

As they rode along, Jerusalem told Kern about her family and then said, "What about you, Kern?"

"Well, I was married, but we didn't have any children. I'm just a lone bachelor now. I suppose you heard the gossip about Tucker and me."

"Yes, I did," she said honestly. "It was too bad."

"Well, it was one of those things. Margaret was engaged to Tucker, and looking back, I think she knew she had made a mistake. I never set out to take her away from him, but, well, that's the way it happened. We fell in love, we married, and Tucker Howard could never forgive us—either of us."

"It must have been very hard living this close to him."

"He never spoke to either one of us again. Hasn't to this day. He didn't even come to Margaret's funeral."

"It must have been difficult having him for a neighbor."

Kern smiled and turned to face her. He was a big-boned man with long arms, and his muscles strained against his shirt. The edge of his jaw was sharp against the heavy, tanned skin, and his nose had a small break at the bridge. He had a rider's looseness about him, and all his features were solid. He had the flat and angular heavy shape of a man who made his living in the saddle. "It will be better now that you're here," he said.

"I'm glad to hear that," Jerusalem said. She hesitated, then said, "I understand that there was a little trouble between Clay and your foreman."

"I heard about that. Burdette's a tough hairpin. Has to be to run a ranch like this. I understand they've had trouble before. Burdette wouldn't say much about it. He told me they were in the mountains trapping together. Did Taliferro say anything to you?"

"Not really. He's not much of one for spreading talk. Well, let's hope they can put it behind them now that we're neighbors."

By the time they pulled up to the house, Jerusalem had decided two things about Kern Herendeen. One, he was an intensely attractive man from a woman's point of view, and two, he was probably one of the strongest men she had ever seen. He was strong physically. That was obvious. But there was an intensity about him that made her know that he was the kind of man who would make a good friend or a bad enemy. He got out and came around, and she waited until he got there and handed her down.

"Most pleasant trip I've had to town in a long time," he smiled.

"Thank you very much for the ride and for the tour."

"I hope you'll come over to Skull and visit. I'd like for you to see my place."

"That would be nice." She nodded and said, "Good-bye. And thanks again." She went into the house and found Julie waiting for her.

"Who was that?" Julie said.

"It's Kern Herendeen. He owns Skull Ranch just across the river."

"He's a good-looking man."

"Is he?"

"Oh, come on, Jerusalem," Julie scoffed. "I could see that much from here, and you were right up in his face."

"Well, he *is* attractive, I suppose. He invited me to come over and see his ranch."

"Not married, is he?"

"No. He lost his wife about two years ago."

"Well, Clay doesn't like you riding with strange men."

Jerusalem turned to stare at her. "What are you talking about?"

Julie laughed. "He came in like a bear with a sore tail. I found out that he was mad because you rode home with Herendeen."

"What did you say?" Jerusalem smiled.

"I told him he ought to say a lot of sweet things to you, and all he could say was, 'I ain't no fancy man.'" Julie laughed. "I told him, 'Then get yourself a squaw if that's the way you have to be.'"

Jerusalem laughed with her and said, "They're building a church in town. We'll go Sunday."

"Not me. But there's a saloon there. I'll tell you what," she said slyly. "You join the church, and I'll join the saloon . . . !"

CHAPTER
THIRTEEN

F all had come to Texas, bringing a thick fragrance from the fields and the grass that was ready to die. The winds had roughed up the plains, and the dissipated heat rising from the earth seemed to whirl in streaky currents. The sun was still warm even the first of November, but the smell of winter hung in the air. So far there had been no rain, and the cattle that Zane and Clay kept circling raised a dust of the thinnest powder.

They had gathered three hundred wild longhorns, and the task of branding them had worn them all down. They had been at it now for three grueling days. Since Clay and Zane were better with the rope than Brodie or Clinton, they rode and roped the steers and dragged them over to the branding fire. It was up to Brodie and Clinton to wrestle them down and slap a branding iron on their hip. Brodie had become fairly adept at throwing a rope over the front legs and felling the steers. As soon as they hit the ground, Clinton would grab one of the branding irons out of the fire, run over, and slap the brand on. The brand was a star with a wavy line under it. The ranch was simply called the Star Ranch. Jerusalem had never told anyone why she had named it that but had simply announced it one day.

Clinton was so covered with dust that his face looked like a chalky mask with only his eyes and lips showing through. He was complaining, as usual, this time about Julie.

"I tell you, Brodie. It ain't right for our aunt to be workin' in a saloon. Nothin' good is gonna come from it. The Bible says lots about the evil of drinking. I think Ma ought to do somethin'."

"Do what?" Brodie asked. He was sick and tired of branding cattle and impatient with Clinton's constant preaching. "What do you expect her to do? You can't *make* people be good."

"Well, I think it's a disgrace."

"You think *everything's* a disgrace. Now slap that brand on and shut up."

He held the steer down, and Clinton said, "I've been readin' about this thing called 'predestination,' and I about decided that's the way things are."

"What in the world is *that?*"

"Predestination? Don't be so ignorant, Brodie. It means that God makes up His mind on what's goin' to happen, and it happens no matter what you do."

"That's the dumbest thing I ever heard of! We can do what we please."

"No, we can't. We do what we have to do. That's what the Bible says, and you can't go against the Bible."

With a snarl of disgust, Brodie slipped the rope off the big steer's front legs and jumped back as he got to his feet. He was wary of these big animals. They were fleet as a deer, almost, and some of them were bad-tempered and could do a lot of harm. He saw this one had a wild look in his eye, and he hollered, "Watch out for him, Clinton!"

The steer suddenly spotted Clinton and took out after him. Clinton started running away, and Brodie hollered out, "Hey, Clinton, slow down and let him get you. If it's the Lord's will for you to get gored, just be still and get it over with."

Zane had been watching, and he headed the steer off. Then he pulled his horse around and said, "Brodie, why didn't you help him?"

"Aw, Zane, I get tired of all his preachin'. He was just tellin' me about predestination, and I told him that the steer was predestined to jab him."

Zane was as dusty as Brodie, but at least he was able to stay on his horse. "You're aggravatin', Brodie. You got to get Serena out of your mind. You've been mad the whole three months we've been here."

Brodie said, "Mind your own business!" He suddenly turned, got on his horse, and rode away.

Clay came up and said, "What's the matter with Brodie?"

"He's tetchy, that's what. He's still moonin' around over Serena."

"Well, it's gettin' pretty late. We've got enough branded for today. They'll be here tomorrow."

"I'm afraid so," Zane said. "Come on, Clinton, let's go get somethin' to eat. That is if you think it's predestined for you to eat."

Clinton glared at Zane and got on his horse. The three made the trip back to the ranch quickly. There was no fear that the cattle would stray very far. The grass was good, and they would still be there grazing the next day.

When they approached the house, Clay said with disgust, "Look, that's Herendeen's horse. He ought to be payin' rent as much as he stays here."

Zane gave a sly smile. "Maybe I'd better ask him if his intentions about my sister are honorable."

"I'll bet they ain't," Clay said, his lips drawn into a tight line.

Clay noticed with resentment that Jerusalem had put on the new dress, the blue one, that made her look so good. He started to challenge her, asking why she didn't ever wear that blue dress for him, but knew that would only cause trouble. He watched as Herendeen smoothly moved and pulled a chair out for Jerusalem, then pushed it forward when she sat down.

"Mighty nice of you to take a lonely bachelor in," he said. "And it looks like a fine meal you've gone to all the trouble to make."

"A lonely bachelor? You've got a cook over there, don't you, Herendeen?" Clay said.

Kern smiled. "Sure I have, Clay, but I bet he can't cook as good as this fine lady."

He took his seat, and Zane nudged Clay, whispering, "You ought to practice up on your manners, boy. Just watch Herendeen. He's slick."

The meal was excellent and had more dishes than normal, Clay noticed. Whenever Kern's plate was empty, Jerusalem was quick to pass him more. And the smiles that passed between them were starting to annoy Clay. Everyone ate heartily, and the talk finally got around to the political situation in Texas. Kern Herendeen was well up on the events. *He doesn't have to work as hard as his neighbors, so he's got more time to hear all that's happening!* Clay thought as they all listened to Kern give his opinion of the current events.

"It's a good thing that you fellows didn't hang Santa Anna when you had the chance, Zane," Kern said.

"There was plenty of us who wanted to because of the Alamo and Goliad, but Houston wouldn't let us."

"Well, like I say, that was a wise decision. Houston made him sign the best kind of a treaty, but we're not out of trouble in this Republic yet."

"Don't you think we'll be admitted to the Union pretty soon, Kern?" Jerusalem asked quickly.

"We would have," Kern nodded, "except for John Quincy Adams."

"Who's he?" Moriah asked.

"Why, he's a congressman. Last May he denounced the whole Texas Revolution."

"Why is it any of his business? He's not from Texas," Clay said sharply.

"That's right. He's not. It's all a matter of slavery. Adams says that this whole Texas Revolution is just a plot to extend slavery."

"Why, that's not so!" Zane exclaimed. "We're just tryin' to save our necks."

"You'll never make Adams believe that or the people up in the north, for that matter. It's gonna be hard to get into the Union. Adams carries a lot of weight in the Congress."

"What about Jackson?"

"Well, he'd like to see Texas taken in, but he won't be in office long enough. No tellin' what will happen when he leaves."

"I heard there ain't no army," Brodie spoke up. "No money to pay them."

"You heard right," Kern said grimly. "If the Mexicans came back now, there wouldn't be anything to stop 'em. As far as I can tell, Houston is determined to avoid a war with Mexico. What he wants most is to get Texas into the Union."

The talk eventually got around to the increasing numbers of Indians. Kern had been keeping up with the growing concern. "What's happening is that people east of us in Arkansas and Tennessee are tired of the Indians, so they're pushin' 'em west. We'll see a lot of 'em coming our way in the coming months. The trouble is they're not Plains Indians. I don't know how they'll make it out here. It's a whole different way of living. A lot tougher."

"What about the Comanches?" Zane said.

"They're always trouble, Zane. It's been real quiet for the last six months, but if they take a notion, they could ride in here with a thousand braves and wipe us all out. We're right on the border, and that means we're trouble to them."

"What about the cattle business? Is there going to be a market?" Jerusalem asked.

"Always a market for cattle." Kern smiled. "Getting them there is the problem."

"It'll have to be New Orleans," Clay spoke up. "No way of driving them north."

"That's right." Kern nodded. "And that's getting to be a bigger problem all the time."

"We'll make it, though. All of us."

Kern stayed late, which irritated Clay, but Jerusalem was enjoying his conversation. He had traveled a great deal and was knowledgeable on many things, which she found quite interesting. After the others had left the main room of the house to go to bed, Kern sat talking with Jerusalem. They were sitting on the leather-covered couch in the living room, and she had asked him about Europe. He had been to England and to Spain and Italy, and she was fascinated by the stories from his extensive traveling.

Finally, Kern said, "Well, I've kept you up late. I should be leaving."

He got to his feet, and Jerusalem rose with him. Before he turned to leave, he stopped still, and at that moment Jerusalem read his intentions. He was a strong, virile man, and when he stepped forward and took her by the arms and bent over and kissed her, she did not resist. Whether it was curiosity or something else, she did not know. His lips pressed hard against hers with a roughness, but for some reason she welcomed it. It had been a long time since she had been kissed like that, and she'd wondered if there was anything more in this man than his rough, rugged good looks. Now, as she received his kiss and responded with her own, she felt stirred in a way that shocked her. Something strong and powerful brushed against her then. She knew she had the power to stir him, but she was more concerned about the emotion she had not anticipated. Putting her hand on his chest, she stepped back, and he released her at once.

"You're going to say I shouldn't have done that. Well, I know it," he said, looking deep into her eyes.

Jerusalem did not answer for a moment. She had known the depth of her loneliness over the years. For that one instant of that caress she had felt a longing for a man, not necessarily this man, but a companion. "Good night, Kern."

"It's been pleasant." He smiled, got his hat, and left.

She heard the sound of his horse moving away and then turned and started for her bedroom. She undressed, got into bed, and knew that she would not forget Kern Herendeen quickly. He was not the sort of man a woman would forget.

During the winter, Herendeen came often to the Hardin house for visits. He took Jerusalem to a dance once during that time and twice to church. And each time Kern would show up at the ranch, Clay would get in a foul mood and head for town. As the winter faded, Jerusalem found herself more and more confused about how she herself felt about Herendeen. Julie, whom she saw only rarely, was living in Jordan City and working in the saloon—something that grieved Jerusalem. Julie had the rare ability to see what was in women and men, and one time she had asked Jerusalem point blank, "Would you marry him if he asked you?"

Jerusalem had said, "Too soon to think of anything like that."

But Julie had smiled knowingly at her and had shaken her head. "Be careful," was all she said.

It was in the middle of March when Kern Herendeen was bringing Jerusalem home from a dance. She had enjoyed the evening, and her cheeks were still flushed with the remembrance of the music and the excitement of going out with Kern. When the buggy pulled up in front of the house, she waited for Herendeen to get out and help her to the ground, but instead he turned to her and said, "Jerusalem, have you thought of me as a man you might marry?"

His words struck hard against Jerusalem, and she could only be honest. "Well, yes, I have. I guess a woman will think about that with any man who pays her attention."

He reached out and took her hand and made no attempt to embrace her. "I'm asking you to be my wife. I know it's soon, but I'm a lonely man, and I think you're a lonely woman."

The suddenness of his words surprised Jerusalem. She had known that he was ambitious and would press people at times to get what he wanted. That was a trait that had made him as successful as he was. He was witty and better educated than most men she knew, but she had not picked him for a man who could look inside a woman's heart and understand her feelings. "How do you know that, Kern?"

"I can't say," he admitted. "Just something I felt about you. I've felt that you are a woman who needs a man just as I'm a man who needs a woman. There's nothing wrong in that," he said quickly. "I think we'd make a good marriage of it."

Jerusalem said instantly, "I can't give you any kind of an answer, Kern. I'm not sure how I feel about marrying anyone right now."

Kern reached forward then, took her in his arms, and kissed her. She did not resist, but when he lifted his lips, she whispered, "Don't press me, Kern."

"I won't," he said. "You're not the kind of woman who can be stampeded. But I wanted you to know how I felt."

He got out of the buggy, came around, and handed her down. As he walked her to the door, she expected him to try to kiss her again, but he was wiser than that.

"Good night. I had a good time."

"So did I, Kern." She hesitated, then said, "I'll think about what you said."

"That's all I ask." Climbing into the buggy, he slapped the reins and drove away.

Jerusalem went into the house and found Clay cracking walnuts on an iron with a hammer. "You should have come to the dance," she said.

"Not much of a dancing man."

"You are, too," Jerusalem argued. "You're a good dancer."

"Well, I didn't want to."

Jerusalem suddenly thought of all that Clay Taliferro had done for her and her family. He had always treated her honorably. In fact, he had never tried to take advantage of her in any way. They were more than friends, but how much more she could not tell. She only knew that he had been good to her, and she needed someone to talk to about what she felt.

"Clay," she said, coming over to sit across from him, "Kern asked me to marry him tonight." She saw the hammer, which was poised to strike, seem to freeze in the air. Clay lowered it then and turned his eyes toward her.

"What'd you tell him?"

"I told him I couldn't think about that right now." Clay was upset. Jerusalem could tell.

"I don't think he's the kind of man that can make you happy," Clay said.

Jerusalem stared at him. "Why do you say that?"

"Just a feelin' I got. I don't think you should marry him."

Jerusalem felt something stronger than aggravation, but less than anger. She got to her feet and stared at him. "Thanks for your advice, Clay. Good night." She turned and walked to her bedroom, slamming the door with more force than necessary.

Clay put a walnut on the iron, raised the hammer, and smashed it with all of his strength. He got up then, tossed the hammer down, and walked outside the house. For a long time he stood staring up at the sky, studying the stars, and then muttered, "He ain't the right man for her."

★ ★ ★

Julie listened as Clay told her what had happened. He had come to the
saloon, and he told her he had to talk with her privately. She had a large
well-furnished room upstairs, and when he came in, he turned to her and
said, "Herendeen has asked Jerusalem to marry him."

"Doesn't surprise me."

Clay stared at her. "You knew it?"

"Of course I did. He's been pretty obvious about it, Clay. If you
weren't half blind, you would know it, too. He's been calling on her off
and on for months."

"Well, I don't think he's the right man for her."

Julie saw that Clay was more agitated than she had ever seen him.
"He's got plenty of money and land. He's educated. Good-looking.
What's wrong with him?"

"He don't—" Clay broke off suddenly. "I can't put it into words," he
said finally. "But he's not the kind of man that can make your sister happy."

"Clay, I used to think you were a pretty smart fellow, but you've been
actin' like a fool lately."

"What are you talkin' about?"

"You've been in love with my sister for a long time. Why don't you
up and tell her so?"

Clay swallowed hard. "Why, I . . . I can't do that."

"Why not?" Julie said impatiently. "You don't have a wife stashed
away somewhere, do you?"

"You know I don't, but I don't have anything to offer her. She's got
a ranch, and all I've got is the clothes I'm standin' in."

"That's foolish! We wouldn't have anything if it wasn't for you.
Jerusalem knows that."

Clay felt terribly uncomfortable. "I can't do it," he said. "I'm leaving.
I can't stand this place no more."

Julie stared at him and then shook her head. "I feel sorry for you, Clay."

"Why?"

"Because you're a fool who doesn't know how to follow his heart. Go
on. Go chase your gold or whatever it is. You won't get any satisfaction
out of it."

"I'm not going back to the ranch for anything. I'm just riding out. You tell Jerusalem I'm leaving."

"You don't even have the guts to face her?"

"It ain't that," Clay said quickly. "I just don't want to."

He turned and left before she could move or speak. Julie walked to the door and stared after him as he went down the stairs. "You fool," she whispered and shook her head sadly.

Clay had been gone for two weeks now. The day he had ridden out, Julie had given his message to Jerusalem, who had stared at her and said, "Did he say why he was leaving?"

"He said he was going to look for gold."

"That's all he said?"

Julie said bluntly, "He's in love with you, and he thinks you're going to marry Herendeen."

"I told him that I wasn't. At least I told him I was just thinking about it."

"That's all Clay needed."

Jerusalem found herself unable to speak about Clay's leaving. Everyone was asking where Clay was gone and why, and all she could say was that he had decided to go prospecting—for a time.

During those two weeks she had asked herself a lot of hard questions, and she had refused Herendeen's invitation and had kept to the house.

She did not sleep well and had lost some of her appetite. Deep down she knew that she felt something in her heart for Clay Taliferro, but his sudden picking up and leaving was too much like something Jake Hardin would do. To simply ride off without a word, that was Jake all over again, and it grieved Jerusalem and brought back too many painful memories of being left alone to care for her family all by herself.

Jerusalem saw Clay ride up and was waiting when he stepped inside the house. "Hello, Clay."

"Hello, Jerusalem."

Clay's clothes were wrinkled, and he had not shaved in days. He stood there staring at her, evidently unable to find words.

"Well, did you find gold?"

"No, I didn't find gold. I didn't even look for gold."

"Julie told me you were leaving to go prospecting. Why didn't you tell me you were leaving?"

"Because I couldn't." He came over to her then and stood in front of her. "I came back because I had to, Jerusalem. I got to tell you something."

Jerusalem felt something stir within her. "What is it?" she whispered.

"Well, I've been makin' a fool of myself. I've been doing it for most of my life," he said, shaking his head with disgust. "But I came back to tell you that I've got feelings for you."

Disappointment filled Jerusalem. She had expected more than this! "You've got feelings for your horse and for Bob!"

"Well, I mean I've got *strong* feelings for you, and I want to tell you that you can't marry Kern Herendeen."

"And why not?"

"He don't want you, Jerusalem. He wants this ranch. He's just using you."

"Oh?" Jerusalem said, and the rivers never ran colder than her tone. "A man couldn't want me?"

"I didn't say that. I didn't mean it that way, anyway. But listen. If you've got to marry somebody, why, you might as well marry me!"

Jerusalem could not believe what she was hearing. "Is that what you call a proposal?"

"Yes, I reckon it is."

"Why, even Jake did better than that."

Clay suddenly seemed to slump. "Well, what do you want, Jerusalem? You want me to write poetry and sing love songs under your window?"

Jerusalem suddenly smiled. "Yes, that's what I want."

"What! You don't mean that."

"Don't I?"

Clay could never quite tell when Jerusalem was dead serious. Well, he could, but he pretended not to. Now suddenly he stepped forward and drew her close. "I might as well warn you," he said. "I'm fixin' to kiss you."

"All right. You warned me. Now, do it."

Clay found her teasing amusing, but he kissed her, holding her tight for a moment, his arms drawing her close. He stepped back, then said, "Now, I'll say it again. I can't write a poem about it, but I love you, Jerusalem."

"Clay, I don't believe you. And I won't spend the next forty years with a man who takes me for granted."

"Takes you for granted! What are you talking about? I'm telling you I love you."

"And I'm telling you that you haven't shown it."

"Well, what do you want me to do?"

Jerusalem stared at Clay and said, "That's for you to find out, Clay. If you really want me, you've got to make me believe it." She turned and walked away from him, going out the back door of the house.

Clay stood there in shock. He had expected anything but having to prove what he felt for her. Suddenly, he felt a weight on his feet, and he looked down to see that Bob had come over and sat down right on the toes of his boots. "I'm going to marry that woman, Bob, no matter what it takes. You hear me?"

Bob lolled his tongue and leaned over against Clay's legs. "Whoof!" he barked.

"If I have to shoot Kern Herendeen, I'll do it. If I have to take a bath every night and shave every day, I'll do that. No matter what it takes, I'm going to marry her. You got that straight?"

Bob looked up, his tongue hanging out like a red necktie, and replied woefully, "Whoof!"

PART THREE:

COURTSHIP

CHAPTER
FOURTEEN

Well, I swan, Clinton. I believe you'd talk to a possum!"

A decrescent afternoon sun sinking in the west cast its last feeble rays on the two riders whose horses plodded slowly along. Clay had taken Clinton and Brodie on a cattle drive to New Orleans, and they were now almost within sight of the ranch. The boys had been excited about the trip and had worked hard. Clay had gotten a good price for the cattle, and the money would come in handy, for the expenses of getting settled in at the new ranch had been heavy.

Brodie had cut away when they had passed within a few miles of their old place. He had said rather defiantly that he was going to see Serena, which Clay had, more or less, expected.

Clay himself had been rather silent on the return journey, thinking a great deal about how he could convince Jerusalem of how he truly felt. Clinton, as usual, spilled over with an unending river of talk the whole way back. Clay had finally burst out with some aggravation. "Don't you ever hush?"

Clinton didn't take offense. He did not really need a big audience, and he always had plenty to talk about when he could get someone to sit still long enough to listen to him. For the past three miles, he had been talking about his views on the book of Revelation, particularly on the Antichrist, and Clay had managed to tune it all out. Now Clinton said, "This is important, Clay. I mean, after all, when the Antichrist comes along, you'd better know who he is or he'll get you."

"You can't tell who the Antichrist is," Clay said with disgust.

"Oh, sure I can!" Clinton nodded firmly. "I know who the scudder is, all right."

Despite his irritation, Clay grinned. Clinton never had any doubts whatsoever about any of his notions. Being proved wrong five times in a row never changed his opinion of his own rightness about theological matters. "Well, who is it, then?" Clay said.

"Why, it's John Quincy Adams."

Clay laughed out loud. "John Quincy Adams! What in the blue-eyed world makes you think John Quincy Adams is the Antichrist?" John Quincy Adams was, indeed, a Yankee, which qualified him in Clinton's view for any depth of villainy, but as far as Clay knew, he did not carry a pitchfork or breathe fire and brimstone.

"Why, that scoundrel has kept Texas from joinin' the Union, Clay!" Clinton said with amazement, staring at Clay. His face was intent, and he nodded firmly. "That's proof enough, ain't it?"

"No, you ignoramus, it's *not* proof enough. There's lots of politicians up North that want to keep Texas out of the Union. They think we're gonna expand the slave states—which we would."

Clinton hesitated, which was rare for him, but then he shot right back, "Well, that ain't the only reason I know he's the Antichrist, Clay. There's his name."

"John Quincy Adams?"

"Yeah, the Bible says that the number of the beast is six-six-six, and that's the number of letters in all of them names of John Quincy Adams."

Clay blinked with surprise. It was difficult sometimes to follow Clinton's strange reasoning at times. "John ain't got but four letters."

"Why, I bet his real name is Johnny, and that's got six letters sure as you're born."

Clay shook his head in disgust. "Clinton, *Quincy* has got six letters. What about *Adams*?"

"Why, it's got six letters, Clay. A-d-d-a-m-s."

"You fool boy! Adams is spelled A-d-a-m-s. That's only *five* letters."

This information set Clinton back momentarily, but at once he said, "Well, if it ain't him, then it's Santa Anna."

Clay took off his hat and wiped his forehead with his sleeve. He was wet clear through, for the day had been hot. Settling his hat back on firmly, he said, "Clinton, you can't make the Antichrist into somebody you just pure don't like. Now, hush up, will you?"

Clinton was silent only for a short time. No matter how many times people told him to hold his tongue, he simply couldn't stop from talking. "Clay, I done figured out a way for you to get Ma to marry up with you."

"Who said I was thinkin' about marryin' anybody?"

"Why, everybody knows it, Clay. Julie told me, and I reckon it's true."

"People ought to have more to do than sit around gossiping." He settled down in his saddle, but curiosity got the best of him. "What's this way you're thinkin' about that I could get your ma to marry me?"

"Well, get converted, join the church, and get baptized."

Clay said shortly, "Listen, Clinton, I can't join the church just to get a woman to marry me. I ain't no Christian, and I know that much. Will you please try to talk sense or else hush up. Talkin' with you is useless! It's like tryin' to shoot pool with a well rope!"

Moriah stood still and looked down pensively at Jerusalem, who was on her knees arranging the hem of a new dress that the two had been working on. There was a dance coming in Jordan City, and Moriah had begged her mother to help make a new dress. Jerusalem had come up with the money to buy the material, and now it was almost finished. She put the last pin in, then stood up and stepped back to admire the dress. "That looks real nice, Moriah. It fits you, too. You were bustin' out of your old dresses."

"I wish we had a long mirror so I could see myself."

"Maybe we'll buy one if Clay gets enough money for the cattle."

"When are they comin' back?"

"Why, they should be back this week sometime. It's hard to tell how fast cow critters will travel."

Moriah turned around and turned her head, trying to see down her back, and then faced her mother. She noticed that Jerusalem had lines of fatigue in her face, and compassion came to her. She walked over to her mother and put her hand around her waist. "You look tired, Ma. This has been a hard four months gettin' settled in here."

"Not as hard as some I've known."

Moriah thought for a moment, and then she said, "How does it make you feel gettin' courted by two men?"

"I think it's foolishness," Jerusalem said.

"Well, Clay and Kern are going to get in a fight over you. Both of them are serious."

"I don't know whether they are or not. Sometimes I think they're both so foolish I wouldn't have either one of them on a bet."

Indeed, the past four months had been hard financially and in other ways, but Clay and Kern Herendeen had indeed driven her nearly to distraction. Kern was straightforward about his intentions and had been quick to ask her out to every social event. He had even taken her to church, which Clay had never offered to do. Kern was not a member of the church, but he was not letting any opportunities slip to spend time with her. Clay, on the other hand, was not so forward. He took occasion to be with her every chance he had, and, as always, Jerusalem enjoyed talking with Clay as much as she had ever enjoyed speaking with anyone. He had a dry wit and a deep wisdom that showed itself in many ways. She had noticed that the two men were becoming more short-tempered and knew that Moriah was right. They were both strong-willed men, and it would not take a great deal to push them into a fight.

"I'm more interested in *your* man, Moriah." Indeed, she was interested in Leonard Pennington, who had been courting Moriah from the first time they had met. Pennington was twenty-five years old, no more than medium height, and very trim. He had crisp brown hair, warm brown eyes, and a neat mustache. He was a lawyer by profession, very proper, and better educated than most. Jerusalem had watched the progress of the courtship, which seemed like a whirlwind in nature, but she was troubled by the thought of Moriah marrying him.

"Do you love this man enough to marry him?"

"Yes, Ma."

"He's not a country man. You said he'll want you to move to St. Louis. He's ambitious, and he won't be satisfied in a little one-horse town like Jordan City. Would you like that?"

Moriah hesitated, then shrugged. "I . . . I think so. It's a wife's place to make her home with her husband, isn't it, Ma?"

"Yes it is, but city living can be hard for a woman who's only known the country like you have."

"Well, how can I know for sure that he is the right man, Ma? Tell me."

Suddenly, Moriah seemed very vulnerable to Jerusalem. She was eighteen years old now, intelligent, pretty, a hard worker, but there was still something of the little girl in her that troubled Jerusalem. She wanted to say, "If you've got doubt about marrying him, don't do it," but that seemed harsh. Instead, she said, "Well, you're asking the wrong woman, Moriah. I've been struggling with what to do with Kern and Clay for months now." She laughed and hugged Moriah. "Maybe we ought to be just maiden aunts or something."

Mary Aidan came bursting in at that instant. She never walked anywhere but plunged forward at a dead run. "Clay and Clinton are here— Clay brought me a present!" She held up a new doll, and her eyes were sparkling. "Her name is Agnes."

Jerusalem was surprised at the sudden relief she felt. She had been worried about Brodie and Clinton, but, as always, whenever Clay left there was something about his absence that disturbed her. She had seen her husband, Jake, ride off so many times and not return for months or even two years on one occasion. Clay, of course, had always talked of going to hunt for gold or going back to the mountains, and she could not afford to tie herself to another wanderer. "Well, let's go see how they did in New Orleans."

The two went downstairs and saw that Clinton and Clay were dirty and exhausted. "You're back." Jerusalem smiled.

"We're back, Ma," Clinton said cheerfully. "I had me a good time in New Orleans. You ought to see what those folks eat there. There's somethin' that looks like bugs."

"That was shrimp, you dummy." Clay grinned. He looked at Jerusalem and Moriah and took his hat off. He slapped it against his leg, and the dust flew. "Well, you got all dressed up for our homecoming?"

"Why, no," Moriah said. "We're going to the dance. Leonard's taking me, and Mr. Herendeen's taking Ma."

Jerusalem saw something pass across Clay's face. Disappointment, she thought, and she said, "We didn't know when you'd be back, Clay, or I'd have waited."

Clay shrugged. "Well, I'll get cleaned up and go by myself. Just save me a dance, Jerusalem."

Jerusalem hesitated for one moment, for she knew that Kern would not like it, but she smiled and said, "Of course I will."

The dance was well attended, for there was little in the way of diversion in the area. Whenever a dance was announced, farmers and ranchers with their wives and dates would come from as far as twenty miles away to the schoolhouse that had been cleared to use for a dance hall. It was really a combination of city hall, school, and anything that called for a larger number of people than could gather together in other buildings.

A fairly good band with guitars, banjos, two fiddlers, and the usual blowers into jugs filled the schoolhouse with lively music.

Leonard Pennington was wearing a new gray suit that fit him perfectly. His low-cut shoes were black and made from patent leather, and a dark brown tie matched the color of his eyes. He was an attractive man, and as Moriah moved around the floor with him, she said, "This is fun, Leonard."

"Well, it's fine, but wait'll we get to St. Louis." He smiled, and his white teeth were perfect. His eyes crinkled when he smiled, and he said, "We'll be dancing at the Rose Ballroom. You could put ten of these places inside of it! You're going to like it in a real city."

As they moved around the floor, Len leaned close and told Moriah how pretty she looked and how well she danced. He was quick to compliment her throughout the dance and felt there was nothing unmanly about it. He was a city man with none of the roughness of most of the men that inhabited Texas. He was quietly witty and courteous and was ambitious almost to a fault.

Looking around the floor, Len said, "It looks like the saints and the sinners are all one tonight. Even the dance hall girls have joined in."

Suddenly, Len missed a step when he saw the hurt look on Moriah's face. "What is it?"

"Well, that's Julie, my aunt."

"Why, I didn't mean to say anything—"

Len halted and tried to make it right, but he saw that he had wandered into an unmentionable territory. It bothered him that Moriah had an aunt who was a dance hall girl, and he rarely spoke of her, though he was polite enough on the few occasions when they met. He changed the subject quickly. "Everybody's wondering if your mother's going to marry Kern Herendeen."

"I don't think she knows. She likes Clay awfully well."

"Why, I like Clay, too," Len said quickly, "but he's got no ambition. Kern will be in the legislature someday. He's a man with vision who's going to make a difference here in Texas."

"I don't think Ma judges a man by his politics. There are other things more important."

"Well, of course you're right. Speaking of marriage, I promised I wouldn't urge you too much, but I'd like for you to set a date, Moriah."

Moriah did not answer right away, and he leaned back and looked into her face. "What's wrong? We're made for each other."

Moriah could not put into words what she was feeling, but finally she said, "I'm not sure I can please you, Leonard. It will be so different for me living in a big city."

"Why, you'll do fine. I'll help you. You'll see." He suddenly lifted his head and said, "Well, there's Clay. I hope he and Kern behave themselves."

Clay had not worn new clothes, although he looked better than he had in the travel-stained ones he had been wearing when he came back from New Orleans. He stood there for a moment, then heard his name called. He turned to see Julie and Frisco Barr approach him.

"How's my darlin' husband tonight?" Julie winked. She loved to tease Clay about the fact that they had pretended to be man and wife simply in order to get the land for Jerusalem and the family. Julie had been willing to marry him legally, but Clay had drawn the line at that, so she had suggested they just *say* they were married, which satisfied Steve Austin. It was not exactly honest, but neither of them was troubled about it too much. They were more interested in finding a place where Jerusalem and the family could sink down roots and get established.

"You ought not to call me that," Clay said. "It gives people the wrong ideas."

Sheriff Joel Bench was standing beside them. He was a tough, little man in his early fifties with white hair and startling blue eyes. "Miss Julie, I think this is our dance, ain't it?"

"Why, I think it is, Sheriff." Julie smiled, took his hand, and went out to the dance floor with him.

Frisco Barr was dressed, as usual, in the latest fashion. As a gambler, he could afford to be flamboyant, and Clay stared at his vest and said, "I ain't sure a man that wears a vest that colorful is to be trusted."

"Probably not," Frisco grinned, "but anybody with a few dollars can buy a vest like this. How's the cattle business, Clay?" The two men talked for a while about the difficulty of running cattle in Texas, and then humor gleamed in Frisco's dark eyes. "Who's runnin' ahead with the widow Hardin?"

"Don't you start on me, Frisco," Clay said, putting a hard glance on the gambler.

"All right, I won't." The two men stood there, and finally Frisco said, "Miss Moriah's doin' right well. Pennington's gonna go up in the world."

"I guess he is," Clay murmured, but his eyes were on Jerusalem. He straightened up and said, "Guess I'll go have myself a dance."

Frisco lifted his eyebrows. "Kern don't take too well to bein' cut in on—in any way. Watch yourself, Clay."

Clay paid no heed but moved right over to where Jerusalem and Herendeen were dancing. He tapped Herendeen on the shoulder, and when Herendeen stopped to turn, he said, "Mind if I cut in, Kern?"

Kern Herendeen was a bigger man than Clay. He was taller and bulkier, and had an aggressiveness about him that flared out at times. "Wait until the next dance, Taliferro," he said.

Kern started to turn, but Clay said, "You know the custom is that gentlemen step aside to give other gents a chance." Kern started to pull away, but Clay put a hand on his arm. "Let's do this easy, Kern."

Kern Herendeen's anger suddenly flared. "Get your hands off me!"

"I don't like your manners much, Kern."

"I don't like yours either."

Jerusalem stood there watching and wanting to separate the two, but it was moving too fast. "If you don't like my ways, Kern, take it up."

"I'll take it up," Kern said, his mouth tightening. "Let's just go outside."

"Stop this!" Jerusalem said. "Behave yourselves, both of you."

"I just wanted to dance with you, Jerusalem. Is that too much to ask?"

"Wait your turn," Kern said and grinned.

Jerusalem had no chance to say anything else. She had been about to say, "Clay, you can have the next dance." But Herendeen swept her away, moving to the other side of the dance floor.

For one instant the wildness that Clay Taliferro tried to keep down way beneath the surface of his manners erupted. An almost irresistible urge to go after Kern, turn him around, and strike him in the face overwhelmed him. He forced himself to take a deep breath, then he turned and walked toward the door. He passed by Julie, who spoke to him, saying, "Clay—" But he ignored her and left the room.

"He's pretty sore," Frisco said, who had come to stand by Julie. "I'm surprised he didn't call Kern out."

"I know him," Julie said. "He'll go away and think about it, and when he gets mad enough, he will take it up again. I hate to see it."

Barr turned and studied Julie, who was looking toward the door that Clay had passed through. "You think pretty highly of Clay, don't you?"

Julie turned and faced Frisco squarely. She said in a level tone, "He's the only man I ever met I'd trust with anything—at any time."

The words seemed to strike Frisco with some force. He chewed his lower lip and then shrugged. "It makes me feel small to hear you say that."

"You'll live. Let's get something to drink."

★   ★   ★

Kern pulled the horses in front of the house, then turned to face Jerusalem. It was past midnight, but the dance had gone on for a long time. Several times Jerusalem had urged Kern to take her home, but he had protested that there were few dances for them to enjoy. Finally, she had said bluntly, "I've got to go, Kern, with you or without you."

He had at once said, "Why, sure, I should have taken you earlier."

The moon was merely a silver crescent in the sky, but the stars shone bright, like diamonds scattered across dark velvet. Jerusalem started to get out, but Kern caught her arm and held her. "I'm sorry about that run-in with Clay," he said.

"It embarrassed me, Kern. I felt like a bone that two dogs were fighting over."

Kern was clearly shocked at her choice of words. "I didn't want it to be like that," he said hurriedly. "But look, if you'd marry me, Jerusalem, there wouldn't be any more of that."

Though she had enjoyed the dance at first, she'd seen another side of Kern when Clay had tried to cut in on them. Kern's spark of anger forced her to make a decision. The dance had begun well, but it had ended badly, and Jerusalem wanted to put an end to their relationship. She turned to him and spoke directly, "Kern, you're a strong man, and I admire strong men—but I can't marry you. I should have told you this weeks ago."

Kern Herendeen was not accustomed to having to beg for anything. He had tried to court other women in his life, but he saw in Jerusalem Hardin a certain strength, which he admired, for he possessed the same quality. She was still an attractive woman, too, young enough to bear a son, which he longed for with all of his soul. He held her arm trying to persuade her, and when she remained adamant, he said roughly, "It's Taliferro, isn't it?"

"That's my business, Kern."

"No, it's not just yours. It's mine, too."

"Plenty of women would jump at the chance to marry you. Find yourself a wife who has no doubts." She pulled away from his grasp and stepped out. She looked at him and said, "Let's not let this turn into something ugly, Kern. We're going to be neighbors. I can't marry you. I wouldn't make you happy if I did."

"I'm not taking that as final, Jerusalem."

"Don't be foolish, Kern," Jerusalem said sharply. "Put me out of your mind. I know your pride hurts, but let that be all that comes of this. Stay away from Clay." She turned and walked into the house, and Herendeen stared after her. Suddenly, he raised the whip and struck the horse, which cried out with a scream, and then drove off at a furious rate.

Jerusalem heard the cry of the horse and knew that Kern Herendeen was not a man who was able to drop things easily. He wanted to hold things, and once he had them, he wouldn't let them go. That was the reason she wouldn't marry him. Jake had not held her at all, but she knew it'd be just as bad for a man who wanted to possess her wholly.

Stepping inside the house, she started toward her room and then suddenly halted abruptly. Clay was sitting at the table watching her. "You're still up," she said.

"Still up." He got up and walked over to stand before her.

He had something in his hand, but she could not make out what it was. He said nothing, but Jerusalem knew he had been hurt. "I didn't mean to put you down, Clay." She wanted to say more, and finally she found the words to express what was in her heart. "No man in this world has ever treated me better than you. Certainly not Jake. I want you to know that every day I thank God for how you've helped me and my family."

Clay looked down at the object in his hand, then held it up. Jerusalem saw that it was something oblong, wrapped in a piece of newspaper.

Clay hesitated, then said quietly, "I guess I don't know the right words to say to a woman like you. I wish I was a little bit better with them, but I love you better than life, Jerusalem." He removed the paper and handed Jerusalem a perfectly shaped rose of a striking yellow color. "I saw this rose, Jerusalem, and it made me think of you for some reason. So beautiful—" He broke off and could not seem to find the words to finish.

For all his toughness, at that moment Clay seemed to Jerusalem to have a gentle spirit, and a tender love filled her heart for him. Taking the rose, Jerusalem held it in her hand. When she looked up, she saw the depth of his love for her in his eyes, and it stirred her. "Thank you, Clay.

It was thoughtful of you to bring it to me—and I'm glad you see something of it in me."

Clay did not move. He was so still that Jerusalem wondered what he was thinking. His eyes were fixed on her, and she wanted him to break the silence.

Finally, he said, "I'm through chasing you, Jerusalem. If you want me, I'll be true to you until the day I die. If you choose Kern, I'll always be a friend to you and to your children and to your grandchildren. You'll always be able to count on me."

He turned and walked away rapidly, his steps echoing on the wooden floor. He ascended the stairway, and Jerusalem stood there. Clay's open expression of love shocked her, and she felt tears gather in her eyes. She held the rose and savored the delicate fragrance, then touched it with her lips. At that moment she wanted to weep and had to struggle to keep the sobs back. She could not tell why Clay's simple gesture had touched her, but she knew that something had happened this night that had changed everything.

CHAPTER
FIFTEEN

Clay and Zane did not urge their horses along but loitered behind the twenty head of bellowing longhorns that raised a cloud of fine dust in front of them. They had strayed over to the east, and the two men had searched for them during the early morning hours and now were headed back with them toward the main herd.

Clay had been silent for most of the day, and Zane finally asked, "What's the matter with you, Clay? You ain't talked as much as a rock for days now."

"Guess I just don't have much to say, Zane."

Zane grinned. He did not speak for a while but lounged in his saddle, then said, "A man in love is a peculiar creature. He will do mighty strange things."

Clay shot him an irritated glance and said, "I hope you get it so bad some day you can't walk straight, Zane."

"Not likely. A man that's escaped marriage for thirty-eight years has got a good chance of makin' it all the way through without all the aggravation of married life."

Clay did not answer, for he suddenly straightened in the saddle. "Look over there," he said abruptly. He lifted his hand and pointed to a slight cloud of dust.

Zane followed his gesture and said, "Can you make out what they are?"

"Well, they ain't Comanches. They're ridin' too slow for that."

The two men kept their eyes on the approaching horsemen, and Clay said, "I can't quite make 'em out. They don't have any cattle, but I don't know what they're doing here." He pulled his horse up, and Zane followed, ignoring the longhorns. As the horsemen approached, Clay murmured quietly, "They look like they're about done in."

As the men came within a hundred yards, it was obvious that their horses were exhausted, and Clay noted quickly that two men were riding with a third between them, holding him up. The leader was a tall man, who was eyeing them cautiously.

"Howdy," Clay said. "It looks like you had some trouble."

"I reckon we have," the leader said. He pulled his horse up and shook his head. "These hosses are about done in." He studied his companions and then said, "My name's Frank Dalton. This here's a ranging company."

Both Zane and Clay had heard of men like this. Sam Houston, not being able to afford to pay much, had persuaded some of the tougher citizens of Texas to serve without pay. They were simply called "ranging companies," and this group looked like they had been used almost beyond their limits.

"I'm Clay Taliferro, and this is Zane Satterfield. Our place is down the way about three miles. Why don't you bring your men in, Captain, and rest your mounts."

"My sister's pretty good at doctorin'," Zane added. "I see you've got a wounded man there."

"That sounds right promisin' to me," Dalton said. There was a weariness in his face, and he said, "We'll limp on in. Could use a little rest."

Dalton kept his mount even with Zane and Clay, and as they followed the longhorns, Clay said, "What sort of chase you been on, Captain?"

"Sam Houston sent us to chase the Comanches up north. They been raidin' real bad out to the west of here."

"It looks like you caught up with 'em," Zane said, glancing back at the battered men. "What happened?"

"We ran into an ambush," Dalton said glumly. "It's a wonder any of us got our scalps. It was about fifty of them, and they had us pinned down in an arroyo. I guess they finally ran out of ammunition. They was mostly shootin' arrows there at the last. We were lucky they didn't get our hosses. We couldn't have walked out of that one."

Zane was pensive and toyed with the reins of his horse as he thought about the report. "Comanches are about the most fearsome Indians there is, I reckon. At least so I hear. Clay here saw some Sioux and Cheyenne. They're pretty bad, too."

"As far as pure meanness, I guess the Comanches might be a little worse," Dalton said. "The worst one is Bear Killer."

"I've heard of him," Zane nodded. "A pretty bad Indian."

"The worst I ever saw. The ranch here is right on the border. You'd better keep an eye out for him, although it's hard to keep an eye out for Comanches."

Dalton fell silent then, whether from weariness or a natural taciturnity, the two men could not figure. They did not attempt to draw him out anymore, for it was obvious he was running on nerve.

Jerusalem and Moriah had busied themselves at once when Clay explained the situation with the rangers. "Bring all of them right on in," she said. "Moriah and me can feed them, and I'll do what I can to patch up any of them that's hurt."

The group of rangers had gotten off their horses wearily, and Brodie had seen to it that the animals were fed and watered. He had come in afterward, saying, "Captain Dalton, them horses is about done in. I watered 'em and fed 'em. Don't see how you can get much farther on 'em, though."

"I guess we'll try to make it into Jordan City and fort up there for a while."

He turned to Jerusalem, who was bandaging the bullet wound in the arm of one of the rangers. She finished fastening the bandage and said, "You keep that clean, and it won't give you any trouble."

"Thank you, ma'am," the ranger said gratefully. He winced as he lifted his arm and said, "I'm glad it was a bullet instead of an arrowhead like poor old Gabe."

The ranger named Gabe had been struck with an arrow in the back, and removing it had required painful surgery. Clay and Zane had held the man down while Jerusalem had dug it out. The man had mercifully passed out, and now he was sleeping fitfully. "I may have given him a bit too much of that pain killer," Jerusalem said.

"I'm glad you had it, Mrs. Hardin," Captain Dalton said. "As a matter of fact, I don't know if we could have made it into Jordan City without you. We're mighty grateful to you."

"It's the least we can do." Jerusalem smiled. "We're very thankful that you and your men are helping to keep the Indians away from us."

"I don't know how much good we're doing with that. There ain't enough of us, and trying to pin a Comanche down is like trying to pin a sunbeam down."

Brodie had been fascinated by the men. He had talked with several of them who, as they ate, were willing enough to describe their mission. Brodie now turned and said, "Captain Dalton, what does a man have to do to join up with you?"

Dalton suddenly laughed. It was a harsh laugh, but not an unkind one. "Well, son, first I reckon you have to be crazy."

Brodie stared at him. "Crazy? Why did you say that?"

"Well, it's a hard and dangerous life. The money is nothing to brag about, and you can lose your scalp. You'd be better off to become a barber."

"A barber!" Brodie snorted. "Not likely, Captain."

Clay, who was across the room standing beside Jerusalem, said, "I'd better disillusion that boy about becomin' an Indian fighter. There ain't no profit in it."

"Talk to him, Clay. I can't afford to lose any more boys."

At the very moment Jerusalem had been taking the arrow out of the wounded man, Moriah was being kissed in Leonard Pennington's office.

She had gone to town to get supplies along with Clinton and had stopped by to visit with Leonard. He had been extremely glad to see her, as he always was, and for a time they had talked about the dance that was coming up. Her eyes had widened when she saw him step closer with a determination in his eyes that she had seen before. He wrapped his arms around her and kissed her, holding her tight, and she clung to him, savoring his caress. After a moment, he lifted his head and grinned. "I like a woman who's got a little tiger in her."

"You shouldn't say things like that, Len!"

"Why, it's true enough. It's what drew me to you in the first place," he said. He still kept his arms around her, and his hands ran up and down her back, sending slight shivers through her.

She liked him very much and knew that he was teasing her. "I hope I'll be a good wife to you."

"You will be. I have no doubt about that." He released her and said, "I got a letter here from my folks. They want you to come and visit in St. Louis. You've got to meet my family. I know they'll love you."

Moriah was apprehensive about meeting Len's family. They were prominent people, and she felt totally inadequate to be thrust into their social circles. Tentatively, she said, "Len, why don't you stay here? You could do great things here in Texas."

"Why, Texas isn't even part of the Union. They may never get in. The way John Quincy Adams is fighting it, it looks that way. Jackson has got more of a vision. He wants Texas because he sees it as a doorway all the way to the Pacific Ocean. That's what he wants. Sam Houston feels the same way. But the northern states will never let it happen. They're too afraid of slavery spreading. So, I've got to get out of here, and you've got to come with me."

He continued to speak to her in this fashion, and Moriah was happy that he was so open with her. Finally, when he kept pressuring her, she said, "Maybe I could go to St. Louis and meet your family."

At her words Len brightened up. He pulled her into his arms and kissed her again. "I love you, Moriah," he said with intensity. "There's nothing that could change me. I'll always love you."

"That's all I want," Moriah whispered. "Just always love me, Len. It doesn't matter where we live as long as you love me."

★ ★ ★

Clay sat beside the creek not moving, but staring rather dully into the river as it flowed by. The Brazos was not an impressive river like the broad Mississippi nor like the Colorado in the mountains to the north that had its own wild, spectacular beauty. The Brazos did bring life with it. Without it there would be nothing but a barren desert.

Overhead a bald eagle soared, and Clay lifted his head to watch the magnificent bird. He loved the predators, the eagles and the hawks and the falcons, and had often thought if he were a bird, he would want to be one of these.

The river made a sibilant murmur at his feet, but the surface was still and smooth. The water seemed to be almost standing still, but it was moving inexorably toward the Gulf, draining the land and bringing life wherever it touched.

Clay glanced suddenly downstream and saw a timber wolf that had caught a frog and was gulping it down. He stared at the rangy animal and admired the strength and the sagacity that wolves had. "Enjoy your frog, boy," he said. The wolf heard his voice, took one look, and then dashed off back toward the trees on the far side of the river.

Clay had come out to the river to think and to get away from things. It was a habit long ingrained in him. That was what he had loved most about the mountains, the solitude. A man could sit down and wouldn't have to be apprehensive that somebody would interrupt him—unless it was an Indian, which might mean a fatal interruption. But it had been quiet there, and he had spent long hours enjoying the natural beauty of the wilderness. Coming back to civilization was like coming out of the silence of the open spaces into a noisy, bustling crowd of people inside a small room. He knew this was why he loved Texas, because of the immense space that stretched for miles on end. He had never been a town man, and the silence and the enormous space that filled the country pleased him and gave him a sense of freedom.

Of late, however, he had been thinking of moving on. He had spoken often of this in jest, but now, more than half in earnest, he had considered going to California to look for gold or return to the north country to join the trappers again. He knew that kind of life was mostly over, but he remembered the good parts of it. His mind and heart were both troubled by a loneliness that he had never known before. Always before, people had been around, and he could take them or walk away from them. But Jerusalem Hardin had made a place inside of him that he could not shake off. Indeed, he had *tried* to put her aside. The struggle between him and Kern Herendeen had been a challenge for him, but he was tired of it. There were longings in him that he could not identify. He remembered times when he was traveling through the country at night and would sight a cabin with a light inside. The sound of happy voices—laughing, and speaking with love and intensity—would make him feel an emptiness inside. Many times he had paused, sitting on his horse outside in the darkness and in the silence, and had simply listened. During these times a longing had developed that only this past year had come to bother him more and more.

He suddenly turned, the old instincts from his days in the mountains still very much alive, and he saw Jerusalem riding her brown mare toward him. He got up as she dismounted, and as she tied her horse to a sapling, he asked, "Is everything all right?"

Jerusalem turned, and her face was still, and yet there was something in her eyes that he could not identify.

"Nobody's sick. Nobody's snakebit. But I guess there's more to being all right than that, don't you think?"

"Come and sit down. I've been sittin' out here feelin' sorry for myself. You can sit down beside me and comfort me."

Jerusalem sat down on the bank, and just the presence of her being near stirred Clay. He had always thought she had the most beautiful mouth he had ever seen. It was rich and self-possessed with a curve that stirred him whenever she smiled. A summer darkness lay over her skin, and her dress fell away from her throat, showing the smooth ivory texture. He was also aware of the smoothness of her figure within her dress, and the sunlight was kind to her, showing the full, soft lines of her body. As she spoke, her lips made small changes in the corners, and from time to time she made a little gesture with her shoulders and expressive turns with her hands. The fragrance of her clothes powerfully touched him, and meeting her glance, he watched the expressions of her face as she spoke of the problems within the family for some time. She was worried about Zane, who had apparently no purpose at all. She was grieved by Julie's working in a saloon and about Brodie, who was so distracted over Serena he couldn't eat. Finally, she said wistfully, "I wish troubles would come one at a time so you could deal with them that way, but they don't. They come in a crowd."

"Did you ever throw a stone in the water?" Clay asked.

Jerusalem laughed, amused at the strange leaps his mind made. "You have a way of saying the craziest things that have nothing at all to do with what I say. I'm talking about my problems, and you're talking about throwing rocks. You've got a mind like a grasshopper!"

Clay smiled at her, picked up a small stone, and tossed it out in the water. It made a pronounced plopping sound, and he nodded. "Look at how perfect the circles are."

Clay seemed to go into fits of philosophy at times, and Jerusalem had learned to listen to him. "They are perfect, aren't they?"

"Well, look at this." He tossed another rock out, which caused another set of circles. "Look how them last circles disturbed the first set. And look at this." He took several stones and threw them, and the concentric circles of the small waves were crisscrossed and had lost their symmetry. "Look how mixed-up they are. They're all crisscrossed." He reached out and touched a lock of her hair without speaking and then dropped his hand. "I guess that's what you mean by wishing troubles would come one at a time. It's like that circle when you throw one rock. It's easy to keep up with that. But most of the time there's about a half a dozen rocks hittin' around us, and they get us all mixed up."

The two sat in silence for a while, and Clay sensed that she was watching him. He turned to meet her gaze, and when she did not speak, he said, "Why are you so quiet?"

Jerusalem seemed to be totally immersed in watching Clay. He had learned that she had this way about her of focusing her entire attention on an object, on a person, or, as now, on a problem

"I think I'd like to get married." She said this much as if she'd said, "I'd like to have a drink of water."

Clay blinked with surprise, and for a moment, he could not speak. "Well, that's what I've been talking about." Suddenly, a thought flashed through Clay's mind. *She's telling me she's going to marry Kern.* A rush of anger and disappointment filled him, and he could not think of a single thing to say.

Jerusalem reached out and put her hand on the back of his neck. He was taken by surprise, for she was not overly prone to show her affection in this way. "Who was it you were thinking of marrying?" he asked cautiously, aware of the warmth and strength of her hand on his bare neck.

"You."

Clay reacted strongly. His torso twisted around, and he said, "Me? I thought it was Kern."

"That's because you don't know anything about women, Clay Taliferro. But I'm going to ask you three questions, and I want you to answer them honestly."

Clay nodded. He could not imagine what the questions were. "Sure, Jerusalem, just ask."

"One. Do you love me?"

"I do."

"Two. Will you stay with me forever and not run off and leave me?"

Instantly, Clay knew she was thinking of Jake and how she had had to raise her family alone. He knew she had desires for a man to fill her loneliness, and yet she had been cut off from her man. "I won't never leave you. I promise."

Jerusalem hesitated, then said, "The third one may be the hardest of all." She hesitated, then said quietly, "Will you stop running from God?"

Clay sat very still. He did not answer at once, and he knew what she was asking. He realized he had been running from God most of his adult life, and he also knew that she longed for his well-being in every way. He had watched her since she had found God in her own life, and now he took a deep breath and said, "Yes, Jerusalem—I'll stop running."

A joy came into Jerusalem's eyes then. She reached out for him, and he turned to meet her. Her arms went around his neck, and she pulled him close. Clay held her tightly as her soft lips responded to his kiss. And in his arms was a sweetness and a richness that filled all the empty places he'd ever felt. At that moment, he was aware of what life's treasure really was. It was here in his arms, and he wanted nothing more than to hold her for the rest of his days.

He lifted his lips, and her eyes were filled with tears, but he knew they were tears of happiness. "You know, by himself a man don't have much purpose. He's just like the wind blowing, with no idea where it's going. But when a man finds his woman, he sees himself, and he knows what he is. And that's what I'm feeling right now, Jerusalem."

The two sat there silently, for both of them were too full of emotion to speak. But finally Jerusalem said, "We'll get married and love each other all of our lives. And whichever of us dies first, the other one will hold their hand. And then the one that goes first will wait on the other side until the homecoming."

Clay smiled and said, "Well, when will it be? Gettin' married, I mean."

"Today's fine with me."

Clay stared at her in shock, then suddenly laughed. "Why, woman, we can't get married today!"

"Why can't we?"

Clay grinned and said, "That's right. Why can't we?"

Jerusalem got to her feet. "You go get the preacher and bring him to the house. Go by the Golden Lady and tell Julie to come. All the children are home, so we'll get married at noon, and we'll leave at one o'clock on our honeymoon."

"Honeymoon? Where will we go?"

"Some place where we'll be alone, and you can tell me over and over again how much you love me and how you'll never leave me."

Clay suddenly grabbed her and began to dance around. His laughter filled the silence, and his horse stared white-eyed at him. Clay kissed Jerusalem, then ran and jumped on his mount, jerked him around, and kicked him into a dead run. He jerked his hat off and was yelling like a wild Comanche, leaving a trail of dust as he headed toward town to find the preacher.

Jerusalem watched him, laughter welling up from deep within her. She watched until all she could see was the cloud of dust that the hooves of his horse stirred up. Finally, she turned to the river and stared at it for a long time. She reached over, picked up a rock, and tossed it out into the river. She watched as the circles spread out, and then she looked up and said, "Lord, take care of my man. Stay on his trail like a blue tick hound hot on the trail of a fat coon. Run him up a tree and keep him there until he gives up and loves You with all of his heart."

Turning, she went and got on her horse. She took the reins, and then for one moment she sat in the saddle silently. Then Jerusalem laughed and said aloud, "They're in for quite a surprise when I get there and tell them Clay and I are getting married today. I hope they like it." She kicked the horse into a gallop and leaned over, urging him to greater speed. As she did, she did what many women had done. "Jerusalem Taliferro," she spoke the name aloud. "Mrs. Clayton Taliferro. That does sound good." Then she began to prepare in her mind the little speech that she would give to her children about their new pa.

CHAPTER
SIXTEEN

Jerusalem stirred herself, moving under the cover for warmth. She stretched luxuriously and slowly came out of a sleep as sound as any she had ever had. She sighed and turned over. When she opened her eyes, she found Clay propped up on one elbow, looking at her and smiling.

"What are you doing?" Jerusalem asked. She reached out and touched his chest, leaving her hand there, feeling his strength and taking in the look of his eyes.

"Well," Clay said, the corners of his mouth twitching, "I'm thinking of taking advantage of you."

Jerusalem laughed, reached out, and pulled him to her. He nudged over and held her tightly. "You can't do it," she whispered in a demure voice

"Why can't I?"

"Because a woman has to be unwilling for a man to take advantage of her." She kissed him, but he pulled his head back and ran his hand down her back, which always drove her crazy. "The next woman I marry," he said, "is gonna be shy. It does purely discombobulate a man to find out he's married a woman with no shame."

"I really don't have any shame." She put herself against him and hugged him. When he moved his head back to stare at her again, she said, "I've got to get up and fix biscuits."

Clay grinned broadly. "I didn't marry you to fix biscuits."

He held her tightly, knowing that she loved to be held. He had found this out four months earlier at the very beginning of their marriage. At night she had to be touching him, even if it was just lightly with her hand on his shoulder or her toes against his feet. She loved to be held as she went to sleep, and now he teased her, as he often did. "You know," he said, his face only inches from hers, "the Bible says that all those old fellows in the Bible had several wives. Maybe that's what I ought to do. I could have one wife to make the biscuits, one wife might wash my clothes, and one wife to do this." He kissed her again, and she held on to him.

Jerusalem's first marriage had never brought her much joy, for Jake had been a rough, careless man seeking his own gratification. Clay had surprised her, for tough as he was on the outside, she discovered from the beginning that he had a deeply tender and sentimental side. Usually, he was careful to keep this concealed from others, but Jerusalem had discovered a genuine tenderness in him. He had taken her to New Orleans for their honeymoon, and she knew she would treasure those memories forever. It had shocked her how he had stirred her from the first, arousing a passion she had never dreamed of. Now she held him and said, "I guess the biscuits will wait . . ."

Moriah was watching her mother closely as Jerusalem took the biscuits out of the oven. "You just look beautiful, Ma. Marriage agrees with you."

Jerusalem shot a glance at her daughter and saw that she was somewhat wistful. "I guess it does. Clay's made me very happy."

"Well, you've made him happy, too. Is Kern Herendeen still mad at you for refusing to marry him?"

"Yes, he is. At Clay, too."

"I'm glad you didn't marry him. I didn't like him."

"I'm glad, too. You know, Moriah, I nearly made a terrible mistake. At times I really thought of marrying him." She put the pan of biscuits down on the table and looked up and saw a look of concern on Moriah's face. "What is it?" Jerusalem asked.

"I hope I'm as happy with Len as you are with Clay."

"I hope you are, too."

"Ma, I want to ask you. How can you be sure you've got the one person in the whole world that's just the right one for you?"

"I think God has to do that. There's too many ways for a woman to make a mistake, but when God puts a couple together, it will be right."

Moriah busied herself setting the table, but Jerusalem could tell something was troubling her. Jerusalem put her hand on her daughter's arm and looked at her. "Something's bothering you. What is it? You can tell me."

"Well, I'm so . . . so *ignorant*, Ma."

"Ignorant! About what?"

Color came into Moriah's face. "You know. About—well, about intimate things."

Jerusalem said gently, "It's better to be ignorant than experienced." As she looked at the girl, she remembered how shy and ignorant she herself had been when she had married Jake. She made a quick decision and said, "After the men have had breakfast and leave, we'll talk. Marriage is always a shock for a pure young girl. It was for me. But I'm going to tell you what to expect. If you and Len love each other, you'll find out eventually how to love. But maybe I can make it a little bit easier . . ."

"Be careful with this hoss, Devoe. He's a good one."

"I'm always careful," Devoe Crutchfield said. He was a young man of twenty-five, strongly built with big, bulky muscles from his blacksmithing trade. He had flaming red hair, mild blue eyes, and a teasing manner. "Haven't seen much of you the last four months, Clay. What you been doin'?"

Clay turned swiftly and stared at Devoe. He knew the blacksmith was teasing him about staying close to home during the early days of his marriage. "You watch yourself, Devoe. I might be forced to shoot the next feller that tries to tease me."

Devoe grinned, not worried in the least. "Well, I figure I might try that marriage bit myself sometime." He ran his hand down the stallion's back, and he looked at Clay with interest. "I was surprised that Herendeen didn't kick up a fuss when you beat him out with Jerusalem."

"He didn't have no chance a'tall." Clay grinned. "I'm downright irresistible."

"Yeah, I bet. When I get ready to go a courtin', you can give me lessons on how to charm the ladies. I'll have this hoss ready in an hour."

"All right, Devoe."

Clay left the stable and headed for the Golden Lady Saloon, but he heard a muffled voice calling his name. "Clay! Clay Taliferro!"

Clay stopped and turned to his right. There in the window was a man's face framed, his hands holding on to the bars. *Who could be calling me from the jail?* Clay wondered. He moved over closer, directly opposite the window.

"It's me, Quaid Shafter. Lordy, it's good to see you, Clay."

"Quaid, is that you?"

Quaid Shafter's face was battered. He had a large scab on his forehead, and his one eye was purple and almost puffed shut. His smile was infectious, however, and Clay thought instantly of how much he resembled his father, Jed Shafter. Jed had been a good friend to Clay during his time in the mountains, and he had fond memories of the man. Quaid, his son, had come just after Clay had left. "What are you doin' in jail, Quaid?"

"I've been arrested. Can't you see?" He grinned. "I was disturbing the peace."

Clay laughed. "That's hard to do in this part of the world. You didn't shoot a lawyer or somethin'?"

"Why, no. Don't matter if you shoot a lawyer now and then. Too many of them anyway. No, I had a little trouble at the Golden Lady. I'd appreciate it," he said, "if you could get me out of here, Clay."

"I'll see what the sheriff says."

"I'll wait for you right here," Quaid said, smiling.

Walking straight to the front door, Clay entered the office and found Sheriff Joel Bench sitting in a chair, tilted back against the wall. "Howdy, Clay. What's goin' on?"

"You got an old friend of mine in there."

"You mean Shafter? If he's your friend, I feel sorry for you."

"He said he was disturbin' the peace."

Sheriff Bench brought his chair down and spread his elbows on the desk. "Disturbin' the peace? That's a nice way of puttin' it! He wrecked the Golden Lady Saloon. Frisco said it'll cost at least a hundred dollars, maybe two, to fix all the damage he did. But I'm fining him twenty-five dollars. He laid out four men and punched me in the ear before I buffaloed him. He can either pay it or squat in a cell for a couple of months."

Clay shook his head. "I'll pay the fine, Sheriff, and I'll settle with Frisco."

Bench stared at Clay and demanded, "Why would you do that? He ain't your kin, is he?"

"No, but his pa was—a real good friend. Jed kept some Cheyenne from lifting my scalp once. He's dead now, and I never could make it up to him. I guess maybe I can help his boy out."

"Well, all right. Never mind the fine, Clay. Just settle with Frisco. Shafter ain't got a dime. He lost his money, his hoss, and his gun. Don't own nothin' but the clothes he's standin' with, and they were pretty tore up in the fracas. I'll get him."

Clay waited as Bench disappeared into the bowels of the jail, wondering if he was doing the right thing. When Quaid Shafter came out, his clothes seemed to be hanging on by a few threads.

"I appreciate this, Clay. I knew the good Lord wouldn't let me stay in this pitiful old jail."

"The Lord ain't got nothin' to do with it, Shafter," Sheriff Bench said sourly. "Clay vouches for you, so you can go. The next time," he warned, "you cut your wolf loose, I won't be so charitable."

"Thanks for the bed." Shafter grinned. "I slept like a baby. You ready, Clay?"

"I guess so." The two left the office, and Shafter seemed to be totally unashamed of what he had done at the Golden Lady Saloon. He was taller than Clay and weighed possibly one eighty-five, a lean, muscular man with a V-shaped face. He had a wide mouth and deep-set, light blue eyes that looked very pale against his tanned features. The most striking feature was his hair, which was pure silver. It had been that way since he was sixteen years old, which was when Clay had first met him. It was glossy and had a wave, and he wore it down long enough to come over his collar. As Clay glanced at him, he thought, *It's funny how that silver hair makes his face seem younger.* "Reckon you could eat somethin', Quaid?"

"I could eat an armadillo!"

"Well, let's get you some new clothes first. I doubt if they'd serve you in the restaurant with those rags."

Clay took Quaid Shafter by Potter's General Store and bought him some new clothes and then took him to the restaurant, where Quaid ate like a starved wolf. Finally, when he finished the last of the breakfast, which included a half-dozen eggs, at least that many biscuits, and a chunk of ham as big as his head, he said, "That was mighty good, Clay. I do appreciate it."

"I'm not a charitable institution, Quaid," Clay said. He was drinking coffee and studying the young man. "You'll work it out at my place."

"Sure, Clay, be glad to."

"Tell me about what you've been doin'. Haven't seen you in a long time. I know you lost your dad. Sorry to hear that."

For an instant the young man's face grew sad. He looked down at the table and nodded. "That was hard when Pa died," he said.

"Good man," Clay remarked.

"Yeah, the best I ever knowed. Well, I've been movin' around, Clay. I went to Santa Fe and drove a freight wagon for a while. Then I got tired of workin' for the other fella, so I bought me some tradin' goods and started tradin' with the Indians. Did pretty good, too."

Clay was interested at once. "Did you do any tradin' with the Comanches?"

"Shore did," Quaid nodded. "They're a tetchy bunch. They like to stake you out on an ant hill or cook you over a fire if the notion strikes them. But most traders steer clear of 'em, so I done pretty good. Almost married me a pretty little squaw, but the chief wanted too much for her."

"You speak any of their talk?"

"Sure, pretty fair."

"Ever meet up with Bear Killer?"

Instantly, Quaid's face grew sober. "Once or twice, and I ain't hankerin' to run into him again. He's the worst of 'em."

"Well, come on if you're through. I'll settle up with the Golden Lady that you busted up. You can work it out."

"Nursin' cow critters?"

"Yes, mostly."

"Well, it beats a few other things I've done."

Clay had put in a hard day, and when he had finally gotten to bed, he had gone to sleep at once. He had been awakened abruptly when Jerusalem had come to bed and had pulled him around so that he had to face her. "Clay, don't go to sleep," she said. She took his hair and shook his head gently. "Talk to me."

Clay groaned. "Woman, I can't talk. I gotta sleep. Runnin' this ranch tires a man out."

"No, you've got to tell me what you did. It's too early to go to sleep."

Clay had discovered that Jerusalem loved to talk in bed. She was not interested in the big picture. She wanted to know the finite details of everything he did during the day, and if he went to sleep before he finished telling her, she would dig her elbow into him and wake him up and make him talk more.

"All right." He groaned, and for a time he lay there flat on his back. He told her mostly about Quaid Shafter, about his times with the young man's father in the mountains and what a good man he was. But he said, "I don't know much about Quaid. He was real young when I knew him. No more than sixteen or seventeen. But he was undependable, I remember, and was a grief to his pa. If he hasn't changed, I'll be lucky if he hangs around long enough to pay Frisco off."

Clay's voice grew fuzzy, and he drifted off. He was awakened by a sharp elbow nudging his side.

"Don't *do* that, woman! I'm so tired I could scrape it off with a stick!"

Jerusalem, however, leaned over him and looked down into his eyes. "I've got some news for you," she said, her eyes dancing.

Clay did not see them, for his own eyes were closed. "Can't it wait until tomorrow? "

"No."

"What is it, then?"

"We're going to have a baby."

Clay did not move for a moment, then his eyes opened, and he stared into her face. "What? A baby! Why, that's impossible!"

Jerusalem put her hands on the sides of his face and kissed him on the nose. "You've made it *very* possible, Clay."

"Why, it just can't be!"

Jerusalem stared at him, shocked at his response. She rolled over and turned her back to him. Clay instantly knew he had hurt her feelings. "What's the matter?"

"You don't want this baby," she said stiffly.

"Why, certain I want it! You just spring that on me of a sudden, and I've got to get used to it." He began to stroke her back, and finally she softened and turned over.

"Would you want a girl or a boy?" she asked.

"Why, it would have to be one or the other, wouldn't it?"

She laughed at him, and the two lay there talking. She was more excited than Clay had ever seen her, but soon she grew sleepy. She turned over and went to sleep almost at once. Clay lay there for a while, his mind racing at the news that he was going to be a father. As the excitement grew inside him, he couldn't keep it inside, so he nudged her and said, "Wake up, Jerusalem."

"What's the matter?"

"I want to talk some more about this baby."

"Not tonight, Clay, I'm so sleepy."

"Too bad. Now you know how I feel. Now, listen," he said, shaking her shoulder, "I've been thinkin' about names. How about if it's a boy we can give him a Bible name."

"I think that would be good—like David or Jeremiah."

"No, I was thinking more about the name that old prophet Isaiah gave his boy."

"I don't remember that."

"Why, he named him Mahershalalhasbaz."

Jerusalem's eyes flew open. She was horrified. "Why, that's *awful!*"

"No, it ain't. We could call him 'Hash' for short. And if we have a girl," he said, "we'll name her Jezebel. We can call her Jez or Jezzy."

Jerusalem began to laugh. "You are absolutely crazy, Clay Taliferro."

Clay put his arms around her and held her close, stroking her hair. "You took me plumb off-guard, wife, but now that I'm used to the idea, I'm plumb proud of myself."

"Proud of *yourself!* What about me? Don't I have any part of having this baby?"

"Well," Clay said thoughtfully, "you can be my helper . . ."

CHAPTER
SEVENTEEN

Moriah sat in the wagon seat beside Quaid Shafter and could not remember a time when she had had such mixed emotions about a human being. She was a young woman who liked to keep things straight and orderly and in proper perspective in every way, but Quaid Shafter had disturbed this equilibrium. As she sat on the far side of the seat so that she would not brush against him, she cast a sideways glance at the young man.

One thing that troubled her was that he was one of the most attractive men she had ever seen. He wasn't neatly handsome in the way of Len Pennington, but there was a ruggedness about him that drew the eyes of women. She studied Shafter as he sat loosely in the seat, whistling cheerfully. His eyes were apparently fixed on nothing more important than the horses. He was clean cut, deeply tanned, and his light blue eyes seemed to leap out from that darkness. They were deep-set, very light, and she felt uncomfortable when he looked at her. It was his hair that set him off from all other men, pure silver and soft, cut now so that it fell on the back of his collar.

Shafter slapped the back of the mules with the line and suddenly turned to face her. He had a very wide mouth, and now he stopped whistling and grinned at her. "My music bother you?"

"No."

"I can't sing much, so I had to learn how to whistle. I expect you sing pretty well."

"Why would you think that?"

Quaid shrugged his shoulders and remarked, "You just look like a woman that can sing."

"That's foolish."

"I expect it is. Most of the things I do and say are pretty foolish. It's a gift I have."

When Moriah had noticed that she was attracted to this young man, it had a reverse effect on her. She grew stiff and answered him only in monosyllables, which he seemed not to notice. This also irritated her, and now she said sharply, "If you'd work a little bit more, you wouldn't have to think up things to occupy your time like whistling."

"Why, I tried work when I was a young fellow, but it just didn't turn out right. I think I'm like a mule we had back when I was a boy growing up. His name was Jesse. Well, Jesse would pull a light load, but if he came out and saw a heavy plow or a wagon heavy loaded, why, he'd turn right around and run back in the barn. I had to put a trace chain around his neck and have a bigger mule drag him out through the gate. He was one cantankerous individual, Jesse was."

"Work never hurt anybody. You might do better if you thought on that more."

"Why, I sure will, Miss Moriah. I'll think on it right hard."

Quaid's voice was cheerful, but there was a slyness that lurked around the corners of his lips. She knew he was teasing her, and it irritated her. She glanced down at the big new gun he wore everywhere he went. Many men carried guns in Texas, but there was something ostentatious about the weapon that Quaid Shafter carried around. The barrel and the cylinder were highly polished, and the handle was carved out of pure ivory. It seemed frivolous, and she asked, "Why do you carry a gun all the time?"

"Why, I reckon because I found out you can get more from folks with a kind word and a gun than you can with a kind word alone."

It was the kind of answer that he made all the time. Moriah had discovered that he was witty enough, and a cheerful young man, though Clay said he was almost worthless at any work unless you posted another man to watch him. "Well, I might as well tell you I don't appreciate the way you've treated our family. Clay got you out of jail and gave you a job, and you haven't been any help at all."

"You know, I expect you're plumb right about that, Miss Moriah. I'm just a no-good bum, is what I am. I've been tryin' to think when it happened to me."

"When *what* happened to you?"

"When I became no good and lost all of the good qualities that a man ought to have. You know," he said thoughtfully, "I'd like to think it all happened in an instant. That I was a good man full of nobility and high ideals, but somebody offered me a passel of money and I sold out and became a crook all in one minute." Shafter shook his head and assumed a look of sadness. "But it wasn't like that. I turned worthless a little at a time. It's like little mice came in the night, startin' a long time ago, and they carried off just a little bit of my honor and goodness. Why, I didn't even notice it! But they kept comin' back night after night, and I looked up one day and found out that they had carried every bit of my goodness off with them! Ain't that a pitiful thing for a man to let happen?"

Moriah suddenly flared out at him. "I believe you've lost your honor, all right!"

"You ain't the only one who thinks that, Miss Moriah. I've got a bad reputation. Why, even the Indians look down on me when I live with 'em. Ain't that a horrible thing to think about?"

The wagon rumbled over the ruts in the road, and the dust rose up behind it. Moriah sat there half fascinated by the rather exotic young man beside her, drawn and repelled at the same time.

Finally, he drew up at a small creek that crossed the road and said, "Better let the horses drink. They're mighty thirsty." He sat there loosely for a time, then straightened up and turned to face her. "So you're gonna get married."

"Yes, I am."

"Well, congratulations. That's a lucky fellow that caught a good-lookin' woman like you."

"Never mind my good looks," she said curtly.

Quaid opened his eyes wide in mock surprise. "Why, a man can't help noticin' a pretty woman. Didn't you know that?" He put his arm up on the back of the seat as he spoke, and Moriah listened, intrigued by his manners. He seemed to be able to take small incidents out of his past and was, despite his laziness and obvious worthless character, able to fascinate people just with his words. As he spoke of his early life, how he had gone with his father into the mountains, he said, "When I left the farm and went to the mountains, everything changed. You know how it is, don't you? Sometimes a man drops something. He bends over, picks it up, and when he gets up and looks around, the whole world has changed all at once. You ever notice that?"

Moriah had noticed that life could suddenly go in a different direction when you least expected it. The biggest change in her life had been when Len Pennington had fallen in love with her. It had happened suddenly, almost as quickly as Quaid Shafter said. She was so engrossed with his talk, she was shocked to feel the touch of his hand on her shoulder. He had moved closer to her, and though the touch of his hand was light, she was intensely aware of it. "Take your hand off of me, Quaid."

But Quaid Shafter was laughing at her. He reached out easily, pulled her around, and his move was so fast that she had no time to think. She started to open her mouth to protest, but his rough kiss prevented her from saying anything. His grip tightened, and for one instant, Moriah was shocked at how his touch stirred her. Then anger filled her at his boldness, and she wrenched her head away and struck at his chest. "You take your hands off of me, you hear me!"

"Well, sure I will," Quaid said. "I didn't—"

"You're nothing but a trashy bum, Quaid Shafter. Get those horses started, and don't say another word to me."

Shafter moved back to his seat and picked up the lines. He slapped the horses and startled them into a fast trot. After a few minutes he turned, and all the laughter had left his face. "I didn't mean anything by it."

"Yes, you did."

"Look, Miss Moriah, it was just a kiss. Don't put a man down when he's drawn to you. That's just something that's in you."

Moriah turned to face him and spoke more sharply than she intended.

"I've told you what I think of you. Now, keep your dirty hands off of me. If you don't, I'll tell Clay, and he'll run you off the ranch."

Moriah saw that her words struck harder than she had intended. The impulse came to soften them, but she had no chance. He turned away from her and slapped the back of the horses, urging them up into a gallop. The road, such as it was, was rutted and filled with potholes, and she had all she could do to hang on.

Ten minutes later they pulled into Jordan City, and she said curtly, "Let me out there at the general store." She waited until he pulled the wagon up and noted he had not said a word. She got out and looked up at him. "It will take me an hour to get my business done. Meet me right here." He did not answer, and she spoke sharply. "Do you hear me, Shafter? Meet me right here."

Quaid turned to face her, and for a moment, it seemed that he would ignore her. But then he nodded and said, "One hour." He slapped the backs of the horses with the lines, and the wagon moved off.

Moriah watched him go. *I didn't handle that well. There was no call for me to be so sharp. Clay said he's had a hard time since his pa died, but he shouldn't have put his hands on me and kissed me.* Troubled by the incident, she turned and walked along the boardwalk, unable to get the incident out of her mind.

It had taken Moriah longer to make her purchases than she had thought, so it was nearly an hour and a half before she returned to where Quaid was supposed to be waiting with the wagon. She expected to find Quaid there, but there was no sign of the wagon. She had a heavy parcel in her arm, and as she glanced up and down the street, she could see no sign of the him.

"Well, hello, Miss Hardin. Come to do a little shoppin'?" Sheriff Bench had approached her. He took off his hat and smiled, saying, "Let me help you with that package."

"How are you, Sheriff?"

"Mighty fine. Where's your wagon?"

"I don't know. Quaid Shafter drove me in. He was supposed to have been here."

Something changed in Sheriff Bench's face. "He's down at the Golden Lady."

"The saloon?"

"Yes, ma'am. As a matter of fact, I don't know if he's able to drive you home. He was pretty drunk. Can I get him for you?"

"No, I'll do it myself. Thank you, Sheriff."

Bench looked alarmed. "You ain't going into the saloon?"

"My aunt works there, so I guess it's safe enough for me to go in and get Shafter out."

"Better let me do that, miss."

"No, thank you, Sheriff."

Moriah smiled, but there was no warmth in it. She turned and walked away, and Sheriff Bench watched her. He muttered to himself, "Them Hardin women sure are stubborn folks. I'd hate to be Quaid Shafter and have one of 'em after me!"

Moriah walked straight to the Golden Lady Saloon and noticed the wagon hidden behind a large freight wagon on a side street. She went to it, deposited her packages, and then went back to the saloon. She had never been in a saloon in her life and was curious. Stepping inside, she saw that the place was occupied only by a few men and two women. One of the women was sitting with Quaid at a table. Her chair was drawn up close, and as Moriah stared at them, the woman reached up and ruffled Quaid's silver hair and laughed shrilly. Everyone in the saloon was watching her, and she wondered where Julie was. Frisco Barr was standing at the bar, leaning against it leisurely. He stood up at once and came over to her.

"Well, hello, Miss Moriah. You come to see Julie?"

"No, I came for that drunk over there." Moriah lifted her voice, and everyone in the saloon heard her. She stared at Quaid, who had realized that the saloon had suddenly grown quiet. He had to struggle to focus his eyes, and he got to his feet slowly.

"Why, hello, Miss Moriah," Quaid said, his speech slurred.

Moriah was disgusted. "Shafter, you're nothing but a drunk. Don't bother coming back to the ranch. You're fired!"

She whirled and walked out of the saloon, hurried to the wagon, and climbed into it. She put the brake off and spoke to the horses sharply, and they started off at a fast clip. Pulling out into the middle of the street, she heard her name, "Miss Moriah!" and turned to see Shafter. He had exited from the saloon and was now running, trying to catch up with her. Anger boiled over in her, and she turned and shouted, "Go on back to your whiskey and your women! That's all you're good for!" She slapped the horses, and they broke into a gallop. When she was down the street, she saw that Shafter had stopped and was staring after her. *I hope he doesn't come back. I don't care what Clay says. We don't need him.*

Back in the middle of the street, Quaid Shafter mumbled, "Go on back to my whiskey? Well, I'll just do that!" He turned and made his way back into the saloon and said, "Come on, Annie, we're behind on our drinking."

He was taken off-guard when Julie Satterfield suddenly spoke. She had come into the saloon during his absence, and she said, "Why aren't you with Moriah?"

"She run off and left me."

"You're supposed to take her home."

"Let her take herself home," Quaid muttered. He moved over toward the dark-haired dance hall girl who was grinning at him. She put her hands out and held herself against him. "Forget about her, honey. Let's have a good time."

Julie stared with disgust at Shafter and shook her head. Frisco came up and said, "I don't know why they put up with Shafter."

"I don't either," Julie said. "I'm going to tell Clay what he's done, and I hope he stomps a mud hole in that worthless Shafter!"

As Moriah rode out of town, she was breathing hard, still angered at what she felt toward Quaid. He had no right to try to force his kiss on her, and now getting drunk made her all the more repulsed by him. Suddenly one of the horses screamed and reared up. Confused, Moriah called out, "What's the matter, Sam?"

And then she saw it. An arrow buried itself halfway of its length into the horse's side. The crimson blood spurted out, and the big horse began to collapse. She turned and saw the Indians then, only five of them, but they were all staring at her. All except one was smiling. The biggest one drew an arrow and notched it and sent it into the other horse directly into the neck. The horse cried piteously, making terrible noises, and Moriah clung to the lines as if they were a lifeline. Horror was a slow-moving thing that ran along her nerves. As the five drew a circle around her, all the horrible memories of being captured by Red Wolf flooded her mind. She knew only too well how the Comanches tortured and killed their captives. The horses were both dying, kicking and uttering plaintive noises, but Moriah could only look at the leader.

He approached the wagon, came off his horse, and handed the lines to another Indian. In one smooth move, he leaped up into the wagon and seized Moriah by the arm. She could smell the wild, rank odor of him—sweat and grease—and his eyes were totally black. She tried to pull away, but his strength was frightening. He simply tightened his arm and pulled her out of the wagon. He uttered a short, guttural phrase, and one of the Indians, who was leading a horse, brought the spare animal forward. He said something, and the other Indians laughed. The leader simply ignored him. He grabbed Moriah and lifted her as easily as if she were nothing but air. She found herself astride the small, stringy mustang, and then the leader tied her feet together, securing the rope under the horse's belly. He leaped on his horse's back. Without another word he drove his horse on. Moriah felt her mount start, bunching his muscles as he ran on. The leader had not said one word to her, which frightened her more than anything else. She clung as best she could to the back of the racing horse and wanted to cry out, but there was no one to cry to. She took one look backward, and although she could not see her home, she wondered if she would ever see it again.

Clay Taliferro was scared, perhaps for the first time in his life. He had faced danger many times, but that was always his own skin. But now, since he had married, he had found a love for Jerusalem so deep that it seemed to be twisted around everything on the inside of him. He could not imagine life without her.

But the pregnancy had not been easy. Jerusalem had never complained, but Clay had learned from talking to the other members of the family that she had never had a hard time like this before. He lay beside her at night listening to her uneven breathing, and knowing she was in difficulty, he was frustrated at not being able to help.

"I reckon I ought to go get Doctor Woods, Jerusalem," he said finally. The two were sitting at the kitchen table, and Jerusalem was peeling potatoes. She always insisted on trying to work all she could, although Moriah and the men did as much as they possibly could to take every burden from her.

"It's way too soon, Clay. Don't worry about me. I'll be all right."

Clay shook his head, unhappiness etched across his features. "I think we ought to go stay in town so we'd be handy to the doctor before the baby comes."

"Why, Clay, I had most of my children without any doctor."

"I know, but this is *my* baby. And besides, well, you're older now." He reached over and took her hand and said, "You don't look it, but you are. I can't have anything happen to you."

Jerusalem felt his hand squeeze hers, and despite the discomfort, she managed a smile. "It's good to have you with me, Clay. I'd be lonely without you."

The two sat there for a time saying little, but then Clay lifted his head. "Somebody comin'," he said, "at a hard run."

Jerusalem rose painfully. She was near her time, and she moved slowly and awkwardly to the window. She saw the horseman riding into the yard at a furious rate. "Something's wrong, Clay."

The two of them moved to the door, and as soon as they were outside, Clay said, "It's Zane."

Fear gripped Jerusalem then, and she stood there clinging to the pillar that held the porch roof up. She saw Zane fall off his horse, his face flushed and covered with a fine dust. His expression told her that something terrible had happened. "What is it, Zane?" she cried.

"I found the team three miles from here, dead. Comanche arrows."

"Where's Moriah?" Jerusalem whispered and knew the answer.

Zane dropped his head for a moment and shook it. He shook his heavy shoulders and said, "Gone. I reckon they took her. I followed their tracks. There's about a dozen horses, then I went back to town to get help."

"Where was Quaid?"

"He was in town drunk at the Golden Lady. He let her go home alone." Rage contorted Zane Satterfield's face. "I wanted to kill him, Clay! I may yet. We're going after them. Sheriff Bench is rounding up all the help he can get."

"I'll get my horse and gun," Clay said and turned away, but Zane's voice caught him almost like a blow. "Clay, you can't go."

Clay whirled. "What are you talking about? 'Course I'm going!"

But Zane was adamant. "You've got to think of Jerusalem."

Clay whirled and saw Jerusalem watching him. He remembered the three things she had asked him before she had agreed to marry him. One of them was that he promised not to leave her.

He did not answer, for Brodie and Clinton had come running out, and Mary Aidan was with them. Clay listened as Zane broke the news to them, but his eyes were fixed on Jerusalem. Mary Aidan burst into tears and buried her face in her mother's skirts. Clay knew they were all thinking of the time they had been captured and dragged off by Red Wolf. He remembered well the night he had walked into Red Wolf's camp and rescued Jerusalem and her daughters. He went over and stood beside her and put his arm around her. She was waiting for him to speak, he knew, and he said the words that came hard. "They'll find her and bring her back, sweetheart."

They'll find her. Jerusalem knew then that Clay would not be leaving her. She clung to him.

"We got a pretty big bunch, according to Sheriff Bench," Zane said. "Even Len's going with us."

"He won't be much help," Clay muttered. He knew Jerusalem was worried about Brodie, but there was no stopping him. Clinton begged to go, but Jerusalem shook her head. "No, Clinton, you stay here."

The three of them watched Zane and Brodie as they rode off on fresh horses. Clay said, "They'll bring her back." But his words were hollow. He knew that the Comanches could outride and outlast any white man that went after them. "Come on in and sit down." He walked inside with Jerusalem, and neither of them spoke as they sat down.

Clinton stood and watched the dust from Zane's and Brodie's horses, and fear had its way with him.

★   ★   ★

Clay heard the sound of the horse coming at a slow walk. Jerusalem was in bed, trying to sleep, so he got up and walked softly out. Clay took one look at Quaid Shafter as he stepped off his horse. Clay walked over and without warning struck Shafter a tremendous blow that caught him high on the cheekbone. It staggered Shafter, and Clay said bitterly, "I ought to kill you!"

The news of Moriah's capture had spread everywhere. After Quaid had learned that Moriah had been captured by a band of Comanches, he had drunk half a bottle of whiskey. Finally, Frisco Barr had told him coldly, "Get out of here, Shafter. We don't need you, and I don't want you in my place."

He had borrowed a horse from Devoe Crutchfield, the blacksmith, and ridden back to the ranch. Now blood ran down his cheek, and he stared at Clay. "I'll go bring her back," he muttered.

Clay shook his head in disgust. "You never came through in your life, Shafter. You're a useless drunk! Get out of my sight!"

For the next two days and nights, the Indians rode at top speed, stopping only twice for rest. The ordeal was a nightmare to Moriah, who was exhausted and frightened, wondering if she would ever see her family again. The Comanches had extra horses and kept swapping them to keep half of the animals fresh. When they had stopped to eat, they only had dried meat to gnaw on.

They had stopped again by a small water hole fed by a spring. One of the Indians dragged Moriah off her horse, and she staggered as the warrior shoved her. She fell down and did not have the strength to get up. She lay there in the dirt unable to move. The farther they rode away from the ranch, she discovered that the horror and the screaming, clawing fear that grew in her could not be maintained. She had become numb inside from that terror of what could happen to her. For all practical purposes, she looked at herself as dead.

Suddenly, the leader of the Comanches stood before her. He extended his hand, and she saw a hunk of greasy, half-cooked meat. She shook her head.

He said, "Eat."

Surprised that he could speak English, she said, "No, I'm not hungry."

"White woman no good. You die if you don't eat."

Knowing it was useless, Moriah struggled to her feet. "Please," she said through parched lips, "let me go."

The Indian stared at her. His dark eyes seemed to have nothing behind them. All the blackness was on the surface. He was a handsome man, his nose aquiline and slightly hooked. He stared at her as if she were some sort of disobedient animal that he had to bend to his will. "White people kill my woman. You will take her place." He watched to see her reaction, and then a cruel grin turned the corners of his lips upward. "I am Bear Killer."

Moriah had heard of him. Clay had told her he was one of the worst of the Comanches, the cruelest and the strongest and the most fearless. She stared at him, knowing that she could expect no mercy. In one smooth motion Bear Killer pulled out his knife. He grabbed Moriah by the hair and tilted her hair back, and she felt the edge of the knife on her throat.

"You will choose," he said. "Live or die."

"What—do you mean?"

"You will be my woman, or I will kill you now. Choose."

Something in Moriah wanted to cry out, "*Kill me*," but the desire to live was strong. She thought, *Somehow there is always hope,* and that hope was like a tiny pinpoint of light amidst the darkness. She shuddered at the guttural laughter of the Indians. She knew the cruelty that women could expect who were captured by the Comanches. The door on the good life she had known with her family had now closed, and the fear of the unknown stalked her like a wild animal. Being loved and protected and honored would no longer be part of her life. She whispered, "I want to live."

Instantly, Bear Killer released her hair. She watched as he put his knife into his belt.

He stared at her, his obsidian eyes filled with an emotion that she could not understand. Finally, he said, "I should kill you. You have brought shame to me."

"No! I never saw you!" Moriah whispered.

"You do not remember me, but I remember you. You were captured with your mother and sister by Red Wolf and brought to our camp. When a Comanche warrior is shamed, he takes revenge on the family of the one who did it."

"My mother never shamed anyone."

"Her man, the White Ghost, he is my enemy." Bear Killer's lips tightened into a thin line, and hatred glittered in his eyes. "He came through all of us, like a spirit, right into the presence of Red Wolf. No man should have been able to do that."

Moriah was frightened by the look on the Comanche's face. "But . . . it wasn't just *you* who let him get through. It was the whole tribe."

"I was next to Red Wolf, his war chief. Anything that happened was *my* shame!"

Moriah had never felt so helpless. She could not run, and her life was in the hands of one of the most murderous Comanche warriors living. He could kill her now, and no one would ever know. Her breathing grew shallow, and she could only pray, *Lord, let me live!*

But then Bear Killer suddenly laughed harshly. "I will take you. That is a shame to white eyes—to have their women taken by one of The People," which is what the Comanches called themselves.

And then he reached for her, and Moriah Hardin closed her eyes as his strong hands gripped her. She tried to pray, but she knew that it was useless.

CHAPTER
EIGHTEEN

I think you'd better go for Doctor Woods, Clay."

Jerusalem's words, though quiet, shocked Clay Taliferro. He had been putting dishes back up into the cabinet when her words came to him. They startled him so much that as he whirled, he dropped a plate, which shattered on the floor. Ignoring it, he took two steps toward Jerusalem, who was sitting in a straight chair. One look at her face, and he said, "I'll send Clinton. I ain't leavin' you."

He whirled and ran outside the house shouting, "Clinton!"

Clinton appeared from the barn, carrying a bucket in his hand. "What is it, Clay?"

"It's your ma's time. Get on your horse and go get Doctor Woods. Break him down if you have to!"

"I will," Clinton yelled. He turned and disappeared into the barn, and in a few moments he came out, not even bothering to saddle his horse but hanging on to the bridle. "I'll get him, Clay!" he shouted as he drove the horse at a dead run out of the yard.

Clay watched him go and had to struggle to make the fear he felt inside subside. Taking a deep breath, he turned and walked back into the house. He went over to Jerusalem and said, "Clinton will get him here quick. Can I do anything?"

"No, this is my job, Clay."

Clay stared at Doctor Woods and swallowed hard. "What do you mean? How is she, Doc?" Woods had just come out of the bedroom, and his face was drawn as he clawed at his whiskers.

"She's in a bad way, Clay," he said, shaking his head.

"You've got to do somethin', Doc. You've got to!" Clay pleaded.

"I'll do all I can, Clay. You know that. But . . . I think . . ." He struggled for words, and then in an unusual gesture, he reached out and gripped Clay's shoulder hard. "I think you'd better prepare yourself."

The stark words struck Clay with all the force and impact of a fist. He looked down at his hands and saw that they were trembling. "Is it . . . is it that bad, Doc?"

"It's not good. I'll do the best I can."

Clay watched as Woods went over, got a drink of water, and then turned and went back toward the bedroom. Turning, Clay moved across the floor, but he felt a numbness. He had been shot once, and what he remembered was not the pain, but the numbness that had spread through him. He felt that way now, as if a bullet had struck him somewhere in a vital place. Though he was walking and thinking, he felt like one on his way to death.

Dusk had come now, and Clay stood on the porch watching the shadows creep across the land. He was alone, and he could hear Jerusalem's moans all the way outside. Every one of them struck him like a blow on an anvil. Jerusalem was not a crying woman, he knew that, and her cries were muted. Still, each one of them revealed the agony that she was suffering.

He began to pace slowly along the long front porch that extended the width of the house. He had walked steadily now for hours, and now, as at other times, he felt the impulse to leave, to get on a horse and run as far away as he could from what was happening inside that bedroom.

Jerusalem said that it was her job to have the baby, and he longed in some way to take some of the pain from her. But that he could not do. He reached out and put both hands against one of the pillars that supported the roof. He gripped it hard until his hands ached, and then he placed his cheek against it and clung to it as a sailor might cling to the rigging on a ship when the wind was about to take it to the bottom. He wanted to close his ears, but that would be cowardly.

As he stood there clinging to the post, everything about Clay Taliferro suddenly became dim and indistinct. He could still hear Jerusalem's moans. He was aware of the stars in the sky vaguely, but a distinct realization was happening on the inside.

It came to him slowly. Then with all the certainty of anything that had ever touched him, Clay knew that his running from God was over. He slumped down to his knees, still clinging to the post. He pressed his face against it, and words of desperation and need for God began to form deep inside him. They did not come out at first, but finally his lips began to move, and he, for the first time in his life, began to call upon God for himself.

Clinton had been out walking in the darkness, getting far away from the cries of his mother. He knew he had to return, and when he did, he rounded the corner and stopped as abruptly as if he had run into a wall. He saw Clay down on his knees and heard his broken cries. Clay Taliferro was weeping, and it shook Clinton down to his foundation. He stood without moving for a time, and then finally Clay grew quiet. Clinton watched as he got to his feet, and when he was standing, he came over and said, "Clay, are you all right?" He watched as Clay turned. The tears had made tracks down his face, and Clinton saw that his mouth was twitching.

"I'm all right, Clint."

"I . . . I was worried about you."

"I called on God, Clint. I think maybe for the first time—and He heard me."

Clinton felt a sudden rush of gratitude and joy, even in the midst of this terrible crisis. "I'm glad, Clay," he said.

"I've been runnin' from God my whole life, but I'm through running."

Jerusalem's voice came then, and Clinton grew silent. Finally, he said, "Do you think there's any hope for Moriah?"

"For her life there is. Any woman taken by the Comanches will have it hard, but she's stronger than she thinks, Clinton. She's like her ma. There's hope."

The bright rays of dawn crept over the horizon. Clay had been standing in the same position for what seemed like hours. Clinton had gone off again. Clay did not know where. Suddenly, he heard the sound of footsteps, and the door opened. Clay turned instantly and could not speak.

Doctor Woods came out and put his arm around Clay's shoulder. "She's all right, Clay."

Clay began to tremble. It was all he could do to keep himself upright. He cleared his throat and blinked his eyes, then asked huskily, "And the baby?"

"Go and see."

Clay walked stiff-legged into the house and down the hall. He turned into the bedroom. The door was open, and he saw the morning light throwing its beam over the figure in the bed. He moved to the bedside and bent over. His eyes were fixed on Jerusalem, and he reached out and touched her cheek. "You all right?"

"Yes." Jerusalem's voice was weak. "I'm fine."

"I got somethin' to tell you." He cleared his throat, tears in his eyes. "You got yourself a new husband. Out there on the porch sometime last night God caught up with me. I reckon you'll have to help me, but I'm going to serve Him as best I can."

Jerusalem uttered a glad cry and reached up. He bent over and buried his face against her hair, and when he lifted his head, she said, "I have a surprise for you." He straightened up and watched as she unfolded a blanket wrapped around a small form. "It's a girl, Clay."

Clay took a deep breath and began to smile. "Just what I wanted—a girl."

Jerusalem was worn and tired, but joy sparkled in her eyes as she said,

"And this"— she loosened another blanket that Clay did not notice—"is your son."

Clay stared at the two babies and could not speak for a moment. "A boy *and* a girl? God is good!"

Jerusalem saw the tears in Clay's eyes, and she reached her free hand out. "I got the right man." He leaned over and kissed her and then picked up his newborn daughter. He looked down into the face of the infant and then smiled at Jerusalem.

"I don't reckon we'll name her Jezebel."

"No, and we're not naming your son Hash, either." Jerusalem felt a deep joy at the new life God had given her with this man she loved with all her heart. "God is so good, Clay, isn't He?"

Clay reached down and picked up his son. He held a baby in each arm and looked from one to the other. "Yes, He is," he said quietly. Then he smiled at Jerusalem and said, "I sure hope they look like you and not me!"

CHAPTER
NINETEEN

C lay finished putting the diaper on his son and then looked up, aware that Julie was watching him. "What are you starin' at?"

"You." Julie smiled. "I can't believe it. A tough hairpin like you—diapering a baby!"

"I think I'm pretty good at it." He held up the baby and admired the red, wrinkled face. "You are going to be as handsome as your pa. Don't you reckon so, Julie?"

"He's already better looking than you are, but he's hungry." She reached over and took the baby from Clay and carried him to Jerusalem, who was already nursing his sister. "Here," she said. "I hope the supply holds out."

"It will," Jerusalem said. "I never had any trouble nursing my babies."

"You never had two at the same time before, either," Julie said, but she was smiling.

She had come to take charge as soon as she had heard of the twins' birth, and Clay had been relieved to see her. He sat down and watched as the babies nursed, and the sight of Jerusalem's tender look at them touched him deeply. He listened as the two women spoke about babies, and finally he said, "We've got to pick names out for these young'uns. I'm tired of calling them number one and number two."

Jerusalem's face was smooth. The birth had been hard, but she had recovered quickly, and she looked up and said, "You find a name for our son. I'll name our daughter."

"I've already got a name for him."

Jerusalem looked surprised. "What is it? You never said."

"I thought you might want to name 'em both."

"No. I want you to name him—but you're not naming him Maher-shalalhasbaz."

"Oh, that was just a joke," Clay said.

"Well, what name do you like?"

"My pa's name was Sam, and I admire Sam Houston mighty well. I'd like to call him Samuel Taliferro."

"That's a fine Bible name." Jerusalem smiled. "I like it." She hugged Sam and leaned over and kissed the top of his fuzzy head. "Samuel it is. Samuel, when you're naughty, and Sam, when you're good."

"What about our daughter? You got any name in your head for her?"

"Yes, I have. I've always liked Rachel for a name. Do you like it, Clay?"

"Rachel Taliferro—I like it! It's got real dignity." Clay got up from his chair and came over to touch both silken heads. "Sam and Rachel. It sounds right natural."

Julie had watched this quietly, and she went about doing the small jobs about the kitchen while the two talked. Finally, she heard Jerusalem say, "Do you think we'll be hearing from the men who went after Moriah pretty soon?"

Clay tried to hide his apprehension, but both women saw that he was troubled. "They may take a long time. Those Comanches can ride a hundred miles in twenty-four hours, I think."

"What about Quaid?" Julie said coldly. "What are you going to do about him?"

"I can't even talk to him," Clay said. "I'd like to shoot him."

Jerusalem reached out then and touched his hand. "He couldn't have saved her, Clay, even if he had been there."

"Don't take up for him," Clay said tersely. "He's a drunken bum. He should have been with her. Even if he got killed, that'd be better than leaving her alone."

"I guess you'll have to forgive him, Clay. That's pretty plain in the Bible for Christians."

Clay swallowed hard and shook his head. "I'll try, but it won't be easy."

Zane and Brodie stepped off their horses, both of them exhausted. Clinton had seen them coming and shouted, bringing those in the house outside. The babies were asleep, so Clay and Jerusalem came out on the porch and stood together, with Julie slightly off to one side.

Even before the two men dismounted, Jerusalem felt a coldness close around her heart. *They didn't find her,* she thought. But she said nothing. Both men were worn down to the point of exhaustion as they approached the house. They could barely walk they were so tired.

"I wish we had better news," Zane said as he looked at Jerusalem.

"You didn't find her?" Jerusalem asked quietly.

"No. We never even seen a trace of them."

"We lost two men," Brodie said. He cleared his throat, for his voice was hoarse. "They came in one night while we was asleep and cut their throats. They were on guard, and we never heard 'em when they died."

"That convinced everybody to come back home. Everybody except me and Brodie here, but we couldn't even figure out which way they went."

"I'm goin' back after her," Brodie said. He lifted his head. His face was planed down, and he had lost weight on the trail.

"We'd lose you, too, Brodie," Clay said quietly, "and your ma can't bear that, and neither can I."

"Come on in the house after you clean up," Jerusalem said. "Me and Julie will fix you something to eat."

Jerusalem and Clay sat on the porch. Jerusalem was holding Rachel, and Clay was holding Samuel. He was looking down into Sam's face and talking to him, as if he were an adult. "Well, son, you sure gave your ma a bunch of grief. I know it wasn't all your fault, but you got a lot of makin' up to do. I want you to listen to your pa now, because we're gonna have lots of long talks, and you don't want to let no pearls drop to the ground."

Jerusalem laughed. "He can't understand a word you're saying."

"Why, sure he can! He's a smart boy, just like I was. When I was his age, I was practically talking."

As she sat there looking at her daughter, she thought of Moriah. She had been grieved over the failure of the riders to find Moriah. Deep in her heart she had known there was little hope, but something inside would not let her give up hope. She would continue to pray for God to protect Moriah and bring her home. She listened as Clay talked to his son. At the same time, she was looking at Rachel on her own lap, wondering what sort of life would lie ahead of her. She caught a sudden motion and looked up quickly. She had not seen Quaid since he had come back from town. She knew Clay had been rough on him, and Quaid Shafter had avoided all of them. He came now slowly dragging his feet and holding his hat in his hands. Jerusalem glanced swiftly at Clay and saw that he was staring at the man, his face hard. Jerusalem said quickly, "You'd better come in and have something to eat, Quaid."

"No, ma'am, don't reckon."

He came to a stop, and Jerusalem saw that all of the happiness and joy that he seemed to carry about with him were gone. His eyes were tragic, and he could not speak for a long time.

Finally, he cleared his throat and said, "Ma'am, I'm sorry for what I done."

"I know you feel bad, Quaid."

" It . . . it ain't *bad* I feel. It's like I'm dead. I wish I was."

Jerusalem said, "We learn from our mistakes. I hope you learned from this, Quaid, to be responsible when people trust you."

"I don't reckon anybody'd ever trust me again."

"You can win their respect, but it will take time," Jerusalem said.

Quaid did not answer. He turned and faced Clay, his back stiff. He did not speak again as Clay glared at him. Quaid broke his gaze away and looked back at Jerusalem. "I'm sorry." He turned and walked quickly away.

"I wish he'd get off the place. It makes me mad just to look at him," Clay muttered.

Jerusalem turned to face him, her eyes fixed on his face. "It's good you never made any mistakes, Clay. It's good to have one perfect man around to point out our faults when the rest of us fail."

Clay was shocked at her tone. "Why, Jerusalem—"

"I told you, Clay, forgiving people isn't something we can choose to do or not to do. You told me you had stopped running from God. If you have, prove it."

Clay stared at her and then smiled. "People say I'm tough, but they don't know tough. Now, *you're* tough, woman."

Jerusalem smiled. "Yes, I am. It won't do any good to beat up on Quaid. He's sorry for what he's done. He'd undo it if he could. That's all any of us can do."

The two sat there, but they were both thinking about Moriah. The silence was broken when Brodie stepped out of the house. He walked purposefully toward them, his tall frame tense, and Jerusalem looked up at him. He had shaved and cleaned himself up and had on clean clothes, but there was a stiffness about him. "What is it, Brodie?" Jerusalem said, although she suspected what he had to say.

"I'm going to try to find Moriah," Brodie said tightly. There was a hardness in his tone, and before either one of them could speak, he said, "There's no point in arguing with me, either of you. It's somethin' I've got to do. It'd be nice if I could go with your blessing."

Clay did not speak. He felt this was Jerusalem's place. He knew better than she the hopelessness of a young man with little experience with Indians starting out to find a woman in Comanche territory, but he said nothing.

Jerusalem surprised them both. "If you have to do it, Brodie, then we'll be proud of you whether you find her or not."

Brodie suddenly seemed to relax. He went over to his mother and put his hand on her shoulder. "Thanks for not tryin' to stop me, Ma. I've got to do it."

"When will you be leaving?"

"First thing in the morning." Brodie turned and said, "Clay, I know you think I'm foolish, and maybe I am, but I hope you understand."

"Sure I do, son. I'm proud of you."

Brodie stared at him and then smiled. "That means a lot to me, Clay."
He turned and walked out in the growing darkness toward the stable.

Brodie had eaten breakfast and then said his good-byes. He leaned over
both the twins, stroked their heads, and said, "You take care of these
young'uns, Ma."

"I will, Brodie."

Brodie came to stand in front of Julie. He did something he had not
done for a long time. He put his arms around her, squeezed her, and then
kissed her on the cheek. "I reckon I never said how much I think of you,
Aunt Julie, but I do."

Julie was stirred by his words. She wanted to beg him not to go, but
she saw the determination on his face. "You take care, Brodie," she whispered and could say no more.

Brodie moved over and put his hand out, and Clay, who was standing
by the door, shook it firmly. "I'll do the best I can."

"Your ma and me are proud of you. We'll be praying for you, Brodie."

"Thanks, Clay." Brodie went to his mother. She was standing with her
eyes fixed on his face. "I'll be as careful as I can, Ma. I promise."

Jerusalem could not answer at first, for the emotions of losing Brodie
too choked her. She reached out, and when he took her in his arms, she
squeezed him hard. She felt the strength of his arms and was determined
not to cry in front of him. "We'll be waiting for you *and* Moriah," she said
and managed a smile.

Brodie turned and walked outside, and the others all followed him.
Brodie stopped abruptly. He had already saddled his horse, but he saw
Quaid Shafter standing on the ground in front of the porch. Brodie did
not speak. He had not spoken to Shafter since his sister had been captured.
He had a deep bitterness against Quaid, and as he stepped to his horse, he
heard Shafter say, "Give me a horse, Clay. I'll go with him."

"What good would you do?" Brodie said roughly. "You'd run away or
get drunk the first chance you got."

"I don't think it'd be a good idea for you two to go together," Clay said, his eyes fixed on Shafter. But he was remembering not Quaid Shafter, but Quaid's father—what a good man he had been. A vague hope stirred within him, and he said, "If you were your pa, it'd be different. He was a real man."

Quaid met Clay's eyes straight forward. "All you're risking is a horse, a gun, and some shells."

A silence fell over the yard, and suddenly Jerusalem said, "Give him what he needs, Clay." Everyone turned to look at Jerusalem, and she said, "Everyone deserves a second chance."

Clay stared at Jerusalem and then looked back at Quaid and nodded. "You're right. I'll let you take that claybank you've always liked. He's got bottom. Wait here." He went inside the house, and Brodie stood beside his horse unhappy, refusing to look at Quaid Shafter.

Clay came out of the house with his own rifle and a pistol and car-tridge belt. "Take these," he said. "They both shoot true."

They all watched as Shafter buckled the gun belt and took the rifle. He looked at Jerusalem but did not speak.

Brodie spoke roughly. "Well, if you're goin', get on your horse."

Brodie stepped into the saddle, and Shafter was right behind him. Brodie said, "I'll be back when I can." He turned his horse and kicked him into a fast trot. Shafter said not a word but pulled the claybank around and started after him.

Jerusalem watched the two disappear. Clay came over and put his arm around her. "It's a mighty thin hope, Jerusalem."

"I'm going to believe God. I don't care how long it takes."

"Then I'll believe with you." His grip tightened around her, and they watched as the two riders faded slowly as they headed north toward Comanche territory.

PART FOUR:

THE CAPTIVE

May 1838—June 1841

CHAPTER
TWENTY

Jerusalem glanced up from where she was sitting in her rocker and smiled at the sight before her. Clay was lying flat on his back, and the twins were cooing on his chest. They were pulling his hair, pounding him with their clenched fists, and screaming like miniature Comanches. The sight of the three of them pleased her inordinately, for before she married Clay she had no idea what he would be like as a husband—much less as a father. His tender love for her had been an immense satisfaction, but when she discovered she was pregnant, she had begun to worry about Clay's attitude. He had been a single man for so long, going where he pleased and doing what he wanted. To be tied down with a wife and a baby—well, that was another matter altogether! Some men, she well knew, were never able to succeed as a father, and she had prayed much that the coming of the baby would be a good thing for Clay.

And then the twins had arrived, and miraculously Clay had been saved on that same day, kneeling on the front porch and calling out to God for His mercy and forgiveness. Since that moment, except for his newfound devotion to Jesus Christ, the most important thing in Clay Taliferro's life had been his wife and his new family. Jerusalem had been delighted and amazed simultaneously. Now, watching them, she offered up a quick thanksgiving to the Lord for the wonderful man that she had married.

Bob had meandered over to watch the antics of the three and joined in by backing up and sitting down on Clay's outstretched legs. Smokey the cat was more dignified and simply watched from his exalted perch on the table. Clay said, "Get off my feet, Bob—you weigh a ton." He sat up and grabbed Rachel under one arm and Samuel under the right. Coming to his feet in one swift movement, he began to turn in circles, eliciting squeals of delight from both of the babies.

"You'll make them sick, Clay."

"No, I won't. They're a tough pair." He stopped turning, however, and stared first in the face of Sam, who immediately reached out and grabbed his nose, then at Rachel, who grabbed two handfuls of his hair. Clay came over and plopped down in the chair across from Jerusalem and endured the punishment that the twins were handing out.

Jerusalem smiled and shook her head in wonder. "I do believe you'd let that pair scalp you! You're a fine father, Clay."

"Well, shucks, who wouldn't be? I'll tell you these are the finest pair of young'uns in Texas. I'm as proud as a cat with two tails!"

Jerusalem laughed out loud. "What a thing to say!" She put her knitting down, went over, and plucked Sam up and bounced him on her knee. "The new herd, is it doing as well as you expected?"

"Why, wife, we're making money hand over fist," Clay said. "If it keeps on going like it's been going for the past year, we'll have enough money to burn a wet mule."

Indeed, Clay had become as good a rancher as he had a husband and father. He had hired Mexicans to help him round up the wild cattle that roamed the plains as well as enough wild horses to form a good-sized remuda. With the help of Zane and Clinton, Star Ranch had, indeed, prospered. They had been able to sell off one sizable herd in New Orleans and make a considerable dent in the loan they owed to Fergus.

Finally, both Jerusalem and Clay put the twins down on the floor. They immediately began to maul Bob, who apparently enjoyed it. Ignoring their squeals, Jerusalem remarked, "I'm worried about the church, Clay."

"Well, I am, too. It looks pretty bad."

"I think maybe you should have let them make you a deacon." The church had approached Clay and had asked him to become a deacon, but he had refused, saying that he was not founded in the faith enough and needed more training. Then three weeks later tragedy had struck when the pastor had left under bad circumstances. He had fallen into an affair with a local woman and had left his wife and two children. Since then the church had wavered, and many had fallen by the wayside.

After speaking about the problems of the church, Jerusalem asked, "Where's Clinton? I haven't seen him all day."

"Oh, he's off girling." Clay grinned briefly and winked at her. "He thinks he's in love with that Abbot girl."

"He's too young to be thinking about things like that."

Clay laughed. "Too young! He's eighteen years old. Why, when I was his age, I had already been in love half a dozen times!"

"I don't want to hear about your old sweethearts again."

"It does you good to hear about 'em. Makes you appreciate being married to a man the gals all liked. You know, one of them gals was the daughter of a millionaire. She was nice. I should have married her. Missed my big chance." Accustomed to his teasing, Jerusalem sat there as he continued to speak. When she didn't say much, he looked at her more closely and said, "I reckon you didn't sleep a whole lot last night. You worried about Moriah?"

"Yes, I am. I know the Bible says it's wrong to worry, but I just can't help it. I keep remembering the time we were attacked and dragged off by Red Wolf. And to think Moriah is suffering the same thing again is more than I can bear at times."

"I know. I've thought a lot about that too," Clay said.

Clay grew more sober. He rose and came over, knelt down beside her rocker, put his arm around her, and squeezed her. "Brodie and Quaid, they won't stop until they find her."

"I was surprised at Quaid. This has shook him up pretty bad. He's not the same man."

"No, he ain't. He's plumb serious now. I think—" He suddenly rose and said, "Somebody's comin'." He walked to the door, opened it, and said, "Well, I guess I'll have to be good for a spell. It's Rice. I hate for a good-lookin' preacher to be hangin' around my wife!"

Jerusalem got up, and stepping around the twins and the big dog, she said, "It's good to see him." The two waited until Rice pulled up and stepped out of his saddle. He tied the reins over the hitching post and then came forward, smiling.

"Well," Rice said, "there's proud I am to see you."

The trip had covered him with a fine coat of dust. He removed his hat as soon as he came to stand before them. His deep-set gray eyes were warm with welcome as he shook hands with both of them. "Has this man been behaving himself, sister?"

"Yes, he has."

"Well, surprised I am to hear it, but proud, too."

"Come on in the house, and I'll tell you all of our problems," Clay said. The three of them went inside, and Rice went over and picked up Samuel. He held him high in the air and got a squeal out of him.

"Is this the lad or the lass?"

"That's Samuel."

"Well, a fine lad you are." He put him down and picked up Rachel, who was studying him soberly. "Come now, admiring you I am, girl! Give me a smile." He continued to hold her, tickling her until finally she squealed. "There's a charmer! You'll be like your ma."

"I never saw a preacher who wasn't hungry." Jerusalem smiled. "I'll fix you something to eat."

"No, thank you. I'm not hungry. I've come to give you some news."

"Good or bad?" Clay said.

"I'm not sure. I'll let you decide. The deacons have asked me to be pastor of the church in Jordan City."

Instantly, both Clay and Jerusalem began to speak. "Why, that's the best news I've had in a long time!" Jerusalem exclaimed.

"Right. You can get this church back where it belongs." Clay nodded.

"Well, the deacons weren't exactly united, but I got a majority. Some of them said I was too plain spoken."

"That's what we need around here," Clay said. "Some straight-forward, turn-or-burn preaching."

"I'm so happy, Rice," Jerusalem smiled, "or I suppose I should say Reverend Morgan?"

Rice simply shook his head. "No titles. I'm the same man I always was, Jerusalem, but I came over to talk to Clinton. He's going to have to give me some help."

Clay suddenly grinned. "Well, he's been waitin' for the chance ever since I've known him. He loves to preach."

"He's a good young man," Rice said quickly. "A little bit too forward at times and maybe a little bit lopsided in his theology."

"Some folks have called him a fanatic," Jerusalem said tentatively.

"Well, I'd rather try to restrain a fanatic than resurrect a corpse." Rice laughed. "God can use fanatics, but not dead people. And," he added quickly, "I'm going to work on Julie."

"Lots of luck." Clay grinned. "She's tougher than old leather."

"She's not too tough for God," Rice said. "Now where's Clinton? I'm ready to start my ministry in Jordan City, Texas! . . ."

Clinton had received Rice's news with great excitement. His eyes had gleamed, and he had done everything but dance. "Well, that's plumb good news, Rice. I mean, Brother Morgan. Now we can start getting something done in that church. Maybe you can shake some of them loose from their money—like old man Morton. That man is so stingy he breathes through his nose to keep from wearing out his false teeth! But you'll stir 'em up!"

"I'm glad you think so, Clinton," Rice said. "We're gonna start right today. That's why I came to get you."

The two were standing out at the corral, where Rice had found Clinton breaking in a new horse, and now he put his hand on the young man's shoulder and smiled broadly. "We're going to start with the Golden Lady Saloon."

Clinton stared at him and suddenly sobered. "The saloon?"

"I'm sure you know the place I mean," Rice said dryly. "So, we'll introduce ourselves to the town there. That'll be the busiest place, if I'm not mistaken."

Clinton perked up at once. "Well, shoot, most of them fellers in there are so drunk they can't see through a ladder, but I'm with you, Preacher. Let me get a horse saddled, and we'll go right in."

Rice watched as Clinton expertly roped a gelding and saddled him efficiently, and in five minutes the two were on their way to Jordan City. The whole way to town, Rice listened mostly as Clinton expanded on his plans of how to handle the situation at the church. It amused Rice that Clinton saw everything in life simply as black or white. There were no gray areas in his mind or in his judgment. *He's a good lad, and grow in faith he will, when life throws its hard edge at him,* Rice thought as they rode along.

When they finally pulled up in front of the saloon and tied their horses to the hitching rail, Rice said, "Clinton, saying nothing against you I am, but maybe it would be better if I did the talking and you did the praying."

Clinton said at once, "Why, sure, Preacher. You just turn your wolf loose!"

The two pushed open the swinging doors and walked into the saloon. They looked around and spotted Julie. She was wearing a low-cut emerald green dress, and her red hair was fixed on top of her head in an ornate hairdo. She wore more makeup than either of them liked, but she smiled as the two crossed the floor, which was already beginning to fill up for the evening's festivities.

"Well, if it's not Rice Morgan and my good-looking nephew. How are you two?"

Morgan took off his hat and smiled, saying, "Why wouldn't I be fine with all that the good Lord has done for me?" He spoke in a normal tone, but several of the men at the bar turned around to stare at him.

Julie was aware of Morgan's rather outspoken ways where God was concerned, and she certainly knew Clinton well enough to expect something of the same. "I hope you two didn't come in here to preach," she said.

"As a matter of fact, I have news. I'm the new preacher at the church here in Jordan City. Clinton and I are making the rounds of the business establishments to invite people to church."

Julie glanced over at Frisco Barr and saw that he was smiling broadly. "What about it, Frisco? We've got two preachers in here. You want to have 'em thrown out?"

Barr shook his head and said, "If you're looking for sinners, Preacher, you've come to the right place. Go ahead and make your pitch."

Taking Barr at his word, Morgan turned from Julie and saw that most of the customers had already sized him up. "It's glad I am to be here with all of you gentlemen and ladies, too," he said. "I am announcing that you are all invited to services Sunday morning at ten o'clock."

A big man named Mick Sullivan with a week's growth of beard was sitting at the poker table. He had been losing, apparently, and was in a bad humor. He had been drinking heavily. Sullivan owned a small ranch south of Jordan City. He stood up and walked over to where Rice Morgan stood beside Julie. He towered over Morgan and said in a loud, surly voice, "I don't remember sendin' for no sorry preachers. Why don't you get yourself out of here and go play church somewhere else?"

Rice's smile did not change. "I don't believe we've met. My name is Rice Morgan."

"This is Mick Sullivan," Julie said, watching with some apprehension. Sullivan was a rough and tumble fighter and had badly broken up several men.

"Get yourself out of here—both of you!" Sullivan said loudly. He was obviously looking for trouble, for he needed fights as other men needed drinks. He had a thick chest, and the muscles in his arms strained against his shirt.

Rice studied the big man and lifted his eyebrow. "Tell me now. Would you be a gambling man?"

Sullivan stared at him. "Sure, I like to gamble. You gonna preach against that?"

"No, I thought I'd make a little wager with you."

"A preacher gambling?"

"Well, in a way. I'll tell you what. Let's you and me have a boxing match." He saw surprise wash across Sullivan's blunt features and continued smoothly. "If you win, I'll come and work for you for a week doing anything you'd like."

Sullivan's broad mouth curved upward in a smile. "And what if you win—which you ain't gonna do?"

"If I win, you come to church next Sunday."

Mick laughed loudly. He turned and winked at his companions, pleased with the wager that he was sure would end in his favor. He was known around the town for beating the best of them. "All right. Let's have this here boxing match."

"If you break any of the furniture, you'll have to pay for it," Frisco called out.

"The only thing I'm going to break is this preacher's face!" Sullivan said.

Immediately, men got up and began to move tables and chairs around. Clinton was watching nervously, and he whispered to Morgan, "This ain't exactly what I thought we'd be doing."

Julie was troubled also. "I think you'd better get out of here, Rice."

"Oh, I will. Just a little matter here of a small wager." He handed his hat to Clinton and said, "Be careful with that. It cost me ten dollars." He turned then and walked toward the cleared space where Sullivan was staring at him in disbelief. "I'm ready now, Mr. Sullivan, any time you are."

Anger ruffled the big man then, for he could not stand a challenge. With a roar and a curse he lunged forward, bringing a punch that would have taken off Rice Morgan's head if it had connected. Rice simply moved his head slightly, and as the big man rushed toward him, he pulled his right arm back, and with his left, he threw three blows so fast that they were almost impossible to see. They all struck Sullivan in the face, bringing him to a stop. Then Rice struck a tremendous blow with his right that caught Mick Sullivan right in the pit of the stomach, exactly at the point where the ribs divide and where the nerves are thick. It made a sound something like "Boom!" And Mick Sullivan suddenly found he could not draw his breath. Everyone in the saloon was staring at the big man as he tried to suck in air. Even as he did, Morgan sent another thunderous right that caught Mick on the side of the neck. It drove him sideways, and as he collapsed, his head hit against the bar with a loud thud. His arms and legs thrashed as he fell to the floor.

Julie stared at Mick Sullivan and then turned her eyes on Morgan. She had never seen a man demolished in such a fashion, nor had anyone else!

"Barkeep, a little water and a cloth, is it?"

Ed Simmons, the barkeep, obeyed silently, and the talk buzzed around the room as Morgan knelt beside the big man. He lifted Sullivan's head, saying quietly, "Now, don't worry. You'll get your breath back in a minute."

Clinton watched in disbelief as Rice bathed the big man's face. As Sullivan began to suck in air in great gulps, Clinton looked up and saw

Julie staring at the two men in disbelief. "Well," Clinton said loudly, "I guess that shows where we stand at the Jordan City Church."

Rice helped Sullivan to his feet, holding on to the big man to keep him steady. Sullivan was holding his head where it had hit the bar, but he was staring at Rice in sheer disbelief. "What did you hit me with, Preacher?" he muttered.

"Just my fist. I did a bit of boxing once. As a matter of fact, I went twenty rounds with the champion of Wales when I was younger. Very few could stand up to me in those days. I guess a little bit is left in me." He looked around the saloon, saying, "Anybody else want to make a little wager?"

Little Jimmy French laughed. "I won't fight you, Preacher, but let me tell you. If me and Mick came to church, your nice little Christians would throw us out."

Instantly, Rice said, "Bring the whole bunch here." He waved at the drinkers and gamblers. "If they give them trouble, you can throw *them* out—and I'll help you do it."

Laughter went around the saloon, and Jimmy French found it amusing. "Fellas, let's do it."

Julie was amazed at how easily Rice had won acceptance from the rough crowd of the saloon. She said little but watched as Rice and Clinton went around getting names and shaking hands.

When they were done talking to everyone, the two came over to her, and Rice said, "Well, I'd like for you to be at church, too, Sunday."

"That would clean the church out," Julie said. "A bad saloon woman in church."

Rice smiled and said quietly, "It would please me a great deal if you would come."

Julie found herself unable to find an answer. She saw Frisco Barr watching her closely and tried to think of a way out. "You sit down," she said, "and play poker with me. If you do that, I'll come to your church Sunday."

Rice said, "All right. Come along." He led her over to a table and pulled the chair out for her and then went over and sat down himself. Clinton walked over and stood there staring at him. "Rice, this ain't right."

"What isn't right?"

"Why, fighting and playing poker in a saloon."

"Well, you know, Clinton, Jesus had the same problem. Every time he ate with sinners, he was in trouble with the real religious folk. We'll probably be in trouble, too, but this is the only way I know." He looked over then, and his eyes were dancing. "Deal the cards, Julie, and I'll see you in church Sunday."

Thirty minutes later, when Clinton and Rice stepped out of the saloon, Clinton was silent. Rice looked at him and said, "I suppose I'm to look for a few words from you?"

"Well, Rice, it don't seem fittin' to me—Christians going into a saloon."

"I imagine that some of the church members will have exactly the same thing to say. Will you stand with me when they say that?"

Clinton felt an enormous liking for Rice Morgan. He did not understand the Welshman, but he knew that there was solid truth in the man. "Sure, Rice. I can do that."

"There's proud, I am, to have a partner like you." Rice slapped him on the back and said, "Come along. We'll do a little bit more hunting for sinners and introduce them to Jesus."

For the next two months, the Reverend Rice Morgan made quite an impression in Jordan City. He made no half-hearted disciples. People were either for him and his methods or against him. Clinton was his shadow, and the two were as likely to show up in a bar as they were in a pulpit. Clay was delighted and often said, "That's the kind of a preacher I needed to meet about twenty years ago."

The deacons split down the middle, half of them admiring Rice and his bold methods, the other half demurring and saying that the ministry had a dignity to maintain. They were all united, however, concerning his preaching, which was excellent and true to the Bible. The church building was running over at every service, not just with aged, old-line believers, but with the disreputable element of Jordan City as well.

Brodie and Quaid came back in early June, both of them thin and worn down. They were met as they rode into the ranch by Jerusalem, who watched them dismount wearily. Both of them looked like tramps, their clothes ragged and patched. The only thing about them that looked clean were the rifles and guns at their sides. Going forward at once, she put her arms around Brodie and pulled his head down and kissed him. "You look half starved," she said.

Brodie grinned. The dust coated his face, and he had not shaved, it seemed, for weeks. "I reckon you're right, Ma. I'm pretty hungry."

"Quaid, it's good to see you." Jerusalem put her hand out, and Quaid, who had been standing back, stepped forward and took it.

"Hello, Miss Jerusalem." He pulled his hat off, and the sun caught his silver hair. His skin was tanned, and his deep-set, light blue eyes made a contrast against his tanned face.

Brodie knew his mother was waiting for news about Moriah, and he shook his head. "We didn't catch up with 'em, Ma, but we're goin' to. We got a trace of a rumor about a white captive held by a Kiowa tribe. It took us a long time to run it down, but she was the wrong woman."

"Did you bring her back?"

"As a matter of fact, she wouldn't come back."

Jerusalem's eyes widened. "She wouldn't come back? Why not?"

It was Quaid who answered. "She'd been a captive since she was ten, ma'am. She didn't even remember how to talk much English. She had become Kiowa, I guess you might say." He shook his head sadly. "She just wouldn't come."

"It'll be different with Moriah, though," Brodie said quickly.

The hope that had risen in Jerusalem seemed to leave all at once. It was that way with her, but she was determined not to show it. "Come on in. I'll feed you. You could use it. . . ."

For two days Quaid and Brodie stayed close to the ranch, mostly sleeping and eating. Everyone was surprised at the difference in Quaid Shafter—Clay most of all. He was filled with anger toward Shafter for letting Moriah get captured, although he finally had admitted that Shafter would have made little difference. Clay saw that there was a new silence about Shafter, and somehow Quaid reminded Clay more of his father, Jed. Clay had thought a lot about what Jerusalem had said about forgiving Quaid. He had struggled with it for weeks, but he knew he had to talk to the young man. Instead of running from his mistake, Quaid had risked his life for months trying to find Moriah in Indian territory. On the second day, he found Quaid brushing down his horse in the barn and said, "I was wrong to bawl you out like I did, Quaid."

"No, you weren't wrong. You had every right for what I done. It was my fault Moriah got captured, 'cause I was drunk." He suddenly shifted his shoulders and said, "I'm pulling out tomorrow. But I reckon Brodie needs to rest up before he goes looking again."

"Pulling out for where?"

"I spent a lot of time with these Comanches, Clay. I think it's going to take a lot of looking to find Miss Moriah, but I've got an idea."

"You'd better stay and rest up."

"I guess not."

Quaid would not change his mind, though all urged him. Brodie was totally exhausted, but after Quaid left, he told the story of how he would have been helpless without Quaid Shafter. "He knows a lot about Indians, and he's tougher than most anybody I've ever seen. Why, he can go forever on half a rabbit and a few sips of water! He had to take care of me most of the time."

Jerusalem listened as Brodie talked, then, "Maybe you don't need to go back with him, Brodie. Maybe it's something he can do better by himself."

"No, I can't quit thinkin' about Moriah," Brodie said. He seemed to have matured considerably in the few months that he had been on the trail with Shafter. "If Quaid don't come back in a few weeks, I'll take off and find him. He told me where he'd be looking, and I can't do anything until I find Moriah."

Bear Killer stared at his brother Lion. They were talking to Runs Fast, the chief of a Kiowa tribe. Runs Fast was a small man, older than most war chiefs, but was one of the most cunning of the Kiowa. The three men had been smoking a pipe inside Bear Killer's teepee. The talk had gone on for a long time, and finally Runs Fast, who had been watching Moriah, said, "Two men came looking for a white woman living with The People."

"Who were they?" Bear Killer said.

"One was very tall. The other had white hair but was not old. The Silverhair could speak our language. The tall one could not. They were looking for a captive, a captive taken by The People."

Lion, at this point, looked across at Bear Killer. "It is as I told you, brother. This woman will cause trouble. Sell her to another tribe."

"I will buy her myself," Runs Fast said at once. "I need a new wife."

Bear Killer shook his head. "No. She carries my child, and I want a son."

Bear Killer had two wives, a young woman named Dove, who had borne him two daughters. His first wife was called Loves The Night. She was childless, but though she bore him no sons Bear Killer loved her the most.

Lion was silent then, for he knew the longing Bear Killer had for a son to lead the tribe when he was gone. Runs Fast studied Bear Killer and offered his opinion. "The Silverhair, he could be trouble."

"He is only one man," Bear Killer said.

"You are only one man." Runs Fast nodded. "But the white eyes fear you. One man can bring down many braves if he is determined."

But Lion knew that Runs Fast was wasting his breath. He shook his head and said no more, but his eyes grew hard as they turned on the white captive. From the beginning he had been in favor of selling her, but Bear Killer would not listen. Many thought that Lion possessed the gift of seeing into the future, and something about this white woman they had come to call The Quiet One disturbed him. *After the child is born I will convince my brother to get rid of the white woman. . . .*

CHAPTER
TWENTY-ONE

Moriah felt the sting of the switch across her back as she strug-gled to carry the heavy buffalo paunch filled with water. She hunched her shoulders and said nothing. She had learned that Bear Killer's youngest wife, Dove, loved nothing better than to hear her cry out or to see her flinch. Ignoring the blow as well as she could, Moriah straightened her back and made for the village as quickly as possible. She was never allowed to go to the river alone. Someone always went with her, lest she try to escape. As she moved across the broken ground, she found it hard to believe that she had been a captive of Bear Killer for six months. When she was exhausted and had been beaten, it seemed more like six years.

Memories now came flooding back on Moriah, and she remembered with vivid intensity the day she had been brought to the camp of Bear Killer. She had been totally exhausted from the hard days of riding from dawn to dusk. Still the memories of the squaws punching her, hitting her with sticks, filled her mind. Even the children had been cruel to her. She even remem-bered how one of the women had thrown her a chunk of liver barely seared over one of the small camp fires and sprinkled with liquid from a buffalo gall-bladder. It had made her nauseous, but she had managed to keep it down. At that moment she knew that she would somehow survive.

The memories of the months that had followed passed through her mind quickly, some of which she would give anything to forget. She had become the third wife of Bear Killer. Trying to shut that out of her mind, she walked as rapidly as possible to keep out of the range of Dove's switch as she hurried back toward the camp.

Looking up, she saw Loves The Night standing over a fire, cooking a chunk of meat, and felt a warmth toward her. This woman alone had shown kindness to her at a time when she had desperately sought it. Many nights after Bear Killer had come to her, she would lie for hours silently weeping. It was Loves The Night who would come in the middle of the night and sit by her and stroke her hair, trying to comfort her. It had taken Moriah a long time to understand the nature of Bear Killer's two wives. Finally, she had come to understand that the younger woman Dove was not the first wife. Dove had borne two daughters to Bear Killer, but no sons. She also had discovered little by little that barren women among the Comanche have little standing. Bear Killer, however, had made it very clear that Loves The Night was his chief wife, and the woman had been as kind as Dove had been cruel.

"Come, you eat." Loves The Night looked up and smiled and came to take the buffalo paunch filled with water from Moriah. She hung it carefully beside the teepee and then saw Dove frowning. Sharply, she said something in Comanche, and Dove went sulkily away. "You eat," Loves The Night said firmly.

As Moriah sat down, she remembered the first bit of hope she had had after being captured. The squaws had been harsh to her, and Bear Killer treated her mostly with indifference except when he would appear at night. But the first week, her dress, which had been torn by the mesquite branches on the way, was practically hanging on her in shreds. Loves The Night had pulled her into the teepee and began making her a dress. She would hold portions of soft animal skins against Moriah's body, mark it with the end of a burned stick, and then cut it into pieces. All the while she had talked, and although she spoke no English, she had been a comfort to Moriah.

As Moriah sat there eating the meat, she let her gaze run over the camp and realized with a slight shock that six months had given her a basic vocabulary to understand more of Comanche than she realized. She watched the children running and playing even as white children would, shouting, pushing, and shoving. She saw Buffalo Heart, one of the warriors, go by wearing a long-fringed deer robe, moving about and ordering his wives with a harsh voice. Across from her, Morning Flower was working on a shield that had four eagle feathers on it, gently brushing the veins. Some women were piling buffalo chips to make fires, and farther off Bear Killer was surrounded by a group of tribal leaders in some kind of meeting.

Even as she watched the activity in the camp, she remembered how the acrid stench of it had almost suffocated her at first, but now, remarkably enough, she had grown accustomed to it. The sounds and the sights and the smells of a Comanche war camp, something that had been foreign to her, now made their way into her mind.

Moriah thought of her first two months in the camp and how she had almost lost her mind. Immediately after her capture, she thought only of rescue, staring to the south every day, hoping to see a large body of men coming to rescue her. But as the weeks had passed, the hope had faded as the tribe had moved farther and farther northward into the dreaded Comanche country, where few white men would dare venture to risk their lives. She had become almost dead with despair, and her thoughts seemed paralyzed at times.

At what point she had passed beyond this despair into some sort of hope, Moriah could not remember. She had gone from a stage of being confused and frightened into insensibility 'til now her mind was clear, and she knew she was stronger than she had ever been. She had heard of the cruelty of the Comanche to those who were not strong enough to meet their standards. She realized that these hard months had been a test for her. Though she had been forced to become Bear Killer's wife, she had determined not to give up. She had worked hard and learned to do all the labor required of all Comanche women. Some of the women who had been cruel to her were now trying to teach her the difficult language.

Then she thought of the terror that had come when she discovered that she was pregnant. That had been worse than any of the physical hardships or torments handed out by Dove or the other squaws. She had always looked forward to having children, but now, carrying the baby of a Comanche war chief seemed to be the most terrible fate that a white woman could endure.

As Moriah finished the meat and sat there quietly, she thought of the hours she had spent praying, accepting the baby that she carried. She knew it had something to do with what Rice Morgan had called a leap of faith.

"It's like you're on a precipice," Rice had said once. You're standing there, and God tells you to jump. And you look down, and see if you do, you'll be smashed. Well, what's for it, then? You either stand there and shrivel up—or you believe God and you jump. Whatever you face is in God's hands then. Nothing you can do about it, so when you get to the point where there's no hope, just jump into the arms of God."

The words came clearly as if they were spoken to Moriah, and she knew she had reconciled a hope that seemed hopeless. She had chosen to believe that they would come for her. She did not know who, but she knew that her mother and Zane and Clay and others would not give up until they found her.

Since that time, each morning her first thought had been, *I will believe in my God, and He will deliver me from the Comanche.* That was also her constant thought during the day and the last thing that was in her mind at night.

Suddenly, she saw Bear Killer coming toward his teepee. He stopped beside her and stared at her for a moment. He was a strong man, and as Moriah waited for him to speak, the sun struck him across his flat, high-cheekboned face. He was, as all Comanche warriors, born and bred as a warrior. Since coming down from the mountain into the high plains, the men of his people had lived to fight, and courage in the face of death was the most valued virtue.

"Quiet One," he said, "we will go to the buffalo hunt. You will help my other wives."

This was not a request, but a command. Moriah had been given the name Quiet One by Bear Killer himself. It was a good name, as most Comanche names were, for indeed for weeks she had said nothing that she was not forced to say. Now she simply nodded and rose to her feet. Bear Killer put out his hand and took her by the arm. She turned, looked up into his face, and he said, "You must forget your people. You are a Comanche woman now."

Moriah said, "Would you forget yours, Bear Killer?"

Bear Killer stared at her. This woman who he had thought much weaker than any Comanche woman was turning out differently than he had expected. She had survived the test of months of hard work. The sun now had baked her, and her hands had grown rough from the demanding labor required of all Comanche women. He had command of her body, but he could never get beyond the quiet that she built around herself like a wall. It aggravated him, and he shook his head and repeated. "You are a Comanche woman. Our son will be a great chief someday."

Despite herself, Moriah found the buffalo hunt to be a fascinating adventure. She had come with the rest of the women to watch the start of the hunt and had been shocked at the size of the massive herd. They scattered all over the plains, grazing slowly and feeding on bunch grass and on anything else in their path. They seemed to be totally unafraid, and Dove, who stood beside her, spoke a phrase, and to Moriah the language was becoming more intelligible. It was almost magic! She had been hearing so many Comanche words, but she had heard these over and over, and now she knew they were real to her. "Many buffalo," she said.

Loves The Night looked at her in astonishment. "Yes, many buffalo," she said in Comanche and was pleased.

The women watched as the hunters moved in on the huge animals. They waited for Bear Killer to move first, and Moriah watched as he guided his horse toward a young bull. He kicked his horse into a full gallop and drove the lance into the shaggy beast, driving the point into the belly just behind the ribs. The pony reared off to one side, and the bull went down head over heels, kicked a few times, and did not get up.

Instantly, the women shouted with excitement and clapped their hands. The other hunters began to charge the herd. Some of them carried lances, and others shot arrows into the buffalo that had begun lumbering at a fast trot. Moriah saw that some of the arrows were buried up to the feathers into the flesh of the buffalo. Sometimes it took as many as half a dozen arrows to bring the beast down. The herd began to move, and the sound was like thunder as they ran across the plain. A cloud of dust rose, cutting off the view of the women, but when the wind cleared it away, many buffalo lay dead or wounded on the plain. Others were still standing, blood soaking their sides. It was now time for the work to start.

The men began to skin and quarter the buffalo, and the young boys rode horses to bring the carcasses home. It was a dangerous time, for some of the beasts were still very much alive. Many were still in position to charge. Moriah watched as the men circled on their horse and drove lances into those, until they fell. Others peeled the hides off easily and then hacked at the carcasses with hatchets. She saw them take out the internal organs, and her stomach turned over as she saw one of them scoop out a buffalo stomach, open it, and eat the half-digested grass. The women hurried back to camp, for it was now time for their work to be done. All seemed to be confusion to Moriah, but she learned quickly. She joined the women, using knives to cut up the meat and help hang it on racks that had been set up to dry it. The livers and the tongues were set aside for immediate roasting over the fires the children had built.

Loves The Night showed her how to take sinew from along the spine and the backs of the leg bones. She had already learned it was used for making the cords for the bows of the warriors. From time to time someone would toss a bloody piece of meat to the dogs that always tried to get as close as possible. Loves The Night pulled out one of the stomachs, of which the buffalo had four, and sliced it, removing some of the half-digested grass. She took a bite of it and, grinning, shoved it at Moriah. Moriah took it and, despite the revulsion she felt, tried a small bite. To her surprise, it had a sweet taste, and she ate it all.

Soon the odor of roasting meat began to fill the air, and the whole camp was abuzz with activity! Children were running everywhere, laughing and pulling off bits of roasted meat from the fires. This went on until the sun dipped below the horizon. And even then the celebration continued as chunks of meat cooked and sizzled over the fires. Though the eating went on constantly, the work of preparing food for the winter never stopped. The women scarcely slept at all that night as they continued to dry the meat, and the men gathered and told one another stories of the hunt.

Moriah found herself exhausted. She was slumped down in the teepee when she heard Bear Killer come in. She turned quickly to face him, her face wary. He put his hand out and touched her head. "You did well," he said. Then his eyes glowed, and he nodded and left the teepee. As always, Moriah had to hold herself still every time Bear Killer touched her. She was helpless against his strength, but something in her spirit rose against him. She touched her belly and thought of the time to come, then lay down, weary in body and spirit. *I will believe in you, O God!* was the prayer that she uttered in her heart, and despite the terrible circumstances, she held on to hope by faith in God.

The fall passed away quickly and soon the cold winds of winter began to blow. Moriah knew that at some point the year 1840 had come, but that meant very little to her. The child inside her had grown, and Bear Killer had given stern commands to Dove to keep her hands off of Quiet One with the switch.

The first few months of winter had been harsh, and yet Moriah had learned to endure it. Loves The Night had watched during her pregnancy as if it were her own child, and in some strange way, Moriah knew, it was. She had accepted Loves The Night's kindness and help, and on one bitterly cold night, Moriah knew that it was time. The pain started in the middle of the night, and when she stirred, Loves The Night was instantly at her side.

"Is it time?" Loves The Night asked.

"Yes, it is time," Moriah said in Comanche. She had made great strides in mastering the language during the past months, and now she was ready to deliver Bear Killer's child. The fact that the child had been forced upon her, she had tried to put behind her. It would be *her* child! She rose and accompanied the women to the birthing teepee. She sat down as the women now came to fill the water pit and took heated stones out of the fire to make steam. Loves The Night rubbed crushed herbs on her belly, and the smell of it in the tent was sharp and pungent.

From time to time the women rubbed her back and made her drink some sort of hot soup. Loves The Night then began to press down on her belly with both hands, gently at first and then stronger as Moriah's pains grew stronger.

Moriah endured in silence, as she was aware that Comanche women would never cry out in pain. The birth was not a hard one, it seemed to Loves The Night, although it was hours of agony to Moriah.

Finally, the child was born, and Moriah lay there exhausted. Loves The Night wrapped the tiny infant in a soft animal skin and placed the bundle in Moriah's arms. Moriah stared into the tiny face, and Loves The Night said, "You have a son." Moriah lay there holding the baby and began to thank God that he was healthy and strong.

Later on Bear Killer came and named him Eethon, which meant "Strong Man" in Comanche. Moriah did not comment but in her heart called him Ethan, which had a good, strong English sound to her.

Bear Killer was very proud of his son, and as Eethon grew, he showed more interest in him than most Comanches did with very small infants. When Eethon was six months old, news came that disturbed Bear Killer. A Kiowa warrior had ridden into camp, and Bear Killer had listened as the Kiowa said, "The Tall One and Silverhair, they ride everywhere in search of the white woman. They are not like other white men. They came north of the Red River where my tribe lives."

"What did they say?"

"They are still looking for the white woman that was stolen. I think they are strong men."

Bear Killer sat listening as the Kiowa described the two men, and later that day he made a decision. He spoke to Lion, saying, "Choose four of our best warriors. Send them to the Kiowa country near the Red River. Tell them to bring back the scalps of Silverhair and the Tall One."

"It would be better to send the woman back. You have your son now."

Bear Killer shook his head. "No. The two must die, and we will move the tribe to the Llano Estacado. The white men cannot move freely there. They don't know water holes, and they can be seen for miles."

Lion did not agree with Bear Killer's instructions, but he knew he had no choice but to obey.

"Do not try to bring back many scalps. Only two. The Kiowa will know where these white men are. Go to their camp. Find the Silverhair and the Tall One. Bring their scalps back."

When Lion chose the warriors to ride with him, they began to shout and raise their weapons in the air at the chance to go on a war party. One of them, Little Antelope, asked, "Can we take other scalps after we have taken these two?"

"Bear Killer wants only these two."

Little Antelope laughed. "We will bring them. Never fear."

Moriah was nursing Eethon as she saw the four warriors all painted for war ride out of camp.

"Where are they going?" she asked Bear Killer.

"On a war party."

Moriah asked no more and watched in silence as they rode off.

CHAPTER
TWENTY-TWO

As Brodie came out of a fitful sleep, he felt so cold that he could not move. The frigid wind that cut across the plain had frozen him, it seemed, into a solid figure. Resisting the temptation to curl up into a ball and seek heat beneath the single blanket, he struggled with the fatigue that seemed to drag him down—and then the smell of cooking meat came to him. The odor caused his stomach to tighten, for he had always been a big eater, but the last few days he'd hardly eaten any of the rough food they could find.

Opening his eyes, he saw Quaid squatting before a small fire, cooking meat in a frying pan. Quaid, outlined against the first beginnings of daylight, looked tough and primitive in the pale morning light. He had not shaved for days now, and the bristles of his beard roughened the outlines of his lean face.

Throwing back his blanket, Brodie came to his feet slowly and stamped the earth to get the numbness out of his feet. He stretched his protesting muscles and looked around and saw the hobbled horses grazing on the scant brown grass that still remained from the previous summer.

He turned back toward Quaid and said, "Well," he muttered, "reckon we still got our scalps."

Quaid looked up and managed a small grin. "So far, but the day's young." He had placed two tin plates in front of him, and now he scraped out half of the antelope meat that looked hard and unappetizing, dividing it into the two plates. "Better enjoy this," he said. "It's the last we got."

Brodie took the plate, bit off a chunk of tough meat, and began trying to chew it. "Antelope is about the worst kind of game there is, I reckon."

"Better than nothing."

Brodie looked over toward the north. They had camped beside a small stream, and now ice covered it. The morning light reflected against the shards of ice, and the stream made a glittering, twisting pattern against the deadness of the earth as it headed off toward the east. "Looks like a blizzard is fixin' to blow in."

"Maybe," Quaid said as he chews on his meat.

Brodie finished his meat and watched as Quaid pulled his heavy coat closer together, then sat staring into the tiny fire that made a colorful red dot in the bleakness of the surroundings. It was a world with no color. During the summer it would be beautiful with wild flowers and green with new leaves on the bushes and tress, but now it was a dreary, colorless world of cold and death.

Brodie stared at Quaid Shafter's face. He had grown accustomed to the man's silences. At first, he had welcomed them, for he had hated the man. He could not help but blame Quaid Shafter for losing Moriah, and he spoke to Quaid only when necessary as they rode the high plains searching for her.

During the first weeks of their search, Brodie had felt his anger and frustration growing. Perhaps two men thrown together into a lonely world would weld their minds together in a single objective and bring them closer together or drive them so far apart that nothing could heal it. But as the days passed, Brodie found his anger toward Quaid slowly begin to change. It was not that Shafter tried to encourage his friendship. Indeed, he seemed to pay no attention to Brodie. Whether they were riding the plains looking for Indians they might question about white captives or sitting at night in the silence of the desert by a crackling fire, Shafter had kept himself wrapped in a stoical silence.

It was this prolonged silence that had troubled Brodie, for Shafter had not been like this when he had first come to Star Ranch. He had been one of the most happy-go-lucky, cheerful, young men that Brodie had ever seen. He was always telling stories or talking to the young women whenever he'd go to town. Brodie had even admired Shafter for this quality, though Clay had warned him that Quaid was not a stable young man. But Brodie had seen another side of Shafter during these months in his company. For one thing, he had learned that Shafter was a tougher man than he was. Quaid endured the burning heat and the numbing cold without complaining. He didn't gripe about the lack of food, nor did he seem to mind the solitude of the great plains of Texas. These hardships seemed not to trouble him as they did Brodie.

Never once has he mentioned turning back or giving up, Brodie thought as he watched the man sitting there like a statue in the gray light of the morning. There was a grim and silent finality in Shafter now, and Brodie had been wondering about it for a long time. He cleared his throat, and said, "Why are you doing this?"

Shafter looked up. His eyes were hooded by the hat that was pulled down low on his head. "Doing what?"

"Risking your life in Comanche territory to get a woman back that's no kin to you." The question lay between them, and Quaid made no attempt to answer. He was silent for so long that Brodie decided that there would be no response.

Finally, Quaid said, "I've been no good all my life." He reached down, picked up a stick out of the fire, held it in the flickering, yellow flame until it caught on fire, then held it up before his eyes like a candle. He watched the flame twist and burn in the morning breeze and then tossed it into the fire. "My pa was a good man, but I wasn't. I never cared that I let everybody down who ever trusted me." He stood to his feet and shook his head. "But when I let the Comanches take your sister, it did something to me."

"Well, you don't even know her."

"That don't matter. I'm going to find her and take her home. I know you hate me, Brodie, and I don't blame you. But if it's any consolation, you don't hate me as much as I hate myself for what I did. And I aim to do what I can to make it right to your family."

Brodie got to his feet slowly and studied the man. "I guess I said some rough things when they first took Moriah, but I've been thinkin' a lot about it, Quaid." He shook his head, for he had gone over this many times in his mind and had tried to find a way to say it. "They would have taken Moriah even if you had been there. And they would have scalped you."

"I should have been there."

Brodie felt the power that lay in the man. Quaid Shafter was standing absolutely still, but Brodie saw in his eyes and in the set of his lips the tremendous energy that Shafter was putting into finding his sister. "What if we can't find her, Quaid?"

"We'll find her no matter how long it takes. I won't never quit until we get her."

Suddenly, Brodie felt a release. He had kept at a distance from Quaid Shafter, but now the two were united in a common goal. He was not alone out here in the vast Texas plains. Quaid was not his friend exactly, but the two of them were linked together in their search for Moriah. He stretched and tried to grin. "Well, I'm glad you're here. I reckon we'd better go to that bunch that the Kiowas told—"

Brodie did not finish his sentence, for he felt as if someone had struck him a sharp blow with a fist in his side. It turned him around, and as he was falling, he felt a tremendous astonishment that anyone would hit him. Then he heard the sound of the shot and knew that it was a bullet and not a fist that had struck him. His gun belt was beside him, and he felt nothing but numbness from the bullet. Glancing up, he saw Indians rushing out of the brush and yelled, "Quaid, there they are!" He made a grab for his gun, but even as he pulled it free, he heard the rapid fire from Quaid's revolver. Quaid had jumped in front of him, and he could not see at first. But then to the left he saw an Indian screaming and running straight for them, a lance in his hand cocked to throw. "Quaid, look out!" he yelled and saw Quaid twist and get off a shot. It caught the Indian in the chest and stopped him dead in his tracks. His lance dropped, and then he collapsed on his face. By this time Brodie had pulled his gun free and gotten off a shot at a shadowy figure he saw. He missed and then he saw Quaid stagger.

"Are you hit, Quaid?"

"Not bad."

"How many are there?"

He saw Quaid turn, but his eyes were searching the brush. "Not many or we'd be dead."

At that moment a bullet kicked up dust right between the two of them, and Quaid leaped forward. He limped as he ran, and Brodie struggled to his feet. Looking down, he saw that his side was soaked with blood, although it still felt numb. He called out, "Quaid, where are they?" but got no answer. He moved toward a tree to take cover but then heard two more shots and a scream that was cut short.

He lifted his gun as someone moved, but he saw Quaid and dropped it again. Quaid came back and shook his head. "I put one more down. There were at least two more, but they ran away. They get you bad?"

"I don't know."

"Let me look at it."

"They got you in the leg?"

"Bullet went right through. Didn't hit a bone, but you're bleedin' like a stuck pig."

Quaid threw more wood on the fire, and then stripping Brodie down, he looked at the wound and said, "It's not bad, but it's gonna hurt. We gotta keep it clean."

Quaid bound up his own wound in his upper thigh and shook his head. "I'm gonna be stiff as a board from this. You, too."

"Quaid, look at that Indian. He's still alive!"

Quaid turned quickly and saw that the first Indian he had shot in the chest was moving. He ran over to him, kicked the lance away, and bent over the figure. He spoke in the Comanche language, and Brodie limped over, holding on to his side, which was beginning to come alive with searing pain now. The Indian's eyes were glazed, and blood was bubbling out of his lips. Suddenly his dark eyes seemed to clear, and he said something that made Quaid glance up at Brodie with astonishment.

"What did he say?" Brodie asked.

"He said for us to forget about the white captive. We'll never get her." He turned back and questioned the Indian, but death was already coming. He made one more statement and then began his death song, but it was cut short with a gurgle as blood flooded his throat. They watched as he died without saying another word.

"What did he mean by that? What did he say there at the last?"

Quaid shook his head. "They were sent to kill us, Brodie. I reckon word's gotten out that we're huntin' for Moriah. We're lucky they didn't send a bigger war party." He looked down at the dead Indian and shook his head. "He's a Comanche all right, but I don't know which band."

"What are we going to do, Quaid?"

"We'll have to go back to the ranch. We can't do anything in this weather. Besides that, we're gonna be stoved up for a while. But we'll be back," he said.

The two packed their few belongings, and Brodie felt tremendous pain as he swung into the saddle. He saw that Quaid was hurting, too. As they rode out, Brodie looked down at the dead Indian and thought, *They could have gotten us easy, but they didn't. I guess the Lord must be with us.*

"Jerusalem, come out here!"

Jerusalem heard Clay's call from the porch and came outside without a coat. The wind was cold. He motioned and said, "There they come."

Jerusalem saw the two horsemen approaching. They were moving slowly, as if they were in the last stages of exhaustion. She waited until they got closer and saw that as Quaid got off his horse, he moved stiffly as he went over to catch Brodie, who fell off his horse. Clay ran forward to help him.

"You fellas hit trouble, I take it."

"Pretty much," Quaid said. "Brodie's hurt worse than me."

Running over, Jerusalem held out her hands and touched Brodie. "Where are you hurt?"

"In the . . . side, Ma." His lips were held tightly together, and his eyes were barely open. "We didn't get Moriah," he whispered.

"Well, you're back alive, and that's somethin'," Clay said briskly. "Come on in."

Clay practically carried Brodie inside the house, and Clinton came in from the back. His eyes widened when he saw that his brother was hurt, and he said, "Did you find her?"

"No," Quaid said. "We got a lead on her, though."

"We'll talk later," Jerusalem said. "I want to look at these wounds."

She began heating water, and for the next half hour, she did not allow any talk. She washed the wounds of both men, bound them with fresh bandages, and then sat them down at the table. She made fresh coffee and a huge panful of scrambled eggs, which she put before them along with the morning's biscuits.

As the two men ate, Brodie became more alert. "Ma, this sure is better than the grub we been eating on the trail." He spoke slowly at first, and as he told them the story of the Comanche attack, he saw that they were staring at him strangely. "If Quaid hadn't been there, my scalp would be on some Comanche's shield."

Jerusalem was sitting across from Quaid, and she reached across the table and took his hand. "Thank you, Quaid."

Quaid stared at her, then finally said, "We had good luck. But those Comanches didn't just happen on us. They came for our scalps. They were sent."

"What do you mean?" Clay said, his glance sharp. "How do you know that?"

"One of them didn't die right off. He told me that we've got names now. I'm Silverhair, and Brodie here is Tall Man. They know we're hunting for Moriah."

Clay stared at them. "I've been talking about getting a bunch of men together and going after them. Maybe even getting some of them ranging men that Sam Houston's organized."

"I don't think it'd do any good, Clay." Quaid shook his head. "If we knew where she was, I'd say yes. But we've got to find her first, and I can do that better than a bunch of men out shooting every Indian they see."

"I think Quaid's right," Brodie said. He looked down at his side and touched it. "This will have to get well first."

"I think we'd better wait until spring," Quaid said, "although I've got some Indian friends, if I can find them, that can help us—if it doesn't kill me first." He smiled grimly then and shook his head. "The Indians are pretty sore about us whites takin' over their land. They're apt to shoot first and ask questions later."

"That's enough of that. I want you two to get in bed right now and get some rest. Both of you are worn down," Jerusalem insisted.

Neither Quaid nor Brodie argued but let Jerusalem hustle them off into the bedroom.

Clay sat there drinking coffee until finally she came back and said, "It's a wonder they're alive."

"It sure is. Four Comanches against two men not lookin' for trouble . . ." He shook his head and said, "That's the good Lord, nothin' else! You know, I'm right glad Quaid is goin' along with Brodie. It seems like he growed up all at once."

Jerusalem sat down and then folded her hands in front of her. "I think you're right. But they're in no condition now to go looking for anyone until they heal up."

"That's right. Be better to wait for good weather."

"You'd like to go with them, wouldn't you, Clay?"

"Well, I'd like to help. But don't worry. My place is here with you." He came over and put his hand on the back of her neck and squeezed it gently. "I've got you, Clinton, Mary Aidan, Sam, and Rachel to think about now."

"Are you sorry?"

"Sorry!" he said with surprise. "I reckon not! I got what I want. If it wasn't for Moriah, everything would be perfect. But we'll get her back. Don't worry."

The two men rested and ate Jerusalem's good cooking for the next week. The time on the trail searching for Moriah had drained and weakened both men more than they realized. They were so worn down that they spent most of their time sleeping and ate enormous meals when they were awake. But both of them were tough men, and by the end of the week, Brodie was getting restless. He had not mentioned Serena, and no one had brought up the subject. But when Clinton went in early one morning, he said, "Ma, Brodie's gone."

"I know. He got up almost before daylight."

"Where'd he go to?"

"He went to find Serena. He left a note."

"But she ain't there, Ma."

"I know." Serena and her mother had left the country. They had sold their place and gone back to Mexico to be with Mateo. Mateo himself had become rather famous, at least along the border. He had gathered a group of discontented men, and they made raids across the Rio Grande on a small scale. After Santa Anna had signed the treaty, Mateo had become bitter at the defeat and took up his own fight against the Texans.

"I'm gonna go find him, Ma, before he gets there."

"He was gonna stop in Jordan City and get his horse shod. You can probably catch him if you hurry. I wish you'd try, Clinton."

"I sure will, Ma. That woman Serena, she ain't worth it. Ever since Brodie left with Quaid, she's was goin' bad, drinkin' and goin' out with all kinds of men."

"I know it, son, but it seems like that doesn't seem to matter much. When a man's got a woman on his mind, his good sense flies out his ears."

Clinton stared at his mother. "Well, maybe some men, but you won't ever have that trouble with me."

Jerusalem began to laugh. She came over and put her arms around him and hugged him. "I love you, Clinton! You don't think anything can ever happen to you, but you're nineteen years old. Just at the right age to get brought down by some woman who pokes a curve at you or flutters her eyelashes."

"Aw, shucks, don't talk like that, Ma! I'm not about to get foolish over any woman."

Jerusalem smiled almost sadly. "You remember the Bible says, 'Let him that thinketh he standeth take heed lest he fall.'"

"Sure, I know it, but I ain't gonna fall," Clinton said stoutly.

"Well, David fell, and he was a man after God's own heart."

"Never understood that. Runnin' around after that old Bathsheba!"

"Men are weak where women are concerned, son."

"Well, I ain't," Clinton protested. "You just don't worry about me, Ma. I'm headed out. I'll catch up with Brodie and bring him back."

"Do that, son."

Jerusalem watched as Clinton left the room, and a sadness filled her. "He's all set for a fall, and he doesn't even know it. Lord, just keep him from total disaster. He's runnin' around in a world full of tigers, and he doesn't even seem to notice!"

★   ★   ★

Clinton pulled up in front of the blacksmith's shop, stepped off his horse, and went over to where Sheriff Joel Bench was talking to Devoe Crutchfield, the blacksmith. "Hi, fellas."

"Hello, Clinton," Devoe said, turning around. He was a burly man with red hair and tremendous upper body strength. "What brings you to town?"

"I'm lookin' for Brodie. Have you seen him?"

"I have," Sheriff Bench said. "He's over at the Golden Lady tryin' to drink all the liquor they got."

"Ah, Sheriff, he ain't either!"

"You go find out. I wouldn't interfere with him if I was you. He's real tetchy. I tried to get him to go home, but he just threatened to fight me if I didn't leave him alone."

"I reckon it's over Serena, ain't it?" Devoe Crutchfield nodded sadly. "A man can sure make a fool out of himself over a woman."

"Well, I'm gonna stop him," Clinton declared stoutly.

Devoe laughed. "You fly right at it, Clinton, but if I was you, I wouldn't go in there doin' a lot of preachin'. He ain't in no mood to listen. I got his horse here all shod, but I don't reckon he'll be goin' home for a spell."

Clinton gave Devoe an offended look and turned and marched off.

Devoe shook his head. "Sheriff, that is one young man that knows everything and never makes a mistake. Must be nice."

Bench grinned. "Just like most of us when we were his age, but we all get the wind taken out of our sails before it's over."

As soon as Clinton stepped into the Golden Lady Saloon, he saw Brodie over at a table by the wall. He had a half-filled bottle of whiskey in front of him and was staring into a glass moodily. Clinton started over, but he was intercepted by Julie, who came and blocked his way.

"Hello, Clinton. What are you doing here?"

"Hello, Julie. I came to take Brodie home."

Julie shook her head. "Right now he's not in the mood to listen to any of your sermons. He's here, and he's getting drunk, and nobody's going to change him."

"Aunt Julie, you shouldn't have let him get drunk."

Impatiently, Julie shook her head. "If he hadn't gotten drunk here, he would have gone somewhere else and maybe got in bad trouble. You just let him alone. Sooner or later he'll pass out. I'll put him to bed and take care of him until he sobers up. Then he'll be all right."

"Did he tell you about not findin' Moriah?"

"Yes. I'd have been surprised if he had. He said him and Quaid both got shot."

"They did, but not bad. And they're goin' back. I'm gonna go with 'em."

"What does your ma say about that?"

Clinton looked uncomfortable. "Well, I ain't exactly mentioned it yet."

"I thought not. Now listen, Clinton. If you got any idea about bawling Brodie out for getting drunk, just turn right around and get yourself out of here."

Clinton stared at her and then said, "I just want to talk to him."

"Talk to him—but no preaching."

Clinton moved over to the table and sat down beside Brodie. "Brodie, I came to find you."

Brodie looked up, and he had trouble focusing his eyes. "Clinton—is zat you?"

"Yeah, it's me."

"Serena's gone."

"Yeah, I know."

"Well, why didn't you tell me?"

"I dunno, Brodie. I thought somebody else might have told you. But anyhow, Mateo's gone plumb bad. He's got a bunch of outlaws and comes raidin' over the border."

Brodie filled the glass and picked it up with an unsteady hand. "Get out of here, Clinton. This ain't no place for a kid like you."

"No place for you either. Come on home, Brodie."

"No. I don't want Ma to see me like this. You go on. Get out of here."

Clinton argued mildly, but he saw Brodie was intent on staying and drinking more. He finally said, "Well, you come home when you can."

He waited for an answer but got none and then walked over and said to Julie, "I'll go tell Ma that Brodie's all right."

Julie smiled and gave him a hug. "You're a good boy, Clinton."

"I ain't no boy! I'm nineteen years old."

"Oh, I'm sorry, sir," Julie said mockingly. She laughed, reached over, and put her hands behind his neck. Pulling him forward, she kissed him on the cheek and said, "You big baby, get out of here!"

As Clinton rode alone, he tried to think of some way he could have handled the situation differently. He was upset with himself, for he always had the idea that he could straighten up any problem—if people would just do what he told them. Repeated failures had not convinced him otherwise.

As he came around a bend in the road, he saw the old Bartley place. It had been vacant for some time now. The family had tried to make a living off of it and had failed. Now he realized he was thirsty and decided to stop in for a drink. They had a good well, and he had often sampled the water. As he came around, he saw two horses standing there and grew suddenly more wary, for he recognized Lou Burdette, the foreman of Skull, and a hulking rider named Dee Nolan, one of Skull's riders. They were facing an older man, one that Clinton did not know, and a boy stood off to one side. Clinton pulled his horse up and nodded, "Howdy."

"What do you want, Hardin?" Burdette said. His hat was shoved back on his head, and his eyes were sharp and cruel. He had locked horns with Clay more than once and had always come out second. For this reason he hated anyone connected with Star Ranch.

"Thought I might get a drink of water." Clinton stepped out of the saddle and moved over and tied his horse up. "Howdy," he said to the older man, nodding. "I'm Clinton Hardin. I don't believe we've met."

The man seemed worried, but he said quickly, "I'm Caleb Stuart. This here is Al."

"Just moved in?" Clinton asked.

"We've been here a week."

Clinton started to speak, but Lou Burdette said, "Get on your way, Hardin."

Clinton stared at Burdette. "I always like to get my walkin' papers from the boss."

Dee Nolan laughed. "They ain't no boss here. These are squatters." He was a big man with broad shoulders and a thatch of bright yellow hair. He had hazel eyes and a cruel twist to his mouth.

"That ain't so," Stuart said quickly. "I'm leasin' this place from the Bartleys. I got the papers right here." He held up a paper in his hand, but Burdette merely laughed harshly. "That don't mean nothin'. You get out of here, old man."

"What's your interest here, Burdette?" Clinton said. He had never liked Burdette, although he had never had words with him, but he knew that the foreman of Skull was an arrogant man who loved to bully everyone. "This ain't Skull ground."

"You keep your oar out of it," Burdette said and abruptly turned and walked over to stand over the older man. "You heard what I said. Get going."

Stuart said, "I got a paper right here—" Suddenly, Burdette grabbed the paper, tore it in two, and threw it in the air. He shoved the old man roughly and cursed, saying, "You heard what I said. Now clear out!"

Clinton Hardin was a mild-mannered young man—except when he saw someone being bullied, and then some of the temper that was so obvious in his uncle Zane and had been in his father would be stirred. Without thought, he walked over and grabbed Burdette's arm. "You didn't have any call to do that, Burdette. This man's not bothering you."

Burdette seemed shocked that Clinton had stepped in. He was a touchy man anyway and always resented anyone trying to interfere with him. His fist shot out and caught Clinton high in the forehead. "Keep your hands off me!"

Clinton was not as tall, but he had gotten strong from hard work on the ranch. He felt the blood running down his face, and without thought, he stepped forward and drove a tremendous blow right into Burdette's face. It drove the foreman of Skull backward. Burdette yelled, "Get him, Dee!"

Dee Nolan came forward, and he towered over Clinton. Clinton was driven backward by the blows, but he fought back as well as he could. He actually got in several good blows, and then he felt himself seized from behind, his arms pinioned.

"Knock his head off, Dee!"

Dee Nolan laughed. "I will. Just hold on to him, Lou." He drew back, and with all his power and might, hit Clinton in the side.

Pain shot through Clinton, and he gasped. But he had no time to do more than that, for another blow took him in the temple, and he dropped into a deep, black hole that had no light and no sound.

CHAPTER
TWENTY-THREE

Clinton tried to open his eyes, but found that they wouldn't open. This puzzled him, because he had always been able to open his eyes before when he came out of a deep sleep. He did not puzzle himself long over that, for when he tried to sit up, a pain ran through his side as if someone had run a cavalry saber through it! He groaned and tried to make sense out of what had happened but couldn't.

"Are you awake?"

With a great effort Clinton managed to open his left eye a slit, and he saw a face bending over him. He couldn't place it at first, and then memory came flooding back. "Mr. Stuart, ain't it?"

"That's right, boy. I expect you're about hurt all over."

"Well, I reckon I hurt all over more than I do any one specific place." Clinton tried to move, which proved to be a mistake. "What's . . . what's the matter with my side?" he asked, grimacing in pain.

Caleb Stuart shook his head. "You took a pretty bad poundin', Hardin. You got kicked in the side, among other things."

Another voice said impatiently, "Grandpa, move out of the way and let me wash his face off."

Clinton managed to turn his head and saw the young fellow, who had witnessed the fight. His vision wasn't good, but he got an impression of a youthful face before a cool cloth began to wash off the blood from his face. "What's your name?" he croaked when the cloth was removed.

"I'm Al Stuart. Your face looks terrible."

"Well, if it looks worse than it feels, I'm in poor condition," Clinton said. He tried to sit up but caught his breath. "He must have kept his spurs on when he put his boots to me."

"We got to get word to your folks. Where do you live?"

"Star Ranch, about six miles beside the river."

"Al, you get on a horse and ride down and tell his folks there about this young feller."

"No, don't do that. I can make it," Clinton said.

"Why, you can't sit on a horse. Looks like you might have a cracked rib."

Clinton struggled to sit up and winced at the pain in his side. His right eye was swollen completely shut, and he had to hold the other open by effort. But he said stubbornly, "Have you got a wagon?"

"Why, shore we got a wagon, but it'd bounce you to pieces to ride in it all that way," Stuart protested.

"Just help me get in the wagon. I want to go home. My ma's a good doctor."

Both of the Stuarts protested, but Clinton was adamant. "I can do it," he insisted. "Just get me in the wagon."

"Al, this young feller is as stubborn as a blue-nosed mule! I'll go hitch up the wagon, but you'll have to take him home. I'd better stay here with your grandma. And I reckon you kin give 'em a big dose of that painkiller, too."

"All right, Grandpa," Al said quickly.

As soon as the older man left, Al moved away, then came back with a large brown bottle. "Take a swig of this. It's powerful stuff. It'll help with the pain."

Clinton took two large swallows and shook his head. "That's laudanum. Ought to dull me up a mite."

"Reckon I better get some quilts and a pillow. Make the ride a bit easier."

"I appreciate that, Al. Sorry to be so much trouble."

"It ain't no trouble after what you done."

Clinton tried to smile but found that his lips were swollen so that he couldn't move them much. "I didn't do much except get my face re-arranged and my ribs kicked in."

"Well, you tried. And we're obliged to you.

"Has Burdette been troublin' you folks before?"

"He came by once and told us to get off, but Grandpa said we wasn't leavin'. We got a right to be here. I picked up the pieces of that agreement that he tore up. I'll glue it back together and show the sheriff."

Clinton only said, "That's good." But he knew that the sheriff's authority did not extend outside the city limits of Jordan City. He sat there while the young Stuart disappeared, then came back carrying an armload of quilts and a pillow. He was beginning to feel dizzy, and he had a hum-ming noise inside his skull. Soon Clinton heard the noise of the team being driven up, and the two came back inside.

"I reckon you'll have to walk, but you can lean on us," Caleb said as he reached down and gave Clinton a hand up.

The pain in his side was so sharp, but Clinton could tell that the lau-danum was working. With Al on one side and Caleb on the other, he man-aged to stay on his feet. They moved slowly, allowing him to set the pace. It was difficult enough getting down the steps, for the effort jarred him.

When they got to the wagon, Al said, "I don't see how you're gonna get up in there. It's gonna hurt something fierce."

"It'll just have to hurt," Clinton said, gritting his teeth. He got to the back of the wagon and saw that Caleb had removed the board, but the level of the bed was still above his waist. He took a deep breath and said, "If you would just give me a shove, don't pay no attention to how I holler."

"Boy, you sure you want to do this?" Caleb said worriedly. "You might have somethin' busted inside of you."

"I got to get home. Give me a push."

Caleb and Al gave him a push, and Clinton felt like he had a knife in his side. He clamped his teeth together, but he couldn't help groaning from the pain. He was glad for the laudanum, or it would have been unbearable. The two of them managed to shove him over, and then Al got in the wagon and guided him to the quilts. "I done made a pallet. Lay down on it here."

Clinton closed his eyes and did not have strength enough to open them. The wagon seemed to be moving in a circle, and he felt sick. But he felt the quilt underneath, and Al's hand guided him down. He lay flat on his back, and a pillow was shoved under his head. "Just lay still there," Al said. "Grandpa, I'll come back as soon as I take this fellow home."

"All right, Al. I'll go tend to your grandma."

"What's wrong with your grandma?" Clinton whispered.

"She's been ailin' ever since we got here. Don't know what it is, but she's powerful sick."

"Doc Woods is a mighty handy man. Have you had him out to look at her?"

"No, but I reckon we're gonna have to. You lay down now. I'll take it slow and easy and try to avoid all the potholes I can."

"Thanks a heap, Al."

The laudanum had taken hold by the time the wagon had traveled a quarter of a mile. The swaying and the bumps seemed to be happening to somebody else, and Clinton tried to call out but only managed a whisper. "Al, the Lord is takin' care of me. I got whipped, but I didn't get kilt." He remembered no more than this, or if he did, it was as if what had happened to him was happening to somebody else in a bad dream.

Twilight had begun to fall across the prairie, and Jerusalem stopped from feeding the chickens to glance around the landscape. It troubled her some how much she had grown to love her home. She had said once to Clay, "It's almost like idolatry, Clay, how much I love this place."

Clay had grinned and said, "This ugly old place called Texas?"

"It's not ugly," she had said. "It's got some size to it. A person ain't all squeezed together on some measly little old thirty-acre hardscrabble farm."

Every evening she would come outside and look across the immense distances of the prairie and thank God that she was here and not back on the farm in Arkansas waiting for a husband who rarely showed up. She started to turn and then narrowed her eyes. She saw a wagon coming over the rise that hid most of the road. She stood there trying to identify the single driver but could not. All of her family were inside getting ready for the supper she had cooked. She waited until the wagon got closer and took in the youthful face of the driver. She did not recognize him.

"I'm lookin' for the Hardin place," the driver called out.

Jerusalem smiled. "This is it. I'm Jerusalem Taliferro." Although she was now a Taliferro instead of a Hardin, the ranch had gotten branded with the Hardin name.

"I'm Al Stuart, Miz Taliferro. I got a feller here who's in the wagon. He's in poor shape. He says his name is Clinton Hardin."

Instantly, a chill ran over Jerusalem. "What's wrong with him?" she said quickly as she made her way to the side of the wagon bed.

"He got beat up. There was two fellers from Skull Ranch. They hurt him pretty bad, ma'am."

Jerusalem was only half listening. She had come to the edge of the wagon and looked down at the distorted face of Clinton and caught her breath. "He looks awful," she whispered.

"Well, his face ain't the worst of it," Al said. "He got kicked, too. His ribs is awful sore. May be busted, Grandpa said."

"Who are you? Where do you live?"

"I'm Al Stuart. We just moved into the old Bartley place a week ago, my grandma and grandpa and me."

"I'll have to hear more about this later, but right now I need to get him in the house."

"I dosed him up with laudanum, ma'am, but it's probably starting to wear off by now."

"Pull up to the front porch. I'll get my menfolk to carry him in."

"Yes, ma'am."

Jerusalem hurried toward the house and entered at once. "Zane, you and Clay come here. Clinton's been hurt."

The two men had been sitting in the big room arguing over something, but they got up at once and hurried toward her. "What's wrong with him?" Clay said.

"Two of the Skull hands beat him up. Some new folks have moved into the Bartleys' place. One of them brought him home in a wagon."

"Is he shot?" Zane said as he hurried out.

"No, but his face is beat up, and his ribs is stove in."

When they got to the wagon, Zane climbed up into it and looked Clinton over and exclaimed, "Why, they beat the poor boy to pieces! Look at that face." He leaned over and said, "Can you hear me, Clinton?"

"Yeah, I hear ya. Zane, ain't it?"

"Yes, it's Zane. Listen, we're gonna move you now. It's gonna hurt. Just grit your teeth. Holler all you want to."

Zane was a large man and strong. He simply picked up Clinton as he would a child and moved to the end of the wagon. He stooped down, and Clay was waiting to take him. When he lowered Clinton, Zane heard the boy gasp and jumped down. "Where do we put him, Jerusalem?"

"Put him in our bedroom."

Clinton tried to argue, saying he wanted to go in his own room, but Jerusalem said, "You shush now, son. Now, do what I tell you, Clay."

Clay walked inside, moving as carefully as he could. Jerusalem ran ahead and opened the doors. Mary Aidan was watching with big eyes and asked, "Is Clinton hurt, Ma?"

"Yes, he's hurt. Now stay out of the way, Mary Aidan."

The two men got Clinton into the bed and Clay said, "What happened? Who done this?"

His eyes were hard as agates, and Jerusalem recognized this mood. She knew she had married a man who could be as hard and tough as he needed to be, and he was very fond of Clinton. "Don't pester him now, Clay," she protested.

"It's all right, Ma," Clinton said. Now that he was lying flat again, the pain had subsided. He managed to open his eyes and look around and said, "I bet I'm a pretty sight, ain't I?"

"Never mind that," Clay said. "Tell us what happened?"

His voice was harsh, and Clinton stared at him. He related his story and ended by saying, "The Stuarts wasn't doin' nothin'. It was that Burdette and Dee Nolan. I tried to fight 'em, but I couldn't handle 'em."

"Well, we're gonna get you fixed up, boy," Clay said gently, but he had a savage glint in his eyes. "What do we do, Jerusalem?"

"I expect we need to get his clothes off and take a look at them ribs."

"Wait a minute, Ma. You can't take my clothes off. It ain't decent!"

"You hush up, Clinton. I don't want any of your foolish modesty. You lay there now while I go get some water.

"You boys take his clothes off."

As Jerusalem went back, she suddenly remembered that she had left the young Stuart outside. She went outside the door and said, "Sorry, I forgot about you."

"Why, that's all right, ma'am. I hope he'll be all right."

"I think he will. You say you folks just moved in?"

"Yes'm, we did. Just Grandma and Grandpa and me."

"Well, we're beholden to you. What's your name?"

"Al. Al Stuart."

"We're mighty grateful to you, Al, for bringing my boy home. I'll have more to say later when we visit. You come in and stay the night."

"No, ma'am. I got to get back. My grandma's poorly, and I don't like to leave the place."

"Let me tell you one thing, Al. Don't you worry about gettin' thrown off your place. I don't know if Kern Herendeen knows about what his foreman did or not, but he's going to hear about it pretty soon. So, you tell your grandparents not to worry, that the Hardins and the Taliferros will be on their side."

The youthful face suddenly lightened. Even under the oversized hat that covered the boy's face, there was a sudden burst of hope. "That sounds good, ma'am. We've had kind of a hard time."

"I'll hear about it later, Al. Now, you scoot on home before it gets dark. I'll be comin' around to visit to see how your grandma is, probably tomorrow."

"Thank you, ma'am. Mighty kind of you."

Jerusalem watched the youth bound into the wagon and line the mules out at a fast clip. She was thinking in her mind of what she might say to Kern Herendeen and looked forward to confronting him. "Kern's gotten too big for his britches, and so has Burdette!" She remembered the look on Clay's face and said grimly, "I imagine Clay and Zane will have a few words to say to Burdette and Dee Nolan . . ."

★   ★   ★

Julie's eyes flashed with anger as Clay finished telling her the story of how Clinton had gotten badly beaten by Lou Burdette and the Dee Nolan from the Skull Ranch. It was nearly evening, and the crowds were beginning to come into the saloon. She had been glad to see Clay and Zane but knew at once that something was wrong from the stern looks on their faces the minute they walked in. She listened while they told her the story, and now she exclaimed, "That no good Burdette! Somebody needs to shoot him!"

"That ain't too far-fetched, Julie," Clay said.

Something in his attitude warned Julie that he had come to town prepared to meet Skull's foreman. He was wearing one of the new repeating pistols on his right hip and the huge bowie knife that he had taken from Jim Bowie's own hand back in earlier days.

"We thought maybe he might be in here," Zane said. He also was armed and had a glint in his eye.

"They don't come in here, Zane, because of me, I guess. I can't stand any of them. They think they own the earth. They spend most of their time over at the Silver Dollar."

"Guess we'll pay the Silver Dollar a call."

Julie said suddenly, "There's usually a bunch of them over there. You'd better get some more help."

"More help for those cowards? I only hope Herendeen's there," Clay said.

"I'm changin' clothes," Julie said. "I'm goin' back and help Jerusalem take care of Clinton."

"Well, that'd be good. She's always glad to see you," Clay said. Without another word he turned, and the two men left the saloon. As they walked along the street toward the Silver Dollar, neither of them spoke.

Finally, Zane said, "I sure wish Julie would get out of that saloon business. I ain't one to talk, for she ain't done nothin' I ain't done, but it bothers me."

"It bothers Rice Morgan, too. I've always thought he's had a special feeling for Julie," Clay said.

"That'd be somethin' to see a preacher marry a saloon girl. He's in enough trouble with church folk already goin' into saloons and draggin' the wild ones into church. I'm surprised he's lasted this long." They were approaching the Silver Dollar now, and Zane said, "Looky there. A bunch of Skull horses tied up out front. Must be six or seven of them."

"We'll divide 'em right down the middle, half for you and half for me," Clay said. "Any odd ones we'll match for it."

The two walked into the saloon and saw that the place was already filled—mostly with Skull riders. They were a rough-looking bunch of cowhands. They looked around and spotted Lou Burdette. He was at a table talking with a woman no longer young but still attractive.

"How do we start the ball, Clay?"

"It's Burdette and Nolan I'm out to get. The rest of them can stay out of it if they want to. If they don't, they take what comes."

"I'll back your play. Let her flicker," Zane said. "I'm ready to teach them cowards a lesson they ain't likely to forget for a long time." He was smiling, and he saw that Burdette had spotted the two of them. "It looks like Burdette's got his eye on us, Clay."

Clay stepped over to the bar at his right, and Zane joined him. When the bartender, a short rotund man with thin, black hair greased against his skull, asked what he'd have, he said, "Give me the best you got in the house." He raised his voice and said, "I hear there's some of them ring-tailed Skull riders in here that think they're tough. You seen any of 'em?"

The bartender's eyes opened, and then in alarm he glanced over toward Burdette and backed away from the bar.

Clay turned around and hooked his elbows over the bar.

"I hear they figure they're some pumpkins because two of 'em were able to take out a boy. I wonder how they'd do with a couple of men."

Silence filled the room, for everyone had heard Clay's voice. Clay grinned and winked across the room at Devoe Crutchfield. "Well, Devoe, you seen any of them big, bad Skull riders?"

"I reckon I seen a few of 'em, Clay." Devoe had been playing poker, but now he laid his hand flat on the table and ran his eyes around the room. "Any of you Skull riders here feelin' froggy I guess now's the time to jump."

Lou Burdette suddenly rose to his feet, shoving the woman away. He moved over to take a stand at the bar some five feet away from Clay. "What's eatin' on you, Taliferro?"

"Well, Lou, my old friend. It's good to see you," Clay said. He smiled and turned to meet Burdette. "Haven't seen much of you lately. I thought we'd pay you a visit."

"You're mighty noisy about it."

"I didn't disturb your siesta, I hope."

"Say what you got to say," Burdette said. He had looked over the room and saw at least six Skull hands, and he knew he had their loyalty. "What's on your mind?"

"Why, you're on my mind, Lou. I come special to see you and your friend Dee over there. Hello, Dee."

Dee stood up and came over to stand beside the foreman. The hulking man with hazel eyes had a reputation as a wicked barroom brawler. "See you come loaded for bear." He grinned and nodded at the big knife. "Where'd you get that little item?"

"I had a fight with Jim Bowie and took it away from him."

A murmur ran around the saloon, for this story had, indeed, been told all over, and it was true.

"You sayin' you whipped Jim Bowie? You're a liar!" Dee Nolan said.

"You're callin' me a liar?"

"That's right," Nolan said. "You make one move for that knife or that gun, and I'll make you eat 'em."

"Why, I don't reckon I need a knife or a gun to handle a weasel like you, Nolan. What do you think, Zane?"

"You ought not pick on the feeble-minded, Clay." Zane grinned. He was enjoying the scene a great deal. His eyes were everywhere though, watching the other Skull riders.

"Never mind all that. Say what you've got to say," Burdette snapped.

"Well, I come to town to whup your tail, Lou, like I've done before. It seems like you don't have a very good memory. If you'll remember, up on the Little Missouri we crossed once, I trounced you good, and you didn't get out of bed for a month."

The memory of the beating that Burdette had taken at Clay Taliferro's hand was like touching acid to a raw wound. He knew the speed with which Clay could draw a gun and held his hands out. "I ain't drawin' on you."

"Well, that's fine. What about the rest of you Skull riders? Anybody want to draw iron?"

The Skull riders were all still, but their eyes were fixed on Burdette, waiting to see what he'd do

Zane said, "Come on, fellas, give us a run for our money. We're gonna beat the soup out of these two, but you can get in on it if you like."

None of the Skull riders said a word. They had heard of Clay Taliferro's skill with a six-gun, and Zane's reputation was almost his equal. Still they were ready.

Devoe Crutchfield got up and came over to join the three. "I wonder if I can get in on the fun."

"You stay out of this, Crutchfield," Burdette snapped. "You'll get hurt."

"Well, I been hurt before, but I'll tell you what. It looks to me like two against six." Crutchfield said, "Zane, if you'll give me the loan of your pistol, I promise to perforate anybody that tries to interfere with the fun."

At once Zane drew his gun and handed it butt forward, grinning. "Don't shoot 'em in the head. That wouldn't hurt 'em. Plug 'em through the gizzard. That'll give 'em to understand you're serious."

Crutchfield made a dangerous-looking figure. He was a big, burly man. His light red hair was bright under the lights of the saloon, and he was known to be a tough fighter himself. He said, "You fly right at it. Any of you Skull riders ready to go meet your Maker, I'll help you along."

"We don't want any trouble," Burdette said, for the odds had suddenly shifted. "I know you're sore about your stepson, but he was interferin' with us."

"You're a liar, Burdette," Clay said calmly. "What do you have? Guns, knife, or fist?"

Burdette licked his lips. His gun was at his side, but he had no delusions that he could beat Clay Taliferro to the draw. He also knew that Taliferro was a fighting machine, but he saw no way out. He looked around and saw that the four other riders were held in place by the gun in Devoe Crutchfield's big hand and knew that he could not count on them.

Clay suddenly stepped forward and slapped Burdette across the face. The blow drove Burdette sideways, and his hand nearly went to his gun. But then he saw that he was too late, for the instant he moved, Clay's own revolver had appeared.

"I ain't drawin'!" Burdette yelled.

Clay reached over and plucked Burdette's revolver from the holster. He laid both guns on the bar and said, "Here, Devoe, take a couple of these. That'll give you enough bullets to shoot every one of them four or five times." He turned then and said, "The two of you beat a boy almost to death. One of you held him, I expect."

Dee grunted, "That's a lie. I don't need no help."

He said no more because Zane stepped forward and like lightning drove a blow straight into Nolan's face. It knocked the big man backward but did not put him down. The blow broke his nose, and Nolan looked down and saw the bright, crimson stain on his shirt. He didn't lack courage, so he threw himself forward, and Zane came at him.

Burdette took this opportunity, when Clay's attention was on the other two, to throw himself at Clay Taliferro. He caught Clay high in the head with a wicked right and drove him backward, then with a fierce yell he threw himself forward. Clay had not gotten his balance and took several wicked punches, for Burdette was a strong man. Clay reached out and grabbed Burdette around the middle. He made a wild swing and lifted Burdette up, then flung him through the air. Burdette struck a table and went down. As he scrambled to his feet, he saw Clay coming forward, his eyes glinting. He knew that no mercy would be given or expected in this fight.

The fight did not last long. Crutchfield, with a gun in each hand, watched it as he could, but he kept his eyes on the Skull riders, all of whom had come to their feet, but none went for their guns. He called out encouragement. "That's it, Clay. Bust him in the belly! He can't take it there!" And then, "Watch out, Zane, he'll use his boots on you."

Zane had his hands full, for Dee Nolan was covered with thick muscles, and his skull was hard as a rock. It had won most of his fights for him, but he was slow and ponderous. He landed a few blows that marked Zane up, but his own face became a mass of blood as Zane danced around, shooting hard lefts, followed by a powerful right. In the blink of an eye, Nolan reached down and pulled a knife from his boot. Zane picked up a chair and swung it over his head. The edge of the seat caught Nolan on the skull and drove him down, as if he had been hammered. It did not knock him out, and Zane dropped the shattered chair, picked up another one, and this time put him down with one terrible blow.

Burdette's face was all bloody now from the blows Clay had rained on him. Clay caught him in the throat with a tremendous blow, and Burdette fell to the floor gagging and choking.

Breathing hard, Clay looked down. He had taken several tough punches himself, but it did him good to see that both of the Skull riders were battered and bleeding. "It hurts me to have to leave you two like this, but you tell your boss if any Skull rider ever so much as even speaks a word to those folks out at the old Bartley place, Zane and I'll be comin' to take it out of his hide. Come along, Zane."

They took their guns, and Zane said, "Come on, Devoe. Let's go down to the Golden Lady. Now, that's a *real* saloon."

As soon as the three left, the Skull riders rushed over to Burdette and Nolan. One of them said, "I think Burdette's dying."

Burdette could not talk, for the blow to his throat had hurt him badly.

Jake Ramsey said, "We'd better get these two to a doctor. They're gonna have to be sewed up and put together again."

They got Burdette to his feet, but it was hard to lift the huge form of Nolan, and Jake said, "We'll have to bring the doc here. He's too big to tote."

"I wonder how Herendeen will take this," a bystander said.

"I expect he'd better take it easy," Jake said, looking at what Clay and Zane had done to Burdette and Nolan. "I'd hate to have them two come callin' on me!"

CHAPTER
TWENTY-FOUR

The last day of September was a blustering windy affair that swept through Jordan City like a miniature tornado. The hornbeam and sycamore trees were swayed by gusts, and the roadrunners seemed to have proliferated. They ran with long, rushing strides, head low and uttering their strange chirping cry. Clay had ridden to the bank to deposit the money he'd gotten for a herd of cattle that he had sent to New Orleans with another rancher. He had not made this trip, a fact that amused him. He had always looked forward to being on the move, but the twins and Jerusalem were like a magnet that drew him closer and refused to release him. Now, as he stepped off of his horse and tied him at the hitching rail in front of the Golden Lady Saloon, he grinned wryly at his own follies.

He pushed the doors of the saloon back and walked over to the bar. "Got any root beer, Butch?"

Butch Landry grinned and nodded. "You're livin' pretty high, ain't you, Clay? Fixin' to let your wolf loose and tree the town?"

"I'm an old family man now, Butch. Them days is far behind me."

Still grinning, Butch went over and pulled a root beer out of a box and set it before Clay, saying, "Don't drink too many of these. You've still got to ride home, you know."

Uncapping the beverage, Clay stood there, his eyes running idly around the saloon. Frisco Barr came over and stood beside him. "Hello, Clay. Haven't seen you much lately."

"Stayin' close to home, Frisco. Julie around?"

"I think she's up in her room." He turned and called out, "Charlie, go tell Julie Clay's down here."

"Right, Frisco."

Clay sipped on the root beer and said, "I guess I've warned you about this before, Frisco, but I'm gonna get Julie out of this place if I can."

"That'd be all right with me." Barr looked down at his boots and studied them as if there were some inherent meaning hidden in the design of the fancy stitching. Finally, he lifted his head and said, "She don't belong in no saloon, Clay, but I can't run her out. It'll have to be her choice."

"Reckon you're right about that."

The two men stood there talking for a time, and Barr spoke of the Texas government, which had begun printing money a couple of years past. "It ain't worth the paper it's written on. Nothin' to back it up," he complained. "You could take a wagon load of it and couldn't buy a bottle of whiskey."

"That's why I always want to take hard money if I can get it."

"And another thing. It was a raw move to change capitals." He spoke of moving the capital of Texas in '40 from Houston to Austin. That move had displeased everyone in Texas pretty much, except, of course, the inhabitants of Austin. Lamar had moved his government to Austin, which at the time only had nine hundred people. It was the wrong decision according to most, for Austin lay far beyond the frontiers of most settlements, and it was on the very edge of Comanche country.

"I don't think anything good has happened since Lamar got to be president."

Clay nodded. "I don't see why Houston couldn't just keep on being president."

"Because the Constitution says that a man can't succeed himself. Anyway, I don't like Lamar."

Clay nodded slowly. "I fought with Lamar at San Jacinto. He's a good fighter, but a bad president, and this burr in his saddle he's got about Indians is gonna mean trouble."

Indeed, President Mirabeau B. Lamar hated Indians with a passion, and upon assuming the office of president, he had begun a series of fierce campaigns against the Indians. He had used the regular Texas army forces and local bands called "ranging companies." Lamar was convinced that all Indians were evil no matter what tribe they came from. He had sent his forces to strike against the southern Indians, including the Cherokee, who were harmless, and several other immigrant tribes who had moved into east Texas after being driven out of the United States.

Clay spoke of this and then shrugged. "I reckon we've got to fight against the Comanches."

"I reckon so," Barr said. "They've been doing lots of raiding against the settlements on the border, but these blasted Indian wars have cost us two and a half million dollars—which we don't have. Lamar tried to establish the Bank of Texas, but it takes plenty of money to found a bank." He grinned wryly and said, "I reckon President Lamar don't understand that, so he up and printed three million dollars in redback notes."

"What are they worth now, Frisco, a dime on the dollar?"

"Not even that much. Did you hear about his latest idiocy?"

"Who? Lamar?"

"Yes." Barr nodded. "He's been talkin' about the borders of Texas goin' all the way to the Pacific Ocean. Can you tie that?"

"Why, that's plumb crazy!" Clay exclaimed.

"I know it is, but he sent an expedition to take over Santa Fe. It come to nothin', of course. The poor fools had to cross thirteen hundred miles of plains right in the middle of Comanches. Them that lived were captured by a Mexican army, only about three hundred of them. They're all in prison now down in Mexico."

Clay sipped his root beer, then set it down on the bar and began to draw figures on the surface. "I heard Lamar was tryin' to get a bunch of Frenchmen to settle along the Rio Grande."

"Another wild scheme of his! They were supposed to form kind of a wall between us and Mexico, to keep the Mexicans out. Wouldn't that make a dog laugh? Imagine Frenchmen bein' able to whip anybody! All they can do is be romantic and eat snails!"

"Well, one good thing about it. Next year we'll have another election," Clay said.

"And we know who our candidate will be."

"Sure. Sam Houston. You hear he got married again?"

"No, I didn't."

"More than that. He got himself converted. Yep, Sam's on the glory road now."

"What brand did he wind up with?" Barr asked.

"A Baptist. I don't expect even the Baptists will be able to tame Sam Houston down, though. I wonder what the issues in his campaign will be?" Clay asked idly.

"Well, I don't know, but Sam will make it interesting." The two stood there talking, when suddenly Barr caught a movement and said, "There comes your dear and beloved friend, Kern Herendeen."

Clay did not turn around, but Barr watched as Herendeen stopped abruptly. He saw the big man's eyes fall on Clay, and he noted the antagonism there. He waved, however, saying, "Come on, Kern, have a drink on the house."

Herendeen hesitated only a moment and then came over and said, "Hello, Barr. I'll take that drink."

After Butch brought the drink, Kern stared at Clay with such animosity that Clay said, "You look like you're about ready to pop, Kern. If you got somethin' to say, why, just set it on the front porch."

"All right, I will. I don't take kindly to your beating up my men."

"Why, Kern, you don't know your Bible well enough. Don't the Good Book say that whatsoever a man soweth that shall he also reap?" Humor played in Clay's eyes, and he said, "I reckon Dee and Lou just did a little sowin', so Zane and me saw that they did a little reaping." His voice grew harder then, a slight edge on it. "Those boys had no business tryin' to run the Stuarts off. That ground don't belong to Skull. The Stuarts are there legally. And Dee and Lou deserve what they got for beating up on my stepson," Clay said coldly. "If they ever do that again, they'll get it worse."

Both men saw that Kern wanted to argue, but he knew he was on shaky ground. Kern Herendeen had hated Clay from the moment that Jerusalem had agreed to marry him. The two men spoke only when necessary, and this was the longest conversation they had had since Clay's marriage.

"All right," Kern said. "I'll let it pass this time."

"I do appreciate it, Kern." The irony in Clay's voice rubbed against Herendeen, but he drank his drink, nodded, and walked away.

He passed Julie on the way but did not glance at her. Julie came over and said, "Hello, Clay. How's Clinton?"

"Oh, he's too holy to hurt."

"Yes, I saw his face, and I'd like to pound Kern Herendeen with a sledgehammer!"

"Guess you'd have to get in line for that," Clay said.

The two stood there talking for a while, and Barr left them alone. Julie seemed to have something on her mind, and Clay said, "I've asked you this before, Julie, but if you want to leave here, we'd be glad to have you."

"Leave me alone, Clay. I don't have any place with you."

"Sure you do. You're family."

"You talk like Rice."

"Smart man. You ought to listen to him."

Julie reached over and picked up Clay's root beer. She smiled at him and shook her head. "You're down to drinkin' root beer, are you? Well, I always knew you'd go downhill when you wouldn't marry me." She tasted the beverage and made a face. "That's awful stuff!"

"Rice is doing fine at the church, isn't he?"

"He's headin' for a fall. He's fillin' that church up with people like me."

"That wouldn't be a bad idea."

Julie seemed moody and restless. She put her elbows on the bar and stared down at it. "I'll tell you the truth, Clay. This life is no fun anymore, but I can't be anything else."

"Sure you can, Julie. You're just like me. I wasn't a candidate for the pearly gates either, but if the good Lord took me in, He'll take anybody." Julie did not look up, and Clay had to lean over to hear what she said.

"I don't know if I'll ever become a Christian, Clay, but if I did— I guess I'd want to be the kind Rice Morgan is."

★ ★ ★

Clinton shoved his plate back and said, "Well, that was a nice breakfast, Ma."

"Six eggs and a half a side of bacon. I think you're gonna founder yourself."

"I got to keep my strength up, Ma. After all, I got to hold this here ranch together."

Jerusalem had to stifle a laugh, for Clinton's enormous self-assurance always amused her. He was always sure that he was right, no matter how many people tried to tell him differently. In others it might have been a rather nasty trait, but somehow Clinton, in all his youthful exuberance, found a way into her heart.

Zane had been sitting to one side listening, and now he winked at Jerusalem and said, "I'm glad it was a fine, upstandin' Christian like you that them two Skull fellers beat up on. Anybody else might be wantin' revenge, but I know a good Christian lad like yourself will have to forgive 'em."

Clinton suddenly looked up. "Forgive 'em!" he said with astonishment. "After they beat me half to death?"

"The Bible says to do it, Clinton. You know that. Forgive your enemies, and it'll pour coals of fire on their heads."

Both Zane and Jerusalem watched as Clinton struggled with the idea, wondering how he would handle it. They both knew that he had been extremely bitter to have been beaten so unfairly and unjustly. At the same time, he was a strict believer in the Bible and took the Scriptures very literally.

"Well," Clinton said, taking a deep breath and then expelling it, "I guess I'll forgive 'em and pour coals of fire on their heads." He nodded firmly and said, "That'll burn their brains out!"

Zane laughed, and Jerusalem had to conceal her own, but she said, "You ought to be ashamed talking like that."

"It's biblical, Ma. Burn their brains out. That's what the Scripture says." He got up and said, "I'm goin' to go huntin'. I think I'll stop by and thank that fella Al for lookin' out for me."

"I think that's a good idea," Jerusalem said. She had visited the Stuarts twice and grown fond of them. Now she added, "I've baked some fresh bread. I want you to take it over to them. Anne is doing much better, but she's still too weak to do much cookin'."

Clinton waited until Jerusalem had wrapped the bread in a cotton sack, and as she handed it to him, he said, "You know, Al seems like a nice young fella. Kind of small, and he shore didn't help much when I was tanglin' with Skull."

Jerusalem smiled at him with something in her eyes. "I think Al Stuart's nice."

"Yeah, he's kind of sissified. You know, Ma, I'm gonna take him in hand. I'll make a tough fella out of him. Maybe some huntin' and helpin' Brodie and me brand some cattle will toughen him up some."

Jerusalem reached out and grabbed a handful of Clinton's thick brown hair and shook his head. "You're always wanting to make people into somethin'. I think you'd better be careful about that."

Clinton grinned, reached up, and moved his mother's hand. He held it for a minute and then reached out and squeezed her arm. "I'm gonna start on you, Ma. I've been thinkin' about some ways to improve your disposition. We'll talk about that when I get back."

Clinton left the room whistling cheerfully, and Jerusalem turned to stare at Zane. "Did I really give birth to that, Zane? He never thinks he's wrong. One day I'm afraid he's gonna have a bad fall."

"He'll be all right, sis." Zane grinned. "And I'm interested to see how he improves your disposition."

"Howdy, Miz Stuart. My ma sent you this bread. Baked it fresh this mornin'."

Anne Stuart was a small woman with silver hair and clear, gray eyes. She had the look of a chronically ill person, but now she smiled cheerfully and said, "Why, thank you, Clinton. That was mighty kind of your ma. Come in, and I'll heat it up and put some plum jelly on it."

"No, thank you, ma'am. Maybe when I come back by." He had removed his hat and looked around, saying, "I'm goin' huntin', and I thought I'd ask Al to go along with me."

"Why, that would be nice. Look out in the barn. Just birthed a new calf last night. Al's mighty handy with animals."

"I'll bring you back a deer, ma'am. I reckon that would go pretty well."

"It sure would. I'm partial to venison stew."

Clinton stepped out on the front porch, turned, and ambled over toward the barn. He stepped inside and found Al crouched beside a newborn calf. "Howdy, Al," he said. "That your new calf?"

Al turned and said, "Sure is. She's a beauty, ain't she?" Al was wearing the same worn clothes, several sizes too large, and the oversized black hat. Clinton noticed the freckles on Al's face, and as he knelt to look at the calf, he saw that Al's eyes were a strange greenish color.

"This is a fine calf," Clinton said as he reached out and stroked the silky hide of the calf. Finally, he said, "I wanted to thank you for helpin' me get home."

"It wasn't nothin'."

"Well, them two Skull lunkheads caught me off-guard. Next time it'll turn out different."

Al smiled, and Clinton noticed that he had regular features and smoother skin than most young men. "Well, I'm goin' huntin'," he said. "I got a fancy for venison. I reckon your folks could use some, too."

"Grandma loves venison. So does Grandpa."

"Well, why don't you come along?"

"Really? You mean it?"

"Sure." Clinton nodded. "Tell you what. You go get your gun, and I'll saddle your horse. Which one is he?"

"That little sorrel out in the corral. The saddle's out on the fence."

"I'll take care of it." Clinton went out to the corral, and the sorrel came to him when he called. "You're a tame little lady," he said. He put the saddle on, and by the time he had it cinched and ready, Al had come out of the house. "Can you shoot that rifle?"

" 'Course I can!" Al said, somewhat offended. "What do you think?"

"Well, I'll be glad to give you some pointers. Let's get on our way."

The sun had fallen deep across the afternoon sky as they rode along side by side. Al told Clay about seeing many tracks at a little creek not far from the Bartley place. When they arrived there, they tied their horses to some low-lying bushes and walked in silence toward the creek. They crouched down, half hidden by a copse of blackjack and post oak saplings, and waited to see if any deer would come to drink. They had a clear view of the creek, and Al said, "Them tracks are right fresh, Clinton. I've seen deer here twice about this time in the afternoon."

"You all loaded and ready to shoot?"

"Of course I am!"

Clinton checked his own rifle, held it across his lap, and then continued to speak. "Like I been sayin', Al, I owe you a lot for takin' me home in the wagon, and I figured on a way to pay you back."

"How's that?" Al said.

He turned and stared at Clinton amongst the shadows of the big brimmed hat. Al's eyes were almond-shaped, and Clinton could not decide if they were blue or green or both.

"Well, you ain't very big, Al, but I reckon you'll get bigger. How old are you? About fourteen?"

Al suddenly smiled. "At least."

"Well, you're just about the age when things get sort of complicated."

"Complicated? Complicated how?"

"Why, a fella starts gettin' notions about that time, and them things ain't good for a fella."

Al was studying Clinton carefully. "What kind of notions you talkin' about?"

Clinton was surprised. "Why, women, of course! You're just about the right age to start gettin' interested in girls. Now, I figure I owe you somethin', so I'm gonna give you some advice on how to handle this problem."

"I'd be right pleased to hear it," Al said.

"Well, the first thing you got to understand, Al, is that you have to stay away from women who ain't following after God. Oh, a few of them ain't like ma and like your grandma, but most of them is tricky. Oh, they are tricky! They're always tryin' to get a man in trouble. Why the Bible says, 'The lips of a strange woman drop as a honeycomb, and her mouth is smoother than oil: but her end is bitter as wormwood, sharp as a two-edged sword.'"

"It says that, does it?"

"Oh, sure, and a lot more. You let me have your Bible, and I'll go through and mark all them parts about bad and sinful women. A young fellow like you needs all the help he can get, especially just comin' into what you're facin'."

"So, women always try to get men in trouble," Al said. "How do they do that?"

"They got ways, Al. Yes, they got ways!"

"What kind of ways?"

"Well, the first thing is they take lots of baths so they smell good."

"And that's a bad thing?"

"Well, I reckon that ain't too bad, but I've always felt like too much bathin' was unseemly."

"What else do they do besides take baths?"

"Why, they use perfume."

"Don't that make 'em smell better?"

"Oh, they don't do it just to smell better. They do it to draw men down into their clutches, don't ya see? And then they paint up their faces, which ain't scriptural."

"Does the Bible say that?"

"Well, I'm studyin' on it right now. I ain't found it yet, but it's in there somewhere. It's got to be, don't it? But I'm tellin' you that paintin' their faces ain't the worst."

"What's the worst, Clinton?"

"Leanin'. That's the worst thing."

"Leaning? What do you mean *leaning*?" Al asked.

Clinton reached down, picked up a straw of grass, and put the end of it between his teeth. His eyes were half closed, as if he were engaged in some sort of deep meditation. "Well, I'll have to be downright specific here, Al. I expect you've noticed that men and women, they're—well, they're built different."

Al stared at Clinton curiously. "Different—how?"

"Oh, you know what I mean. And you'll sure be noticin' it a lot more. They're just—different."

"You mean men are bigger than women?"

"Well, of course they're bigger, but it ain't just that. Oh, confound it, Al, you just take a look at a woman and then take a look at a man. You'll see the difference."

"All right, I will. But what about leaning?"

"Oh, they *do* that. They put on perfume, and then they come around you, and then they *lean* on you, you know? And that can get a fella all mixed up. You got to watch that leanin', Al. It can tempt a man something fierce."

Al's voice was shaded with admiration. "I just don't understand how you managed to stay out of their clutches, Clinton. There must be a powerful heap of girls been leaning on you."

"I'm wise to 'em, Al! They can't fool me! No siree! And you see, the thing is . . ." He took the straw out of his mouth and waved it as if it were a wand. "You got to keep 'em in their place, don't you see? A firm hand, that's what it takes."

"Well, what if they won't mind?"

"Well, then it's just like breaking a horse. You got to give 'em discipline."

"I see, and have you had to discipline many, Clinton?"

Al's voice was slow, and there was a tenor in it that caused Clinton to turn and look.

"Oh, it wouldn't be proper of me to speak of it. Not to a young feller like you. Look, Al, you just take my word for it. Women are a snare and a trap, and a man's got to keep himself thinkin' about that all the time. Now, there's a few more things I need to—"

Suddenly, Al reached out and clutched Clinton's arm and pointed toward the creek. Clinton looked up and saw two deer step out of the underbrush. He watched carefully, then leaned over and whispered, "You take the doe, and I'll take the buck. You shoot first."

Al nodded, and they both slowly raised their rifles into position. Clinton waited, and when Al's rifle sounded, he was disconcerted when the doe leaped straight up, covering the form of the buck. The doe was hit, but by the time she had fallen, the buck had whirled and was headed away. Clinton took a quick shot but missed.

"Confound it," Clinton said. "Shucks!" He saw Al looking at him and said, "I got somethin' in my eye just about the time you fired. Come on. We got one anyway."

"Yes, *we* did," Al said.

They walked over, and Clinton began to point out Al's errors. "You didn't aim quite low enough. Next time lower your rifle just a bit and move that shot a bit forward."

Al stared at Clinton and then suddenly laughed. "All right, I'll write

all that down when I get a chance. Now, let's get this meat back home."
Al pulled out a skinning knife from beneath the bulky coat that he wore,
but Clinton shook his head. "Nah, we'll put her on your horse and dress
her out at your place."

"You want me to walk?" Al asked, frowning.

"No, we'll ride double."

All the way back Al rode behind Clinton, but he glanced from time to time
at the doe that was tied securely down on the sorrel. Clinton had talked
continually. *Listening's what seems to be what you do when you're around
Clinton,* Al thought.

Clinton said, "I've been thinkin' about all this stuff I've been tryin' to
teach you about men and women, and I decided what I got to do."

"What's that, Clinton?"

"I'm gonna look for a nice young girl for you to start courtin'."

"Why, that's thoughtful of you, Clinton! You sure it won't be too
much trouble?"

"Oh, I don't mind trouble. After all, we're buddies, ain't we?"

"We sure are."

Al said nothing for a time, and then asked curiously, "How are you
going to be sure it's the right girl for me?"

"Well, I'll test her out."

"Test her! Test her how?"

"Well, the first thing, of course, I'll test her theology."

"Theology? You mean what she thinks about God?"

"Oh, sure. That's *real* important. Got to be sure we get you a woman
who ain't got any off-breed ideas about religion."

"I see. Anything else?"

"Well, got to be sure that whoever this gal is that she understands a
woman's place."

"A woman's place?"

"Well, I mean so far as men are concerned. You know, Al, the Bible
says that a woman's made out of the rib. You wouldn't expect a rib to be
uppity, but they get that way sometimes. So, I'll have to be sure that she's

read that part in the Bible that talks about how a woman's supposed to be submissive to her husband."

"Submissive?"

"Oh, yeah, submissive. You know what that means?"

"You mean a woman always lets a man have his way?"

"Well, that's scriptural right there. You hang on to that idea, Al. And the next thing—" Clinton did not finish his sentence, for a sharp, dry buzzing almost beneath them startled both horses. Clinton's gelding reared so suddenly that Al suddenly disappeared. Clinton yelled and pulled his gelding back. As he came off the horse, he pulled his pistol and shot one time. The shot blasted the six-foot rattler, his body as thick as Clint's wrist. Both horses galloped away at the explosion of the pistol, but Clinton shoved his pistol back in his holster and knelt down beside Al, who lay crumpled up. "Hey now, you all right, Al?" Anxiety coursed through him. He had not seen Al hit the ground, but he had known people could break their necks when they were thrown from a horse.

"Al, are you all right?" He picked the limp figure up into a sitting position and said, "Come on, now. Don't be hurt. Did you hit your head?" He reached up, knowing he had to examine the head for bruises or cuts, and yanked off Al's wide-brimmed black hat.

The instant the hat came off, he froze and stared at the long, blond hair that fell all the way down to Al's shoulders. He could not speak for a moment, and he reached out with his free hand and touched the hair as if he didn't believe it.

Al's eyes suddenly opened, and Clinton was relieved. "Are you all right, Al? I was afraid you broke your neck."

"No, I'm okay. Let me get up."

"Here, I'll help you."

Clinton pulled the young woman to her feet, for obviously that's what she was. As soon as she was upright, she said, "I don't usually fall off horses, but—" She reached up to touch her hat, and a look of confusion crossed her face. She felt the hair down around her shoulders and then glanced down and saw her hat on the ground. She whirled then and saw that Clinton Hardin was staring at her in absolute astonishment. "Well, what are you staring at?" she said.

"You ain't no boy!"

"Well, now, ain't you *clever*! You found that out all by yourself." She pulled away from his grip, reached down, and picked up the hat. She put it on her head and shoved the golden hair up under it. Her face was flushed, and she waited for Clinton to speak, but at that moment he could not think of a thing to say—a rare moment in Clinton Hardin's life!

Finally, Clinton cleared his throat and said, "Oh, shucks! I knowed you were a girl all the time."

"Oh, really? Why didn't you mention it?"

Clinton was rapidly inventing a scenario he fervently wished had happened. "Well, I seen you was tryin' to keep it a secret, so I thought it might be best not to mention it. And, anyway, you got a boy's name. There ain't no girls named Al."

"My name is Aldora—Aldora Catherine Stuart."

"Well—I knowed you was a girl, anyway."

"Why, you . . . you *liar*!"

Clinton noticed that Al's eyes were enormous, and now that he was in on her secret, he could see the planes of her face were not those of a man. And he had never seen a boy or a man with such smooth complexion as that of Al Stuart.

Al waited for him to speak and then said, "You give me all this dumb advice about how a man ought to treat a girl, and yet you're telling me you knew I was a girl?"

"Well, no, not exactly. I was just—"

"I'm going home." She put two fingers in her mouth, whistled, and the sorrel came trotting back. She swung up behind the deer and turned the mare's head toward the house.

Clinton watched her ride off and yelled, "Hey, get my horse, will you, Al?"

Al turned and yelled back, "Use your charm on her like you do with all those women who lean on you!"

Clinton stood there as shocked and spellbound as he had ever been in his life. He watched until she was a hundred yards away and then muttered, "Just like I always said, women are plumb deceitful!"

Turning toward his horse, he felt immensely sorry for himself. He yelled, "Come here, you no-account critter!" But the horse had a mind of its own and wandered farther off. Finally, after half an hour, he managed to sneak up on the horse and get into the saddle. He thought once about going to the Stuart house, but then decided that would not be the best. "I better not bother them," he said. "I'll just go on home and let 'em have all the meat."

He rode home, talking to himself all the way, and when he dismounted, unsaddled, and went into the house, he found Jerusalem sitting in the living room sewing.

"Did you get a deer?" she asked.

"Well, I got one, but I gave it to the Stuarts. It was just a doe."

Jerusalem looked up, for something in the sound of Clinton's voice struck her as being odd. "What's wrong?"

"Well, shoot, Ma, I hate to tell you this, but I got bad news."

"What's the matter?"

"Well, that Al Stuart, the one that brought me home? Why, she ain't a boy at all. She's a girl."

Jerusalem laughed loudly and put her sewing aside. She came to Clinton and put her hand on his shoulder. "Well, of *course* she's a girl, and a very nice one, too."

Clinton stared at her and exclaimed, "You knew she was a female?"

"Yes, I did!"

"Well—when did you find out?"

"The first time I saw her, of course."

Clinton stared at her, and then he could not bear the thought of being wrong. So he blustered, saying, "Well, she's mighty close to being a . . . a *hussy*, that's what! Running around with a man's name and dressin' like a man!"

"I expect she'll outgrow that." Jerusalem grew curious. "What did you two talk about when you thought she was a boy?"

Clinton's face instantly reddened. "I . . . I don't rightly remember, Ma."

"Clinton Hardin, you are absolutely the worst liar that I have ever met in my whole life!"

Clinton's face flushed, and he turned and walked away, saying over his shoulder, "Well, I'm going to tell her about the way she's acting." He hesitated, then said firmly, "It's *unseemly*, that's what it is!"

CHAPTER
TWENTY-FIVE

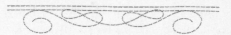

Moriah sat perfectly still as Loves The Night took one of the long spines pulled from a prickly pear plant. She watched as the woman heated it in the small fire, then bent over and took Moriah's earlobe between her fingers. Moriah sat still, ignoring the pain as the barb went through her flesh. Loves The Night perforated the other ear and then drew three lengths of horse hair knotted at one-inch intervals through. Moriah knew that each day they would pull one of the knots through each ear, and by the time the horse hair was through, the ears would be healed.

Loves The Night smiled then. "It will be a good, clean wound," she said. "We will not paint you now, but sometime soon you will learn." She explained the process carefully. "The black paint is never worn by women except in mourning, but we will find reds and yellows that will make you beautiful." She reached out and ran her hand down Moriah's hair, which was not braided and hung below her waist. "We will start using ochre in your hair to give it color."

Ethan was standing to one side watching the ear piercing silently. He was fourteen months old now, and like most Comanche children, he had learned the habit of silence. Moriah could not understand how this would happen, but she knew that it was true. Ethan had cried like any white child at first, but somehow binding one onto the cradle board did something to them that she could not fathom.

Loves The Night saw Moriah glancing at Ethan and nodded. "He will be a great chief of The People. He has some of his father and some of you."

Moriah knew what she said was true. Ethan's features did have some of Bear Killer's appearance—the high cheekbones and the wide mouth made Moriah think of the man who called her his wife. Ethan was much fairer, however, than any of the other children, taking his coloration, apparently, from Moriah herself. She looked over and saw that Loves The Night was staring at Ethan. She knew that the woman loved him almost as if he were her own. It pleased her, and she said, "I want him to be a good man."

Loves The Night suddenly looked at Moriah. "Will he serve the Jesus God or the gods of The People?"

Moriah could not answer, for the religion of the Comanches seemed strange indeed to her. From what she had learned, they worshiped the world of nature. Gods were everywhere, and it was so confusing that she had given up trying to understand it all.

Her own faith had grown stronger. It was the world inside that she kept inviolate from the indignities of the life that were forced upon her among The People. As soon as the shock of her captivity had worn off, she had vowed to God she would be faithful. And every day she prayed to Him to deliver her, and every day she spoke English to Ethan, determined that he would know English words.

"He will serve the Jesus God," she said firmly.

At once Loves The Night said, "Tell me again how the Jesus God died."

The story of the death of Jesus fascinated the Indian woman. She was shocked the first time Moriah had shared her faith, but since then many times she had made this same request. "Tell me how the Jesus God died."

Patiently, Moriah spoke of the death of Jesus, and she saw a longing in Loves The Night's eyes.

"Why did the Jesus God die?"

"Because He loves us. His father, the Great Spirit, loves us, and He sent His Son to become a man like all men, and as a man He died for the sins of everyone."

"He does not know me. How could He know my sins?"

"He knows everything about us. Every Indian, every white person, everyone in the whole world. And Jesus loves everyone."

Loves the Night sat for a long time as Moriah continued to speak of the love of Jesus for sinners. Finally, she said, "It would be good. I wish I had this Jesus."

"You can have Him," Moriah said simply.

"How? Do I bring Him a sacrifice?"

"He has said that the sacrifice He wants is a humble heart, and that anyone who believes in Him can ask forgiveness and receive it."

Moriah waited breathlessly, and Loves The Night said, "I will think on this."

Moriah felt a glow of happiness. She said no more, for she had learned enough of the Comanche mind to know that Loves The Night would ponder the words she had heard.

The two women heard a babbling outside the tent, and they rose and went outside, followed by Ethan. Loves The Night whispered, "I never saw children like that. They're black!"

Indeed, there were three black children tied together at the neck with a slip of rawhide. Their captors were Pawnees, and the two women listened as they spoke of their pride in their capture.

"Have you ever seen black people before?"

"Many times," Moriah said. She felt a tug of compassion for the children who were frightened out of their wits. She wanted to go to them and comfort them, but they were the captives of the Pawnee, and Bear Killer would never permit that. She turned away grieved, knowing that the fate of the three would not be good. They would suffer more than she had.

Bear Killer had seen her, and he came to her as she moved away. "We will move tomorrow," he said, watching her intently.

"As you say."

"Why do you never smile? I never see you laugh." He waited, but she gave no answer. "They call you the Quiet One even to me."

Moriah had no words to say. She had told Bear Killer shortly after her captivity that she would not be a good wife for him. She had urged him to take her for a ransom, but he had been adamantly against it. And he still was. "You will become a woman of The People. It may take a long time, but you will forget your life from before."

Moriah turned and faced him squarely. "I will not forget," she said.

Bear Killer knew how to fight men, but he had no way to fight this woman. He said, "We will entertain the Pawnee."

"Yes, as you say."

Moriah had helped Dove and Loves The Night feed the Pawnees. They had gambled until very late, and both Dove and Loves The Night had gone to sleep. Moriah was restless as she lay there listening. One of the Pawnee spoke Comanche, and she was shocked suddenly to hear him say, "There were two of them as we have heard. Tall Man and Silverhair."

Instantly, Moriah grew still. Bear Killer said, "Where did you see them?"

"To the south."

"That is where I captured her, on the river called the Brazos."

"These two are killers, and there may be others. The men in black coats that have pistols that fire many times, they will come for the woman, the Quiet One."

"I will not give her up."

"Better you should go kill all the men of that family."

Bear Killer did not answer, and they did not speak anymore of the two, but Moriah knew the truth. She reached over and took Ethan in her arms. "It's Brodie and Quaid," she whispered. She thought of Brodie as a very young boy, but he was a man now, very tall. And Quaid, she thought of him, whom she had hated, and now he was risking his life trying to find her. She remembered his silver hair but could not remember what his face looked like.

Finally, Moriah, captive of The People, hugged Ethan, who was almost a year and a half old now, and she whispered, "They will find us, Ethan! Brodie and Quaid, they will find us! God will lead them to us! . . ."

PART FIVE:

DELIVERANCE

CHAPTER
TWENTY-SIX

A s Al Stuart rode up to the front yard of the Taliferro house, she glanced around quickly but saw no sign of Clinton. She stepped to the ground in one easy motion, tied her horse to the rail, then walked over to where Clay was standing with a rope around the head of the small roan. The twins were sitting on the back of the horse, Sam in front and Rachel behind. As soon as they saw her, they started calling her name, and Clay turned around.

"Whoa up there, Buster!" The horse stopped obediently, and Al approached with a smile.

"You've got two fine future hands for Star Ranch, Mr. Taliferro."

"Why, these young'uns of mine beat hens a-pacin'." Clay grinned. He moved over to the pair, ruffled their hair, and said affectionately, "You two are about ready to tackle a wild bronco." Turning, he grinned and said, "This is their birthday, Al. Four years I've had to put up with these sorry critters."

"They're fine-lookin' young'uns," Al smiled. "They look just like their daddy."

"Shucks, I hope not!" Clay exclaimed. "There's enough problems in this world without two ugly young'uns around."

Al smiled, for she had watched the pride that Clay had in his children for some time. "I brought back the bowls that your wife sent food over with."

"Why, you take 'em right on inside. How is your grandma?"

"Not too well. We keep hopin', but she don't seem to get no better. She was feeling fine for a long spell, but for the last year, she's been seeming to get worse." She looked around and said, "Is Clinton on the place?"

"Why no, he ain't." Clay shook his head and looked somewhat uncomfortable.

"He asked me to come over and go huntin' with him. Where might he be?"

"Well, he went to town, Al. He's havin' supper with the Abbots." Clay saw something cross Al's face then and said quickly, "I expect it slipped his mind. That boy's plumb forgetful."

"Oh, it's okay. We can go some other time. I'll just take these bowls in."

Al crossed the yard and knocked on the door, and almost at once Mary Aidan was there. "Hi, Al. Come on in," she said. At the age of twelve, Mary Aidan Hardin was all arms and legs, a bundle of energy, who had one pitch used for every statement—at the top of her lungs. "Ma," she yelled, "Al's here."

"Will you stop yelling, Mary Aidan! You're gonna deafen me. Come on in, Al, and set. I got some coffee on the stove."

"Oh no, ma'am. I just brought these here bowls back. Shore do thank you for all the fine grub you sent over."

Jerusalem took the bowls but kept her eyes on Al's face. She had developed a liking for the young girl—and a sympathy. Aldora Stuart only wore two outfits, oversized men's clothes that enveloped her, with a hat pulled down clear to her ears, or on Sundays for church she would wear a too-large, shapeless, faded brown dress that evidently had belonged to someone else. Her blond hair was beautiful and glossy when clean, but she took little care with it usually, just twisting it up in a bun or braiding it in pigtails. She had none of the graces of a young woman and did most of the work at her grandparents' place. Glancing down at her hands, Jerusalem saw that Aldora's hands were tanned and looked hard as any working man's. "I got some gingerbread ready to take out of the oven. It won't be more than ten minutes."

"I'll entertain her, Ma," Mary Aidan said.

"Watch out for this one. She'd talk the horns off of a steer."

As Jerusalem went to the other room to check on the gingerbread, Mary Aidan began to pepper Al with questions. She had an insatiable curiosity and had no inhibitions at all about the nature of her questions. No sooner had Al sat down than Mary Aidan sat down across the table from her and said, "How come you got a boy's name, Al? Did your ma and pa want a boy and couldn't have one, so they gave you a boy's name?"

"My name's Aldora. My pa's name was Al, and ma's name was Dora, so they made it up."

"Does it bother you that people call you Al?"

"No, not a bit."

"How come you always wear a man's clothes? Don't you like to wear dresses?"

"It's hard to wear dresses when you're plowin' or doin' other hard work."

Mary Aidan kept up her barrage of questions until finally Jerusalem came over with a pan filled with warm gingerbread. "Will you shush for just one minute, Mary Aidan! If you don't, I won't give you any gingerbread." The threat silenced Mary Aidan, and she sat there until she got her piece of gingerbread, which she stuffed into her mouth as if someone were going to snatch it from her.

Al ate more daintily and asked finally, "Have you heard anything about your daughter?"

"No, Quaid and Brodie are still out lookin' for her. It's been hard. She's been gone a long time, but I pray every day that they find her."

Mary Aidan swallowed the last of her gingerbread and said, "Ma, can I have another piece?"

"Just one, and no more." Mary Aidan quickly ate another piece and then began talking about Lucy Abbot. "I don't like her," she said loudly. "She thinks she's smarter than anybody else. I don't know why Clinton wants to run around with her for. I don't think boys have very much sense about girls, do you?"

Al smiled and said, "I don't know about things like that."

Jerusalem listened as Mary Aidan kept her incessant questioning going, and finally when she had half of the gingerbread up in a pan and covered with a cloth, she handed it to Al and said, "I'll be over to see your grandma sometime tomorrow."

"Thanks, Mrs. Taliferro."

As soon as Al left, Jerusalem turned and said sternly, "Mary Aidan, I want you to stop asking so many questions."

"Well, how am I gonna learn if I don't ask questions?" Without waiting for an answer, she said, "I wish I was a boy."

"Why would you wish a thing like that?"

"I think they get to do more stuff than girls."

"Most of that 'stuff' they do don't need to be done, anyhow. Now, you come on. We've got washin' to do. . . ."

As Professor Fergus St. John Nightingale III pulled into Jordan City, he attracted as much attention as if he were a Fourth of July parade with an elephant. The lead wagon was enough to catch every eye, for it was furnished with what appeared to be a silk canopy of brilliant red. Actually it was canvas, but it had been coated with a dye that made it glimmer in the sun.

Nightingale himself was six feet two but weighed less than a hundred and fifty pounds. He was wearing a pair of fine brown trousers, a white shirt with a tie, and a top hat that would have done justice to any gentleman in London at the opera. Pulling up in front of the Golden Lady Saloon, Fergus turned and descended to the ground as limber as a spider and reached up with his hand. A young Indian woman wearing a beautifully textured, white deerskin dress stepped to the ground. She had a smooth light complexion for an Indian woman, and her eyes were beautifully shaped. Every man within seeing distance stopped immediately and turned to look at her. "Come down, my dear," he said. "It's time for refreshment." He turned and said, "James, find a place to stable the horses. Wynona and I will be in the Golden Lady Saloon. Then get yourself something to eat."

"Very well, Sir Fergus."

"Come along, my dear. Time for liquid refreshment." He opened the door, and the woman named Wynona stepped inside, and immediately every man in the saloon turned to stare at her. Some of them knew Fergus Nightingale, and all who did were puzzled by him. He was a titled nobleman from England who was fascinated by Comanche Indians. He had practically gone to live with them, learning their language, their customs, and their diet with the aim of writing a book about them.

Julie came over, smiling. "Why, Fergus, you're back!" She put her hand out, and Fergus, instead of shaking it, bowed gracefully and lifted it to his lips.

"Why, you look more beautiful than ever, my dear."

"You flatterer! When did you get in?"

"Just now. Oh, may I introduce to you Wynona. Wynona, this is one of Jordan City's premier subjects, Miss Julie Satterfield."

"How do you do, Wynona?"

Wynona had been unsmiling, but now a smile touched the corners of her lips. "How do you do?" She spoke carefully, pronouncing each word and studying Julie carefully. "I am pleased to meet you."

"Well, Fergus, come and have some refreshments."

The three sat down at a table, and Fergus ordered champagne, but there being none, he settled for a more Texas-style drink. He ordered a soft drink for Wynona, and she made no comment.

"Wynona is my teacher," he said solemnly, but humor danced in his eyes. "She's been teaching me the language and customs of the Comanche."

Julie laughed. "Well, I'll bet you never picked an ugly teacher, only a pretty one."

"Oh, I assure you, my dear Julie, I have only a platonic interest in this young lady."

"What's platonic mean?"

"Why, we're just good friends. Like David and Jonathan, don't you know? I'm just about finished collecting material, so I'm ready to start my book." He downed his drink as if it were spring water, then said, "What about the Hardins?"

"Well, Clay and Jerusalem have twins. They're just four years old and doing fine. Clay's dotty over them. You'd think nobody ever had a child before. I don't think he credits Jerusalem with having much to do with their existence."

"How about the ranch?"

"Oh, it's much bigger now. They nearly doubled the size of it. Got a big piece of land for almost nothing after they sold a big herd in New Orleans."

"And Miss Moriah? Any word?"

"No. Brodie and Quaid are still looking. Wearing themselves out the last year riding all over creation." Julie went on to speak of the rest of the family, when suddenly Hack Wilson, one of Skull's punchers, came over. Wilson was a regular customer, a hard drinker, and typical of Skull's riders. He stood there staring at Wynona and reached over and squeezed her arm.

"Good-lookin' squaw you got here, Englishman. Where'd you get her? I might want one like her myself."

Fergus came out of his chair and said frostily, "If you would please remove your hand, it would be greatly appreciated."

Wilson ignored him, and his hand caressed Wynona's arm. "What do you say I rent this one out? She wouldn't—"

Julie was watching, but it happened so quickly she had barely time to catch the action. A full long-neck bottle of whiskey was on the table, and Fergus reached out, lifted it high in the air, and brought it down full force on Wilson's head. He did it with no more emotion than if he had been swatting a fly. The bottle broke and left a bloody track down Wilson's face as he collapsed. He fell to the floor and didn't move.

Julie laughed and called out, "Charlie, throw this trash outside, will you, please?"

"Why, sure, Miss Julie."

Charlie Hendricks came over, grabbed one arm, and simply dragged Wilson outside. There was a slight crash as he hit the sidewalk, and Charlie came in with a big grin on his face.

Fergus looked at Wynona and said, "Pay no attention to that ill-mannered cretin, my dear."

"I hope you killed him!" she said.

"Not very likely. His head's probably the hardest part of him." Fergus turned and studied Julie for a moment. "I've thought about you considerably, my dear, since I've been gone."

Julie smiled at Wynona. "I'll bet you didn't think much, not with this young lady around."

"Oh, but I have." Suddenly, Fergus Nightingale grew serious. "You're not happy."

Julie shrugged. "I don't guess I deserve to be happy."

"You were made for better things than working in a saloon, Miss Julie Satterfield."

Julie did not know what to make of Nightingale, nor did anyone else. She stared at him, trying to find the hidden meaning of his words and decided that he meant exactly what he said.

"Well," she said, "you'll be happy to hear that I've been going to church."

"Splendid! Glad to hear it!"

"I lost a bet with Rice Morgan, so I have to go." She laughed. "I really do it to irritate the congregation. Last Sunday I took five of the worst drunks you've ever seen. Got them sobered up enough to move, and then we all walked in right in the middle of the sermon. Rice didn't miss a word, but some of the congregation got upset about it. I know that was wrong. I won't do it again."

Nightingale looked at her intensely, pondering his thoughts, then said, "I'm not a very religious man myself, Miss Julie, but I see something in you that God wants and that He can use. Well, come along, Wynona. We'll go eat and then get us rooms in the finest hotel in Jordan City. Since there is only one, I know what it will be."

Julie sat there as the two left, thinking of what Fergus had said. She had confessed it to no one, but although she went to church complaining, Rice Morgan's preaching had stirred her more than she wanted to admit. She had tried to shake it off, but she couldn't. *What could be in me that God would want?* she thought bitterly, then poured a drink and downed it quickly.

Dinner at the Abbots was an awkward event for Clinton. He had managed to finagle an invitation, and now as he sat there, he felt totally out of place. Donald Abbot owned the bank, and his wife had come from the top of St.

Louis society. The Abbots had only the cream of Jordan City society for visitors to dinner, and Clinton had been silent most of the night except to answer a few questions.

The meal itself was very fine, and a maid served it expertly, but Clinton had been confused at which fork to use. He had secretly watched Lucy and imitated her actions.

"And what are your goals, Clinton?" Donald Abbot asked. He was a small dapper man with a large mustache, and he kept his eyes fixed on Clinton, as if the young man were a bug under a microscope. "What are your goals?" he repeated when Clinton did not answer.

"Well, sir, I reckon I'll keep on punchin' cows." This seemed to be a reasonable enough ambition to Clinton. The ranch was getting bigger all the time. Clay had told him that in ten years they might well have the biggest ranch in all of Texas. "That's what I do best, I guess."

Mrs. Abbot stared at the young man and said, "But surely you have higher ambition than to be a cow puncher?"

"Oh, Mother, Clinton's parents own a fine ranch. They're adding to it all the time, and I suppose Clinton will own it one day," Lucy said.

"Well, I don't know about that," Clinton said hurriedly. "There's quite a bunch of us to divide it up, and I got an older brother named Brodie. He'd probably get the ranch if anything happened to Ma and Pa."

Donald Abbot stared at the young man without speaking for a moment, then changed the subject. Clinton knew that somehow he had been crossed off the list of suitors that the Abbots would approve, and the thought depressed him.

The rest of the evening was a failure. He sat in the parlor across the room from Lucy while Mr. and Mrs. Abbot sat together on a couch. The three of them seemed to do most of the talking, and Clinton could not think of a single thing to say. Finally, the Abbots excused themselves, and Clinton noticed they did not speak of his coming back again. As soon as they left, he turned to Lucy and said, "I guess I didn't make much of an impression on your folks."

"Oh, they just don't know you very well."

Lucy came over and sat down beside Clinton, and he was fascinated with her. She was a blond-haired, blue-eyed beauty, wearing the latest fashions from the East, and the faint aura of her perfume seemed to make him dizzy. He reached over and took her hand. She did not resist, and then taking his courage in both hands, he did what he had wanted to do the first time he saw her. He put his arms around her and, pulling her close, kissed her. Her lips were soft beneath his, and her perfume seemed to be an incense that intoxicated his feelings.

But Lucy pulled away all at once, saying, "Oh, you mustn't do that, Clinton!"

"Why not?"

"Just because." Lucy Abbot, as a matter of fact, was an accomplished tease. She had learned at a much earlier age how to make men desire her. She would coyly let them pursue her with their attentions, and then she'd push them away at the moment when they were most stirred.

Clinton did not know how to behave with Lucy. He had been interested in several of the local girls and felt very much at home with them, but with Lucy he was almost tongue-tied. Finally, he said, "I'd like to take you to that dance next week, Lucy."

"Oh, I'm sorry, Clinton. I've already agreed to go with Tom Ellis."

"Tom Ellis!"

"Yes. You should have asked me earlier, Clinton."

Clinton got to his feet. "Well, I don't know how much earlier I have to ask. What about next year?"

"Don't be angry," she said softly. She came and pressed herself against him and put her hand along his cheek. "I really like you, but Tom asked first. I'll save you a dance. Maybe two." Clinton started to put his arms around her, but she stepped back and whispered, "You'd better go now. It's getting late."

"All right. You save me them dances now."

"Oh, I will."

Clinton left the house feeling confused and upset. As he stepped onto his horse, he stared at the Abbot house and said loudly, "Well, Tom Ellis, you might as well step aside because I'm gonna beat your time!" Turning the horse around, he kicked the animal into a dead run as he left Jordan City. When he was almost halfway home, a thought came to him, and he spoke aloud again, "Shoot, I was supposed to take Al huntin'! Forgot all about it. Well, I'll make it up to her . . ."

CHAPTER
TWENTY-SEVEN

Clinton had finished dressing for the dance and now stood in the center of his room trying to think if he had left anything out. He had begun getting ready almost in midafternoon. Taking baths had not been one of his favorite habits, but he had heated water and taken a bath in the big tub, which he had moved into his bedroom. He had lathered with a great deal of the soft soap that his mother made and then had shaved carefully, as if getting every hair down to the level of the skin was an all important thing. He had given particular attention to his hair, anointing it with Macassar oil and plastering it close to his skull. To crown all this, he had put on a special lotion guaranteed to charm the birds out of the trees, then had dressed in new clothes that he had kept for such an occasion. He had no large mirror, but looking down, he admired the gray trousers, the snowy white shirt, the carefully tied string tie, and the multicolored vest that would have done honor to a gambler on a Mississippi riverboat!

Carefully, he picked up his new light brown leather hat and set it squarely on his head. "Well, now, that ought to do it," he said, feeling satisfied with the results. He stepped outside of his room, turned down the hall, and as soon as he stepped into the big room, as they called it, Bob, the big dog, came out of a sound sleep and approached him stiff-legged, his lips drawn back exposing bright, sharp teeth and uttering a ferocious, deep-pitched growl.

"Well, I swear to my never!" Clay exclaimed, putting down the paper he had been reading. "If you don't look like the big dog at the meat house! Ol' Bob there don't even know ya. He thinks you're some kind of handsome stranger come in from Chicago."

"Shut up, Bob!" Clinton said sharply. "Go somewhere and go to sleep." Bob hung his head when he recognized Clinton and came over and tried to sit on his feet. "Get off of my new boots, you no-account hound!"

Clay had gotten up and was walking around Clinton with obvious admiration. "Wife, look at this boy. Wouldn't that cock your pistol?"

Jerusalem said at once, "You leave him alone, Clay." Getting up, she walked over and stood in front of Clinton. "You look just fine, son. Your new clothes fit like a glove."

Mary Aidan had come over and now wrinkled up her nose. "What's that I smell?"

Clinton stared at her with indignation. "That's me! I ordered that lotion all the way from Buffalo, New York."

"Well, it stinks!"

"You hush, girl," Jerusalem said. "It does not stink. It smells fine."

Zane had been working on a new sheath for his knife, for he was very good at leatherwork. Now, from where he sat, he shaded his tone with admiration. "Why, you look pretty as a speckled pup under a wagon, Clinton. Danged if you don't! You're gonna have to fight them girls off with a stick. And what's more, if you drop dead, we won't have to do a thing to you but stick a lily in your hand."

"You all leave him alone," Jerusalem said sharply. "I wish the rest of you paid as much attention to your appearance as Clinton does. You go on and have a good time at the dance, son."

Clay was not through. He grinned and said, "I ain't sure all that ornament is scriptural, Clinton. You may be committin' a sin by dressin' up that fancy."

"You hush, Clay," Jerusalem said. "Clinton, I want you to take some food by the Stuart place. Anne Stuart isn't doing well at all."

"Sure, Ma." Clinton looked around at his tormentors and said, "Blessed are ye when you are persecuted for righteousness sake." He took the food from his mother and walked with righteous indignation out the door.

Clinton took the food by the Stuarts and was met by Caleb. "Ma sent this food by, Mr. Stuart."

"Why, that was right thoughty of her, Clinton. Won't you come in and set?"

"No, I got to get on. I'm going to a dance."

Stuart said, "What's that I smell?"

"That's *me*," Clinton said with intense satisfaction. "Lotion come all the way from Buffalo, New York."

"Well, it's mighty fine."

"How's Mrs. Stuart?"

"She ain't too pert, son. I done sent Al into town to get some more medicine from Doctor Wood."

"Well, I'll ask the preacher to come by and pray for your wife. He's right good at prayin' for sick folk."

"I appreciate that, son."

Rice Morgan was sitting in his room, his Bible on his lap, but his eyes were closed. He had been praying for various members of his church, for he was aware that many of them needed it. He knew that he hung on to his position as pastor by a very slim majority and that he very likely would not be pastor for much longer. A number of the church members were outraged at the people he would invite from the saloons to come hear the gospel. In fact, the last time some of them had walked into the church, a few church members had up and walked out.

As he sat there in the stillness, not praying exactly, he waited for a time for something to come into his heart. He had discovered that he often got closer to God by listening than by talking. He heard the sounds of wagons passing in the street outside, people calling greetings to one another. From far away came the sound of a pistol shot, muffled but definite, but he paid no heed to any of those.

Finally, after a long time, he began to speak to the Lord aloud. It was a habit he had formed, for he had discovered that if he prayed aloud, his mind was less likely to wander. "Lord," he said, "I've been praying for a long time for You to give me a companion, and I just have to admit to You, Lord—which You already know—that I'm lonely. I don't want to run ahead of You, but a man needs a wife and children. You haven't said I couldn't have them, so I ask You right now to give me some kind of a promise. Whatever it is, Lord, if I'm not to have a wife and that's Your will, so be it. But if You can give me a great gift like that, a family, I'd be grateful."

He sat there as still as a statue for a long time, and then he opened his eyes and looked down at his Bible. An impulse came to him, and he shoved it away, but it returned again and then a third time. He had learned over long experience that when something kept returning, it sometimes came from God. He laid his hand on the Bible and struggled with the impulse. "Lord, I know so many who have tried to find guidance by reading the Bible and taking what they find when they open it as a sign. That never seemed right to me. I've always felt like searching the Scriptures. But I've been searching the Scriptures and praying for a long time, and You haven't given me an answer. So, I may be losing my senses, but I'm goin' to open the Bible. Lord, it would be very fine, and very proud I'd be, if You'd lead me to some verse that would help me." He put his hands on the Bible and hesitated. "Right you! Now, open it." He opened the Bible and stared down at it. He had turned to the book of Hosea. He read aloud the first verse, then part of the second verse, and then broke off. He read the third verse, "'So he went and took Gomer the daughter of Diblaim; which conceived and bare him a son.'"

A hope came to Rice then as he sat there with the Bible open before him. He knew the book of Hosea very well and had often been touched by the history in it. The prophet Hosea had had a wife who had gone away from him with other men, had become a harlot, in fact, but God had said in the third verse that Hosea was to go take this woman, for she was his wife.

Rice sat there, saying nothing aloud, but reading the verses over and over again. Finally, he closed the Bible and held it in his hands, his head bowed. He closed his eyes and said, "Well, Lord, I may be wrong, but I'm going to take this as a word from You that I am to marry Julie Satterfield! If I'm wrong, please strike me dead or do something to head me off!" He got up then, tucked the Bible under his arm, and left his room, headed for the Golden Lady Saloon.

Julie stood looking out the window, not that there was anything that she cared to see, but she had grown tired of lying on the bed, staring at the ceiling. Lately, she had been feeling that her life was missing something. Sure, there was always the excitement of the saloons, the men, the drinking, but it wasn't the same anymore. She had gone to hear Rice preach once with some of her friends from the saloon, and one thought had stuck with her. Rice had said that Jesus had come to give life to the fullest. *My life is full, but not with the right things,* she mused as her mind wandered. She watched as a freighter tried to replace a wheel that had come off of his wagon. His cursing filled the air but did not seem to help with the work. The streets of Jordan City were half full now. She knew there was a dance somewhere in town, but she had no interest in going.

Abruptly, Julie turned and went over to the dresser. She was wearing a thin robe tied with a sash over her gown, and she leaned over and looked into the mirror over her dressing table. The left side of her face was discolored, and her eye was almost closed. She stared at it, filled with disgust at what had happened, when suddenly a knock drew her attention. She had asked for some hot water to be sent to her room, and thinking it was Eddy bringing it, she went to the door, but when she opened it, she saw Rice Morgan standing there.

Quickly, Julie turned the bruised side of her face away and asked sharply, "What do you want, Rice?"

"I need to talk to you."

Instantly, Julie said, "Is somebody hurt in my family?"

"No, it's not that."

Julie started to close the door. "I don't want any of your preaching, Rice. I've heard enough of it."

"I didn't come for that," Rice said. "May I come in for a minute?"

Julie struggled, then shrugged. "If you want to, I suppose." She turned and went over to the sofa and sat down.

As Rice entered, he ran his eyes around the room. Julie had taken two rooms that made a suite, the bedroom in one side and then a sitting room in the other. The lamp was not on, for it was not completely dark outside, and the last pale vestiges of the afternoon sun cast its golden shadows over the room. Tiny mites swirled in the pale sunbeams, and Rice noticed that Julie was behaving rather strangely. He went over and stood beside her and said, "May I sit down beside you?"

"If you want to, I suppose."

Rice saw that she kept her face averted. He sat down and said what he had come to say. "I'm a very lonely man, Julie."

The words hit Julie with a force that surprised her. She was so shocked she turned to face him, forgetful of the sight she must have made with her closed eye. "So, you're *lonely*," she said bitterly. "I thought you were the one man in the world who would never come to me like this! How many 'lonely' men have I had crying on my shoulder? You almost had me going, Rice, with all this preaching of yours, and to tell the truth—well, I was beginning to think there was something to all of it. And now you come here like this!"

Rice's face changed only when he saw the bruises and the closed eye. "What happened?"

"Oh, this?" Julie said bitterly. "Another *lonely* man came in here. I had to fight him off, so he hit me."

"Julie, when I say I'm lonely, I don't mean anything like that." He sat there quietly, trying to put his thoughts together, and finally said, "I never have anyone to talk to. When I've taken a beating, or made a fool out of myself, or when I'm scared out of my wits, who am I going to tell it to? I don't have anyone."

Julie was shocked at his words. "Rice, I never think of you as being scared or making a fool out of yourself."

Rice smiled, yet there was a bitterness in it. "There is soft you are, Julie! I'd hate for you to know all the things I do. We're all of us, every man and woman in the world, frightened about something. We're scared, and we all make fools out of ourselves from time to time. Me especially."

Rice continued to speak, not looking at Julie, but she was staring at him. Finally, he turned to her, lifted his head, and a wry smile turned the corners of his lips. "God took one look at man, and he said, 'Adam, you need help,' and He was right, Julie."

Julie Satterfield had been pursued by men since she was in her early teens. A bitterness filled her now as she realized that she had not followed the right path. Her past was always a specter that haunted her at night when she was alone. This was one reason why she drank—to cover up and obliterate the memories of what she had been and what she had become. Now, as she listened to Rice, she was amazed to find that he had weaknesses—the same weaknesses in some ways that she had, for she, too, was afraid.

"What do you want me to do, Rice? I can't even help myself." Rice seemed to straighten, and she saw a steadfastness in his eyes.

"I want you to marry me," he said plainly.

Julie thought she had not understood Rice. She stared at him and couldn't speak, and then she laughed bitterly. "Why, you're crazy, Rice! I'm a saloon woman. They'd throw you out of church!"

"That would be their problem, not mine."

Julie suddenly stood up, and Rice rose with her. She could not think clearly. Other men had asked her to marry them, but they had been as depraved as she felt herself to be. She knew Rice Morgan was a good man, good to the bone, that he was steadfast and honorable, and that a woman could depend on him to the very end of life.

Rice reached out gently and took Julie by the shoulders. He turned her around and pulled her closer. He did not kiss her on the lips but kissed her bruised face very gently, almost like the touch of a butterfly. She had not known much gentleness like this. As she stared into his eyes, she felt something that moved her deeply. He accepted her and loved her just as she was with no judgment.

"I need you, Julie, in every way. I want to wake up every morning of my life and see your face, and I want to know you love me all that day. I want to hold a child in my arms someday, and I want to see your beauty in our child's face. I want us to grow old together, and when your hair is white and I've lost all mine, I want to hold on to you and have you hold on to me in love."

Julie was absolutely shocked into immobility. She could not move. She waited for him to say more. She waited for him to kiss her, and the thought came to her, *This is some new kind of a trick!*

But Rice released her and said, "I'll wait for your answer, and I know it will come one day." He turned and walked to the door, but before he left, he turned and faced her, and then he smiled. "If you could ever come to love me, Julie Satterfield, I'd count myself a king among men."

He turned and shut the door behind him, and Julie stared after him. Then suddenly her shoulders began to shake. Tears filled her eyes and rolled down her cheeks. She made her way into the bedroom, fell across the bed, and pressed her face into the coverlet, her entire body shaking as she wept with an abandon such as she had never known.

Clinton stepped off of his horse, tied him to a hitching rail, and then started down the streets of Jordan City. He was excited about going to the dance, and Lucy, who had promised him one or two dances, didn't know that he intended to have far more than that. As he came by the stairway that led up to Doctor Woods' office, he saw someone coming down and turned to see it was Al. "Hello, Al," he said. "I stopped by and took some food for your grandma."

"Thanks, Clinton. Your mother is always good about that."

Clinton saw the sadness on the girl's face and impulsively laid his hand on her shoulder. She looked rather pathetic in the baggy clothes she insisted on wearing, and he bent down to peer at her face. "Now looky here. It'll be all right, Al. Why, I'm goin' by to ask Brother Morgan to pray for your grandma."

"Thanks, Clinton."

Al's voice was so miserable that Clinton felt a wave of compassion. He had always liked Al, and now he put his arm around her and squeezed her. "It's gonna be all right. You wait and see!"

Just at that moment a voice came to him, and Clinton looked up to see Tom Ellis, who was walking down the street with Lucy, headed for the dance. The two had stopped, and Clinton felt uneasy about having his arm around Al's shoulder. He dropped it at once, but Tom Ellis was laughing.

"I'm glad you got yourself a girl there, Clinton." He turned and said, "Lucy, Clinton's got himself a woman. You'd better watch out, or you're going to have competition."

Ellis was an overbearing oaf as far as Clinton was concerned. He was large and heavy and had a tiny mustache that made him look like an idiot—or so Clinton had always thought.

Ellis leaned forward and peered at Al and said, "Where'd you buy your dress, girlie?"

Clinton sensed Al's tensing and glanced down at her face and saw embarrassment and shame there. Anger rushed through Clinton, and he said, "Ellis, you got a big mouth. Keep it closed, or I'll close it for you."

"Why, you're a preacher, ain't ya? But you'd better get your sweetie lookin' more like a lady before you come to the dance."

Clinton stepped forward and grabbed Ellis by the shirt front. "I told you to shut up!"

Ellis hit Clinton in the chest, and Clinton fell backward. He heard Lucy scream, but that was all he heard, for the temper that he worked to control suddenly spilled over. He threw himself at Ellis, struck him in the middle of the body, and wrapped his arms around him. The two of them hit the hitching rail, and it snapped beneath their combined weight. The force of Clinton's plunging attack drove Ellis backward, and the back of his knees hit the edge of the large horse trough.

"Hey, you—" Ellis yelled, but then he fell into the horse trough with Clinton on top of him. The tremendous splash of their bodies rose up and engulfed Lucy, who caught the force of it right in her face and down the front of her dress.

The shock of the water brought Clinton to himself. He scrambled out sopping wet and saw Lucy standing there, her mouth open, uttering a soundless scream.

"Lucy," he said, "I didn't mean—"

"You stay away from me, Clinton Hardin!"

Ellis was scrambling out, too, and yelling, and he started for Clinton, but at that instant Rice suddenly appeared. He put a hand on Ellis' chest and held him there. "What's this all about?"

Ellis was shouting, and Rice could make no sense of what he said. He looked over and saw Clinton dripping wet with Al Stuart standing by, her eyes large under the shadow of the broad-brimmed hat she wore. "What's this all about? Who started it?"

Clinton sputtered, "Well, he used rude language to Al here. I can't abide rude behavior, Rice. You know that."

Al suddenly pulled a big red bandanna from her hip pocket, a grin on her face. She extended it to Lucy, saying, "You need to borrow my hand-kerchief? It ain't big enough to dry you all off, but maybe you can get your face clean."

Lucy glared at her, then whirled and started away at a run. Ellis took off after her. "I'll take you home, Lucy." He yelled back, "I'll get you, Clinton. You see if I don't!"

Rice stared at the two and by supreme effort was able to keep from laughing at the scene. "You'd better come up to my room and dry off, Clinton."

"No, I ain't gonna do it. I'm goin' home."

Rice watched as Clinton stalked away, the water squishing out of his boots. As the young man got on his horse and rode out of town, Rice turned and said, "Well, that was unpleasant, wasn't it, Aldora?"

"I guess it was. He was takin' up for me, though."

"I'm sure he was. Look, why don't you ride after him? Maybe you can talk to him and make him feel better."

"Yes, sir, I'll do that."

She got on her own horse and took off after Clinton. She caught up with him when they were about two miles out of town, and when she came up beside him, he gave her a look such as she had never seen on his face.

To tell the truth, Clinton was mortified. He knew he had made a fool out of himself, but he refused to speak.

After they rode along in silence for a while, Al said in a small voice, "I'm right sorry I caused you trouble, Clinton."

Clinton gave his shoulders a shake, but he turned to her and shook his head. "It wasn't you, Al. It was that no-account Tom Ellis!"

"Well, anyway, I thank you for takin' up for me."

Clinton rode for a few moments without answering, and then he turned to her and managed a grin. "Well, I reckon you're almost as much a sister to me as Mary Aidan is. A fella's got to take up if a man insults his sister, ain't he now?"

Clinton expected Al to agree with this sentiment. It seemed reason-able enough to him, but she glared at him and said in a tight voice, "I *ain't* your sister, Clinton!"

Staring at her, Clinton shook his head. "Well, maybe not. But I couldn't stand it when he made fun of you."

Suddenly, Al laughed. It made a musical sound on the air. "It was somethin' to see you dunk that ol' Tom Ellis!"

Clinton was a bit shocked at how fast he had lost his temper, and now the memory amused him. "I've been wantin' to do somethin' like that for a long time."

The two of them rode along talking about the incident. Clinton was able to laugh, and Al's laughter made a counterpoint to his.

A wolf came out of the night with a lizard in his mouth. He stared at the two, his green eyes glowing beneath the moon. Seeing them, he turned and loped away into the darkness.

CHAPTER
TWENTY-EIGHT

The country that Brodie and Quaid moved through was lined with deep canyons and heavy strands of straight pines. The smell of the pines was rich, but as they traveled northward, they left the trees and came out into the great plains again. For two days now they had been aware that they were being trailed by a single rider. Quaid had spotted him first, and they had pulled up and waited for him to catch up, but the rider had simply hung back. The next day he had been there again, a dot that kept with their pace.

"Well, he ain't tryin' to hide, is he?" Brodie observed as they pulled up for camp on the second night. "He's been behind us all day there."

"He's come closer," Quaid said. "It's like he wanted to catch us, but he's afraid to."

"Well, there's just one of him, so I don't reckon he'll be that much trouble."

The two men unsaddled their horses, hobbled them, and then turned to the business of making supper. Both were wearing two pistols and cartridge belts, and their heavy rifles were in the saddle holsters. They had

ridden heavily armed so long that they were completely unaware of the
guns now, but they would have felt incomplete without them.

Brodie cooked up a supper of two prairie hens he had managed to
shoot. He had decided to broil them, since the meat would be tough and
stringy if they roasted too close to the fire. He found some narrow
branches with a crook in each one. He drove them into the ground away
from the fire so they wouldn't catch. Then he stripped a narrow branch
and pierced the hens and then hung them above the fire. The shadows
drew longer, and when the fowls were done, Brodie gave one of them to
Quaid, and the two sat back and began picking at the flesh. The birds were
soon devoured and Brodie observed, "We're gonna run out of salt pretty
soon."

Quaid did not answer but suddenly came to his feet. "He's comin'
in!"

Brodie leaped up, for he had heard the sound of a horse coming
toward them. Quickly, without saying a word, they moved apart, taking
cover with their guns half lifted.

A voice called out to them out of the darkness. Brodie said, "You
understand him, Quaid?"

"Yes, he's a Pawnee. Says for us not to shoot. " He lifted his voice and
said, "Come in slow."

Both men watched cautiously as the horseman came slowly forward
and pulled up ten feet away from the fire. He held one hand out in the
universal sign of peace and said again, "Do not shoot."

Quaid moved forward cautiously and saw that Brodie was staying
back. He approached the Indian, and by the light of the fire, he saw that
he was a short, squatty man with terrible scars on his chest. "Who are you?
Why have you been following us?" he asked in Pawnee.

"My name is Steals Many Horses." He sat there and looked around in
the direction of Brodie and waited until he came out, holding his gun
directly on the Indian.

"I think he's alone," Quaid said.

"What does he want?"

"I don't know. His name is Steals Many Horses. He's Pawnee, all
right. "Get down from your horse," Quaid said and waited until the
Indian got down. "We have a little food. You're welcome to it."

Steals Many Horses hobbled his horse, watching as the two men holstered their guns. He carried a knife in his belt, and on the saddle hung a bow with a quiver of arrows. He sat down and ate the meat that Brodie set before him, drank thirstily of the water, and then he said, "I have heard much of you. You are Silverhair, and you are Tall Man."

Quaid interpreted his words to Brodie, then said, "Why are you following us?"

"You seek the white woman, the captive of The People."

Quaid said, "He's talking about Moriah."

"Does he know where she is?" Brodie said tensely.

"What do you know about the white woman?" Quaid asked.

Steals Many Horses turned his eyes on Quaid. The Indian's scarred face was emotionless, but his dark eyes glittered. He was cautious, but finally he said, "Maybe I know."

"He knows where she is," Quaid said. "Don't show any excitement, though. He'll want to bargain for her." He spoke to the Indian, "Where is she, Steals Many Horses?"

He had expected no answer, and he got none. His experience in trading with the Indians had taught him that it was best not to rush them.

The fire crackled in the silence, and from far off a coyote howled, wailing his sad, mournful song. Steals Many Horses finally said, "I went on a raid with our warriors. We went to steal horses from The People." He paused, looked into the fire, and then shook his head. "It did not go well. Four of our warriors were killed."

Quaid did not take his eyes from Steals Many Horses. He knew that it was useless to hurry the man, and he listened as the Pawnee spoke of the raid.

"I was wounded," he said, "and captured. They were going to put me to the fire the next day, but I escaped that night."

Quaid waited until he had finished, then said, "What about the white captive woman?"

"They call her the Quiet One. I saw her. She had red hair, and she had eyes that were brown, and she had a scar by her eye here."

Quaid took a deep breath. "He's describing her. He knows about the scar on her face."

"She got that scar when she was six years old. Fell against a post and cut her face pretty bad." Brodie stood absolutely still. "That's got to be her!"

Quaid said, "Which tribe holds her, Steals Many Horses?"

"What will you give me if I tell? That is why I followed you."

Quaid had expected this. "What do you want?"

"I want one of your pistols that shoots many times, and I want many bullets for it."

At once Quaid unbuckled the cartridge belt with the pistol on it and handed it to Steals Many Horses.

"You're giving him your gun?" Brodie asked with surprise.

"That's his price. I'm not arguing," Quaid said. Turning to Steals Many Horses, he said, "I will teach you how to shoot it in the morning."

Steals Many Horses pulled the gun from the holster. He ran his hands over it, then looked up and said, "She is with Bear Killer."

"Bear Killer of The People?" Quaid said.

"Yes. He is a mighty warrior. He killed my brother, and he would have burned me. But I will kill him now that I have the pistol."

"Where are they, Steals Many Horses?"

"Bear Killer always winters in what white men call The Staked Plains. . . ."

Quaid listened as the Indian gave the location of the tribe. Steals Many Horses was still fascinated by the pistol. He put the belt around his waist and buckled it awkwardly and then looked up.

"You will not take the woman with only two of you. It will take many warriors. Bear Killer is well named."

"We will take her," Quaid said, and a hard finality edged his tone. "Will you sleep here?"

"No, I will go back now that I have the pistol." He got to his feet and walked to his horse. He slipped off the hobbles and in one smooth move mounted. For one second he looked at them and said, "You will not take Bear Killer unless you have many warriors." Without another word he turned, and the horse leaped forward, disappearing into the darkness.

"What did he say, Quaid?"

"He said the two of us wouldn't take a captive away from Bear Killer."

"Did he say where she was?"

"Llano Estacado."

"The Staked Plains." Brodie made a face. "I wish he was someplace else."

Quaid turned to face him. "I'd go after him if he was at the North Pole."

"I don't know, Quaid. I've heard he's got a big band. Maybe we need to go get some of the rangers to help us."

"We don't know where he is, Brodie. We've got to find him first then we'll see."

Moriah had worked with Dove and Loves The Night getting ready for the winter. They had picked wild plums, mesquite beans, sometimes wild cherries. They had added this to ground-up dried buffalo meat. The two of them had packed the mixture in the bladders of buffalo sealed with tallow. As she worked, she often thought of how much like canning garden vegetables this process was.

Bear Killer had gone to meet with a small group of chiefs of several tribes, and Lion had been left to guard the camp. Lion had been angered because he had not been permitted to go. He came in now to Bear Killer's teepee, where the three wives of Bear Killer worked, a scowl on his face, and snatched up one of the small bundles that Moriah had made and snapped, "This is bad work!" He threw it down, causing it to burst.

"There's nothing wrong with it, Lion," Loves The Night said. She knew that Lion hated the Quiet One and stood between the two of them as much as possible.

Lion merely laughed. "Pick it up, Quiet One, and do it again!" He had always believed that Bear Killer's white wife expected to be rescued. He stared at her with obsidian eyes for a moment, then said loudly, "Don't think about anybody coming after you. The Silverhair and the Tall Man, they are dead."

Moriah looked up at once and stared at him. Something she saw in his eyes made her say, "You are a liar. They are not dead."

Instantly, Lion stepped forward and swung his hand. It caught Moriah on the cheek. She staggered but did not go down.

Loves The Night stepped between the two. "I will see if you will beat Bear Killer when he hears of how you struck his wife!"

Lion glared at her and would have said more, but she suddenly drew a knife and said, "Leave here, or I'll cut your liver out!"

Lion stared at her with hatred but knew that he had gone too far. He turned abruptly and stalked away. As soon as he was out of the teepee, Moriah went to Loves The Night. She put her arms around the woman and said, "Thank you, sister."

"He is a coward. Pay him no heed. I will tell Bear Killer when he comes back—and we will see what will happen!"

The two women were finished with their work, so they sat down and from time to time looked over at Ethan, who was asleep on his pad of animals furs. Loves The Night said warmly, "He is a fine boy. He will bring you much joy."

"Do you think so, Loves The Night?"

"Yes. I have been watching him, and he has the strength of Bear Killer, but he has your gentleness." The two women sat there silently, and finally Loves The Night reached over and put her hand on Moriah's shoulder. "I've always watched you since you came. You are strong inside."

"I feel very weak."

"I want to ask you why you will not have our god." From the time of her capture, Moriah had never made any secret of the fact that she was not at all interested in the vague gods of The People. "You are true to your Jesus God?"

"I hope I am. He is the mighty God above all gods."

"Tell me about Him."

Moriah felt a sudden warmth for this woman who had become her dearest friend in this alien world. "He loves you. He loves everyone, and He wants for you to love Him."

"Tell me."

Moriah talked for a long time softly and gently. It was difficult to tell what impression she made, for Loves The Night did not show her emotion openly. But there was a glow in the woman's eyes, and Moriah prayed. *God, let her listen to my words and touch her heart.*

CHAPTER
TWENTY-NINE

Well, plague take it, Zane. You shore picked a sorry time to get piled up by a hoss!"

Zane looked up from where he was eating his bacon and eggs and frowned at Clay, who sat across from him. "I didn't exactly plan for it to happen like it did," he said petulantly. "If I remember correctly, you've been piled up by a few hosses yourself."

"Zane didn't get hurt on purpose, Clay, so leave him alone," Jerusalem said. She looked at Clinton, who was eating furiously, as if his life depended on it. "Don't eat so fast, Clinton, you'll choke yourself."

Clinton said with his mouth full, "But, Ma, the Lord might come back before we finish, and I'd hate to miss out on this here good food you made."

Mary Aidan was sitting next to Clinton and said, "You need to put on some more of that lotion you got from back east. It'll make you smell better."

Jerusalem said sharply, "If you'd take more baths, you wouldn't need any lotion to make you smell good!"

Clinton swallowed an enormous bite of his breakfast and then looked around the table defiantly. "It ain't scriptural to take baths."

"What are you talkin' about?" Jerusalem said. "Of course it is."

"No, the Bible says it ain't." He nodded vigorously, adding, "I got that out of the Bible."

Jerusalem shook her head in dismay. "You must have got it *out* of the Bible because you didn't find it *in* the Bible."

"Did too!"

"Well, where is it?" Clay grinned. "I might use it myself."

"It's in the last book of the whole Bible, chapter twenty-two and the eleventh verse."

"What does it say? I can't remember the whole Bible," Zane said.

"It says, 'Let him that is filthy be filthy still.' Now, I hope that settled this bathin' question once and for all!"

Clay listened half-heartedly as Clinton defended his idea of not bathing, but finally he lifted his head and said, "I guess we'll have to put off drivin' that herd to New Orleans. You can't go with that bad leg, Zane, and I can't go because Rachel and Sam have both got the chicken pox."

"I can take care of them. You can go," Jerusalem said quickly.

"No, I don't want to go off and leave 'em. We'll just put the drive off for a bit."

Clinton looked up from his plate and said, "I don't see what the fuss is about. I can make that drive."

Clay stared at Clinton. "Why, you've never handled a drive by yourself, Clinton."

"No, but I've been with you and Zane. New Orleans is in the same place, ain't it? I reckon I can find it, and there ain't nothin' hard about drivin' critters. You just get behind 'em and holler and whoop, and you steer 'em in the right direction."

Clay considered Clinton steadily for a moment and then said, "I just don't know if you can take care of all the details."

Clinton's face grew red. "I don't know why you don't trust me. I've worked as hard as anybody on this ranch."

"He's right about that, Clay." Zane nodded. "Clinton's a mighty good hand."

"I know he is, Zane, but he might make a mistake."

"I ain't *never* made a mistake," Clinton said loftily. "And I don't ever plan to."

Jerusalem threw up her hands. "My land, what a boy!"

"Oh, come on, Ma. I'm twenty-one years old. If I can't take a bunch of dumb cattle to New Orleans on a little old drive, I might as well give up ranchin' and go and become an ol' salesman."

Clay had been thinking hard, and now he grinned. "I got to admit you're a good man with critters, Clinton, and we need the money. I got my eye on a piece of land that we can get cheap." He looked at Jerusalem and winked. "I guess we can trust him to get a bunch of cows to New Orleans. He ain't likely to lose 'em. The worst thing that can happen is a bunch of Mexicans could steal 'em, or the Comanches might come in from the north and scalp him and take all the cattle."

Clinton brightened up at once. "You just wait! I'll dicker with them cattle buyers down in New Orleans and make 'em think that they been hit by a tornado."

"They're liable to skin you," Zane said. "They're pretty sharp dealers down there."

"They ain't skinnin' me, not as long as geese go barefooted," Clinton declared. "I got to hire me some Mexican drovers."

Clay looked at Jerusalem and said, "Well, your baby boy's growin' up. It's time he learns to take some responsibility."

"He'll do fine, Clay," Jerusalem said. "I'm real proud that you trust him enough to go."

Clinton had hired four Mexican drovers to make the trip to New Orleans. He knew them all well, for they had made the trip twice before with Clay and Zane. Clinton had been busy getting things ready and listening to a great deal of advice from Clay and Zane, which he paid little heed to. The day before the drive was to start, he left the drovers holding the cattle in a bunch and rode over to see the Stuarts. He had promised his mother to check on Anne Stuart, and when he dismounted and walked up to the house, he found her sitting out on a cane-bottom chair. "Well, Miss

Stuart," he said, his face lighting up. "Good to see you up and around. Ma sent me over to find out how you were."

Anne Stuart smiled and said, "I'm doing much better, Clinton. You thank your mama also for all she's done for us. She is one kind lady."

"Where's Mr. Stuart?"

"He went out to see if he could bag a deer."

"What about Al?"

"She's out back behind the house tryin' to find some worms. She wants to go fishin' in the river. I tell her it ain't a good time, but you know Aldora. She's gonna do what she says."

Clinton grinned and said, "I'm leavin' for New Orleans with a herd tomorrow. I'll just go say good-bye to Al."

He shoved his hat back on his head and walked around the house. He found Al out by the barn digging and turning over dirt. "Findin' any worms?" he said cheerfully.

"No, I reckon they've went down deep. But I can use chicken guts." Al turned to him and said, "What are you doing over this way?"

"I came to see how your grandma was. She's doin' a heap better, it appears like."

"Yes, she is."

"Did you hear about me takin' a herd down to New Orleans to sell?"

"I thought Zane was going to do that."

"Oh, he got piled up by a hoss, so I jumped in and offered to take the herd."

"You mean all by yourself?"

Giving her an offended look, he said, "No, not by myself. I've hired four hands to go with me. They ain't enough, but that was all I could get."

Al leaned on her shovel and unexpectedly said, "Let me go with you, Clinton."

"What! On a cattle drive?"

"You know I can ride herd on cattle. You won't be brandin' 'em or anything like that. Just keepin' 'em in the road, ain't it?"

"Well, that's right, but there could be trouble. It could be dangerous. We might meet up with some Comanches or a bear."

Al didn't speak again, but something passed across her face. Clinton studied her more closely and could tell something was bothering her. "What's wrong, Al? Ain't you feelin' good?"

"I'm feelin' fine, but—well, we're powerful short of money, Clinton. I hate to mention it, but we could sure use some extra cash. That's why I asked for the job."

Clinton Hardin had a tender heart, and he had become very fond of Al. They had fished and hunted together, and although he didn't understand her moods at times, he felt an obligation to the whole family. "Well, shucks, if that's the case, you might as well ride along. You can be the cook. We're leavin' early in the morning."

"Oh, thanks, Clinton! I'll be ready."

"You ain't asked what I'm payin'."

"Whatever it is, it'll be more than I'm making here."

"You be over at our place about daylight. I want to get a good day's start." He reached over and shoved her hat down over her eyes. "Better wear some warm clothes." He grinned. "And don't wear your hat over your face like that. Makes you look foolish." He turned and moved away quickly, calling back, "Better bring a pistol if you got one. We might run into some bandits."

Al pulled her hat up and watched him go, her eyes warm. She began to grow excited, for she had never been to New Orleans or any big city, for that matter. *Maybe we'll get to go downtown and see some of the fancy hotels and restaurants there,* she thought. *It'll be fun!*

The drive to New Orleans had been as easy as Clinton had hoped. The cattle had not stampeded. There had been no bandits and no storms. The October weather had been nippy, but not bitter. Each night they had built up a fire, and Al had appointed herself cook, and, indeed, she proved to be a good one. She had slept at night away from the men wrapped in a blanket and had been the first one up in the morning so that breakfast was always ready. Once Clinton had said to her, "You're a right good hand, Al. I'm gonna take you on all my cattle drives." The remark had pleased her, and she had looked forward to more of the same.

The sale of the cattle went better than Clinton was expecting. Clay had told Clinton what he should get for the cattle, and to Clinton's surprise, the first offer he had received was only a dollar a head less than Clay had mentioned. He bargained with the buyers and managed to get a better price than Clay had mentioned.

He came back to where the crew was camped and said, "Payday, fellas." They gathered around, and he paid them off with a bonus. "You fellas might as well go on back when you take a notion, if you can find your way home. Al and me are gonna go see the sights of New Orleans."

Al brightened up at the chance to see some of New Orleans. After the Mexicans had left, Clinton counted out some bills to her and grinned. "A little bonus there for that good cookin' of yours."

"Thanks, Clinton. This will help out at home."

"Well, what do you say we go see what New Orleans looks like? I don't figure on leavin' here until we seen the sights. Tell you what, let's go get a couple of hotel rooms. Then we can go out and eat and see what the French Quarters have got to offer to a couple of Texans."

"I didn't bring any clothes to wear to go out."

"Well, I didn't either, so maybe they won't let us into the fanciest place, but I betcha we won't starve. Come on, we'll find someplace."

Aldora Stuart was excited as they rode around. She had never been in a large city like this, and all the sights and sounds fascinated her. She knew she would have the best time in New Orleans with Clinton that she had ever had in her life. They had cleaned up as best they could, and Clinton had asked a carriage driver for a good place to eat.

"Money is no object," he had said loftily.

The carriage driver had grinned and said, "You might try Mulate's. They make mighty good food."

"Thanks."

They had taken the driver's advice, and twenty minutes later, they were standing in front of Mulate's. When they walked through the doors, a waiter wearing a fancy suit with a white shirt looked aslant at their garb, but Clinton had slipped him five dollars and said, "We want the best treatment you got." The waiter had grinned and said, "Right over here, sir and madam" then led them to a corner table set with fine china and a crisp white tablecloth.

They waited until the waiter gave them a menu, and Clinton looked at it. "Why, I can't read this. It ain't English."

"No, sir, it's French."

"Look, you just bring us what's good in there. I trust your judgment."

"Why, thank you, sir. I'll see that you have a fine meal."

When he returned a few minutes later, he was carrying a bowl which he identified as gumbo.

"What's in it?" Clinton asked.

"Well, it is one of our specialties with shrimp and a few other things. I think you'll find it quite enjoyable."

The two ate their gumbo while the rest of the meal was coming, and they liked it very much. They had samplings of something called shrimp Creole, and then the waiter brought in a platter full of something that made Clinton exclaim, "What is it, some kind of bug?"

"No, sir, these are crawfish."

"Why we use them things for fishbait! I ain't eatin' no fishbait! Go serve 'em to the cats. They'll probably cover it up."

The waiter could not hide his grin. "Yes, sir. Could you eat some fish?"

"Fish sounds mighty good."

The two ate more samples of the Creole food and finally ended up with something called chocolate *mousse*, as the waiter identified it.

"Moose? You got to kill a whole big moose to make this?" Clinton said with astonishment.

The waiter tried to hide his amusement but said, "Sir, it is a special dessert quite palatable to the taste."

The two ate until they could hold no more, and then they left the restaurant. They walked the streets of New Orleans, and Al said once, "I didn't know there was a place this big."

"It is fair size, but—" He was interrupted when suddenly two women came out of the shadows. They were on one of the side streets only partially lit by lanterns.

"Hey, fellas, you lookin' for a good time?" one of the women said.

Clinton could barely see the two women in the feeble darkness, but he could smell their strong perfume. One of them grabbed his arm, and the other one moved to stand beside Al. The one holding Al's arm said, "Come on. I'll show you a good time, honey."

Al made an odd croaking sound and pulled away, saying, "Take your hands off me!"

Quickly Clinton said, "I guess you girls better go find other customers. Come on, Al." He grabbed Al by the arm and pulled her away. The women's curses filled the air behind them, and Clinton was laughing. "They took you for a fella."

"Those are bad women, Clinton."

"They sure enough are."

The two were walking rapidly away toward the main street, and Al said, "Did you ever—"

"Did I ever what?"

"You know. Did you ever have anything to do with women like that?"

"What do you take me for? Why, a fellow would have to be dumber than a hairball to mess with evil women like that! Don't you know what the Bible says about them? Their steps lead down to hell. I'm surprised you'd even think such a thing of me."

"I'm sorry, Clinton. I didn't really think so. They looked awful, didn't they?"

"I couldn't see 'em all that well, but they probably did."

After crossing a few streets, they found the hotel, and both of them went to bed at once.

Clinton said good night and added, "No reason to get up early. We can make good time without those dumb cows to hold us back."

Al smiled at him. "I had such a good time. I'll never forget it, Clinton."

Clinton reached over and squeezed her arm. "You'd better not tell your folks about them two women."

"I won't. Good night."

"Good night, Al."

They slept out each night on their return trip, exactly as they had before. They had brought enough food on the packhorse for the trip home. Each day when they stopped for the night, Clinton would gather the firewood. Al would cook a good supper, and afterward they would sit around the fire. Clinton was a great talker, as Al already knew, but she found herself getting more vocal than she had ever been with anyone.

After they had eaten and washed out their dishes in the creek that ran by their campsite, Clinton said, "We'll be back home tomorrow. You know, Al, I'm kind of sorry it's over."

"So am I. It's been the most fun I've ever had."

"Well, me too, I guess." He got up, poured coffee into two cups, and came over and sat down beside her.

Al looked up at the skies, which were adorned with glittering stars, and began to recite:

"Star light, star bright
First star I've seen tonight,
Wish I may, wish I might
Have the wish I wish tonight.

"I say that every night when I see the first star."

Clinton sipped his coffee and said, "What'd you wish for?"

"You can't tell what you wish for. It won't come true if you tell someone."

"Well, I ain't superstitious. I'll tell you what I wish. I wish Brodie and Quaid would find my sister. That's what I want most in the world. She's been gone a long time."

"That's a good wish, Clinton. I'll wish that, too."

"You know, I've been worried about my Aunt Julie."

"She's really nice."

"She sure is, but she's workin' in a saloon, and you know what that means. I've talked to her a whole lot, but she just laughs when I try to tell her she's livin' wrong."

"I guess people have to come to find out what they are by themselves."

Clinton drained the rest of the coffee, set the cup down, and turned to face her. The moon was full, and he was struck by her even features. "I don't know what you mean by that. There's got to be folks to tell us what's right and what's wrong—like preachers and parents and people like your grandma and grandpa."

Al did not argue with him. She had discovered that arguing with Clinton was like arguing with an anvil. It made no impression whatsoever.

Clinton finally sighed and said, "It seems like I spend half my time tryin' to straighten people out."

Al suddenly laughed. "You certainly do. Maybe I need to spend a little while straightening you out."

"Me?" Clinton said, staring at her with blank astonishment. "Why, I don't need no straightin' out."

"Yes, you do."

Clinton glared at her. "What would you straighten me out about?"

"Well, for one thing, you make an absolute fool over yourself running around after Lucy Abbot."

Al's words touched a sore spot, and Clinton said, "I ain't neither. I'm gonna keep on chasin' her, too."

"You won't catch her. Everybody knows it except you."

"What do you know about it?"

"I know what everybody knows. She's a stuck-up, spoiled young woman who will marry a rich man 'cause that's what her parents want. That's what she wants, too."

Clinton reached over and grabbed her arm and shook it. "Don't you talk like that about Lucy!"

"Turn loose of me!" Al said. She tried to jerk away, but Clinton took her other arm and pulled her around.

"Listen to me," he said, "I'm tellin' you—"

Al wrenched aside and slapped at Clinton. She had not intended to hit his face, but she did. Instantly, she was sorry.

"Why, you little varmint!" He grabbed her shoulders to shake her, and she pulled away. Clinton was pulled off-balance, and when she fell backward, he kept his grip on her. Her hat fell off, and her soft hair that had been tucked up underneath fell down in soft waves around her face. Clinton was a strong young man, and he pinned her to the ground, "Now, you just listen to me, Aldora Stuart. I won't have no kid tellin' me how to run my life!"

"I'm not a kid! Let me go!"

Clinton's face was over Al's, and her struggles were nothing to him. He was looking at her lips and was shocked when he realized how beautifully shaped they were. They were round and curved, and his whole attention fastened on them. Al grew very still, and he looked deeply into her eyes. He saw something in them he didn't understand and was uncomfortably aware of the rounded form that he rested on. Clinton Hardin, for all his purity, suddenly lowered his head and kissed Aldora. The softness of her lips came as a shock to him, and he sensed her response, which he had not expected. He had grown so used to thinking of Al as a good friend, someone to fish and hunt with, but now he was aware that she was a woman, soft and desirable.

Al twisted her head away and said, "Let me go!" He released her at once, and she shoved him away.

"I . . . I'm sorry, Al. I didn't know—I mean, I didn't mean—"

"You get away from me, Clinton Hardin!" She scrambled to her feet and gave him one withering look. "Go on and make a fool out of yourself over that ol' Lucy Abbot!"

She marched off to where she had placed her blankets ten yards beyond the fire. Clinton struggled to find something to say, then called out, "Hey, Al, we'd better leave early in the morning." He got no answer, and he sat down before the fire staring at it for a long time. He was confused and upset with himself. *What's the matter with me? I must be losing my mind. I'll be glad when we get home!*

Jerusalem had sensed that something was wrong with Clinton the minute he returned from the cattle drive to New Orleans. Two days later he came out with it when they were alone. He told her the whole story and said, "I don't know what got into me, Ma, but we was wrestling around, and suddenly my face was right next to hers, and I just—well, I up and kissed her."

Jerusalem sat silent for a moment, then said, "And how do you feel about kissing her?"

Clinton did not answer for a time, and he finally stammered, "Well, you . . . you know, Ma, sometimes I think I'm not as smart as I think I am."

Jerusalem laughed and hugged him. "You'll be all right, Clinton. You're just growing up."

CHAPTER
THIRTY

The Staked Plains encompassed an enormous amount of ground, most of which was uninhabitable, as Quaid and Brodie discovered. They had only a vague idea concerning the exact location of Bear Killer's camp, so their only hope was to either happen upon it by luck, which would be dangerous and perhaps even fatal, or to find someone who would be willing to divulge its location.

As they wandered through the area, Brodie was impressed at how time and weather had etched a great chasm into the high plains. Some of the canyons dropped away beneath their feet so suddenly that it took his breath away. The horizon stretched away forever, so it seemed, and one day when the sun was still high in the sky, Brodie said, "Quaid, we could wander around like this for a year and never find Bear Killer's camp!"

"You got another plan?"

"Another plan? Don't seem to me like we have *a* plan. To tell the truth, I'm gettin' a little bit desperate."

Quaid sat easily in his saddle, letting his gelding pick its way across the sandy soil. He kept a sharp look ahead, taking in the stunted pinyon junipers, but the only moving thing he saw was a roadrunner dashing ahead of him with long, rushing strides. Winter had come, and the cold had swept across the country, dropping ice and snow across the land. But the weather was unpredictable. The sudden, violent chills could come, and the next day a warm breeze would come, so there was no way to prepare for it. The Indians, of course, thought that spirits controlled the weather and pummeled the land with violence to show their displeasure.

The two rode steadily for two hours, and finally Quaid drew his horse up sharply. "Something up ahead," he said. "Can't make it out."

Drawing in his reins, Brodie stared. "I see it. It ain't an animal."

"No. Let's see what's up."

The two kicked their horses into a gallop, and shortly afterward Quaid said, "It's an Indian all by himself."

Indeed, it was an Indian, but it was an old woman, they discovered. They kept their eyes constantly moving, looking for danger, but they saw no signs of others. When they pulled up in front of the old woman, she was sitting with her eyes closed and singing a song.

"Singing her death song," Quaid said. He stepped off his horse and moved over and spoke to her in Comanche. "Old mother, what are you doing here?"

The old woman stopped singing and slowly opened her eyes. "I go to the spirit land," she whispered. Her lips were dry, and her tongue seemed thick in her mouth. "Bring some of that water over here, Brodie."

Brodie came out of his saddle, pulled off a canteen, and handed it to Quaid. Quaid unscrewed the top of the wooden canteen and held it to the old woman's lips. Some of it went down her chin, but she drank eagerly.

"That's enough for now. You can have all you want later."

The woman's face was wrinkled, and she studied the two white men. "Will you kill me now?" she asked in Comanche, as she watched them without fear.

"No, we do not kill women. Where are your people? Are you Comanche?"

"No, Kiowa."

"Did they leave you to die?"

"No. Our camp was raided. I was in the bushes, and they did not see me. I started walking back, but I am too old now."

"We'll help you find your people if you'll tell me where they are."

"My name is Sky Woman," the old woman said. "I am of One Ear's band."

"Well, do you know where we could find him?"

"Yes, I will guide you."

"I think we'd better take her back, Brodie. This One Ear, whoever he is, may be able to give us some information about Bear Killer."

The two made a quick meal, for they had shot an antelope earlier in the day. They had to pound it to make it easier for the old woman to eat, but as she ate, she became more curious. She kept looking at them, and finally when she had eaten and drunk her fill of water, she sat quietly by the fire, saying, "You are Silverhair, and you are Tall One. There are tales about you."

Quaid interpreted this for Brodie and said, "What have you heard about us?"

"That you seek for the white woman, the captive of Bear Killer."

"Yes. That is true. We want to take her home to her people."

"Bear Killer will never let her go. He is a mighty warrior."

"We will take her," Quaid said quietly. Then he asked idly, "I don't guess you know where Bear Killer is?"

"Yes, his camp is beside the two mountains."

Quaid stiffened, unable to believe what he was hearing. "Two mountains? Where are they?"

"That way. One day's ride in a canyon. His people camp there during the winter."

Quaid turned to Brodie, his eyes flashing. "We've got him! He's by two mountains, a day's ride that way."

"That's what she said?"

"Yes. Now, we've got to get her back to her people." He turned and said, "Old woman, can you sit on a horse?"

She smiled at him. "I was sitting on a horse before you were born. Take me to my people. . . ."

Getting the old woman back to One Ear proved to be an easy ride. She had led them to a Kiowa camp, but One Ear was not there. Instead, the old woman presented them to a subchief named Antoine. He had been surprised at the two white men worrying themselves over an old Kiowa woman, but he had said, "She is the grandmother of One Ear. He will be happy to see her." On being questioned about Bear Killer's location, he confirmed what the old woman had said. "Yes, Bear Killer always winters in the big canyon beside the two mountains."

"We will leave, then."

"One Ear would help if you would wait."

"No, we will do this alone."

Antoine shook his head. "You will not take the woman alone. Bear Killer's band is large, and he is the most fierce warrior among The People. You will die if you try."

Quaid had grinned at him. "Well, Antoine, they can't kill us but once, can they, now?"

Antoine laughed. "You have good medicine, Silverhair. May the spirits go with you."

With Antoine's advice, finding the two mountains had not been difficult, for they had risen up against the horizon, making an obvious target. As they approached where Bear Killer had taken his band for the winter, Brodie said, "I don't know what we think we're doing. According to Antoine, Bear Killer's got a big band. He might have as many as fifty warriors there. Who knows?"

"I thought we might go back and get help, but by the time we do, they might've moved. Let's go look it over first and see what we're up against."

They approached the mountains gradually, and according to the description given by the old woman and Antoine, Bear Killer's band stayed in a large canyon that was almost hidden from view. As they drew closer, they found that the trees were thicker here, not tall, but of many varieties, including hornbrim, sycamore, and blackjack. Quaid said, "We don't know what we're running into, Brodie. We'd better stake the horses out here and go ahead on foot until we find them."

The two dismounted, hobbled the horses, and tied them for extra security with their ropes to the tops of large saplings. When the horses pulled, the saplings would give, but the lariats would not break.

For several hours they carefully made their way forward, going according to Antoine's directions. They found the main canyon just as dusk was beginning to fall. Crawling up to the edge of it, they looked down and could see a large stream cut down through the middle of the canyon. The canyon itself was covered with mesquite and dried buffalo grass. Along the edge of the stream were cottonwoods and prickly pear.

They scouted down the rim of the canyon and noted that there were knolls and mounds and bluffs and that the walls ran straight to the plains above without footholds in many places.

"Well, Bear Killer found him a good place to winter," Quaid murmured. "If I'm not mistaken, I see smoke over there, probably their camp. It'll be too dark soon. We'd better get back to the horses. First thing in the morning, we'll come and scout out the camp."

The two made their way back, and as they ate the last of the antelope, Brodie said, "We won't be able to shoot any game."

"That's right. Too much danger of some of Bear Killer's band hearing us."

"Well, we'll have to find some food quick, or we'll starve."

"Let's get all the sleep we can. We may need it. I sure wish we had brought some more grub."

"I wish we had another horse. If we get Moriah back, one of us will have to ride double. I don't fancy that with Bear Killer's band chasing after us."

"We haven't got her yet," Quaid said soberly. Then he smiled and said, "But we will. I think we're gonna do it, Brodie. Now, let's get some sleep."

The next morning, shortly after daylight, the two went back to scout out the camp down in the canyon. "That's got to be Bear Killer's camp. He wouldn't allow any other Indians to stay here," Quaid said. They had moved up and down the canyon walls searching for a way down. Finally they found one passageway where the horses could make it down, for there were many prints on the ground. "I expect this is the way the tribe gets in and out of this canyon."

They made their way down and stayed inside the shelter of the cottonwoods until they came to a spot where they could see the smoke of the camp easily. "I don't think we ought to get much closer than this in the daytime," Quaid said. "Let's just stake out here and see if we can spot anything."

They stayed there all day watching for any movement, and from time to time, Indian women would come to the river for water. They would fill their pots and then walk back to the clearing of teepees.

At sundown they were about to go back when suddenly Brodie, who was keeping watch while Quaid sat with his back against one of the trees dozing, said, "Quaid, look."

At once Quaid came out away from the tree and moved to stand beside Brodie. He looked across the creek and saw two women coming. "What is it?" he said.

"That one on the left—it's Moriah!"

Quaid had good eyes, but he had simply seen two Indian women accompanied by a small boy. He focused on the one that Brodie had indicated and said, "You're right, Brodie. That's her!"

Brodie slapped Quaid on the back, and the look on his face was exultant. "We found her, Quaid; we found her after all this time!"

"Some doubt in your mind about that?"

"I reckon so, to be truthful."

"If we had the horses, we could get her right now. But that won't work."

"Well, we know she comes to the river for water. What we'll have to do is bring the horses up as close as we can and wait for a chance like this. I wouldn't doubt if she'd come every day or two." Brodie was speaking, but his eyes were fixed on Moriah. "Look at her," he said. "She's laughing."

Quaid watched, and sure enough, he could see Moriah's teeth flash as she smiled at the other woman. "She seems to be all right," he said. "That's a relief."

"From a distance she looks just like a Comanche."

They watched as the two women filled their pots and started back. The boy followed them slowly, and they saw Moriah reach down and touch his head to urge him forward. Neither of them said anything, but both had their long thoughts about the boy walking beside Moriah.

"We'll bring the horses here in the morning, but we can't go in that camp. There's too many of them."

"We'll find a way. Don't worry."

Finding a way to get Moriah away proved to be more difficult than either of them had thought. They watched constantly for four days. They were about to starve, so Brodie had taken a horse and ridden back half a day's ride, where he shot a deer and brought it back. They had to go back up and away from the canyon to roast it so the smoke wouldn't be seen by anyone from the camp.

They had established that the camp was big, for many of the braves came down, from time to time, to the river. The camp was no more than a quarter of a mile away, or a half a mile at most, according to their calculations, but to try to sneak into it was impossible.

On the sixth day of their watch, Brodie said, "I think we'd better go back and get some help. If we had a band of rangers here, we could surround the camp and go in and get her."

"And maybe get her killed," Quaid said. "When the shootin' starts, those rangers aren't too careful about who they shoot from what I've heard."

"Oh, that's not true. Just stories."

"Maybe it is, but if we could just snatch her away when she comes down to the river, we'd have a better chance of getting out of here."

They watched the rest of the day and slept that night next to the horses. When they went back the next morning, Brodie said, "Look, somethin's happenin'. Look at that bunch of warriors."

Quaid stared at them for a moment, then said, "It's a war party. Look at that paint. That's what it means."

Indeed, a large group of warriors was coming out of the camp, mounted with their shields and lances. There were at least twenty of them, and Quaid said quickly, "Let's get out of their way. They're comin' up that defile that we found."

They watched as the group left. They were close enough that Quaid got a good look at the leader. "I bet that's Bear Killer! You can almost bet on that. He's takin' his warriors for a raid on somebody."

"Then this is our chance," Brodie said.

"You may be right. As soon as they're gone, bring the horses here. The first time Moriah comes back to the river, no matter who's with her, we move in, take her, and make a run for it."

"We can't make it ridin' double," Brodie said.

"No, I think you're right. What we've got to do is sneak in there tonight and steal one of their horses."

"Steal horses from an Indian?"

"It can be done," Quaid said.

The two talked about the matter of an extra horse, and finally late that night, past midnight, the two of them went down to the horse herd. It was a large herd of horses. Most of them snorted and ran away when they caught scent of the strangers, but they saw no signs of a guard. "They usually leave very young boys to guard the herd at night. Maybe we'll get lucky."

Every time they tried to get near a horse, it would nicker and move away. For a time it seemed hopeless, but then one of the horses did not bolt as they approached. Quaid stood watching them, outlined by the pale moonlight. He moved slowly, holding his hand out and speaking softly. The horse dipped his head but made no attempt to run this time. When Quaid got to him, the horse stuck his head out and allowed Quaid to stroke his nose. "This is a tame one. He's about half broke." He slipped the rawhide halter over the horse and walked away. The horse followed as obediently as a dog.

When the two of them got back across the river, Brodie said, "I'll go get the other horses, and we'll hope that Moriah shows up in the morning."

"She'd better," Quaid said. "We can't hang around here. We're liable to be caught and lose our scalps. That raid may be on a bunch not far from here. It's now or never, Brodie." He added, "I wish I was a prayin' man."

"Well, I'll do the best I can, but I wish Ma knew about this. She'd pray up a storm," he said as he turned to go get the horses.

Jerusalem had been baking biscuits, but she had been troubled all day. Something had come to her spirit, and she could not identify it. Finally,

Clay came in at noon, and she said, "Clay, I'm worried. Something's wrong."

"Are you sick?"

"No, but I want you to go get Rice," she said with finality in her voice.

"Rice? What for?"

"God's laid it on my heart to fast and pray for Brodie and Quaid and for Moriah. You go get Rice. We want all the praying folks we can. I don't know what it is, but God's told me we need to pray."

Clay took one look at her, but he never questioned things like this from Jerusalem. "I'll be back as quick as I can get him," he said. He turned and left the room, and Jerusalem went over and sat down in a chair. She closed her eyes and began to pray soundlessly.

CHAPTER
THIRTY-ONE

L ook, Quaid, there they come!"

Quaid looked up to see Moriah and the Indian woman who had accompanied her days before along with the boy emerge from the trees headed toward the river. They walked quickly, for it was a cold day, and he knew they would have but little chance to take her. "Come on. Get the horses," he said.

"What if the other woman hollers?"

"I don't think she could holler enough to reach back to the camp, at least I hope not, but we've got to take a chance."

The two stood up and suddenly Brodie said, "Wait a minute. Look, there's an Indian with them."

Quaid turned to look and a tall Comanche emerged from the trees. He was obviously following the two, and Quaid shook his head. "Why did he have to come along? Well, we can't wait. We may not get another chance like this."

"What will we do? Just run down on him?"

"No, he could duck back in those trees as soon as he saw our horses."

Quaid scanned the terrain and said, "Look, I'll go down and cross the river around that bend. There's a chance he won't see me, and I can come in behind him. I'll sneak around and take him with my knife. It'll have to be quiet. As soon as I do, you bring the horses on across—all three of 'em."

"I don't like it, Quaid. The woman might run off and get help from the village. And those Comanches have knives, too. Look, he's got a tom-ahawk in his belt."

"It's the best chance we got," Quaid said impatiently. "We don't have time to argue about it."

"But what if he kills you?"

"He may do that, but I'll take him with me. You come in and take Moriah home." He stood up and started to leave, then turned and said, "Tell Moriah I'm sorry I let her get took." Without another word, he turned and ran through the brush, dodging from tree to tree.

"I wish that Indian hadn't come along! I could take him out with a rifle from right here, but that won't do. Lord, help Quaid to take care of that Indian, because if he don't, we're gonna end up dead!"

Moriah was carrying two empty water skins in her left hand, and with her right hand she was holding on to Ethan. Looking back over her shoulder, she asked, "Why is Lion following us?"

Loves The Night had been very much aware of Lion's presence. "He thinks you might run away. Probably Bear Killer told him to keep a closer watch on you while they were gone."

"Run away on foot? I wouldn't get far."

"Lion's a stubborn man."

Moriah put Lion out of her mind. She did not like the man, and nei-ther she nor Loves The Night had told Bear Killer about how he had struck her. As she made her way down to the river, she looked down at Ethan, who clung to her hand. He was two years old now, a sturdy boy, who gave evidence of being very tall. The sun had burned him a golden color, not coppery like the Indians. The sun glinted on his hair, which was dark but had a touch of red. When he looked up and smiled at her, he called her name and pointed at the river.

"Yes, river," she said. She was glad that his eyes were a dark blue. No one could ever mistake her part in him, for although he had the high cheekbones of Bear Killer, his face had more the shape of Moriah's. She thought he looked like his grandfather Jake, and this made her happy. She had cherished every trace of her past before being captured by Bear Killer, and now as they walked down toward the river, she said, "Go throw a rock. See if you can throw it across."

Moriah let go of his hand, and Ethan ran toward the river and began to pick up stones and throw them into the water.

The day was warmer than usual, and, as always, Moriah relished getting out of the camp. She had never gotten completely accustomed to the smells of an Indian camp, which was unpleasant after the tribe stayed in one place for a long time. The sun glittered on the river, which looked very clear. There was no ice on it, but when she bent over to fill the water skin, it numbed her hand. "I wish it were warm enough to take a bath," she said.

Loves The Night said, "It will be a long time before the spring comes." She filled one of the water skins she had brought and then said, "Let's come back to fish later in the day. I would like some fish. I get tired of dried meat."

Lion stood close beside and said, "Women cannot fish."

Loves The Night carried on a running argument with Bear Killer's brother. "I can fish better than you can."

Lion laughed and said, "You talk too much. If you were my wife, I would cut your tongue out."

"If I were your wife, I'd kill myself!"

Lion's voice rose, and he began to argue loudly with Loves The Night. He argued so loudly that he did not hear the sounds of steps rapidly approaching him from behind. He did, however, see Ethan turn from the river, and he saw the boy's eyes open wide, and he lifted his hand to point, saying, "Man," to his mother.

Lion turned quickly, and a shock ran over him, for he saw a silver-haired man running directly for him, the knife in his hand flashing as it caught the light of the sun. He had little time to think, but as the man rushed at him, he seized the tomahawk in his belt and threw it, shouting, "Run for the village!" The tomahawk missed, and he pulled his knife as the silver-haired man was upon him.

Moriah whirled at Lion's shout, and when she saw the figure running across the broken ground at full speed, the first thing she noticed was the silver hair, and she knew instantly who this man was. "Quaid!" she cried, but then the two men collided. She saw Quaid throw himself forward even as Lion raised his knife. Quaid struck him, and as Lion's arm fell, she saw the blood leap along Lion's left arm—very bright red as it flowed freely. It was not a killing wound, and Lion slung the body of Quaid off. Quaid rolled over once and was up like a cat. He stood up crouching, holding the knife out in front of him with his right hand.

Again Lion cried out, "Go to the village. Tell them that Silverhair is here. Go quickly!"

"It's too late. Don't let her go, Moriah," Quaid cried. He did not take his eyes off of Lion, and the two men circled each other, moving in a clockwise direction. Moriah could not speak, and she glanced once at Loves The Night, whose eyes were on the two men. She was making no move at all to run but was watching with a fierce intensity in her eyes.

The knives flashed in the sunlight, and soon both men were bleeding. The blood ran down Quaid's face, for the blade had opened up a cut in his left cheek. His left hand also was bleeding, but Lion was in worse shape. He was an expert knife fighter, and time and again his blade leaped out as fast as a snake striking. Again and again Quaid blocked it and drew back. Moriah gasped as the two men came together with a grunt. Each of them had made a grab for the wrist of the other, and the two men stood there straining. Lion was a very strong man, one of the strongest of the Comanches. She saw his arm slowly rise despite Quaid's attempt to hold it. The two men fell to the ground with Lion on top. Slowly, the blade was being forced down. He was stronger than Quaid, and Moriah, without thinking, ran forward and grabbed the scalp lock of Lion and jerked at it with all her strength. Lion uttered a cry and released his grip. He fell back and sliced at Moriah with his knife, but even as he did, he knew he made a mistake. He turned, but Quaid was upon him.

Quaid drove the knife hard, and the blade sliced downward, opening up Lion's chest and part of his stomach. Lion looked down and saw the opening and knew that it would be fatal. Still, he threw himself at Quaid. Quaid stepped back, and when Lion fell, he reached down and kicked the knife away. Quickly, he lifted his head and motioned, and Brodie came galloping madly toward the river, leading two horses. He turned quickly to see what the woman would do. She was standing there watching, making no attempt to run.

"Will this woman give us away? We need time."

Moriah could barely speak. She saw that Quaid was bleeding badly from several cuts. It had all come as such a surprise she could not believe it, but then she said quickly, "No, she is my friend."

Loves The Night looked at Quaid, then said, "He has come for you. I knew he would."

Moriah faced Quaid and could not speak. He said, "We've got to get away."

"But you're wounded."

"Yes. He will bleed to death. Quick, sit down," Loves The Night said.

Quaid was already feeling a lightness of head. He stared at the Comanche woman, and then at Moriah, and said, "All right." He sat down, and the Indian woman came and took his shirt off. She began to rip it into strips and began binding his wounds. Moriah came to help her. She heard the sound of horses splashing across the river, and she cried out, "Brodie!" as the tall man that she scarcely recognized came off the horse. He kept the lines in one hand, but she rose and went to him.

Brodie put his arms around her and whispered huskily, "Sister." He was choked with emotion and could say no more, nor could she.

"You must get away quickly."

Brodie said, "How bad is it, Quaid?"

"It's bad enough," Moriah said. "You have a spare shirt?"

"In the saddle roll."

She quickly went to the saddle roll, stripped it off, and took out a shirt and a pair of pants. Using the bloody knife that Lion had dropped, she sliced the strips, and the two women bound up Quaid's knife wounds.

"You must go now before Bear Killer returns," Loves The Night said.

Quaid got to his feet and staggered to the horse. He managed to pull himself up and then whispered, "Quickly. We must go."

"Bear Killer will come for you."

Moriah was shocked. She looked over to see that Lion had risen up. He was weltering in his own blood, holding his stomach, which had a large gash in it. He was a dying man, but he was staring at her. "He will come for his son, and he will kill you and you, too, Silverhair."

"Go quickly," Loves The Night said.

Moriah went to her at once. She threw her arms around Loves The Night and said, "You have been my friend."

Loves The Night's face was stiff. "And you have been my friend. Take care of Ethan. You have told me about Jesus. I have Him in my heart now."

"I'm so glad."

"Be careful. Bear Killer will come."

Brodie watched as Moriah spoke to the other woman, and then his eyes turned to the boy. "Is he your boy, Moriah?"

"Yes."

"What's his name?"

"Ethan." She saw something change in Brodie's face, and she was afraid he would reject her son. But she saw Brodie go over and kneel by the boy and say, "Come along, Ethan Hardin. I'm your uncle. You're going to ride that big horse right there." He picked the boy up, and Ethan cried aloud.

Moriah said, "It's all right, son. This is our kin. You ride with him." She walked quickly to the mustang that Quaid had stolen, leaped up, and straddled him.

Brodie spoke to the horse and turned his own. He held Ethan tightly in front of him and started across. "Come on," he shouted. "Hang on, Quaid."

Moriah gave one look at Loves The Night, and the Indian woman cried out, "I will not tell them. You will need all the time to get away. Good-bye."

Moriah could not speak. Tears filled her eyes, but she knew she had to get away. She kicked her mount in the side, and at once the pony drove forward, splashing through the freezing water. As she crossed the river she saw that Quaid was reeling in the saddle, and she was afraid he would fall, but he held on. She looked back as they entered the pass that led out of the canyon and saw Lion lying still and Loves The Night watching her. She lifted her hand and waved and cried out, "Good-bye," and saw Loves The Night lift her own hand in a final gesture.

CHAPTER
THIRTY-TWO

I think he's going to die, Brodie," Moriah said.

Brodie had been sitting away from the fire talking to Ethan. Now he rose and came over and, stooping low, looked into Quaid's face. "He does look bad, don't he?"

"He's lost so much blood," Moriah said. She looked down into the pale face of Quaid Shafter, reached out, and put her hand on his forehead. "He seems so cold."

"I don't know what we can do, Moriah. It's gonna take at least two or three more days to get back. We have to go so slow, hauling him in this travois."

Quaid had been unable to keep his seat on his horse. They had been forced to stop and put together a travois out of saplings and saddle blankets. When it was finished, they tied Quaid into it and pulled him behind the horse slowly. Both Moriah and Brodie kept looking over their shoulders, expecting at any time to see Bear Killer thundering in with his warriors. Brodie had shot a longhorn and dressed it out, and Moriah had cut it up into pieces and made a stew out of it. She had practically forced Quaid to eat it in his brief moments of consciousness.

Ethan had come over to stand beside Moriah, looking down into the face of the wounded man. He said, "Man sick?"

"Very sick, son," Moriah said.

Brodie put his hand on the boy's shoulder and nodded. "He's gonna be all right, though. Now, don't you worry about it."

Brodie rose to his feet and said, "We'd better keep that fire out." He picked up a rifle and disappeared into the darkness. For a time Moriah sat there silently. Her mind was swimming with thoughts. Everything had happened so quickly. It had been hard to believe that she was actually delivered from the hands of the Comanches. Now as she sat there, she looked up at the stars glittering overhead for a long time, and then she said quietly, "Lord, I thank You for Your deliverance, and now I pray that You would deliver this man. He needs Your help, Lord."

Ethan grew sleepy as time passed. Moriah rolled him up in a blanket, and he went to sleep instantly. She leaned over and kissed him on the forehead, and as she went back to take up her vigil beside Quaid, her thoughts were filled with what it would be like to be home again. She knew that people could be cruel, and she had heard talk all of her life about how worthless half-breeds were. One had lived near them when they had first come to Texas. He was a drunken old man and was called "Breed" by everyone. Moriah thought with a pang how she had treated him as inferior, as had everyone else.

A sound caught her attention, and she looked down and saw that Quaid had his eyes open. Quickly, she leaned over and said, "Are you hurting, Quaid?"

He looked at her for a time, licked his lips, and shook his head. "Not bad."

"I think you are. You took some terrible wounds."

"Where are we?"

"About three days from home, Brodie says. I want you to eat something and drink something."

"Not hungry."

"That doesn't matter. You've got to eat and drink as much as you can. You have to keep your strength up." She moved over to the pot of stew, which was still warm over the fire that had been extinguished. She picked up the pot and came back and said, "You'll have to sit up."

She leaned forward and pulled him into a sitting position, her left arm around him. She waited to see if he could hold it as she set the pot on the ground. Spooning out a portion of the stew, she held it to his lips, and he accepted it. She watched him carefully as he chewed, and she continued to slowly feed him.

"I feel like a blasted baby!"

Moriah shook her head. "You saved Ethan and me. Don't try to talk. Just eat." She fed him more stew and then water from a cup. "Do you want to lie down again?"

"No, it feels better to sit up, but it seems like the whole world is swimmin' around."

"You lost far too much blood. Some of those wounds should be stitched up, but we had no way to do it." They had been in such a hurry to put as much distance between themselves and the Comanche camp that there had been no time. Quaid said, "There's a needle in my kit bag and some stout thread that might do."

"We'll have to do that, but we'll need light. First thing in the morning. I'm afraid it will hurt a great deal."

Quaid did not answer. He sat there, and she continued to feed him more of the stew. It came to Moriah then how strange it was that this man, whom she had hated so bitterly when she had first been captive, had become the one who had saved her. He was studying her face, and she said, "What are you thinking about?"

"I'm thinkin' about—how I let you down, Moriah. I never regretted anything more than letting you go home alone that night. I know you must hate me."

"It was not the right thing to do, but then we all do things that aren't right."

"Not like that. It's been eatin' at me ever since."

"That's why you came after me. Brodie told me how all this time you've had one thought, and that was to get me back. So that makes up for everything."

"So you don't hate me anymore?"

"I did, but that's gone now."

Quaid smiled then, the first smile she had seen, and said, "I feel better." He looked over at Ethan. "That's a fine boy you've got there."

When she did not answer, he looked at her in surprise. "What's the matter?"

"He's half Comanche. You know what that means, Quaid. He'll be called a half-breed."

"Maybe not."

"You know Texans better than that. You know how they hate the Indians."

"Not all of them."

"Most of them do."

"This will be different, Moriah. He'll be a Hardin. That means everything. Everybody respects the Hardins and the Taliferros."

A tiny bit of hope began to stir within Moriah, and she whispered, "Do you really think so, Quaid?"

"Oh, there will always be knotheads who have no better sense, but he'll be a good man, and everybody in the whole family will love him. He'll have brothers and sisters. It'll be good."

Moriah saw that he was tiring and said, "You'd better lie down and rest now. We want to make a lot of time tomorrow." She helped Quaid to lie down and said, "We'll put those stitches in tomorrow morning, then we'll travel hard."

"Bear Killer will come after him just like that Indian said."

"I know it. He's a strong man, and he never gives up."

Quaid reached out and touched her hand. "He won't get him. We won't let him. Me and Brodie and Clay and Zane—we won't let him."

Moriah watched Quaid's eyes begin to flutter, and he went to sleep with an abrupt suddenness, a sure sign of weakness.

"You never gave up," she whispered.

Brodie had been on guard and came in later that night to sleep some. "How has he been?"

"He ate a lot of stew, and he talked. He's feeling better."

"That's good."

"He's got some thread and a needle in his kit bag. We need to sew those wounds up in the morning."

"I wish we had some liquor to put him out."

"It'll hurt, but it'll have to be done."

The next morning they rose, and getting the needle and thread,

Moriah sewed Quaid's wounds together. She had seen this done often enough before but had never helped. Quaid did not make a sound, although it must have been extremely painful. Tying up the wounds, she said, "Now, they can start to heal, but they're going to leave scars, but they'll be honorable scars."

"Can't hurt my manly beauty none," Quaid whispered. He got into the travois, and Moriah bound him in. Then she got on his horse with Ethan behind her.

"We'll make as good a time as we can. I'll feel a heap better when we get home," Brodie said. They moved forward, and all that day they looked over their shoulder for sign of Bear Killer but saw nothing.

They traveled hard all day, stopping frequently to give water to Quaid, and that night when they camped again, Moriah said, "He never gave up, Brodie."

"No, he never did, and Ma, she didn't either. She always thought you'd come home, no matter how the rest of us doubted. I don't think she ever did doubt. And I know she prayed for you every day."

The two sat in the darkness until Quaid woke up. They fed him one more time, and Brodie said, "I think we might make it in tomorrow night if we have a good day. Next day if not. That'll be good, Moriah. We're gonna see a celebration like none of us ever seen before."

Mary Aidan was milking Esther the goat. She always talked to her exactly as if the goat understood every word she said, but then Mary Aidan talked to Bob the dog, Smokey the cat, and any other sort of animal life that happened to be close.

"Esther, if you'd just be still, this wouldn't take as long. Now, like I was tellin' you. This boy that lives down the road, his name is Harold, and I think he likes me. But he likes Mary Sue Gaston, too. She's a year older than I am, and I'm worried because she's already shapin' up, and I'm shaped like an old rake handle. So, what I been thinkin' about doin' is sort of paddin' myself up, you know, to make myself look better. Kind of catch Harold's attention."

Continuing with her talk at a steady rate, Mary Aidan filled two buckets and then freed the goat and started walking toward the house. It was a cold December afternoon, and she stepped up on the porch, when suddenly a movement caught her eye. She looked at the road, and then her eyes flew open. Dropping both buckets and letting the milk splash on the porch, she hit the door hollering, "Ma—Ma, it's Brodie and Quaid, and they got Moriah with them!"

Jerusalem had been cooking supper, and at Mary Aidan's wild cry she turned pale, whirled, and ran through the house. She opened the door and almost fell outside with the twins running right behind her. She saw the travois behind one of the horse, and then quickly saw that Brodie was astride his horse and knew that it was Quaid who was hurt. She ran forward and saw Moriah dressed as an Indian with braids and skin burned by the sun, but all she saw were the tears running down her daughter's face. She grabbed Moriah and squeezed her with all her might while the twins danced around, with Mary Aidan popping questions a mile a minute.

As for Moriah, to be enfolded by her mother's arms brought a sense of peace and security and love she had longed for. She put her head against her mother's neck and simply stood there crying from joy. Her mother was stroking her back and making comforting noises and calling her name tenderly, tears streaming down her face.

"Ma, give us a chance. We ain't got to do no huggin'!" Mary Aidan protested.

Jerusalem's eyes were wet, but she gave a half laugh. "Well, I reckon that you deserve it." She stepped back, and as Moriah took Mary Aidan and hugged her, Jerusalem turned to Brodie, who had stepped off his horse and was grinning at her.

"Well, we done got her, Ma."

"You did. We'll have to hear all about it, but what about Quaid?"

"It was quite a thing, Ma. He had a knife fight with one of the subchiefs of the band. Got cut up pretty bad. We wasn't shore he'd live, but he's doin' better now."

Jerusalem went at once to the travois. She knelt down beside Quaid and saw that the dust had gathered on him. She took out her handkerchief and wiped his face and smiled at him. "How are you, Quaid?"

"Fine, ma'am, just fine."

Jerusalem leaned over and kissed him and then put her hands on his cheeks. "We'll always be beholden to you, Quaid, for bringing my girl back."

"I'm glad it turned out like this."

The twins had gone over to the horse where Ethan still sat perched in the saddle. "What's his name? Who is he?" Sam demanded.

"He's an Indian boy," Rachel said. "Can't you see? Where'd you get him?"

Moriah went over and lifted him out of the saddle. She held him and looked at her family and said, "This is my son, Ethan."

At once, without a moment's hesitation, Jerusalem said, "Well, ain't that fine! Look at him. Why, he looks like Jake, Mary Aidan! Look at him."

"I always thought so, Ma," Moriah said as she held Ethan.

"You reckon he'd let me hold him?"

"He's a little shy, but you can try."

Jerusalem smiled and coaxed Ethan until finally he released his mother and came to Jerusalem. "Wait until Clay sees this boy. He'll be proud as a strutting peacock!"

"Let me hold him, Ma," Mary Aidan said.

"Now, you kids don't pesterfy him. Brodie, you come on in the house. I'll make a bed for Quaid. I want to look and see what kind of treatment you gave this poor fella."

"Well, he got cut up like chicken for the pot, Ma, but we done the best we could."

Moriah watched as her mother, not releasing Ethan, carried him into the house. The children all followed, and she turned to Brodie and said with a tremor in her voice, "It's good to be home."

"They're gonna love that little feller just like I do, sis. Don't you worry now. Come on. Let's get Quaid in the house. Quaid," he said, "you soldiered long enough in that blasted travois. You want me to carry you in like a sack of meal, or do you want to walk like a man?"

"I think I can make it," Quaid said. They helped him out of the travois. His clothes were hanging on him, sliced by the knife and blood-stained.

When they got him in the house, Jerusalem fixed a bed for him and said, "You put him down right there. We want to wash him off, and I'll see about them wounds. Supper's almost ready. As soon as we get him cleaned up, we'll all eat."

"Where's Clinton and Pa?" Brodie asked.

"They went huntin', wouldn't you know it! They ought to be back soon. He promised me they'd be back before dark." She went over and put her arm around Moriah again. "They both worried about you more than you'd think."

Moriah could not speak, her heart was so full of emotion. Jerusalem, seeing her almost starting to cry again, said, "Why don't you go to your room and get you some clean clothes. They're right where you left 'em."

Moriah nodded, and Brodie said, "Ethan, why don't you come outside with me. I'll show you some fine horses out there."

"Yes!"

As soon as the two left, Jerusalem said, "You taught him English."

"Every day of his life, I've talked to him in English. He's not very good, but he'll learn fast." Then she hesitated and said, "I'm afraid what people will say, not about me, but about Ethan. That he's a half-breed."

"Well, God's answered one prayer to get you home safely. Now we'll take it a day at a time." Jerusalem came over and kissed Moriah and said gently, "Now, I'll bring you up some hot water. You can take a good bath and put on fresh new clothes, and we'll start all over again."

The twins were fascinated by Ethan. They were almost five now and talked almost as much as Mary Aidan. Ethan was silent at first, but he could not resist them. He was an inquisitive two-year-old, and soon the twins were busy showing him their possessions and their pet coon, of which they were very proud.

Jerusalem was finishing up supper and talking to Brodie, who was telling her a great deal of the fight between Quaid and Lion. "It was some fight. I was across the river, but I seen them knives a-flashin'. It's a wonder they didn't both die, Ma."

Even as he spoke, Jerusalem lifted her head and said, "Listen. There comes Pa and Clinton and Zane, and I'll reckon they'll be plenty surprised."

The three came in and took one look at Brodie, and Clinton let out a wild holler and came forward at once. "Well, you come back, you son of a gun!" All three of them came over and began to shake hands with Brodie.

"I didn't come alone."

"Oh, where's Quaid?"

"He's in the back room. He got hurt," Jerusalem said. She walked over and picked up Ethan, who had learned to trust her by now. "This is Ethan Hardin." She said no more and watched the reaction of the men. It was Clay who moved first and said, "Well, praise the good Lord. You got her, did you?"

"Shore did, Pa. She's up now gettin' prettied up. Ain't that a fine boy?"

"He sure is," Clay said with admiration. "What do you think, Clinton?"

"Why, he's nearly as good-lookin' as I am."

"You knucklehead!" Zane said. "He's ten times better lookin' than you are."

"No, he ain't," Clinton said indignantly. "There ain't nobody better lookin' than I am!"

Even as he spoke they heard steps, and they all turned to look at the stairs that led to the second story.

As soon as Moriah had entered her old room and shut the door, she felt very weak. It was all so familiar! She stood for a moment, then walked around, touching the furniture and letting her hand run across the colorful quilt on the bed. It all came back to her how much time she had spent in this room. She finally went over and sat down in the chair, unable to think clearly. Her mother brought hot water up and left to finish the meal. Taking a sponge bath and drying off, Moriah went to the drawer and began to dress. She put on clean underthings and the blue dress that had been her favorite. She noticed that it still fit her. She went to the mirror over the dresser and undid her braids, parted her hair in the middle, then tied it up in a bun. When she slipped on her shoes, they felt tight and uncomfortable after the loose moccasins she had worn for so long. She stood there feeling like a stranger in the clothes, but then she held her head up and said, "I'm home now, and that's the way it is." She heard voices down below and picked out the voice of Clinton louder than others and then Clay's. She was almost afraid to go down, but she knew that Ethan would receive nothing but love from these men. She turned slowly and left the room and walked down the stairs.

"Well, look at that girl, she's done got plumb prettified!" Clay said. He came forward at once, holding Ethan in the crook of his arm, reached out, squeezed Moriah, and kissed her on the cheek. "Daughter," he said, "thank the Lord you're back."

Moriah reached up and touched his cheeks with tears brimming in her eyes. "It's good to be home, Pa."

Clinton came over, his voice loud as always, and hugged her and swung her around the room. "Why, you're prettier than a speckled pup under a wagon! And that boy child you brung in, I'm gonna take him under my wing and teach him everything I know!"

Zane laughed. "Well, that won't take long. How are you? You look good, Moriah."

"Uncle Zane, it's so good to see you."

"You say Quaid got sliced up pretty bad?" Clay said.

"He's better now," Brodie said. "Moriah sewed him up. He shore saved our bacon, though. Why, I've got to tell you about it. You see, we was—"

"Not now. We're going to sit down and eat this food," Jerusalem said.

It took some doing to get every one quieted down, but Quaid was able to come to the table holding on to Brodie. All through the meal, Brodie told the story of how they had located Bear Killer's winter camp and rode in and rescued Moriah and Ethan. He made little of his part in it, and finally said, "It was all Quaid there. If he hadn't stopped Lion, we'd have been dead meat."

"That's right," Moriah said, looking at Quaid. "I'll never thank you enough, Quaid, and you, Brodie."

Quaid tired quickly, and immediately after the meal, he said, "I reckon I'll lie down."

"I'll go with you," Clinton said. "I want to hear some more about all this."

"You will not, Clinton," Jerusalem said. "Quaid needs to rest. More storytelling can wait for another time."

Clinton grumbled but then contented himself with sitting down cross-legged on the floor, talking to Ethan. The children gathered around him, and Clay said to Moriah, "I feel like a new man just seeing you here, daughter." He hesitated, then said, "Was it bad?"

"Some of it was very bad."

Jerusalem was sitting on the other side of her on the couch. She put her arm around her and said, "Well, God brought you back."

Moriah was quiet, then she said, "I may as well tell you. Bear Killer will come for Ethan. Not for me, but for him. You know how Comanches love their children, and he's a determined man. He wants Ethan to be chief of his band someday."

"Don't you worry about that. He won't get within ten miles of this place, not the way we'll watch."

Moriah took Clay's hand and held it. He patted it and said, "It's gonna be fine."

"I worry about Ethan. They'll call him names like half-breed."

Clay's face darkened. "Why, they'd better not. Not in front of me! I'd cut 'em off at the neck—and so would Clint and Zane and Brodie." He looked over where Clinton was still sitting on the floor playing some game with the children, and he noticed that Ethan had joined in. "You know, I got a feelin'. That boy is gonna be the best of the Hardins, Moriah. You wait and see."

Moriah squeezed his hand and sat there, pondering all that had happened since that day she had been captured. After the years of fright and humiliation, she was home again, and she knew that there would be hard times ahead. But she had family now, and that gave her the courage to go on. God had been faithful, and she would continue to trust Him.

CHAPTER
THIRTY-THREE

Brodie came into the room he shared with Quaid. Christmastime had come, and the weather was cold, but the sun was bright as it beamed through the window. "You'd better get yourself ready, Quaid. Ma's been cookin' on this meal for two days now. I aim to plumb founder myself."

Quaid leaned over to pull on his boots and made a face as he did so.

"Them cuts still a-hurtin', ain't they, Quaid?"

"Not bad." Quaid straightened up and smiled. "I appreciate you buyin' me these new clothes, Brodie. My old ones was about past goin'."

"Well, I got them clothes put away."

"Put away? What for?"

Brodie grinned and came over and tapped Quaid on the shoulder gently. "Why, them's gonna be famous clothes, worth a heap of money someday."

"What are you talkin' about? They're nothin' but bloody old rags."

"I can see it now," Brodie said, waving his hand in an eloquent gesture. "For only one dollar you can see the very bloodstained clothes that the great Comanche killer Quaid Shafter wore when he fought the chief of the Comanches, Bloody Hand, to the death!"

"His name wasn't Bloody Hand. It was Lion, and nobody would pay a dollar to see any bloody old clothes."

Brodie laughed. "I'm keepin' 'em anyway. Someday you'll get to be a crotchety old grandpa, and when they don't treat you right, you can drag out them bloody old rags and say, 'I expect a little bit more honor around here. After all, looky here what I done.'"

"You do carry on, Brodie, but I'd never made it back if it wasn't for you and Moriah."

"Well, we wouldn't have rescued Moriah if it wasn't for you, so we can settle down and brag on each other for the rest of our lives. Now, come on. Let's go down and see if we can destroy ourselves with Ma's cookin'."

The two men went downstairs, and they were greeted on all sides. Everyone was there, Clay and Jerusalem, of course, with Rachel and Sam, the twins. Mary Aidan peppered everyone with questions. Clinton and Brodie, Zane, Moriah and Ethan, and Julie and Rice Morgan were standing around talking, waiting to sit down and enjoy the meal Jerusalem had labored to make.

Jerusalem said, "Will you children be quiet, and you, too, Clinton! I declare, you get louder every year."

"I do not," Clinton argued. "I talk just like I always done."

"Well, anyway, all of you sit down and try to eat what Moriah, Julie, and me fixed."

The women had worked for hours doing all the cooking. There was wild turkey, cornbread dressing, sweet potato pie, pecan pie, and fresh bread.

Quaid was quiet during most of the meal. Brodie, who sat beside him, kept his plate filled until finally he protested. "I'm about to bust now, Brodie."

"Why, you ain't hardly ate nothin'," Clinton said loudly. "You got to keep your strength up. That's what the Bible says."

Everyone laughed, and Rice Morgan said, "Where does it say that a man ought to eat until he nearly busts?"

"Well, I ain't exactly sure, Reverend, but it says it somewhere. If it don't, it ought to."

"You ought to write a book, Clinton," Zane grinned. "It'd be called *Things the Bible Don't Say but Ort To.*"

Quaid felt very strange, and his eyes kept going back to Moriah. She was wearing a simple light blue dress and no jewelry at all. Her hair had been cut and was no longer in pigtails but formed a soft red wreath around her head. He noted that her hands were hardened and scarred by the hard work during her time as a captive. Aside from that and the darkness that the sun had left, she looked much the same as he remembered her. More than once she looked up and caught his eyes and smiled, and he returned the smile.

Clinton piped up, "Quaid, I want to hear that story about how you killed that Indian."

"Not at the table," Julie said. "Don't you have any manners at all, Clinton?"

"I got perfect manners," Clinton said indignantly. "I'd like to know anyone who ever found any fault with my manners."

As always, when Clinton made an outlandish statement like this, everyone laughed, and he stared around, saying, "What's so funny about that?"

"Nothing, Clinton, and we'd all like to hear Quaid tell the story, but not at the table."

It was a happy time for them to all be back together, and eventually the talk turned to politics. It was Zane who started it by saying, "I'm beginning to doubt if Texas will ever make it into the Union."

"We'll get there someday, Zane," Clay said quickly.

"Well, it don't look like it." Zane shook his head with disgust. "I've heard talk that we might join up with England."

"How would we join with them? They're over the water," Clinton said. "Who needs them Limeys anyway, or them Frenchmen either."

The talk went on, but Clay turned and said, "Well, Brodie, you've had a nice long vacation chasin' after Comanches. Now you can come back to work."

Brodie was sitting next to Moriah, and he had taken Ethan from her and was holding him on his lap, feeding him bites of the pie from the plate in front of him. "No, sir," he said. "Don't reckon so."

Everyone turned to look at Brodie, and Jerusalem said, "What do you mean, son?"

"I've decided to join the rangers."

No one spoke for a moment, and then Clay shook his head. "All they do is get shot and fight Indians and Mexican bandits."

As soon as Clay mentioned the word "Indians," Quaid glanced quickly at Moriah, who showed nothing. But she spoke up and said, "Don't do it, Brodie, not on my account."

"It's somethin' I want to do. I can't say why."

"But, Brodie, this place will belong to you one day, or part of it," Clay said. "That's what Jerusalem and me have always wanted, to have family here, and have the biggest ranch in Texas."

"I guess I got a taste of runnin' free, Pa." Brodie grinned. "I wish you wouldn't pester me about it because my mind's made up."

Brodie's news came as a shock and a disappointment, for Jerusalem, especially, had looked forward to the time when Brodie would be back. He had always been a favorite of hers, and she had missed him greatly while he and Quaid were out hunting for Moriah. To hide her disappointment, she turned to Quaid and said, "What will you be doing, Quaid, when you get your strength back?"

"I thought I might go back to Santa Fe."

"Santa Fe," Clay said, frowning. "There ain't no point in goin' back to Santa Fe."

"Why, I reckon not," Clinton said. "There's plenty of work on this place. I do most of it myself, so I ought to know!"

Clay shot Clinton a disgusted look and shook his head. "I can't let you go back to Santa Fe, Quaid. With Brodie leavin', I got to have help. This ranch is growin' faster than I can keep up with."

Quaid glanced over at Moriah, who was looking at him intently. He could not read her expression but said, "Well, that's a mighty kind offer, Clay, but I'll have to think on it."

Afterward, when the women were cleaning up and the men were sitting over at one end of the big room singing with the youngsters, Moriah said, "It's the best Christmas I could have imagined, Ma."

"It is with you back." She shook her head. "I wish Brodie wouldn't go off and join the rangers. It's a hard, dangerous life with no reward to it."

"I think it's something he just has to do."

★　★　★

Two days after Christmas, at Jerusalem's insistence, Moriah climbed into the wagon with Ethan, and the two women drove toward Jordan City. The sun had come out and was bright as they bumped along the rutted road. Jerusalem had waited for Moriah to tell more about her experiences during her captivity, but she had kept silent. Now, however, as they rode along the open spaces, something seemed to break within Moriah, and she began telling her mother about her time with the Comanches. She spoke slowly at first and then more freely, and finally she said, "Ma, when I first was captured, I thought the Indians were nothing but beasts. But after I'd been there awhile, I began to see them as real people. They're not what I expected."

"How do you mean, Moriah?"

"Well, when we think of them, it's always of a warrior comin' in with a scalping knife to kill us or ambush settlers, but when you're with them, you find out that they love their children and they laugh a lot. That surprised me, Ma. I didn't think about Indians laughing. They love a good joke. They love their children better than white people do, I think." She went on speaking of how she'd had her eyes opened. She told her of how she had suffered from the other women, and then she told her of Loves The Night, saying, "Loves The Night was the best friend I had. I'll always miss her."

"Maybe you'll see her again."

"No," Moriah said quickly. "I'd have to go back to their camp for that, and that's the last thing I want to do."

The two women looked back at Clinton, who was riding his horse behind them and singing to himself loudly as usual. "Clinton's plumb foolish about Ethan," she said. "All of us are. I don't want you to worry about him, daughter."

"Ma, I'm scared to death to go into town. Everybody knows about me now and about my Indian husband." She was silent for a moment, then said, "I never thought of him as a husband. I didn't have any choice about that."

"Of course you didn't. Everybody understands that. And as for Ethan . . . he's a fine boy. Aren't you, Ethan?" Ethan was wearing cast-off clothes from Sam. They had been cut down and, more or less, tailored to fit him. He had on a bright red knit cap that covered his ears, but he looked up and smiled.

"Yes," he said, then he looked back and called, "Clinton!" He watched as Clinton waved his hat and then turned around and sat quietly.

"He's a quiet boy, isn't he?" Jerusalem said.

"Most Indian babies are very quiet. Of course, when they get to be as old as Clinton, they play and shout and carry on and fight just like we do."

After a few more miles, the outline of Jordan City came to view, and Moriah grew quieter and quieter. Clinton rode up beside the wagon and said, "Let me give that boy a ride on a real horse." He reached over and took Ethan as Moriah handed him up and put him in front of him on the saddle. "Hang on, Ethan. I'll show you how a real Texas cowboy can ride." He spurred his horse, and the gelding shot ahead as if shot out of a gun.

Moriah watched them go, but her face was still cloudy.

When they reached town, Moriah pulled the wagon up in front of the general store. Clinton came galloping up, pulled the horse up short, and stepped out of the saddle. "Come on, Ethan. Me and you are goin' in there and buy some store-bought candy."

"Candy?" Ethan said. He had no chance to ask more, for Clinton snatched him up, tossed him up on his shoulder and swaggered over the boardwalk and disappeared into the store.

The two women walked toward the store and had not gone more than ten feet when suddenly a voice behind them called out, "Well, I swan, it's Miss Moriah!"

Moriah turned, along with Jerusalem, to see Sheriff Bench headed for them, his face wreathed in a smile. He came forward and said, "You look good enough to hug." He put out his hand instead, and when Moriah took it, he covered it with both of his. "I tell you, Moriah. It's a sight for these old eyes to see you. I thank the good Lord for bringin' you back."

"Thank you, Sheriff Bench. It's good to be back."

"You're gonna find how many friends you got. The whole town's talkin' about how Quaid and Brodie snatched you right out from the middle of them Comanches."

"It was God's doing," Moriah said.

"Where's that boy of yours? I want to see him."

Nervously, Moriah said, "He went in the general store there with Clinton."

"Well, I'll just go along and make my howdys to him. Welcome home, girl!"

Bench was just the first of many who came to Moriah, all delighted to see her. She gradually began to relax, and after making some purchases in the store, Clinton came and said, "Come on, let's all of us go and see if we can get somethin' fit to eat down at the restaurant."

There was no resisting Clinton when he made up his mind on something, and the four of them made their way down the boardwalk. They passed by the Silver Dollar Saloon, and the usual loafers were sitting there. They had passed by them, and Moriah saw every man's eyes were on her—and on Ethan.

They were ten feet away when the voice of one of them came clear enough to understand. "There's the squaw and her papoose. I reckon she might be gettin' cold this winter without her buck to keep her warm. Maybe I can do somethin' about that."

Instantly, Clinton whirled and started back, but Moriah grabbed him by the arm. "Don't go, Clinton."

"Don't go? You reckon I'm gonna let scum like that talk about my sister? I don't reckon!"

"You can't fight everybody, Clinton. Come along," Moriah said.

Clinton struggled to control his anger and glared fiercely at the men who had fallen silent. He said loudly, "My womenfolk are with me now, but I got you fellers all in my mind's eye. The next time I meet one of you, you'd better take off because I'm gonna skin ya. You hear me?" He glared at them but got no answer and turned and walked away.

Moriah held on to his arm and said quietly, "Thank you, Clinton, but don't fight over me or over Ethan."

"Why, I certainly will!" Clinton said with astonishment. "The Bible says that."

"Says what?" Jerusalem demanded.

"It says to stomp any scum who talk bad about your sister."

Moriah could not help but smile a little, although her heart was grieved. "It doesn't say that. It says pray for those that despitefully use you. Now, you behave, Clinton."

"Why, I always do," he said. Then he reached down and picked up Ethan and said, "Tell you what. Maybe they got some candy. You like candy?"

"He doesn't know what candy is, Clinton."

"Well, he's in for a treat. I'm gonna teach him."

Neither Moriah nor Jerusalem mentioned the incident of the roughs in front of the saloon, but, of course, Clinton did. He told the story to Quaid, saying, "I got their faces all in my mind's eye, Quaid. I plan to accidentally run into 'em, and then I'm gonna stomp a mud hole in 'em!"

"You don't even know which one it was."

"Don't make no never mind. I'll whup every last one of 'em. That way I'll be shore to get the right one."

"But the others didn't do anything!"

"They deserve a whuppin' for hanging out with a skunk like that!"

Quaid shook his head but said little about it. After Clinton left, he went to find Moriah, who was in the kitchen by herself.

She greeted him with a smile and saw that he was disturbed. "What's wrong, Quaid?"

"Clinton told me about what happened in town. I wish I had been there," he said grimly.

Moriah turned and faced him squarely. "Would you have shot him, Quaid?" He did not answer, and she said, "Would you have beaten him up?" Still no answer, and she shook her head. "You and the rest of my family can't shoot every man who makes a remark about me and Ethan."

"It's not right," Quaid said, his jaw clenched tight. The scar on the left side of his face was healing, but it would always be there—a reminder of his knife fight with Lion.

Moriah had intended to say nothing, but she turned then, and her voice was a mere whisper. "It's worse than being taken."

"Don't say that, Moriah," Quaid said. He came over to stand behind her and tried to see her face, but she kept it averted. "You can leave this place."

"And go where? I can't leave Texas. It's my home. It'd be the same anyplace Ethan and I go." Quaid reached out and touched her arm, and when she turned to face him, he saw the tears in her eyes. "And Bear Killer will come for Ethan. You know he will, Quaid. He'll kill anyone who tries to stop him."

"We won't let him do that."

"You won't be here. You'll be in Santa Fe."

"I been thinkin' about it. Haven't made up my mind."

Moriah saw that he was troubled about her and the remark. *There's nothing he can do about it*, she thought. *There's nothing anybody can do about it.*

By the time a week had gone by, Quaid was feeling well enough to go outside and even to ride for short periods. He volunteered to go to work, but Clay had said, "There ain't much work to do in the wintertime. Them cows ain't goin' nowhere, or if they do, we can catch 'em up again. Now, come spring, we'll have a roundup and take another bunch to New Orleans. And you forget about goin' to Santa Fe. There ain't nothin' there for you, and there is something here."

It was a few days later during the afternoon when Quaid had gone out to ride for the exercise. He had been shocked at how the ranch had grown and how Clay now had to keep half-a-dozen Mexican riders at all times to keep up with the cattle. It was a big job and was going to get bigger because Clay had thrown all his strength into enlarging the ranch. Across the river Kern Herendeen was doing the same thing, and once Clay had said to Quaid, "We're gonna have trouble with Herendeen sooner or later. He wants all the land that joins his. He thinks he's some kind of a little god in tin pants, and somebody's gonna have to cut him down to size someday. I'll need help when that time comes, Quaid."

Quaid had thought about Clay's offer for him to stay and work for him, and now as he turned back toward the house, he saw Moriah come out and walk along the tree line. She was looking down at the ground, and when he approached, she looked up and smiled.

"Quaid, where have you been?"

"Just riding." He stepped off his horse and said, "Mind if I join ya?"

"No, of course not."

The two walked along, and Quaid said, "I can't hardly believe how much the ranch has grown."

"I know it. It's amazing. My folks don't have much money, but they've got a lot of land now. The ranch is twice as big as it was when I was taken."

"It's going to be bigger yet, according to Clay."

"It's strange. He never wanted anything much, and then he married Ma and had the twins. Now he's determined to have the biggest ranch in Texas."

The two walked until they reached a small creek that bordered the tree line. Quaid reached down, picked up a stone, tossed it in, and watched the ripples it caused. "You're much better. You couldn't have done that a few days ago," Moriah said.

"I'm too mean to kill, I guess." He said. "Are you all right, Moriah?"

Moriah looked at him quickly but knew what he meant. "It was almost as much of a shock coming home as it was being carried off to live with the Comanches, but it's all coming back now. Of course, everything has changed."

"What do you mean?"

Moriah looked at him directly. "I'll never marry now. No man will ever have me."

"Well, that ain't so. Lots of men would be glad to have a woman like you."

She turned then, but she said, "There's Ethan. How many men would want an Indian son?"

"He's a fine boy. His father was a strong man, and you are a good woman."

Moriah had shared some of her thoughts with her mother, but not everything, but she felt she could say things to this man who had given his life to find her. "I can't tell you how ashamed I am, Quaid."

"Why, that's plumb foolish! You didn't ask to be taken. You were a captive."

Moriah stared at him expressionless for a time, and then she said, "Have you made up your mind what to do?"

"I think I'll stick around." Quaid was surprised, for he had made that decision on a moment. He had thought of going away, but Clay was right.

There was nothing for him in Santa Fe. He had no family, and now he smiled. "Maybe me and Ethan could get to be partners. And I'd like to have a word or two with Bear Killer when he comes pokin' around."

"I hope you will. Ethan needs a man to look up to."

"Well, he's got some good men, Clay and the Hardin men." He hesitated, then said, "I want you to do something, Moriah."

"Do what?"

"I'd like to take you and Ethan to church next Sunday." He saw the fear in her face and said, "Don't be afraid. You faced the Comanches and won. I want you to keep your head high. You're a good woman. You've got a good boy, and you need to say so by lettin' people see you together."

Moriah could not answer for a moment. She had fared well enough with the townspeople, but she knew that some of the members of Rice's church were prejudiced to the bone. But she felt Quaid's eyes on her and said, "All right, Quaid. I'll do it if you go with me."

"Why, the whole bunch of Taliferros and Hardins will go!" He grinned and said, "The whole Comanche nation couldn't face us if we get our backs up!"

CHAPTER
THIRTY-FOUR

M oriah stood at the window of her room looking out as the morning unveiled itself. The sun stretched long fingers of light through the trees over to the west, touching the earth with gentleness. As she watched them, it seemed that the trees stood in disorganized ranks like a regiment at ease, laying their shadows on the ground in long lines. Farther over in the corral, a young colt ran around friskily, gleaming like light on water in the early morning sunrise.

For a moment she stood there thinking about how her life had changed. It had taken a different shape and already had begun to grow new branches, and the old branches were withering away. After all she had been through in these last few years, she had hoped and prayed for such a thing, for she knew that the constant of nature was discard and then growth. Old things had passed away, and new things had to come. Suddenly below she saw Ethan bundled up in an old coat that had belonged to Sam. He was running headlong across the frozen ground. Sam and Rachel chased after him, and the sound of their laughter was like music on the air to her.

Her glance shifted, and she saw that the men had already gathered, bringing the buggy and a wagon out for the trip to church. Clinton's voice was loud as he supervised the arrangement of boxes and threw together seats in the back of the wagon. The horses' breath made puffs of heavy white mist, as if they were breathing smoke. One of the mules hitched to the wagon suddenly kicked, his feet striking the wood, making a hollow sound on the cold, dead air. Steps sounded outside her door, and when a knock came, she turned and moved across the room to open it. Her mother stood there in her best dress with a heavy coat on, smiling and saying, "Come along, Moriah. We'll be late for church. Everybody's waiting on you."

"All right, Ma." Taking her heavy coat from the bed where she had laid it, Moriah slipped it on and then put on a hat made of black felt. She pulled it down, fastened it with a pin, and saw that her mother was watching her carefully. She made herself smile and said, "I'm ready."

"You look just fine, daughter."

"So do you, Ma." The two women went downstairs, and when they stepped out on the porch, the cold air brushed itself like a hand against Moriah's face. When Ethan saw her, he came running across the yard. She stepped off the porch, leaned over, and hugged him, pulling him off the ground and swinging his feet back and forth.

"Going to church," he chirped and grinned at her.

"That's right. Going to church."

"Let him ride with us in the wagon, Moriah," Mary Aidan said.

"All right. You watch after him. But he'll have to sit with me in church. I don't trust you."

"That's right. I don't trust you either," Clinton announced. He had come up and squeezed Ethan's shoulder. "You sit on my lap when we get to church."

"No, I don't trust *you*." Jerusalem smiled. "Ethan will sit with me. Now, let's go."

Moriah climbed into the back of the buggy with the twins, and Jerusalem and Clay waited until they were settled and Jerusalem was sitting beside him. "Let's go to church," he said, smiling. He slapped the lines on the back of the horses, and they started out at a brisk trot.

As they left the yard, Moriah glanced back and saw Zane driving the wagon with Quaid sitting beside him. Clinton was in the back, and his voice carried even over the sound of the horses' hooves. Brodie sat across from him, and Moriah settled back for the ride back to town.

Moriah had not slept well that night, for somehow this first Sunday of 1843 was a momentous time for her. As the distance passed—she could not remember where or when exactly—she remembered her father Jacob talking about going back to old places. She must not have been over five or six years old, but she had been sitting in his lap on one of his rare visits home, and he had been talking to someone—she didn't remember who. He had said, "You can go back to some place where you used to live, but it won't be the same place. You could walk over it and find an old path, and you can say 'Why, sure I remember this,' or you can look in a valley that used to know you, but it don't know you no more." The words seemed to swim together inside Moriah's head, and she refused to think of what it would be like when they got to the church. She knew Rice would be preaching. Julie had said that she wanted to be with the family on her first day back, and promised to meet them there. But there would be other eyes watching her—hard, critical, judgmental eyes. As the buggy moved along, crushing the frozen grass under its spinning wheels, Moriah Hardin straightened and made a vow to God that she would let no sign of weakness show in her. *You've been good to me, God, to bring me back, and I won't dishonor You by showing shame.*

When they pulled up in front of the church, Fergus Nightingale III was waiting. He came forward and removed his stovepipe hat and said, "Good day to you all. A fine day for church. I haven't been in so long I've forgotten how to act, so, Clinton, you keep an eye on me, and if I misbehave, put me right, eh?"

Clinton grinned. "I shore wish you'd get a big dose of religion, Fergus. An Englishman like you needs it to cheer him up."

As soon as Moriah stepped to the ground, she found Julie waiting for her. Julie was wearing a more subdued dress than she usually did, a plain light brown dress that showed beneath the long wool coat she wore. Her eyes were bright, and she came over to hug Moriah.

"I'm glad to see you, sweetie. You look beautiful."

"Thank you, Aunt Julie."

"We're late," Clay said. "It's all you primpin' so long, so let's get on in there."

They heard the sound of singing as they approached the simple white church, which was nothing but a rectangle with a small steeple on the top. The windows were closed, but Moriah could see the worshipers inside. They were singing a hymn that had long been a favorite of hers, "Rock of Ages." It brought back memories of the years she had sat in church beside Jerusalem. Now as Zane opened the door, Jerusalem was close behind her, holding Ethan. Moriah turned and said, "Let me have him, Ma."

"All right, daughter." Moriah took Ethan and whispered, "You be a good boy now," then stepped inside. The church, she saw, was full, and her eyes fell on Rice Morgan, who was standing in front of the congregation leading the song. He had a fine, clear, tenor voice, and when he saw her, he smiled brilliantly and stopped singing.

"Well, I hate to interrupt a good hymn, but we need to make room for our latecomers. Some of you folks on the front are gonna have to move over. Make room for the Taliferros and the Hardins."

Moriah knew that her face was flushed, but she held her head high, and Jerusalem stepped up beside her.

"Well," Jerusalem whispered, "we've got a place right down front. Come along, daughter."

Moriah made her way up the front aisle, and every head in the church turned to face her. She held tightly to Ethan, and when she got to the front, the people in the first two pews had moved out, going to find another place. Rice stepped down off of the low platform and came to her. "We have some distinguished visitors. Sir Fergus Nightingale is with us this morning for the first time, I believe. Sir, it's good to have you here."

"A pleasure to be here, Reverend, a pleasure." Fergus beamed.

"And then the rest of the visitors you know except one. We rejoice to have two very special visitors." Rice was beaming, his eyes dancing. "We're glad to have Miss Moriah Hardin back with us again, and for his first visit we have Master Ethan Hardin, Esquire. We don't usually applaud in church, but I think it would be fitting to clap our hands as a praise offering to God for bringing Moriah and Ethan back into the heart of their family and all of us." He began clapping, and the entire congregation joined in, it seemed, and the sound reverberated throughout the small wooden building.

Moriah stood there, and a feeling of gladness filled her heart. She took her seat alongside Jerusalem, and when everyone was seated, Rice went back to take his stand on the platform.

"Now we will sing the doxology. Let's make the rafters ring as we thank God for His mercy."

Praise God from whom all blessings flow.
Praise Him all creatures here below.
Praise Him above ye heavenly hosts.
Praise Father, Son, and Holy Ghost.

Moriah stood there holding Ethan. She felt her mother leaning against her, touching her on one side, and Clay moved until his shoulder was rubbing against hers. Right behind her she heard Clinton's voice, then Quaid singing with enthusiasm along with Brodie.

She took a deep breath and joined in the song, and in her heart she was giving praises to God as she had not since she had been rescued from Bear Killer's camp.

Rice led the congregation in two more hymns and then asked them to be seated.

Taking his Bible, he said, "This morning I am going to speak to you very simply about the most important subject in the world. When the Lord Jesus was on this earth, He was accused of what many people saw as a crime, at least as a disgrace. He was called 'the friend of sinners.'"

Rice shook his head, and there was wonder in his dark eyes as his rich voice filled the building effortlessly. "If any of you here this morning feel yourself to be a sinner, then rejoice, for you have a friend, Jesus Christ of Nazareth. He delighted in finding the outcasts, the harlots, the drunks, and the murderers. All that the world had spurned, Jesus found them out. You will remember at one point in His life He was on a journey, and the Scriptures say that, 'Jesus needs to go through Samaria.' He had to go through Samaria because there was a sinner there, a woman that He met at a well. You know the story, but I'll read it again. . . ."

The congregation listened as Rice went through the Gospels, reading the story of person after person lost in sin, condemned by the world, but loved by Jesus. His face glowed as he spoke of how Jesus sought out the demoniac with a legion of demons and delivered him from oppression and gave him peace and joy and life. His voice lifted as he spoke of the ragged lepers that Jesus not only spoke to, but actually touched, which was foreign to every follower of Judaism! He spoke of the rough fishermen He called from mending their nets, and the tax collector named Matthew who He chose as His apostle—a sinner in the eyes of the Pharisees if there ever was one! He spoke of the woman who anointed His feet with her tears and dried them with her hair.

"That woman was the object of scorn by every self-righteous, religious Jew in Jerusalem, but Jesus loved her. And when she fell before Him, He praised her for loving Him with all her heart. I'm sure, for that time and for now and all eternity, she'll be singing the praises of Jesus the friend of sinners."

Finally, Rice said, "I could go on forever. I could tell you about my own life as a sinner when Jesus found me. You heard me tell it many times. It was the greatest time of my life, dear friends, and I will never forget it. But now it's time for those of you who are not believers. Perhaps some of you have reached the lowest point in your life. The world may have turned against you, but I'm here to tell you that Jesus is the friend of sinners. He will make you, no matter what you've done, as white as snow. We're going to sing a hymn now, and during this time, I want you to imagine that Jesus is here as He is in spirit. But just imagine He came down the aisle, and He came to you where you're sitting. Picture Him reaching out His hand and saying, 'I am your friend. Will you love Me as I love you?' Can you imagine that? I feel the Spirit of God moving strongly this morning, and as we sing, I'm going to ask you to come and let the Lord Jesus Christ come into your life as your best friend."

The congregation stood up, and Rice began singing an old hymn, but he had not sung more than a few words when suddenly he stopped and Jerusalem saw his eyes widen and shock run over his face—and then pure joy.

Indeed, Rice was transfixed and could not move for a moment, for there coming down the aisle was *Julie Satterfield*, tears running down her face. He saw that she walked unsteadily and her hands were trembling, and immediately he stepped down from the pulpit and said, "My sister, you've come to find the Lord."

"Yes." Julie said that one word and then could say no more. She had listened to the sermon as she had to others, but the thought of Jesus being her friend and making her white as snow had moved her. Halfway through the sermon she had felt as if she were before the very eyes of God. All of her past suddenly came to her, and she had sat there stiffly, trying to ignore Rice's words. But she could not, and now as she came, she could barely stand up.

Rice whispered, "We will pray, Julie. It's your time. Just tell the Lord Jesus that you love Him, that you're sorry for every sin, and He will come into your heart."

The church was shocked and stunned. Several hardened sinners had been saved in this very church under righteous preaching, but Julie Satterfield! Several of the church members came and fell on the altar and began to pray. Jerusalem held tightly to Ethan and could not see for the tears that ran down her face. She heard others weeping.

And then Rice rose and pulled Julie to her feet. Her face was wet with tears, but there was a new light in her eyes, and Rice's voice was triumphant as he said, "Beloved, I have to announce the death of one of our members." Everyone stared at him, and he lifted his hand, the sign of victory. "The old Julie Satterfield has died, and now we have a new Julie Satterfield. Come and welcome her into the family of God."

Julie stood there as people came forward to hug her and welcome her to the church. Then her sister's arms were around her, and she was sobbing. But she whispered in her ear, "Praise God, sister." And then Julie—Satterfield—the new Julie Satterfield—took a deep breath, for she knew that she had come home, the home she had longed for all of her life without even knowing it!

CHAPTER
THIRTY-FIVE

The weather through March of the new year had been bitter cold, but now on the first day of April of 1843, a large crowd had gathered at the Brazos River for a baptizing. Clinton Hardin had proclaimed himself to be the "feeler."

Fergus Nightingale had been puzzled by the ritual. "Is this some sort of a theological office, my boy?" he asked as Clinton stood dressed in old clothes, faded jeans, and a white shirt by the riverside.

"Well, I thought you was an educated man, but you never heard of a feeler? I swan, your education's been neglected!" Clinton said. He waved at the river and said, "There's deep holes that wear themselves into this river. It wouldn't do for one of our new believers to step off into one and get sucked away, so a feeler is the fellow that goes out and feels around to be sure that there ain't no holes to lose nobody in."

As Clinton was explaining the importance of his task to Fergus, Rice waded out into the main stream of the section of the river that had already been approved by Clinton. He was wearing a pair of light gray pants and a white shirt, and the wind blew his black hair over his forehead. He brushed it back and looked at those gathered on the riverbank to be baptized. All of them were wearing older clothes, and two tents had been set up for them to change into dry clothes afterward. His eyes fell on Julie, and she smiled back at him. Then he lifted his voice and began to speak. "Baptism is the command of the Lord Jesus. It is the sign for all who wish to follow Him." He went on to speak of baptism and finally looked at the new believers and said, "These have come now to proclaim their faith in Jesus, and we as a church take them in. They are a part of the family of God, and we are charged to nourish them, to love them, and to help them stay on the straight and narrow path." Looking over all those who had come to faith, he said, "Each one of these is precious in God's sight."

He held out his hand, and a line began to form, managed by Clinton, of course. He put Julie at the last of the line, and she stood there patiently watching. The first candidate, a short man who had been converted from a dreadful life of drinking, approached and waded out tentatively. His face was pale, but Rice smiled and took his place beside him. "This is Brother Al Dearing, a brother indeed." He arranged Dearing's hands and murmured, "Just grab your nose, Al, when you go under." Then he put his right hand on Al's neck, held his left hand up, and said in ringing tones, "And now in obedience to the commands of our Lord and Savior Jesus Christ, I baptize you, my brother, in the name of the Father and of the Son and of the Holy Ghost." He lowered Dearing down, completely submerged him, and then pulled him easily up. Dearing came out wiping his nose.

Clinton let out with a rousing, "Amen! Amen, brother!" And others joined him.

One new believer after another came until finally it was Julie's turn. As had the other women, she had sewn heavy weights in the hem of her dress so that it would not float up. When she came to Rice, she saw that his lips were trembling, and suddenly tears filled her eyes. "Dear Rice," she whispered, "you never thought it would come to this."

"You're mistaken there, Julie Satterfield. I knew it would. God answered my prayers." He put her into position, and Julie folded her hands as he covered them with his. She heard Rice speak the words, and then as she went under she felt the coldness of the water. When she came up, her hair streaming and the water flowing from her face, she heard

Clinton shouting. For that one moment Rice did not let her go but kept his left hand on hers, his right hand behind her back. He said nothing, but when she turned to look at him, she saw the tenderness in his eyes that she could not mistake.

"Shall I say it now?"

"Yes, Rice."

He stepped closer, and Julie stood beside him. "You remember that Solomon's Song speaks of one called his sister and his spouse. For a long time I couldn't figure out how a woman could be both a sister and a wife, but now I know. And I can't think of a better time"—his voice lifted and carried on the afternoon air—"to announce that Miss Julie Satterfield will be married to the Reverend Rice Morgan next Saturday afternoon. All are invited."

Applause began then, and laughter, and as Julie and Rice came to the bank, they were congratulated on every hand—first by the family, who were aware of this beforehand, and then by others who came eager to say a word.

Julie went to change clothes with the other women, and Rice stood there smiling. Jerusalem and Clay came to stand beside him. "There is proud I am to be a part of your family, Sister Jerusalem."

"And there is proud I am to have you in the family," Clay said, and they both shook hands with Rice firmly.

"I didn't tell the other part," Rice said.

"The other part? What do you mean?" he said.

"The deacon said if I married Julie, I'd have to resign as pastor."

Clay started to speak, but Jerusalem put her hand on his arm. "The best day's work they've ever done! It's time to start a new church!"

Rice Morgan suddenly laughed. "Just what I had in mind, sister. Just what I had in mind!"

"What's the matter with you, Clinton? You got a face as long as a mule eatin' briars," Jerusalem said.

"Oh, it ain't nothin', Ma."

But Jerusalem knew better. Clinton, who was usually cheerful and smiling, had been strangely silent for the past two days. He was standing now leaning against the door, staring off in the distance. Bob came up and sat down on his feet, and Clinton, who usually shoved him off, absent-mindedly leaned down and touched the big dog's head.

"There's something wrong with you," Jerusalem said, coming over and putting her hand on his shoulder.

"Well, Lucy won't go to that dance next Saturday with me."

"She going with that man named Tom?"

"No, it's some stuck-up shrimp from Philadelphia." Clinton shook his shoulders and said, "Get off my feet, Bob!" and pushed Bob away. "She ain't got no manners treatin' me like that. It's unseemly, that's what it is!"

"Well, I'm ashamed of you lettin' a woman get you down in the mulligrubs like this. Go find yourself another girl. Buy yourself some new clothes and go in there and show that Abbot girl she can't get to you."

"Oh, Ma, all the gals have already paired off."

"Nonsense. You can find someone to go to the dance with you."

"No, I can't."

"Listen to me, Clinton. You go buy yourself a new suit and a fine pair of boots. Get yourself some good-smelling lotion. You'll show that Lucy Abbot she can't put you down."

"I don't want to go by myself."

"You won't go by yourself," Jerusalem said. "I'm going to have a girl ready for you."

Clinton stared at his mother, unable to believe what he was hearing. "What are you talkin' about, Ma?" he said.

"I'm talkin' about you goin' to that dance with a girl I pick."

"Ah, you'd pick that old Maggie Birchwood. She's homely as a stump full of spiders."

"Clinton, have I ever let you down in your whole life?"

"Well, I reckon not, Ma, but—"

"You do what I tell you. You get yourself all slicked up and ready, and next Saturday night you'll set that Abbot girl upside down."

Clinton stared at his mother and said, "Well, Ma, you ain't never failed me, so I'm trustin' you."

"You won't be sorry. Now, go buy you some new clothes."

* * *

By the time Saturday night had arrived, Clinton was as nervous as a man could be. He had pestered his mother to tell him the name of the girl she had chosen, but she had remained adamant. "I'm not telling you a thing. You're always talkin' about how much faith you've got, so have a little faith in your ma."

The dance began at seven o'clock, and at five-thirty Clinton came down the stairs wearing his new suit. It was light blue, and he had on a white shirt and a new tie. His face glowed from the razor, and at his mother's insistence, he had not slicked his hair down but merely brushed it back.

"Why, you look downright handsome, Clinton Hardin."

"Ah, Ma, don't be puttin' me on. Who is this girl that you picked out for me to go with? I sure hope it ain't Sarah Magnunson. She's so skinny she could take a bath in a gun barrel!"

"No, it's not her. Now listen, we agreed that you're taking whoever I picked, and you haven't lied to me very often, Clinton."

"Why, I ain't *never* lied to you or anybody else!"

"All right. You'll take her, then, no matter who I say?"

"Yes, Ma," Clinton said with resignation. "Now who is she?"

"It's Aldora."

"Aldora! Are you crazy, Ma? Why, she don't even have a dress—except that baggy old brown one she wears to church!"

"She does now. I went with her to town and helped her pick out a dress and gave it to her for her birthday. Got her new shoes, too. Now you get on over there. She's waitin' for you."

"Ma, she can't even dance."

"How do you know?"

"Why, I don't know. She just don't *look* like she can dance. She's mighty good at coon huntin', and she ain't a-scared of snakes, but she ain't the kind of girl a fellow would take to a dance."

"You gave me your word, Clinton. Now, you get on your way. Take the buggy."

"All right, Ma—but it's just because you forced me into it."

Clinton left looking gloomy, and Jerusalem stood watching him, smiling as he went. "That young man needs to be cut down to size, and I think this might be what does it!"

Clinton was in no hurry. He dreaded going to the dance, and memories of how he had had a fight with Tom Ellis, who had insulted Al, came back to him. "Maybe we can be real late and leave real early," he said to the horses. "That's about the only hope I got."

He drove the horses at a leisurely walk, and when he pulled up at the Stuart house, it was nearly six-thirty. "Still too early," he muttered. "Maybe one of the horses will break a leg or something, or maybe she decided not to go." Holding this hope, he jumped out of the wagon and walked up the steps. He knocked on the door and was met by Al's grandmother, Anne.

"Howdy, Miz Stuart."

"Why, come in, Clinton." As soon as Clinton stepped inside, Mrs. Stuart opened her eyes and shook her head in admiration. "Well, ain't you the finest-lookin' thing I ever seen! You look like a Philadelphia lawyer."

"I hope not," Clinton said, trying to smile. He looked around and said, "Is Al sick, maybe, not able to go?"

"No. She ought to be ready by now. I'll go get her."

Caleb Stuart came in from the kitchen and admired Clinton duly and then said, "I tell you what. I never seen Al look so happy as when she found out you had asked her to go to this dance."

"Well—I'm proud she feels that way, Mr. Stuart." Guilt rose in him, for he knew that he on his own would never have asked Al Stuart to go anywhere except maybe fishing on the river.

He heard the sound of Mrs. Stuart's voice and turned. She was coming down the hall, and he could see Al behind her, but not until Mrs. Stuart said, "Here she is, Clinton," and stepped aside did Clinton get a full view of Aldora Stuart. For a moment he was unable to speak, and he thought, *There's got to be some big mistake here. This ain't Al.*

Indeed, Aldora Stuart was not wearing baggy overalls. She did not have a hat on that was too big for her pulled down over her ears, and she was not wearing the large men's shoes that she usually wore while working around the homestead. She was dressed in one of the prettiest dresses Clinton had ever seen. It was made of a light pink silk that complemented her blond hair, which had been pulled back from her face, curled into long ringlets, and held in place with mother-of-pearl combs in the back. The dress had a long-waisted bodice of white taffeta that draped with folds to form a V-shape to the waist. A dark pink sash was tied into a bow at the back, and the neckline was edged with a delicate white lace. The sleeves were straight and came to her wrists and ended with the same lace, and the full, long skirt had three deep flounces also edged with more of the same lace.

"Hello, Clinton," Aldora said.

When she smiled, her lips curved up in such a way that reminded Clinton of the time he had kissed her on the way back from New Orleans. He'd always felt that was one of the rare mistakes in his life, but now as he stared at her, he could not think of a single thing to say—perhaps a mile-stone in the life of Clinton Hardin!

"Well, aren't you going to say anything?" Al said.

"You . . . you look real nice, Al."

"Thank you, Clinton."

Clinton stood there staring at her until finally Mrs. Stuart said nervously. "Is something wrong, Clinton?"

"What? Oh no, not at all. I guess we'll be on our way. May be a little late, but these dances last a long time."

"We trust you, Clinton. You stay until it's all over," Mr. Stuart said.

The two went out on the porch and stepped toward the buggy. Clinton started around the horses, when he suddenly realized that Al was standing, waiting.

"What's wrong?" he said, coming back.

"I want you to help me in the buggy."

It had never occurred to Clinton to help Al do anything, for she was so self-sufficient. But now he flushed and said, "I guess I forgot."

"I guess you did." Al held her hand out, and Clinton put his own out and helped her in. She had on perfume that brushed against his senses, and when she settled down, he stood there staring at her. "Something wrong?"

"No, nothing's wrong."

"Then why are you staring at me?"

"I don't know. I guess I just—"

Clinton could not complete a sentence, it seemed. He hurried around, got in the seat beside her, and took up the lines. "Your ma is so nice to me, Clinton. She bought me these new clothes, and she helped me do my hair and gave me some perfume. You've got the best mother in the whole world!"

"I reckon that's right."

"She said you wanted so much to take me to the dance."

Clinton's head seemed to give off an alarm. *Well, that's the first lie my ma ever told in her whole life. I'll have to speak to her about that!*

"I guess I did," he said.

"Why didn't you ask me yourself, Clinton?"

"I guess I was workin' too hard, but I knew Ma would take care of it. We'd better get on our way now. I don't want us to be late." He slapped the horses with the lines, and they broke out into a fast clip.

"What's your hurry? You're going to turn us over."

"No, I won't. I never turn buggies over."

They were barely half a mile down the road when the left wheel hit a pothole, and the buggy careened wildly. Aldora was thrown against Clinton, and he put his arm around her. "I guess I'd better hold on to you. I don't want to lose my girl on the way to the dance."

"You never worried about it before."

"Well, you've changed a lot, Al, and I've had some serious thoughts myself about you."

Aldora was pressed against Clinton now, and she said, "You don't have to hold me so tight."

"Oh, it's dangerous. A wild pair of horses like this, you just can't control 'em."

"That's Bess and Herman. They're the mildest and gentlest horses you folks have got."

"Oh, well, I mistook 'em for a couple of other horses."

Al laughed. "Well, let me go. You're messing up my dress."

Clinton took his arm away, but he kept stealing glances as he slowed the horses down. Usually, as Clay had remarked, Clinton could talk the legs off a kitchen stove, but he had very little to say on the way to the dance. This stranger riding beside him was so different! He kept looking for signs of the old Al with whom he had fished crawdads out of the river for bait, but he saw very little of her there. When they rode into town, he said, "I guess I'd better tell you, Al. I don't much care for my girl dancin' with other fellas."

"You don't?"

He turned to her and said, "You do dance, don't you?"

"A little bit."

"Well, I'm the best dancer in Texas, so you'd better just stay with me."

"But what if someone asks me for a dance?"

"You just tell 'em to come to me. I'll handle it."

Al hid her smile behind her hand and did not answer. She knew very well that Clinton's mother had arranged all this, and it somehow did her good to see Clinton becoming possessive. No one had ever acted this way toward her before, and she determined to make the most of it.

To say that Aldora Stuart created a sensation among the young, unmarried segment of Jordan City's young men would be an understatement. The minute Clinton walked in with her on his arm every unattached young man in the hall had made it his business to try to secure a dance with her. Clinton had fought them off as best he could. He had tried every trick he knew, saying to one, "Aldora here is not a very good dancer," but Tom Hicks had said, "That's all right. I'm a good teacher," and had swung off with her.

Indeed, no matter how much Clinton protested, Aldora was certainly the belle of the ball!

He was standing beside the refreshment table with Brodie and Zane, who were enjoying watching Clinton's futile attempts to keep Al away from the young men.

Clinton watched Aldora moving around the room with Kurt Beals and muttered, "Would you look at that Kurt Beals? I'm gonna punch his head!"

"What for?" Brodie asked, winking at Zane.

"Why, he's holdin' Al too tight. It's *unseemly*, that's what it is!"

"Everything you don't like is unseemly," Zane said, grinning.

"Well, look at it my way," Clinton said with intensity in every line of his body. "For years now I've been takin' care of Aldora, and I've been teachin' her how to act. And now that she's sort of blossomed out, it's all due to my upright teachin'."

"I'm sure she's grateful. Yes, I remember all the times you took Al out to dances and things. How many times was that, Clinton?" Brodie asked innocently.

"Well, she wasn't ready. I had to teach her so much, don't you see? It takes a while to get a young woman all trained up—" Clinton broke off and said angrily, "Look at that! Beals has gone too far!"

"You'd better let Kurt alone. He's a pretty rough cob," Zane said. But Clinton, as usual, paid no attention, and made straight for the pair. "He's gonna get his hair parted if he bumps into Kurt."

"It wouldn't be the first time for Clinton. We'd better be there to pull him out from under Kurt before he gets hurt bad."

Actually there was no fight, but Clinton did have an argument with Beals, who insisted on finishing the dance.

"Well, don't hold her so tight."

"Why don't you mind your own business?"

"This is *my* girl. Go find your own, or I'll inundate you with bodily harm!"

Finally, Beals threw up his hands. "All right, Clinton, you're always right. I'm sorry, Aldora."

"That's all right, Kurt. I enjoyed the dance."

Clinton came to Aldora and said, "I'll finish this dance."

"I thought you were very impolite."

"He wasn't actin' right, Aldora. I've got to talk to you about that."

"He wasn't doing anything!"

"He was holding you too tight."

"What about you? You're holding me tight."

"Well . . . that's different."

"Why is it different?"

"Because those other fellas, they don't understand how to handle a woman like I do. They might take liberties."

Aldora was enjoying Clinton's attention immensely. "And you're not going to take liberties?"

"Why, did you ever know me to take a liberty?"

"Yes, I did. That time we were on the way back from New Orleans you forced your attentions on me."

"Well, shucks, that was *your* fault."

"*My* fault!" Aldora stopped dancing in the middle of the floor and stared at him. "Why was it my fault?"

"Well, because women know how to lure a man on."

"I didn't lure you on. If I remember right, we were wrestling, and I was trying to get away from you, and you just kissed me."

Clinton could not think of any way to get out of that, so he changed the subject. "Well, I'm glad you've come to the dance with me."

"Clinton, tell me the truth. Your ma made you bring me, didn't she?"

Clinton struggled with his conscience and then said, "Well, I guess she was in favor of it, but she won't ever have to make me take you anywhere else. Now, it seems to me that we've got that all settled—"

"Got *what* all settled? You've been walking around like an idiot chasing after Lucy Abbot, and now you bring me to one dance and somehow *it's all settled*."

The argument continued until the end of the dance, at which time Aldora was claimed by Devoe Crutchfield, the burly blacksmith. "Devoe, you don't be holdin' her too tight."

"How tight can I hold her, Clint?"

Clinton stared at him. "You behave yourself now. I'm watchin' ya."

"Oh, I'll be careful."

As Devoe moved out onto the dance floor, he said, "You tell me now if I hold you too tight, Miss Aldora."

"Oh, don't pay any attention to Clinton."

She danced around the floor, her eyes sparkling, and finally she said, "You know, this is the first dance I was ever at in my life, Devoe."

"Well, I'd never know it. You look like a million dollars, and you dance like a dream. Maybe I'll come courtin' myself."

"That'd be all right. I wouldn't mind," Aldora said.

Clinton made up for his silence on the way to the dance by talking constantly all the way home. He went over all of the dances that Aldora had danced with other men, illuminating the dangers of each one of them. Finally, they approached the house, and when he pulled the horses up, he got out and helped her out without being told. When they got to the porch, she turned to him and smiled. It was a smile to cause Clinton to notice, as he had once before, the richness of her lips. Under the light of the stars he could see the rich, yellow gleaming of her hair and could not help but notice the smooth roundness of her shoulders. The moonlight ran over her, accentuating her figure, and her face was like a mirror reflecting her feelings.

"Devoe Crutchfield asked me if he could come calling."

Clinton blinked. "What did you tell him?"

"I said it'd be all right."

"Well, I don't think—"

When he did not complete his sentence, she said, "You don't think what?"

"I don't think you ought to go out with Devoe. I mean, after all, he's the blacksmith."

She stared at him. "What's wrong with blacksmiths?"

"They ain't trustworthy."

"Why, Clinton Hardin, you must have lost your mind! Devoe Crutchfield is one of the finest young men in town, and you know it!"

"Well, I guess he's all right, but you and me, we been friends for a long time."

"Yes, we have. I guess you've been my best friend, Clinton."

Clinton perked up at her words. "Now that sounds better."

"But a girl can have more than one friend."

"I reckon maybe we need to be closer friends. That's it—closer friends. That's what I want."

"How close?" Aldora asked. Clinton was not tall, but Aldora was four inches shorter. She was looking up at him now, and he became rather uncomfortable.

"Well, real close," he said. "You know, at times like this I reckon that it's probably good for good friends to do something to show how much they care for each other." He saw Al was smiling at him.

"Like what?" she said.

"Well, maybe I could kiss you good night. But the last time I kissed you, you gave me a black eye." Suddenly, Clinton saw something in Aldora's eyes, and he said, "I guess you'd better get ready to black the other eye. I never realized how pretty you were, Aldora, never."

He reached over, and she did not resist as he put his arms around her. But as his lips touched hers and he smelled the faint perfume, something stirred within him. He held her tightly and felt her arms go around his neck. The kiss lasted longer than he intended, and finally she drew away.

Her voice was husky as she said, "This was the best time I ever had in my life, Clinton."

"We'll do it again."

"All right."

"Maybe I'd better come by tomorrow, and we can go riding."

"You mean do something like digging fish worms and going fishing in the river?"

"No, maybe we'll have a picnic. We ain't done that in a long time."

"We've *never* done that," she said. She put her hand on his chest and said, "You're a fine man, Clinton, even if your ma did force you to go with me. I enjoyed myself. Good night."

She turned and walked quickly away, and Clinton called out, "Well, she's not makin' me go on no picnic with you."

"Good night, Clinton."

Clinton stood there for a moment, thinking that somehow she had gotten the best of him. "Why, shoot, *that* can't be right," he muttered. "No woman could ever get the best of me!" He went back, settled down in the buggy, and then bellowed, "I'll be here about noon. You be ready, you hear me?" Then he slapped the lines on the horses and said, "Get up," and the horses moved off obediently.

Jerusalem was in bed reading her Bible, an old one that she'd put away long ago. The cover was frayed, and the pages were yellow with age and worn thin. She smiled as she read some of the comments she'd written in the margins. Then she turned to a page and stopped dead still, catching her breath.

With fingers not steady, she carefully picked up the pressed flower that she'd placed there years ago. It was fragile, but the yellow rose still maintained its rich color. Tenderly, she traced the blossom as memories of the night that Clay had given it to her came flooding into her spirit. It had been the night she'd told Kern Herendeen that she'd never marry him. She remembered how Clay had been waiting for her when she got home. He'd told her he'd always love her and had given her this very flower. She'd pressed it in her Bible, and now here it was in her hand. She thought of how their love had grown steadily, and she closed her eyes and breathed a prayer of thanksgiving to God for giving her such a good and loving man.

Clay had gone to sleep long ago. She had been talking, and Clay had just simply fallen asleep, as he did at times, and now she dug her elbow into him and said, "Wake up!"

Clay groaned but rolled over. "What is it?" he said. "Can't it wait until tomorrow?"

"No, it can't."

"Well, Jerusalem, you've talked like a parrot all night! You told me everything you could possibly know, and I'm sleepy."

"I want to call our ranch The Yellow Rose Ranch."

Clay blinked like an owl staring at her. "That ain't no name for a ranch!"

"Why not?"

"Why, the name of a ranch ought to be tough—like The Wild Steer or some such name."

"No, it's going to be The Yellow Rose."

Clay groaned and shut his eyes. "All right, then, call it the Purple Daisy if you want to. Just let me get some sleep."

Jerusalem reached out and grabbed a handful of his hair. "There's one thing I haven't told you."

"Well, what is it?"

"You and I are going to have another baby."

Clay jumped and sat straight up in the bed. "Another baby! Why, I'm too old to have another baby!"

Jerusalem began to laugh. "No, you're not."

Clay was wide awake now. He reached over and pulled her to him until their faces were inches apart. "That's wonderful! You can't get too many good babies, I always say, but I'm worried about you. You're a little bit old for havin' babies."

"God is giving us this baby," Jerusalem said. "It's going to be all right."

Clay was silent for a moment, thinking it all over, and finally he said, "Hey, maybe it'll be twins again. We can name them Huz and Buz just like in the Bible."

"Clay Taliferro, you are impossible! We're not naming any helpless infants Huz and Buz!" She stroked his cheek and said, "It's going to be a girl, and her name will be Rose."

"A mighty fine name—for a girl or a ranch." He held her in his arms, and for a long time the two talked quietly, and then he said, "Well, I've said something nice to you. Now you say somethin' nice to me."

"All right, I will. Clay Taliferro—you're not as bad as you used to be."

"Why, wife, that's the nicest thing you've ever said to me. I'm gonna give you an award for them kind words," he said as he drew her closer.

Jerusalem laughed deeply and murmured, "I can't guess what it might be! . . ."

THE LONE STAR LEGACY BEGAN WITH BOOK 1

DEEP IN THE HEART

They came to Texas to make their family whole.
They stayed to fight for the land they'd come to love.
An unforgettable saga of faith, love and loyalty that
will find its place deep in your heart.

In the days when Texas was the northern edge of Mexico, when Bowie and Houston and Crockett were men and not yet legends, when the Alamo was still a scruffy mission on the banks of the San Antonio River, this unorthodox family struggled to make a wild but beautiful land their own.

This is the tale of Jerusalem Ann, who is willing to take whatever life dishes out in order to make a life for her family. It's the story of Clay, who finds himself protecting another man's family—and in love with another man's wife. It's about Jake, who loves two women and can't do right by either . . . and Julie, who'd rather be free than respectable. . . and Bowie, who can handle war but might not survive his first love.

It's the story of Comanches and fiestas, hunting parties and courting parties, of battles and massacres and beautiful calm nights under a canopy of stars. Wide as the prairies, warm as a San Antonio breeze, spiced with adventure and romance, this Texas-sized saga of faith from a beloved storyteller will quickly find its place deep in your heart . . . and never let you go.

You can find *Deep in the Heart*
wherever good books are sold!

THE LONE STAR LEGACY
CONTINUES WITH BOOK 3

After the battles of the Alamo and San Jacinto, Texas remains a dangerous land. The bloody war for independence has been won, but now begins another war—one of survival.

Clay and Jerusalem Ann Taliferro are determined to make the Yellow Rose Ranch into a cattle kingdom—a dynasty that they can bequeath to their children. First, though, they must reckon with two deadly enemies: Mexican banditos from the south, who make periodic raids on the Taliferros' herds; and wandering bands of savage Comanches who ride in from the north, killing and kidnapping Texicans.

The entire cattle empire of the newly formed state of Texas could be crushed by its enemies, if not for a small force of men who stand against them. A small but mighty force known as the Texas Rangers.

As the Taliferro family and their fellow Texans fight to preserve the freedom they've won, Jerusalem Ann's son is in a battle of his own. When Clint joins the Rangers, he finds all the adventure he's desired as these hard riding, quick shooting men throw themselves into a deadly conflict against the Mexican *pistoleros* and the bloodthirsty Comanches. But Clint turns into one of the most deadly of the Rangers, and is in danger of becoming nothing but a killing machine.

Two young women will seek to save him from himself. One is a half-Comanche whose beauty and courage Clint can't help but admire. The other is a young Welsh missionary with flaming hair and flashing green eyes who is drawing him to the call of Christ.

You won't want to miss what's ahead in the unfolding drama of Book 3! Be on the lookout for this action-packed volume in the Lone Star Legacy, coming soon.